The
STOLEN
DAUGHTER

BOOKS BY FLORENCE ỌLÁJÍDÉ

Coconut

The

STOLEN
DAUGHTER

FLORENCE ỌLÁJÍDÉ

bookouture

Published by Bookouture in 2024

An imprint of Storyfire Ltd.
Carmelite House
50 Victoria Embankment
London EC4Y 0DZ

www.bookouture.com

ISBN: 978-1-83525-299-4
eBook ISBN: 978-1-83525-298-7

To my great-grandparents, who lived through a turbulent time in British-African history.

CONTENT NOTE

This book contains slavery, sexual assault and children being harmed.

ONE

The sun hung low on the horizon, with only half of the golden
disc visible as Ṣìkẹ́mi and her younger brother trudged into the
family compound. Her narrow hips swayed in tandem with the
heavy stack of trussed firewood on her head. Beside her, ten-
year-old Kúnlé balanced a smaller stack. She'd planned to get
back long before the women started preparing the evening
meal. But she'd lost track of time while foraging for the giant
African snails in the sack hanging from her shoulder. Unless she
could join them unnoticed, she was certain her aunts would
have something unsavoury to say about her tardiness.

The rectangular structures they called home contained
several rooms for her family, including each of her father's
brothers and his older widowed sister, Màmá Aláṣọ. They
enclosed a courtyard, where the family spent most of their
waking hours. Hoping to sneak in without being noticed,
Ṣìkẹ́mi tiptoed into the open courtyard through the archway in
the middle of one wall.

She and Kúnlé headed for the wood store in the corner and,
after setting down her axe and load, she helped Kúnlé with his.

He rewarded her with a flash of white teeth before running off to join his cousins. She returned the smile as he disappeared among the flurry of heads. Her eyes followed him until they landed on Fọlárìn, the current bane of her life, sitting by himself on a stool. Their eyes met and held and, although she felt the rush of blood to her face, she held his gaze. After all, this was her territory. Fọlárìn broke eye contact first and looked away. Ṣìkẹ́mi sighed. She stored the axe out of reach of the younger children, picked up the sack and looked around.

The courtyard bustled with several aunties hovering over large cauldrons of food, perched above tripods filled with three-way mounds of burning firewood. An aunt, bent over her haunches, blew air at the base of a tripod, trying to coax the fire to life. In response, wisps of white smoky film swirled up to the heavens, filling the air with an acrid smell and causing those nearby to splutter. Cousins who were old enough to help scurried around gathering the serving bowls, while younger ones watched the food, their hungry eyes tracking its progress.

As she crossed the courtyard, Ṣìkẹ́mi wondered what Fọlárìn was doing in their compound. Then she noticed his father, sitting with Màmá Aláṣọ, and several uncles on wooden stools beneath the thatched roof's overhanging eaves. From there, they conversed, while enjoying the shade and cooling breeze easing the afternoon's stickiness away. Ṣìkẹ́mi spied her màmá near a tripod and made a beeline for her.

'I see the princess has returned.' The sneer from Màmá Péjú, her least favourite aunt, who stood barring her way with crossed arms and a deep scowl, stopped her in her tracks.

'Please do not be cross, Màmá Péjú. I lost track of time.'

'Of course you did. You always lose track of time when there is cooking to be done.' Her aunt spat the words with a baleful glare.

Ṣìkẹ́mi bit her lips. It was the only way to keep her mouth

from uttering the words itching to escape. Out of the corner of her eye, she spied Fọlárìn watching, a nasty smirk on his face. He could smirk all he liked.

'That's unlike you. Aren't you going to speak?'

She knew what her aunt was doing, but she ignored the challenge. Her aunt looked her up and down, kissed her teeth, and walked away. Ṣìkẹ́mi let out one breath and drew a large one in its place. Then she walked over to her màmá.

'Ẹkú ilé,' she said as she knelt to greet her màmá. She pulled the heavy sack off her shoulder and opened it, exposing Màmá's favourite delicacy. She hoped the offering would atone for her lateness.

'Kú àbọ̀,' Màmá said without pausing, as her hands smashed yam flour paste against the side of the enormous pot wedged between her feet. Then she lifted her head and scanned the courtyard for Kúnlé. Happy her son had returned unscathed, she nodded. 'Were you fighting with your aunt again?'

'Màámi, I never said a word.'

Màmá chuckled. 'I can't imagine how hard that was.' Then she looked at the snails and the shadow of a smile hovered on her lips. 'Did you see Fọlárìn?'

Ṣìkẹ́mi felt her skin burn again. She refused to meet her mother's gaze but nodded in response. After a moment's pause, Màmá spoke. 'It's too late to cook them today. Put them away, and then come back and help me.'

As she left to do Màmá's bidding, Ṣìkẹ́mi noticed several aunts eyeing her, their lips pressed into angry grimaces. It had been like that for as long as she could remember; their disapproval of everything about her, from the way she spoke or sat to her penchant for climbing trees and hunting. But she knew of no other way to be and had long given up trying to please them. She used to retaliate with her mouth, back in the days when she had Bàbá's support. Then, they couldn't touch her, no matter what she said. These days, she chose her battles with care.

With her eyes averted, she tried picking her way around the courtyard's circumference. It was longer than cutting through the middle, but she'd avoid Fọlárìn. She'd had all the smirking she could handle in one day.

'Where are you off to now?'

Ṣìkẹ́mi sighed. If only Màmá Péjú would leave her alone.

'I just need to store the snails under a basket.' She kept her voice neutral, not wanting Fọlárìn and his father to witness her arguing with her aunt.

'So why are you skulking around like you haven't got things to do?'

Ṣìkẹ́mi stood silently until her aunt shook her head. With a perplexed frown on her face, she dismissed Ṣìkẹ́mi. Ṣìkẹ́mi continued on her way, but she couldn't resist a peek in Fọlárìn's direction. And there it was again. That stupid smirk. She kissed her teeth and gave him an eye-roll. His grin widened.

Ṣìkẹ́mi returned to her mother's side and for the rest of the evening refused to look in Fọlárìn's direction until he and his father took their leave. They were forever linked by an act of their parents' will that neither of them had control over. Still, she had no intentions of making it easy for any of them. Later that night, she fell asleep wondering what else she could do to dissuade her parents from their plans for her and Fọlárìn. Nothing she tried had worked so far.

Ṣìkẹ́mi's eyes snapped open like a surprised catfish, her heart thudding like she'd run a race. In her dream she was drowning, but she'd also heard the shrill cries of '*fire*', which didn't make sense. Alerted by the smell of acrid smoke in the air, her body stilled. She scrambled off her sleeping mat, coughing, her eyes searching the darkness. Where were Màmá and Kúnlé? 'Màá-mi?' she spluttered into the dark, but got no reply. Then she remembered Màmá allowed her to sleep in Bàbá's room whenever he visited the family farm, as long as she left his things alone.

With speed, Ṣìkẹ́mi plucked her wrapper off the floor, draping the cotton sheet around her body before tucking the ends into tight folds under her armpit. *Krakaka!* The unfamiliar sound of gunfire made her flinch. She'd heard that sound only once before, at Bàbá's farm, when he'd needed to scare off thieves with the white man's musket. She darted to the doorway, opened the wooden door, and froze, her eyes widening.

Red tongues of fire licked the thatched roof of the adjacent row of rooms in the family compound; the horror the villagers feared most was happening right before her eyes. Through the haze, she spotted people scurrying out of the courtyard towards the bushes and wondered if Màmá and Kúnlé were among them. Before leaving for the forest farm, Bàbá had said, 'If you see fire, or hear gunshots, run! And don't look back.' But she needed to find Kúnlé and Màmá first. In Bàbá's absence, the role of protector fell to her.

Ṣìkẹ́mi's feet pounded the dust as she sped across the courtyard to Màmá's room, where she found the door open. She peered inside the smoke-filled room and hollered, 'Màámi?' She got no reply but caught a throat full of smoke for her trouble. Spluttering, she doubled over, trying to snatch some fresh air. Her heart roared in her ears and a tiny, panicked sob caught the back of her throat. Still, she took a clean breath, hitched the lower corner of her wrapper over her nose and dived in. She could barely see through the thick smoke and her eyes stung. A single bead of sweat rolled down her temple. The intense heat warned her to get out, fast! Instead she dropped to her knees, searching with wobbling hands. Her smarting eyes adjusted, and a quick sweep reassured her there was no one inside.

Convinced of her family's escape, Ṣìkẹ́mi sprang for the door and, as fast as her feet could carry her, headed for the bushes. Halfway through the compound, she paused, turned and headed back to Bàbá's room. '*What are you doing?*' the voice inside her head screamed, but she ignored it, pressing forward. She reached the room to find the fire licking the edges of the thatched roof, the insides filled with wavy columns of smoke.

Holding her breath, she moved towards the rectangular raised mound of earth Bàbá slept on, knowing exactly what she wanted. She'd seen him put it there many a night, and she hoped he hadn't taken it to the farm. Her hand circled under the mat until it hit its target. The small, leather-sheathed metal would do. The nearby sound of crackling warned her of impending doom. Heart thumping, she fled.

TWO

Ṣìkẹ́mi rushed out of the compound into the open space, her eyes searching the distance. The faint silhouette of a mother and child appeared through the trees. The woman stopped and yelled and Ṣìkẹ́mi heard the echo of her name carried on the wind. She sped up, intent on reaching them. Just as she reached the first row of trees marking the village boundary, a hand snaked out of the darkness and caught her ankle. Her heart clawed its way up her throat as she stumbled before tumbling to the floor. But she was back on her feet in seconds, lashing out at her assailant with the weapon she had snagged from Bàbá's room. She heard a grunt as the knife slashed through flesh. Stunned by the surprise counter-attack, her assailant faltered and, in that moment, Ṣìkẹ́mi bolted.

After several minutes of careering through the forest, Ṣìkẹ́mi paused and caught her breath. Then she tucked the knife under her *igbàdí*, the traditional beads strung round her waistline. Inside, her heart thundered like a thousand *gbẹ̀du* drums, but the surrounding forest stayed eerily silent. Only then did she realise she had lost everyone.

Under the cover of darkness, the bush looked different. But this was her childhood playground; her escape from the day-to-day flurry of her family's existence and where, for years, she and Bàbá had set traps for bushmeat. The realisation slowed her heartbeat down to a steadier rhythm, allowing her brain to register other sensations. A heavy mist cloaked the vegetation, and she wrinkled her nose at the dank, musky smell of rotting wild mushrooms. Shivering, she rubbed her arms as the cold from the damp undergrowth seeped through her bare feet. She wished she had an extra wrapper to cloak her shoulders.

Unsure of where the villagers or her family were hiding, she decided to keep moving. Head down, she felt her way using her hands, the darkness and nocturnal sounds heightening her senses. A feathery object brushed against her bare arm, making her shudder, but she refused to think of the potential dangers. Soon, she came to the boulder demarcating the bush from the real forest. She had been here many times, and it was the furthest she had ever travelled alone.

If she stood on the boulder in daylight, she could see the village rooftops. Now in the dark, the sky offered an eerie amber glow; the silence was punctuated by the occasional sound of crackling or hissing. An unfamiliar flutter echoed nearby. She stilled as the snapping of twigs underfoot warned her of company. She ducked behind the boulder, held her breath and waited.

Startled at a light tap on the shoulder, Ṣìkẹ́mi jumped and opened her mouth, but a palm clamped over it from behind, stifling the scream.

'Shush! It's me. Look!'

Ṣìkẹ́mi's shoulders sagged at Fọlárìn's familiar voice and her eyes followed the direction of his fingers. Four shadowy figures crept through the forest, each holding a sword. Wordlessly,

Fọlárìn and Ṣìkẹ́mi melded their backs into the boulder until the shadows faded into the distance.

'Follow me,' Fọlárìn said.

Ṣìkẹ́mi stared at the tendon pulsating at the base of Fọlárìn's neck. Despite his bravado, he was as scared as she was. 'I need to find Màmá and Kúnlé,' she said.

'Do you know which way they went?'

Ṣìkẹ́mi's palms clenched as she shook her head. Without knowing which direction they had fled in, how would she find them?

'Then we need to find safety first.'

He was right, but she hated agreeing with anything he said.

'You know I'm right. Come on!' His tone held a hint of impatience.

Her face tightened, but she nodded. He turned, and she followed his lithe frame as his shoulders heaved left and right through the dense forest. As they moved in the direction opposite to that of their would-be assailants, she hoped she wasn't making a mistake.

Fọlárìn's stronger arms cut through the forest faster than Ṣìkẹ́mi's ever could, although she'd never admit it. But given, age wise, he was two years her senior at twenty minus four, she supposed that was to be expected. Behind him, she ducked through the vegetation, leaving behind the glowing skyline. They trekked for hours, until a faint light on the horizon heralded dawn, and dawn turned into morning. Then, suddenly, they burst out of the forest at a three-pronged cross-roads. The well-worn dirt tracks suggested the roads led to major towns or markets; however, the *ẹbọ* dotting the roadside, placed in offering to the gods, posed a stark reminder not to linger. Everyone knew the first person to stumble across someone else's sacrifice would be afflicted with that person's bad luck.

Hoping none of the sacrifices were fresh, Ṣìkẹ́mi used her left hand to draw three invisible circles around her head, finishing the ritual with a click of her thumb and middle finger. This invoked the protection of her *orí*, the personal god responsible for her welfare on earth. Taking his cue from her, Fọlárìn repeated the ritual. Then he turned his full gaze on Ṣìkẹ́mi and asked, 'Which road shall we take?'

Instead of replying, Ṣìkẹ́mi stared at her would-be husband. His father, the village ironmonger, had paid half of her bride price three months after Kúnlé's birth. Until that moment, she had been her father's pride and joy, and a suitable replacement for the male heir her mother couldn't supply. But Kúnlé's birth changed that, and she'd been primed and prepared for wifehood ever since.

At the prolonged silence, Fọlárìn repeated his question, his voice tinged with frustration.

Ṣìkẹ́mi shrugged. 'I don't know. I've never been this far from the village through the route we took, and these roads could lead anywhere. We should probably search for food and water first.'

'Well, that's not helpful. We won't find food out here. We need to find help.'

Ṣìkẹ́mi noted the upturned curve in Fọlárìn's upper lip. He never took her seriously.

'I can catch the food we need,' she said.

'With what? Your teeth?'

Ṣìkẹ́mi's skin tingled as a flash of anger coiled through her. She pulled up the lower end of her wrapper, revealed the small knife and crowed. 'With this.'

But Fọlárìn's sneer deepened. 'You think the bush rats will stay still long enough for you to pierce them with that?'

'No, idiot. I'll use it to fashion a bow and arrow and kill the rats with that.'

She made a loud hiss, releasing some of the pent-up fear and adrenalin she'd suppressed all morning.

'Shush, keep your voice down. I think I can hear footsteps,' Fọlárìn said.

But the warning came too late as several warriors carrying an assortment of swords and spears sprang from the forest and surrounded them. Alert, hunger and thirst forgotten, Ṣìkẹ́mi braced herself and crouched, searching for an escape.

'Don't worry. We can fight our way out,' she whispered to Fọlárìn.

'Really?' he said, and, to her horror, dropped to his backside and hugged his knees in total surrender. With barely concealed fury, Ṣìkẹ́mi rushed at the legs. But sturdy hands seized her arms, pinning them to her waist before tying them together behind her back. Then, they did the same to Fọlárìn. Refusing to concede, Ṣìkẹ́mi screamed, but someone threw a sack over a head. She gagged and spluttered as a plume of dust filled the back of her throat.

'Move!'

A hard prod in the back propelled Ṣìkẹ́mi forward, and she stumbled as her feet caught the gnarled roots of a tree. Someone pulled off the sack and replaced it with a filthy gag. As her eyes adjusted to her surroundings, the sun's warmth disappeared off her skin. The last place she wanted to be was back in the forest, yet here she was.

Ṣìkẹ́mi took quick shallow breaths as she concentrated on putting one foot in front of the other. Several thoughts raced through her mind, but one thought dominated the others. How did she escape her captors? She remembered Bàbá saying none of the disappeared ever returned and her stomach dropped, twisting down to her gut. She tested the ropes tying her hands, but the knot held firm. Two warriors led from the front. She looked behind her to count the others and was rewarded with a vicious prod.

She gave up, and, to distract herself, turned her mind to the past. Before Kúnlé's birth and despite Màmá's protests, Bàbá had treated her like a boy, taking her on forest jaunts and teaching her things only boys knew. Those were joyful times. After Kúnlé's birth, the hunting trips lessened until, one day, Bàbá spoke the words forever seared into her memory.

'Ṣìkẹ́mi, it is time to grow up. You are a girl, not a boy, and one day you will marry and leave our family. Now you must learn to be a good wife for your future husband and his family.'

Even now, the betrayal still hurt. She'd blamed Kúnlé for her predicament and given him a wide berth for months. However, one day curiosity drew her to her mother's side as she bathed the infant. 'Can I hold him?' she asked. To her delight, Màmá nodded, and, after drying the child, placed him in her arms. Ṣìkẹ́mi held on firmly as the baby squiggled. Then his upturned face stared at her. Time stopped as her eyes met her brother's for the first time, hers searching, his surprised.

Then a most beautiful thing occurred. Kúnlé's face creased into the widest toothless grin Ṣìkẹ́mi had ever seen, and out of the depths of her belly she felt something move and rise. She closed her eyes and, with trembling arms, clasped the boy to her chest, rocking him on the spot as she'd seen Màmá do a thousand times. Kúnlé giggled in response and squirmed harder. Màmá prised the wriggling child out of her arms, but Ṣìkẹ́mi's body still tingled all over from the wonder of it. She knew then that she still loved her brother and always would.

For a while afterwards, Bàbá took her on the occasional trip to the forest, allowing Ṣìkẹ́mi to improve her hunting skills. However, when Kúnlé became old enough to traipse behind Bàbá, he'd stopped taking her. Ṣìkẹ́mi was thankful that as her brother grew he showered her with affection, following her everywhere, filling the void created by Bàbá's defection, and their bond grew stronger.

A sob welled at the back of her throat as she contemplated never seeing him again, but before it burst from her lips she caught it and swallowed. Hard. She would not give in to the fear. She could still escape if she kept her ears and eyes open.

Ṣìkẹ́mi heaved a heartfelt sigh when the group stopped to rest in a small clearing. A warrior pulled the gag out of her mouth and cautioned, 'If you don't scream, you can have some water.'

Ṣìkẹ́mi nodded.

'Cup your hands.'

The warrior pulled a gourd, fashioned into a water bottle, off a shoulder and offered her the drink. Ṣìkẹ́mi lapped at the water with haste, her tongue chasing the droplets seeping through her fingers. Her thirst assuaged, she cast a forlorn glance about her surroundings as her captor moved on to Fọlárìn. The sun, its visage partly obscured by tall, vertical rows of trees, painted the sky indigo and red, signalling the fast-approaching dusk. A butterfly perched nearby on the leaves of a fern, its beautiful black wings be-speckled with yellow dots. At any other time she would have marvelled at the work of art, but not today. The forest, filled with nature's own music, invited her to listen: birds tweeting, insects chirping, the sounds filling her with sorrow.

Next to her, Fọlárìn sat with hunched shoulders. Their gaze met; his frightened, hers defiant. She cut her eye at him, leaving him in no doubt of her feelings. A fine husband he would have turned out to be.

For the next few minutes Ṣìkẹ́mi studied her captors, an odd band of eight, with unfamiliar tribal marks on their faces and arms covered in interlaced scars. Although they'd spoken Yorùbá to her, they sounded odd, and now they conversed in a foreign language. Instead of *dànṣíkís*, their lithe frames were clad in mid-thigh, sleeveless tunics and *ṣòkòtòs* that stopped just above the knee, flashing muscled but slim calves and ankles. Their chests seemed somewhat fuller than normal, and the softer, less angular faces sported no facial hair. Despite the short haircuts, their voices lacked the depth and huskiness that signified maleness. The sum of Ṣìkẹ́mi's observations led her to one incredible conclusion; one she struggled to comprehend.

The captors appeared quite relaxed as they snacked on sweet potatoes wrapped in banana leaves. As she mulled over her findings, a warrior left for the trees to answer the call of nature, and, instead of standing and spouting an arc in the air like a man, the warrior squatted. Ṣìkẹ́mi knew without a doubt these warriors were female, and decided that ought to make her escape easier. She wondered if Fọlárìn harboured similar ideas, then remembered his dismal capitulation. Perhaps it was best if she made her escape alone, since he'd already proved himself unreliable.

Soon, the warriors began packing up, their heads bent over, stuffing things into the satchels they carried round their necks. After a quick headcount, Ṣìkẹ́mi took her chance. Headlong, she rushed through the trees, weaving and diving. Behind her she heard shouts and thundering feet, then out of nowhere came a tackle and Ṣìkẹ́mi hurtled to the ground. Rough hands manhandled her to her feet and she faced another warrior, who was still trying to tie the strings holding up her *ṣòkòtò*. She had miscounted and run smack into a warrior who had walked deeper in the forest for more toileting privacy. As the warriors led her back to the clearing, she met Fọlárìn's accusing eyes. She looked away, refusing to feel guilty. She wasn't giving up. She would try again the first chance she got.

THREE

Dusk descended, and Ṣìkẹ́mi concentrated on staying alive. The twilight cast tall shadows across the dense forest vegetation, and Ṣìkẹ́mi shuddered at the thought of the potential unseen terrors lurking in the dark. Unfamiliar noises filled the forest, every sound amplified by the stillness of the approaching night. She remembered Bàbá's stories of hunting big game deep in the forest, and the darkness left her feeling like a lion's easy meal. At least during the daytime they could see the danger coming. She hoped her captors were able and willing to protect her if necessary.

To her relief, the warriors paused their journey to fashion makeshift lamps from oil-soaked rags wrapped round wooden stakes. But Ṣìkẹ́mi's relief was short-lived. The fire invited a variety of insects, who homed in on the banquet before them with ferocious determination. Ṣìkẹ́mi's bound hands made it impossible for her to swat the offenders away and, with senses heightened by hunger and exhaustion, each bite packed a punch.

As each weary step took her further away from home, the need to escape and find her brother grew. But she had to wait until the morning, since she wasn't brave enough to tackle the forest at night on her own. It upset her to think her last adventure with Kúnlé was just the previous day. She remembered his unbridled excitement. After cutting the firewood they needed, they had practised who could shoot the furthest arrows using the weapons they sneaked out of Bàbá's room, when the adults weren't paying attention.

The scene flashed through her mind. Kúnlé had grumbled when her arrow flew past his. 'Watch me,' she'd said. Planting her feet firmly on the ground, she'd gripped the bow in her left hand and raised her arm. Then, with her right hand, she rested another arrow in the groove between her thumb and forefinger, closed her left eye and looked down the spine of the arrow.

'Elbow!' She heard her father's imaginary growl and lifted her elbow until it was level with her shoulder. Then she pulled the string back as far as possible and let the arrow fly. It hit a tree several strides away with a satisfying thud. Her face split into a grin. As she ran to retrieve her arrow, Kúnlé jumped up and down as if he'd trodden on soldier ants. 'My turn, my turn.'

'Yes, calm down,' she'd said. 'Now stand up straight.'

Her brother had straightened his spine, just as she had for Bàbá, and, when he let it fly, his arrow had travelled further than ever before. He'd celebrated with a whoop and a somersault, sheer joy radiating from every pore. On the way home, he'd lamented the fact that they wouldn't be able to do this once she married Fọlárìn. She'd pulled the beaded bracelet Màmá gave her when he was born off her wrist and given it to him. 'Wear this and no matter where you are, I'll always be close to you,' she said, as she slipped it on his wrist.

Ṣìkẹ́mi's mind grew quiet, and a heavy pressure built inside her chest until it flooded her entire being with an intense shaft of anguish. Her skin prickled at the intensity and a sob rose at the back of her throat. She shoved a fist in her mouth to hold it back and stumbled forward. Whatever it took, she would find him, she vowed.

Surrounded by darkness save for the torches, the group trekked in silence, breaking it only to issue instructions. When the orange glow of a campfire appeared in the distance, and the group picked up pace, Ṣìkẹ́mi guessed they were near their destination. They were less than a hundred strides away when Ṣìkẹ́mi's captors stopped suddenly. In a clearing in the middle of the forest huddled dozens of captives. Their hands were bound behind their backs, and the air carried the soft whimpers of sorrowful women and children. Yet, there wasn't a single guard in sight. Alert and on guard, the warriors formed two rows, weapons handy. With Fọlárìn and Ṣìkẹ́mi sandwiched in the middle, one row walked backward protecting the group's rear, while the other advanced towards the camp.

As they closed in on the centre, a shrill whistle pierced the air. Out charged dozens of new warriors, chanting a war cry, and mayhem ensued. Ṣìkẹ́mi ducked and dived between the warring factions and made a beeline for the trees. She looked over her shoulder to see if Fọlárìn had followed her, but he was nowhere in sight. At the first tree, she stopped, panting, giving her body a chance to recover from the sprint. Using her teeth, she worked the rope until she freed her hands. Then she paused. Should she run or go back for him? She shook her head in exasperation. The boy was more trouble than he was worth, yet now, with her initial anger gone, she felt a slight twinge of guilt at leaving him behind.

For a moment, Ṣìkẹ́mi hovered while her head battled with her heart. Her innate sense of fairness reminded her of Fọlárìn's help earlier on in the forest. Also, as Bàbá used to say, you need two hands to beat your chest. They might stand a better chance of making it through the night, and home, if they worked together. Her mind made up, she ran back to the edge of the clearing. The combatants were still fighting, with several of her initial captors dead. The new warriors, taller and heavier, swung their weapons with a dexterity their opponents could not match. She spotted Fọlárìn crouched near the other captives, a terrified look on his face.

Ṣìkẹ́mi's brain worked furiously as she considered how to help him. From the safety of the trees, she skirted the perimeter of the clearing, edging her way towards him. The battle still raged; the sound of clashing blades was almost deafening. Near Fọlárìn, two warriors parried with each other in a death dance. Almost transfixed, she watched and waited until one thrust his blade into the other's chest. The wounded fighter tumbled backward, and his opponent moved on, leaving the area clear of soldiers. Ṣìkẹ́mi ran to Fọlárìn. 'Come with me,' she said. But Fọlárìn seemed rooted to the spot. She tugged on his arm and that woke him from his stupor. Together, they ran for the trees.

They'd almost made it when an arrow whizzed past Ṣìkẹ́mi's ear. A command rang out: 'Stop, or that will be your last step.'

But Ṣìkẹ́mi kept moving. A second arrow flew past, grazing her arm. Ṣìkẹ́mi gasped and her steps faltered as the sting registered. She looked behind and found Fọlárìn had already stopped. His head shook in a silent plea, doleful eyes entreating her to back down. She couldn't outrun the arrows. Her heart knew it, though she hated giving in. Dejected, she sank to her knees. Tears rose unbidden and squeezed past her closed eyes. A man grabbed her hands and tied them, before running his hands all over her body. His hands stilled as they slid over Bàbá's knife. He removed it, and Ṣìkẹ́mi's throat thickened at the loss of her last link to Bàbá and the only means of defending herself. Then the man led her and Fọlárìn back to the clearing, where the fighting had stopped, with her original captors vanquished or in retreat. As she joined the other captives, she let the tears fall. Her destiny, it seemed, was written and there was nothing she could do about it.

A few hours later, Ṣìkẹ́mi tried to make herself comfortable on the hard floor. Their captors had ordered them to rest ahead of the morning's trek, but Ṣìkẹ́mi's thoughts encircled her head like an irritating fly, making sleep impossible. So, while others slept, she studied her new captors. Men, she surmised, as a few relieved themselves standing up. Although they spoke a dialect of Yorùbá, most of them had three long horizontal marks carved into each cheek, showing they were not *Ẹ̀gbádò* like her.

At dawn, Ṣìkẹ́mi found herself lined up and chained to the other prisoners at the neck, each captive with about an arm's length of slack rope between them. Thankfully, their captors left their hands unbound. Somehow, she found herself in front of Fọlárìn, shoulders hunched, the heavy and unfamiliar rope weighing her down.

'You won't be able to run away this time,' he said.

The barb hit its mark. Ṣìkẹ́mi's body grew rigid and her mouth twisted with venom. 'You are the reason I am in this mess. I should have left you behind.'

Unable to think up a suitable rejoinder, Fọlárìn stayed silent.

A soldier hollered at the group. 'Move!'

Dread permeated the air and, as if frozen in time, the group stood silent. The soldier hissed, then issued the order again, this time accompanied by the crack of a cowhide whip. The whip sizzled in the air for a few seconds. Then, like a flash of lightning, it drew a trail across the row of exposed flesh. Ṣìkẹ́mi flinched as the whip's tip connected with her lower arm. She drew a sharp breath and tears rose unbidden to her eyes. Then the human train lurched forward.

FOUR

Ṣìkẹ́mi gulped and held her breath as an enormous wave crashed over her. One, two, three... Her head broke through the surface. She flapped her arms wildly and looked around. The water extended as far as she could see. How did I get here? I can't swim. What's keeping me afloat? How do I escape this? The thoughts crashed through her head in quick succession.

'Ṣìkẹ́mi! Ṣìkẹ́mi, you can do this! Swim!' She heard the faint echo of her name.

She tried turning her head, following the sound of the voice. But a mountain of water rose out of the sea and sped towards her. Ṣìkẹ́mi opened her mouth and screamed as the darkness sucked her under.

'Ṣìkẹ́mi! Ṣìkẹ́mi! Wake up!'

The urgent whisper in her ear snapped Ṣìkẹ́mi out of the dream. She could feel her heart pumping, and beads of sweat rolled down her forehead. She searched her surroundings with wild eyes, then sank back against the tree trunk as she recognised Fọlárìn and remembered they had been allowed a short rest.

'You screamed in your sleep,' he said. 'Are you all right?'

Ṣìkẹ́mi ignored him. She hadn't forgiven him yet for her recapture. Had she listened to her head, she might well have been on the way to finding her family by now. Instead, she was stuck, heading to only the gods knew where. Her palpitating heart slowed its rhythm, although she still remembered the taste of her fear as the water crashed over her. The dream was always the same. Màmá took her to the village seer once because of it. He predicted she would embark on a long journey that would last for years. His ramblings made little sense then. Now she reconsidered his words, and her heart grew heavier. But she held on to a single hope. The seer had said she'd return home, so she believed somehow an escape was still possible.

The trek resumed, and they trudged through the dense vegetation of the tropical forest, down into valleys and over hills. Despite the relentless march, the heavy restraints and the torturous environment, she began paying attention to the terrain, hoping to create a mental map for her way back home. Giant mahogany trees lined their path, their grey barks a soothing contrast to the lush green background. As the captives moved, they trampled the trees' fallen, perfumed flowers. The flowers retaliated by releasing a cloying scent, almost a funeral dirge of sorts, paying homage to the misery of the passing travellers.

Ṣìkẹ́mi also tracked the position of the sun at the hottest point of the day, and knew they were heading south. She waved her hands frequently to deter the tsetse flies. A single bite could induce a sickness that sent you into a coma before it killed you and she had no desire for death. Throughout the day, the warriors allowed their captives the shortest of breaks, fed them stale bean cakes and allowed them sips of water. Neither was enough to assuage Ṣìkẹ́mi's thirst or hunger, and in those moments she imagined her family gathered around the cooking pots in the courtyard, preparing the evening meals. What she wouldn't give to be back there, even under the censure of angry aunts.

Still, she was grateful for the tropical storms that came on as suddenly as they dissipated. Often, they were accompanied by flashes of blue lightning and booming thunder from which the ground shook. Then, as if the gods were weeping, the waters fell like almond slivers from the sky, drenching both captor and captive, cooling them down and providing an additional source of drinking water.

That night they made camp, allowing for more rest, while the warriors took turns to stand on guard. By now, a small rip in her wrapper from when she made her initial escape from the compound had grown into a much wider tear. When her captors weren't watching, Ṣìkẹ́mi tore a strip off the edge and tied it to a branch, hoping this, too, would guide her way home. The warriors insisted on silence and discouraged their captives from talking to each other. So, when sleep evaded her, Ṣìkẹ́mi spent the time listening to their chatter. That was how she learned they were heading to the coast, to the Fẹlẹkẹtẹ slave market in a town called Bàdágrì. Based on what she knew about Bàdágrì, she was fast reaching the point of no return. Still, she dug deep. There was always hope for tomorrow.

Ṣìkẹ́mi lost track of time as the sunrise rolled into evening and the day became one monotonous rhythm of trekking interspersed with brief moments of rest. As her hunger grew, she paid more attention to the trees and recognised the ùbé tree, whose fruit was a well-known snack. Ṣìkẹ́mi preferred it cooked, but the debilitating hunger overrode her fussiness. Every so often she snagged the low-hanging, ripened fruits with her hands, to supplement the meagre food offerings from her captors.

During the next rest break, Ṣìkẹ́mi glanced at Fọlárìn, realising the future their parents had planned for them was now on a divergent path. She didn't want to marry anybody, let alone Fọlárìn, although she'd had little say in the matter. Still, she knew he was handsome. The problem was Fọlárìn knew it too, because the villagers kept telling him so. *Dúdúlẹ́wà*, they called him – Black is handsome. Every time, he preened at the compliment like one of Màmá's prized peacocks. Worse still, his family kept calling her their 'wife' in a tone that suggested she ought to be grateful for the privilege.

She studied him in the silence. A gaunt hopelessness had replaced his usual cocky arrogance and his face had lost its sparkle. *All her life, she'd been her brother's protector, but what kind of protector would she be if she let someone else die needlessly of hunger?* Careful to avoid the guards' attention, she twisted sideways and offered him one of the ùbé fruits she'd kept hold of during the day's trek. Fọlárìn gawked at the purple cylindrical object with a frown.

'Eat it. It will help with the hunger.'

How do you know? Ṣìkẹ́mi saw the question in his eyes.

She raised an eyebrow and glared at him. Her annoyance dissipated when he snatched it off her hand and shoved it into his mouth.

'Careful! It's got a hard core. You can't eat that. Gnaw around it as best you can.'

Fọlárìn nodded and thanked her in between mouthfuls. After that, whenever she found an ùbé tree Ṣìkẹ́mi used the backs of her elbows to alert him, until he started recognising the fruit by himself.

The next time Fọlárìn sank down beside Ṣìkẹ́mi, he whispered into her ears, 'Thank you.'

Ṣìkẹ́mi thought of saying 'what for?' Then she changed her mind and nodded. It was the first time he'd said something nice to her.

'How come you know so much about the trees?' he asked.

Ṣìkẹ́mi smiled at his awe-tinged tone. 'Bàbá taught me every time we went hunting in the bushes. Have you ever been hunting?'

He shook his head. 'My uncles do the hunting for the entire family. I was following in my father's footsteps and training to be an ironsmith.'

'Did you like it?'

His shoulders lifted. 'It is all I know.'

Ṣìkẹ́mi acknowledged the truth in his words. It was the Yorùbá way; sons following their fathers' footsteps and learning the family trade. She supposed she'd been too hard on him for not wanting to fight. He clearly had no experience of it. Ṣìkẹ́mi realised this was the first time they had ever had a meaningful conversation. All their past interactions had been full of derision and sarcasm. Now that he wasn't mocking her, she found herself warming to him.

'Did you enjoy hunting?' he asked.

'I loved it. Bàbá started taking me when I was young, even though every woman in my family objected. They thought the time would have been better spent teaching me how to be a woman and a good wife.'

An uncomfortable silence descended as they both remembered she was supposed to be his future wife.

'Well, your knowledge has helped me, and I won't forget it.' He flashed her a dazzling smile and Ṣìkẹ́mi's heart did a somersault. A warm tingly feeling snaked up her insides, and she suddenly had an inkling why the villagers loved him so much.

Lanky with a square jawline, full brows and long eyelashes that could rival any woman's, he was still a very handsome boy, gauntness and all. And she was glad she had at least one friendly person with her on this perilous journey.

A day later, four days after her capture, the vegetation changed as they left the rainforest and emerged into a terrain altogether different. Ṣìkẹ́mi found herself wading through water, sometimes knee deep, often waist high. The mutterings of the warriors alerted her to the fact that they were in the mangrove swamp and near their destination. The warriors cut a path through the tangled branches blocking their passage, but Ṣìkẹ́mi's feet still got caught in underwater branches. For once, she was glad of the rope at her neck tethering her to others, since it prevented her from slipping under water and drowning.

The group followed the course of the nearby river. Ṣìkẹ́mi noted its colour, often a muddy brown, sometimes an alluring aquamarine green, inviting her for a swim. Much more impressive were the trees, whose many roots stood proud of the water, spread out like giant ropes, anchoring them to the lagoon basin. Ṣìkẹ́mi named them the walking trees, since their roots looked like legs.

Further into the mangroves, the ùbé trees disappeared, removing the extra food source, and the hunger returned. Weaker captives collapsed, unable to walk, holding up the transit. The captors responded by cutting them loose and pushing them into the river. Ṣìkẹ́mi wondered if she should take her chances with the water, but she wasn't sure she was strong enough.

. . .

Days later, heads hung low, feet weary and bodies battered, the bedraggled group trooped into Bàdágrì town. Despite the loss of any chance of escape, Ṣìkẹ́mi's posture perked up. Her innate curiosity overrode her exhaustion as she took in the feather-like roofs thatched with dried palm leaves. Her eyes scanned the rows of densely packed, oblong bamboo dwellings, so unlike the clusters of well-spaced mud houses in her village. The atmosphere felt different, and a cool breeze blew through the town, reducing the effect of the scorching sun.

The children playing in the streets stopped and gawked at the strangers, while their mothers hurriedly ushered them back indoors.

'Why do those people have a rope round their necks?' a child asked her mother.

Her mother replied in hushed tones, 'That's what happens to people who don't do what they are told.'

Ṣìkẹ́mi's head hung low and, even though she knew she had done nothing to deserve this, shame and humiliation washed over her.

FIVE

As the group marched through Bàdágrì town, the street noises grew louder, the narrow, criss-crossed streets thrumming with traders carrying their wares. They had arrived on a market day, the last day of the four-day week. The squawking seagulls signalled they were close to a harbour, and Ṣìkẹ́mi wrinkled her nose at the rotten, fishy odour permeating the air. The closer they got to the sea, the fouler the smell became, until the group turned into a different street. Here, mud houses with doors secured on the outside with giant iron chains and locks lined the street.

Ṣìkẹ́mi pulled in a ragged breath and gagged at the overpowering stench. Through the tiniest of windows, people moaned and pleaded for help. Her heart sank when she realised these were captives like her and what she smelt was a combination of unwashed bodies, vomit, urine and other things she didn't want to think about. Was this to be her fate? Locked up like cattle?

Her captors kept the group moving straight past the mud houses, down to the Fẹlẹkẹtẹ slave market. Soon they arrived at their destination, an open square, framed by the picturesque turquoise sea, complete with a slave ship in the harbour. Ṣìkẹ́mi's eyes bulged at the towering ship, large enough to swallow a village's entire fishing fleet. It rose majestically in the background, its sails swaying in the breeze. Then she caught her first glimpse of a European and her eyes nearly fell out.

At first, Ṣìkẹ́mi thought he resembled a person with albinism. She'd seen such a person once, when she'd followed her mother to the market. However, this man, with straight silky hair the colour of red clay and a narrow beak of a nose, was different. Other foreigners soon came into view. Some bore the colour of the cows she'd seen in the village, a faint yellow-tan. Others were so pale they resembled *efun*, the local chalk that the Ifá priest used in his divination.

The captors led the group to the raised platform in the middle of the open square and prepared them for the sale. Ṣìkẹ́mi cast wild eyes around the square, her brain searching for a new plan, but she came up empty. The captors removed the neck chains and separated the captives by age and gender. Ṣìkẹ́mi stifled a sob as the slavers led Fọlárìn and a group of boys to another part of the square. She wondered if she'd ever see him again. Although sometimes annoying, he'd been a lifeline through the trek; her only connection to her home, and she had drawn comfort from this. Now, with the last link broken, tears fell silently down her cheeks.

Then a rustling in the market square caught her attention as traders parted for some newcomers. A tall Black woman appeared, followed by a retinue of servants and guards. She cut a formidable but lonely figure, shrouded in a cloak of melancholy. Ṣìkẹ́mi observed the heart-shaped face, structured cheekbones, downturned lips and dead eyes. The woman wore a wrapper, woven in a tapestry of dark colours, round her body, cinched at the waist with a sash. Her head looked regal, decorated with a tall headpiece from which a black veil fell to the ground, and the row of red coral beads round her neck suggested great wealth. A servant held a massive canopy of ostrich feathers over her head to shade her from the scorching sun and a younger, well-dressed woman walked a few paces behind her.

Ṣ̀ikẹ́mi's gaze connected with the young woman's and an unbidden plea rose from within her. 'Ẹ gbà mí!' she mouthed silently, opening both palms in helpless supplication. The younger woman's gaze held for a moment before she turned away. In that instant, Ṣ̀ikẹ́mi's last hope died. She closed her eyes, waiting for the inevitable.

The sale began and the first person in Ṣ̀ikẹ́mi's group was led forward. All around her, the gut-wrenching sobs of captives filled the air, but Ṣ̀ikẹ́mi refused to give in to the lump in her throat. In her peripheral vision she spied a group being led to the white man's ship, and shuddered. Her journey home would be so much harder if she had to cross an ocean. Her attention turned back to the captive on the auctioneer's block. She listened as the buyers wrangled and the auctioneer's price rose. The bidding ended with an exchange of goods, two bottles of whisky for the slave. Then it was Ṣ̀ikẹ́mi's turn. The auctioneer tried to rip her half-torn wrapper from her body, but she held on firm, causing a titter to spread among the hagglers. Hoping to make herself a less desirable buy, she closed her eyes and lifted her chin to a proud angle.

The auctioneer extolled her features, noting the strength in her arms and thighs. 'She'll make a good workhorse,' he announced in a leering tone. For a short while, the roar of haggling voices deafened Ṣ̀ikẹ́mi's ears. Then a soft hand touched her shoulder. She opened her eyes and saw the well-dressed young woman in front of her, beckoning her to follow. Not comprehending, Ṣìkẹ́mi stared in confusion.

'Come,' the woman said. 'You are Madam's now.'

In a dazed stupor, Ṣìkẹ́mi gaped at the offered hand. Then, as if awakening from a deep sleep, she grasped and held on to the lifeline. A man stepped forward and handed the younger woman a clean wrapper, which she draped round Ṣìkẹ́mi's shoulders. Ṣìkẹ́mi clutched the wrapper. Did this mean she was safe from the ship in the harbour? Sensing the unspoken question, the young woman spoke. 'My full name is Adérónkẹ́, but you may call me Ẹ̀gbọ́n Rónkẹ́ to show your respect. You are now the slave of the Olorì, the former queen consort and sister-in-law of the current Ọba of Èkó. Her name is Màmá Ẹfún-pọ̀róyè Ọ̀ṣuntinúbú, although everyone calls her Madam Tinúbú. Do you understand?'

Ṣìkẹ́mi nodded, still trying to fathom this turn of events. She knew of Èkó, also called Lagos, a powerful city that her parents mentioned often, because their kings, the Ọbas, kept changing. She peeked at the madam in question, but Madam's expressionless gaze stayed fixed on the horizon.

Rónkẹ́ continued. 'You will return to the palace with us, where you can eat and bathe.'

At the mention of food, Ṣìkẹ́mi's tummy groaned, although she wasn't sure she could cope with more trekking. Rónkẹ́ signalled Madam's guards, and the group started their return journey. 'What is your name?' she asked, as they walked behind Madam.

Ṣìkẹ́mi found her voice and squeaked, 'Adéṣìkẹ́mi, but my family call me Ṣìkẹ́mi.'

A short walk later, they stopped in front of two giant wooden gates marking the entrance to a palace. Ṣìkẹ́mi's eyes lit up in surprise. She'd expected a long trek to Lagos, not this.

Despite her weariness, her eyes took in the mural of intricate carvings depicting the gods, humans and various sacred animals covering the gates' entire surface. The carvings' dark wood glistened as if recently oiled, and the sun struck the figures at just the right angle, making them appear almost lifelike. Ṣìkẹ́mi itched to run her fingers over the surface, but she restrained herself.

The gates opened to allow the group entry. A broad road drew Ṣìkẹ́mi's eyes forward to the majestic, thatched palace roof rising like a row of dense dried-out treetops on the distant skyline. On either side, clusters of compounds, each with their own courtyard, lined the road to the main building, which stood enclosed behind a tall boundary wall shielding it from view. Ṣìkẹ́mi shook her head from side to side. It made no sense that the *Ọba* of Lagos owned a palace in Bàdágrì, a completely different town. But that, she decided, was a puzzle for another day.

For now, relief flooded her at the thought that she might be able to rest soon. Then doubts assailed her. As a slave, she might not get any rest. They might work her hard all day long. Perhaps even beat her. She clutched the wrapper around her shoulders like a talisman, thoughts of escape once more flooding her mind. But, every few steps she took up the road, she spotted armed guards pacing the perimeter wall. Escape would be impossible from this enclave. In a flash of understanding, she realised the long journey predicted by the seer wasn't just about the distance. It would be a long time before she saw her kin again. A sudden pain speared her heart, the ache, almost physical, spreading down to her toes. Her steps faltered as she suppressed a deep moan.

Rónkẹ́ paused and looked at her. 'What's the matter?' she asked.

'Nothing,' Ṣìkẹ́mi said, keeping her head down. No more tears henceforth, she vowed, as she forced her feet forward.

Ṣìkẹ́mi soon found herself opposite the main compound located almost at the centre of the complex. Like her family compound, the thatched roof overhung the rafters, creating a shaded veranda along the entire front façade, but there the similarities ended. The roof stood at least a tree-span high, along the entire undulating rectangular length, the eaves resting on carved cylindrical wooden pillars. Well-spaced, carved wooden doors lined the front of the building, each door a miniature of the palace's main gates. Between the doors, several small, square, wooden doors covered holes carved into the walls. Ṣìkẹ́mi pondered their use, since they did not reach the floor.

To complete the compound, two similar buildings with slightly lowered rooflines flanked the main building on either side. The rest of the courtyard, an open space large enough to house a village, enclosed a variety of shrubbery, adding colour and softening the palace's character. Around them, servants scurrying about their duties paused and bowed or curtsied as Madam and her entourage passed by. When the guards led Madam and Rónkẹ́ to the building on the left, a restraining hand on the shoulder held Ṣìkẹ́mi back. She looked at the man who had supplied her new wrapper. 'Follow me,' he said.

Ṣìkẹ́mi took note as he led her to a compound that seemed hidden in the back of the complex and north of the main palace courtyard. It stood isolated and set further back than the other courtyards. As soon as she entered, Ṣìkẹ́mi understood why. The village-sized courtyard teemed with workers, many who she presumed were slaves like her scurrying about and engaged in an activity of some sort. She spied some washing clothing near a well, while others sorted farm produce into large baskets. A few girls and women in a corner wove baskets with straw bales. Some separated strands of palm-fronds into broom-stick batches. Others fetched and carried bundles of firewood strung together. The thrum of activity overwhelmed her. She'd never seen so many busy people in one place all at once. The man led her to a thin man barking orders at a group of slaves. He barely acknowledged her before yelling for someone called Gàniyátù.

'What's your name?' The man directed the question at Ṣìkẹ́mi just as Gàniyátù appeared before him.

'Ṣìkẹ́mi.'

He gave Gàniyátù a nod. 'Settle her in.' Then he was off barking at other people.

Gàniyátù turned and moved towards the edge of the court-yard. 'Come with me. You can wash, eat, and get a little sleep. You will soon feel human again.'

Ṣìkẹ́mi's lips twisted at the irony, given her recent ordeal. To feel human again was more than she'd hoped for. The girl led her to the bathing area, a large shack within the compound but behind the main building. From here, Ṣìkẹ́mi noticed a forest formed a backdrop along the entire back wall of the rectangular building. Her mind ticked furiously at the opportunity it presented, but she was too tired to contemplate running. It would have to wait.

A short while later, cleaned and fed, Ṣìkẹ́mi shuffled into an extra-large empty room with a row of mats stacked against the wall. 'Catch some sleep,' her guide said. 'I will wake you later for the afternoon shift.'

Ṣìkẹ́mi yawned, then remembered her manners. 'Thank you. May I call you Gàni?'

When the girl nodded, Ṣìkẹ́mi thanked her again, before pulling a mat off the stack and spreading it out. Her eyes closed, and her thoughts drifted to Fọlárìn. She hoped he wasn't in the belly of the white man's ship because that would be awful. She was grateful her *orí* had saved her from being taken across the sea. As darkness enfolded her, she murmured her thanks and prayed her family's *orís* had done the same. For now, she would concentrate on regaining her strength. Then she would plan her escape.

SIX

Ṣìkẹ́mi kept her head down as she lifted her axe and swung it in a downward motion. The axe hit the wood dead centre and split into two even parts. She used her hands to arrange the two pieces on top of the growing bundle beside her. She still had two more bundles to produce to complete her afternoon quota of four. Behind her, Gbénga, the reedy head slave, was busy screaming at another hapless slave, his booming voice compensating for his lack of stature.

Out of the corner of her eye Ṣìkẹ́mi spied a young boy nearby, probably about Kúnlé's age, trying to split a chunky piece of wood into smaller bits. The ache, now familiar, hit her in the belly, but she ignored it. The boy lifted the heavy axe at an awkward angle and swung it down with minimal force. The axe hit the wood's bark and barely dented it.

'How many times do I have to show you how to chop wood?'

The boy flinched at Gbénga's roar, lifting a trembling chin as the head slave bore down on him. Ṣìkẹ́mi paused her task and gawked, as did most of the others.

'Now do it again.'

The order only made the boy more nervous. With trembling fingers, he lifted the axe and, with all his might, brought it down on the wood. The wood split just as a projected piece flew into the air before embedding itself in the boy's hand. The boy flinched and yelped. Ṣìkẹ́mi dropped her axe and ran to his side.

'Who asked for your help?'

Ṣìkẹ́mi kept her voice low, practising the patience Màmá had urged to use when dealing with her aunts. 'I'm just going to help him remove the splinter so he can finish his quota.'

'I said, who asked you? This is not your business.'

Ṣìkẹ́mi ignored the head slave and took the boy's hand. 'Here, let me see.'

Behind her, Gbénga ranted about her impudence, but she drowned him out. She inspected the boy's hand. The splinter was tiny, but a visible bit protruded out of the boy's palm. 'I can get it out for you. It won't hurt.'

The boy nodded. Bending her head, Ṣìkẹ́mi grabbed the protruding bit and pinched it between her fingers, then in one swift motion pulled it out. 'Press your finger over it to stop the bleeding,' she said.

The boy obeyed her, and Ṣìkẹ́mi stood upright, prepared to go back to her work. Then she noticed her almost-completed last two bundles of wood were missing. 'Who took my wood?'

No one answered as all the slaves returned to their tasks. Gbénga glared at Ṣìkẹ́mi, a triumphant smirk on his face. 'You have four more bundles to produce before sunset.'

Ṣìkẹ́mi squared up to him. 'No, I had two left to submit. I have already produced two today.'

'I am the boss and I say you have four more bundles to submit today.' He turned and left.

Ṣìkẹ́mi hissed, knowing she wouldn't complete the task before night-time.

. . .

It was way past mealtime by the time a weary Ṣìkẹ́mi completed her last bundle and stumbled back to the room she shared with the other slaves. Inside, slaves banded together in small groups on the sleeping mats. Ṣìkẹ́mi found an empty corner and tried to lie down. A small tap on her shoulder made her turn round, and there stood the boy and Gàni. 'We saved you some food,' the boy whispered as he offered her some èkọ wrapped in banana leaves and two small bean cakes. Ṣìkẹ́mi bestowed a grateful smile on them as she wolfed down the food, while Gàni and the boy shielded her from view, since food wasn't allowed indoors.

'What's your name and how old are you?' Ṣìkẹ́mi nodded at the boy as she swallowed her last morsel.

'I am Kàmọ́rù, and I am ten,' he said with a smile.

'Thank you, Kàmọ́rù.' She ruffled his woolly hair, and the action brought back memories of her interactions with Kúnlé. A lump formed in her throat as she settled down to sleep. She'd just completed her first day in slavery and trouble had already found her.

Within minutes of awakening, Ṣìkẹ́mi bathed, ate and presented herself for duty. The slaves all gathered in the courtyard as Gbénga called out names and assigned duties. Today, Ṣìkẹ́mi planned to keep her head down and out of other people's affairs. As much as she had done the right thing the previous day, common sense told her making an enemy of the boss was unwise. She wondered if she should apologise but wasn't ready to be that humble.

'Ṣìkẹ́mi!' She heard her name ring out. 'Woodcutting, twelve bundles!'

A loud gasp echoed round the courtyard, and Ṣìkẹ́mi knew why. He'd increased her daily allocation by a third.

'*Ẹ̀hn, that's too much! What did she expect, standing up to him? She doesn't know her position yet.*' The other slaves' whispered commentary reached her ears. For a minute Ṣìkẹ́mi considered her plight, then she stepped forward.

'*Ọ̀gá* Gbénga, you punished me yesterday, so why are you doing so again today?'

Someone bumped into her back and hissed in her ear. 'You are still talking, ẹhn? Haven't you learned anything?'

Gbénga gave her the full benefit of his stare. 'Ṣìkẹ́mi, your punishment is only just beginning. You will produce twelve bundles each day for the next three days.'

'You better keep quiet before he doubles it again,' someone said in the crowd.

'*Ọ̀gá*, can we please have our own allocation so we can get to work? Ẹhn? Time is passing by o.'

A murmur of agreement echoed around the courtyard and people elbowed Ṣìkẹ́mi out of the way as Gbénga called their names and sent them off to their duties.

Ṣìkẹ́mi seethed as she dragged her feet to the tool store in search of an axe. Outside among the trees surrounding the compound, others allocated to woodcutting had already picked a spot. As she picked a felled tree, Ṣìkẹ́mi heard the others still talking about her. Some thought her arrogant and full of herself. Others said she was stupid for courting controversy, and there were those who agreed she would learn soon enough. Ṣìkẹ́mi almost laughed. It felt like she was back in her father's compound amid her garrulous aunties. She knuckled down to work, thinking if she avoided breaks and worked through the worst of the midday sun she just might finish her quota by night-time.

She had begun the day with good intentions, and wondered

how she was going to survive slavery if she couldn't go an hour without finding trouble. Throughout the day she cleaved through the wood and, by the time the others returned from their afternoon break, six bundles of wood lay stacked beside her. But she was flagging, and she knew it. Her pace slowed and her breathing became laboured. Muscles and joints ached in places she didn't know she possessed, and her palms smarted where new blisters were forming. Still, she kept going, until a small shadow fell across her path. She looked up and found Kàmọ̀rù holding two logs in his hands.

'I've finished mine,' he said, 'so I am going to help you.'

Ṣìkẹ́mi melted. His generosity reminded her so much of her brother. Pretending to rub some dust out of her eyes, she swallowed a sob and accepted his paltry offering with a watery smile. Side by side they worked until sundown and, although his efforts made little difference to her growing pile, just having his company was enough. On the bright side, the boy copied her movements and was becoming adept at splitting wood.

That evening, as Ṣìkẹ́mi held out her hand for her supper, the cook dishing out food paused. 'You are the newcomer with the big mouth, right?'

Ṣìkẹ́mi bristled, but the woman was as old as her mother, so she held her tongue.

'You should watch yourself around here, or you'll soon be back to the Fẹlẹkẹtẹ market.'

The stark warning sent chills down Ṣìkẹ́mi's spine. She wasn't sure whether it came from kindness or spitefulness, but she couldn't ignore it.

As if testing her, the woman sliced a piece from the chunk of ẹ̀bà nestling in her hand and handed Ṣìkẹ́mi the rest. Outraged at receiving a portion half the size of everyone else's, Ṣìkẹ́mi opened her mouth to protest and caught the woman's smug smile. She clamped her mouth shut. Spite, she decided, or maybe a bit of both, but she wouldn't let her win. That night, she drank extra cups of water to fill her stomach. After all, it wasn't as if she hadn't gone hungry before.

One week later, Ṣìkẹ́mi's life had settled into a routine. After serving her punishment, Gbénga left her alone, and she stayed out of his way, the threat of being resold too big a danger to ignore. Despite the compound's size, Ṣìkẹ́mi felt trapped and, everywhere she went, the cook's eyes seem to follow her, daring her to trip up. She yearned for her family and often spent her breaks eyeing the trees with longing. Most of the slaves rarely left the compound or its immediate environs, since they had their own bathing and cooking areas. However, she'd seen a privileged few carrying bundles of firewood to other compounds, escorted by a single guard.

Guards watched the compound day and night, working in two shifts from sunrise to high noon and from noon to sundown, with an increased presence during the daytime. Ṣìkẹ́mi knew their compound was the northernmost within the complex and furthest from the main entrance. She had wondered why no one tried to escape through the surrounding trees, especially since there appeared to be no boundary wall beyond them.

The day before, she'd found herself beside Gàni, and they worked in a companionable silence all day. At sundown, as they packed up, ready to return to the courtyard, Ṣìkẹ́mi watched some guards leave. She'd observed the strange pattern all week. She nodded at the guards as she spoke. 'Why are there only two guards left by sunset? Aren't they worried people will try to escape at night?'

Gàni chuckled. 'And go where?'

'They could escape through the trees.'

Gàni shook her head, a rueful smile playing on her lips. 'In the dark? They'd be crocodile food before morning.'

Ṣìkẹ́mi's eyes widened. 'What did you say?'

'There's a swamp full of crocodiles beyond the trees. They wouldn't survive the night.'

Ṣìkẹ́mi was glad she hadn't attempted her escape yet. 'Has anyone tried?'

'Not since I arrived, but the others tell stories.'

A thought crossed Ṣìkẹ́mi's mind. 'What if the guards invented the story to deter us from trying?'

Gàni shrugged. 'Do you want to test that idea?'

Ṣìkẹ́mi chuckled. 'No.' Then she had another thought. 'So, what's stopping the crocodiles from attacking us while we work?'

'They won't come this far from the swamp. They prefer staying close to the water.'

Gàni's answers had been plausible, but Ṣìkẹ́mi wasn't giving up. She needed to study the palace layout and find its weaknesses, but the first step would be understanding Gbénga's criteria for choosing those allowed out of the compound.

Still deep in thought, Ṣìkẹ́mi flinched as a chilling scream pierced the air, followed by the sound of a whip striking flesh. The victim screamed again, and Ṣìkẹ́mi tried to tune out the sound. A murmur travelled through the slaves, and Ṣìkẹ́mi picked up key words – *thieving*, *food*. They were fed well. Nothing fancy, but enough to fill their stomachs, so Ṣìkẹ́mi could not understand why a slave would steal food, of all things.

Ṣìkẹ́mi heaved her completed bundle of wood onto her head and took it to the wood store in the courtyard. She'd learned a hard lesson from her first day and now delivered each bundle when she completed it, to prevent anyone stealing the fruit of her labour.

Inside the courtyard, she found the newly whipped slave tied to a tree, stripped naked except for a tiny loincloth. Large, oozing weals from the beating stood in sharp relief against his dark skin. He looked young, about Ṣìkẹ́mi's age. She pondered his fate but didn't linger, delivering the wood and returning in haste to her woodcutting station.

Later that evening, when all the slaves downed tools and returned to the courtyard for supper, Ṣìkẹ́mi looked for the slave. Not finding him, she asked Gàni. Gàni shrugged. 'He's probably been taken to town already. It's market day tomorrow. They'll sell him on.'

Ṣìkẹ́mi shuddered, realising the cook's threat wasn't an idle one, and she would need to pay it good heed.

SEVEN

The next day, Ṣìkẹ́mi stood at the edge of the large gathering and observed how Gbénga assigned tasks. That she was taller than most for her age, a trait she had inherited from her father, helped her see above the numerous heads in front of her. Gbénga began giving out orders. 'Ṣìkẹ́mi; laundry duties.'

Ṣìkẹ́mi sighed in relief at her name call. Although the daily woodcutting was helping to build strength in her arms, it was backbreaking work, and her hands needed the break too. She was pleased when Kàmọ́rù was also assigned to duties within the courtyard; she could watch out for him. Most of the slaves kept to themselves, but she'd noticed a few liked to pick on the smaller children. A welcome outcome of her altercation with Gbénga was that most of the slaves avoided her, knowing she was more than capable of defending herself.

By noon, she had some insight into Gbénga's methods. As she rubbed black soap into the dirty laundry and ground it against the wooden basin, she watched as those assigned the lightest duties came up to Gbénga.

'Ọ̀gá Gbénga, would you like some water?' Someone cooed

the same words every few minutes. If he were to drink all the water offered, he'd probably drown.

A girl returned from carrying a bundle of wood to another compound. 'Ọ̀gá Gbénga, is there anything else you would like me to do?' She batted her eyelids at him.

Ṣikẹ́mi got the gist of it. The slaves traded favours such as seeing to Gbénga's personal needs for lighter duties or the opportunity to escape the compound. Could she do it? she wondered.

The idea of simpering up to Gbénga left a bitter taste in her mouth. But she was pragmatic. Gritting her teeth, the next time he walked by she gave him a brittle smile, although she suspected it looked more like a grimace. 'Ẹ pẹ̀lẹ́,' she said, acknowledging his presence with the general Yorùbá greeting. Later that day, after spending several minutes whipping up some courage, she walked up to him.

'Ọ̀gá Gbénga.'

'Uh-uh?'

'Would you like me to fetch your bathwater in the morning?' She cringed and almost gagged on the words.

Gbénga nodded and thanked her, but she swore she caught a gleeful grin as he went on his way. It reminded her of her interactions with Fọlárìn. He thought he had crushed her spirit. But Ṣikẹ́mi would show him, eventually. The following morning and for the next six days, she fetched Gbénga's bathwater, but to her dismay she remained assigned to laundry duty.

Despite her tiredness from the daily grind, Ṣikẹ́mi found it hard to sleep at night, when images of her family intruded. Thoughts of how to win Gbénga's favour also occupied her mind into the early hours. She studied the other slaves and wondered how they coped with their captivity. Some older ones bore an air of resignation. Others appeared quite indifferent to their lot, but some barely spoke to anyone during the day and curled up into a ball and wept at night. The latter were mostly the young, who were probably new to captivity, she surmised.

She wondered who she would become a few years down the line. Resigned to her fate like the older ones? She shook her head. That would not be her lot. It was time to offer Gbénga more.

It was the first day of the week, a day dedicated to Ògún, the god of iron and thunder, and a new beginning, Ṣìkẹ́mi hoped. She stood in the open courtyard as Gbénga sent the slaves off one at a time. Ṣìkẹ́mi remained hopeful that she would be rewarded for a week of fetching his bathwater, but one never knew.

'Ṣìkẹ́mi: laundry, and take some time off this afternoon.'

Her heart swooped and lifted as a brainwave hit her. All the slaves were given a few hours off one afternoon a week to attend to personal chores, such as hair grooming or their personal laundry. Ṣìkẹ́mi didn't need to groom her hair, having always worn it short like a boy's. It had been the bane of her mother's life, and she had spent many hours evading her mother's eager clutches until Bàbá ordered her mother to leave her alone. Màmá relented and allowed her to keep it just short enough that it didn't need plaiting without making her look like a boy. That gave her some spare time to play with.

As the courtyard emptied, Ṣìkẹ́mi sauntered across to Gbénga. 'Ọ̀gá, do you have any laundry that needs doing? I can wash it with mine.' She watched his eyes light up, a mischievous twinkle flashing back at her. Was he reading her mind?

'Yes. Thank you,' he said. 'You can collect them later.'

Ṣìkẹ́mi gave him a polite knee dip as she left to collect the main laundry, but that twinkle left her wary and second-guessing herself. Perhaps she should have thought it through before acting.

After eating her lunch she went to the men's wing, where she found Gbénga among other senior slaves, munching through his *ẹ̀bà* and *ẹ̀gúsí* stew.

'I came for the laundry,' she said.

Gbénga pointed to a huge pile in a corner. 'There they are.'

Ṣìkẹ́mi's eyes widened, and a gasp escaped before she could hold it back. The mountain of clothes could not possibly all belong to him. The other men sniggered, confirming her fears. Determined not to be browbeaten, she mustered what dignity she could, bent and picked up an armful of clothes and carted them to the wash area. It took two additional trips to move all the clothes and the entire afternoon to wash them. When she went to gather the clothes from the rocks she'd spread them on to dry, some remained damp. A delighted smile lit her face. Damp clothes in the morning were exactly what they deserved. She itched to teach them a bigger lesson or give Gbénga a piece of her mind, but knew she was powerless. Patience, she realised, was a virtue she needed to cultivate, much as it pained her to admit it.

On the first day of her fourth week, Gbénga announced Ṣìkẹ́mi was on log-ferrying duty. Given the gasp that followed the announcement, Ṣìkẹ́mi reckoned she wasn't the only one who was surprised. She'd almost given up hope of getting out of the compound. Now she felt like singing, but contained her joy for fear of making the others jealous. The opportunity to escape the compound was reward enough. Learning the layout of the complex while doing so would be a bonus.

After the others left the compound, Gbénga assigned them a guard and explained that they would deliver logs to four different compounds. Ṣìkẹ́mi did a little jig, but stopped herself when one of the girls gave her a quizzical frown. The first three drops went without incident. Ṣìkẹ́mi delivered logs to a compound run by the chief cook, Màmá Lékan, who provided meals for the *Ọba* and for Madam Tinúbú. One was for the compound housing senior staff, including Madam's foreman, who oversaw her businesses. Bàbá Kékeré, the others called him, suggesting he was a very small man, and Ṣìkẹ́mi wondered just how tiny he was to earn such a moniker. By the time they had completed the third round, it was time for their lunch break and the group returned to their courtyard.

As they walked past the main compound on their way back, Ṣìkẹ́mi remembered something she'd seen on her first day. She nudged the girl beside her. 'What are the small wooden doors on the buildings in the main compound for?'

'Those allow in light during the day and make the rooms appear bigger.'

Ṣìkẹ́mi processed that, thinking of the differences between town and rural life. Back in her village, rooms, used only for sleeping, had no need of extra light. Life happened in the court-yard and those confined to rooms during the day, for whatever reason, used oil lamps.

After lunch, the group prepared for the final delivery round to the guards' compound. Ṣìkẹ́mi took her *oṣùka*, a small padding made of rags wound in a circle, which cushioned her head from the wood bundle, and placed it on her head. She bent to pick up the heavy load just as Gbénga's voice rang out. 'Ṣìkẹ́mi, stop! I have another task for you.'

A sinking feeling flooded Ṣìkẹ́mi's being. She saw this trip as the best opportunity for reconnaissance. Their destination was the nearest compound to the main gates, requiring a walk through the length of the complex. 'Can't someone else do it,' she whined.

Gbénga's eyebrows bowed to each other and Ṣìkẹ́mi realised her error. She snapped her mouth shut, knowing there was no point in antagonising him or she'd never get another chance. As she ran his errand, she wondered if she was just unlucky or whether Gbénga could really read her mind. She hoped with all her heart that it wasn't the latter and that she'd get another chance.

EIGHT

Ṣìkẹ́mi lay back and floated as the waves gently lapped her shoulders. Her eyes scanned the horizon, searching. A thin line in the distance presented the only possibility of refuge. While the water soothed her nerves, common sense told her she needed to get to shore. Did she have sufficient energy to swim that far? A black cloud chased the yellow streaks in the sky. Màmá and Bàbá's voices called to her, urging her home, and her instincts asserted themselves. Ṣìkẹ́mi kicked her legs and headed for shore, aiming to beat the cloud.

As if aware of her intent, the clouds moved, chasing her faster than she could swim. Now they hovered overhead. The sea grew rough, threatening to suck her under. She dug down deep and pulled on her last dregs of strength, but her arms flailed and the water sucked her under. Her last thought before everything turned black was, 'Why won't Màmá and Bàbá save me?'

Hours later, Ṣìkẹ́mi fiddled with the edge of her wrapper as she awaited her turn at the back of the wood store queue. Her enforced diligence had finally paid off and, after washing several more rounds of Gbénga's laundry, she was on wood delivery duty again. As the last person ahead picked a bundle and disappeared, Ṣìkẹ́mi rubbed the back of her neck and eyed the stacked bundles like they were poison. The dream had punctuated her sleep, leaving her with a deep sense of foreboding. *You should be more excited*, she chided herself. But her instincts told her she would be better off doing something else today.

'What is holding you up?'

The impatient query from those waiting for her intruded on her thoughts. Biting her lips, she picked a bundle and heaved it onto her head. The group filed out of the compound, with Ṣìkẹ́mi trailing from the rear. She hoped whatever troubles faced them today would affect those in front of her first. *Ṣìkẹ́mi, what an evil thought*, Màmá's imaginary voice chirped in her head. She shrugged; it was a matter of self-preservation.

The drop included the same four compounds as her first time and, as she passed the main one on her way to Màmá Lékan's, thoughts of Madam and Rónkẹ́ flitted through her mind. She hadn't seen either woman since the day she arrived and wondered if they remembered her at all. From the snippets she gathered from the slaves and guards, the Ọba was very much in residence, as was Madam, who bankrolled him. She still didn't know why the Ọba was in Bàdágrì instead of Lagos.

Màmá Lékan's compound buzzed with scores of people at various stages of food preparation. Ṣìkẹ́mi and her companions untied their bundles and began stacking the wood pieces into the compound's wood store. As she worked, Ṣìkẹ́mi spied a little boy playing with a worm and a familiar scene flashed through her mind, transporting her to an earlier time. It was the first time she'd taken Kúnlé into the bushes without Bàbá.

'Look, Ṣìkẹ́mi!'

She'd paused at his unbridled excitement and looked over

her shoulder. The chubby five-year-old squatted over a tiny creature writhing on the ground, his face bathed in wonder. Ṣìkẹ́mi walked over to inspect the insect.

'*Ekòló*?' he asked.

Ṣìkẹ́mi shook her head, moved closer and pointed. 'No, *Ọkùn*. Can you see it has many legs?' She understood the boy's confusion. The millipede looked like a bigger version of the earthworm he had played with earlier. He peered closer.

'I see them. There are so many!'

'Touch it gently with your stick.'

The child obeyed, and the millipede responded by curling into a circle. Kúnlé dropped his stick and clapped with glee, as if it was the most exciting thing he'd ever seen. She'd ruffled his head before drawing him close and cupping his face between her hands. The action elongated the three tribal marks, just like hers, on each of his cheeks. Her heart had bled for him when Bàbá performed the ritual when he was just four months old. But the scarification, the only means of distinguishing friend from foe, hadn't saved either of them in the end.

Ṣìkẹ́mi pushed the unhappy thoughts away and, as she filed the last log, a familiar voice imprinted on her consciousness. She looked up and saw Màmá Lékan chatting with none other than Rónkẹ́. On her way out, she dipped her knee as she passed them and said goodbye. Only Màmá Lékan responded, and Ṣìkẹ́mi let out a sad whoosh of air. She'd expected Rónkẹ́ to recognise her and say something.

'You there, stop!'

Ṣìkẹ́mi flinched. She paused and turned round slowly.

'What is your name?' Màmá Lékan asked.

'Ṣìkẹ́mi,' Rónkẹ́ supplied.

So, she remembered! Ṣìkẹ́mi waited for Màmá Lékan to continue.

'We need a lot more wood today as the palace has guests. Can you bring back one more bundle?'

Ṣìkẹ́mi nodded, relief flowing through her veins. 'I shall tell Ọ̀gá.'

'How are you?'

Ṣìkẹ́mi's eyes widened in surprise. After her initial snub, she hadn't expected Rónkẹ́ to address her.

'I am well,' she said with an uncharacteristic shyness.

Rónkẹ́ nodded and turned back to Màmá Lékan. Dismissed, Ṣìkẹ́mi left.

After lunch, Ṣìkẹ́mi sought Gbénga and relayed Màmá Lékan's request. Gbénga remained silent for aeons, and Ṣìkẹ́mi read the undisguised suspicion on his face.

She lifted both her hands. 'Ọ̀gá, if you don't believe me, ask the others or the guard.'

Gbénga chewed his lips for a moment, as if undecided. 'I don't have another guard to escort a single slave to that compound.'

Ṣìkẹ́mi saw his dilemma, since she and the others were heading south.

Gbénga's cloud cleared. 'I know. You take the logs, then come straight back here.'

Ṣìkẹ́mi's nose flared as an angry retort rose inside her throat. It was the second time he was preventing her from venturing near the gates. Then, another thought swiftly followed. On her way back, she could explore the north of the compound unaccompanied!

She bit back her annoyance and nodded.

Gbénga's stare probed, as if trying to read her mind. 'You should know the guards have instructions to shoot any unaccompanied slaves near the gates.'

Ṣìkẹ́mi kept her face passive and gave a small nod.

The unease returned as Ṣìkẹ́mi and the group started out. At Màmá Lékan's, they parted ways, and the others continued south. Màmá Lékan's courtyard was quieter, although a fair bit of cooking was still ongoing. As she walked across to the wood store, she saw the little boy again. Their eyes met, and his uncanny resemblance to Kúnlé at the same age struck her. She smiled at him. 'What is your name?'

'Bíọ́dún,' he said, returning her smile as she passed by.

As Ṣìkẹ́mi occupied herself with stacking the extra bundle of wood, she considered what to do with the opportunity she had. She decided she would explore the rear of each of the nearby compounds and check if they were bordered by a swampy forest. If yes, they could be crocodile-infested. If not, they might provide an opportunity for escape. She stored the last few pieces of wood atop the stack and dusted the grime off her hands. Then she noticed Bíọ́dún nearby, squatting, with a thin stick in his hand, prodding something writhing in the dust.

At first, Ṣìkẹ́mi's brain barely registered the squirming object, then something in the recesses of her memory stirred. Alert, she zoomed in on the object – and froze. It was a black-necked spitting cobra. A baby one, but a cobra, nonetheless. At once, lessons from Bàbá rose to her mind. First: back away slowly. Two: keep your eyes averted to avoid being blinded by a spit-full of venom. How could she do both and save the child who was completely oblivious to the impending mortal danger?

The snake slithered on its belly into a protective coil and completed a turning circle. Now facing the child, it fanned out the venom glands on its neck, ready for attack. Ṣìkẹ́mi let out an almighty howl and, acting on pure instinct, grabbed the child's arm and hurled him as far away as possible. In the same instant, she felt something cool hit the corner of her eye, which exploded in searing pain. The child landed in a heap, his screams joining Ṣìkẹ́mi's, and pandemonium let loose.

The hysterical screams brought adults thundering to the scene, just as the snake slithered back underneath the rest of the firewood.

'Did it bite you?' a voice asked.

'My eye! The snake spat in my eye.' Ṣìkẹ́mi screamed, howled and hopped, pointing to her right eye, now clamped shut. The pain felt like a thousand tiny knife stabs. The adults grappled with her, trying to make her stand still so they could examine the eye.

'Breast milk,' someone said in the background. 'We need breast milk. Get some from Màmá Bíọ́dún.'

Someone else produced a bowl of water. 'Here, dip your eye in here and let it rinse out the venom.'

But the words failed to register through the fog of Ṣìkẹ́mi's pain. Then muscular arms wrestled her to the ground and held her arms and legs. Someone prised her right eye open and poured some water over it. Ṣìkẹ́mi barely noticed the frantic conversation in the background.

'We need breast milk. Hurry!'

'You have to wait. She's still expressing it.'

'Tell her to come and do it here, straight into the eye.'

The water helped and Ṣìkẹ́mi's writhing lessened at the slight reduction in the intensity of the stabs, but the pain remained unbearable. Then she felt someone cradle her head. An unfamiliar voice spoke in the background. 'What's her name?'

'It's Ṣìkẹ́mi,' Màmá Lékan said.

'Come on, Ṣìkẹ́mi. Open your eye for me. I am Bíọ́dún's mother.'

Then the woman squeezed her breast, expressing a steady stream into Ṣìkẹ́mi's eye. The milk stung and Ṣìkẹ́mi struggled, but firm hands kept her still. Soon, it was all over, and she relaxed into the arms that held her, just as a lethargic feeling wormed its way over her legs up towards her chest. Her chest tightened. *I can't breathe*, she thought. *I can't breathe!*

'Look! There's blood on her foot.' The voice sounded far away.

'The snake bit her, too. This must be the devil's handiwork.'

'Look, she's fainting!'

Ṣìkẹ́mi processed the last sentence just as her world turned black.

A searing pain in her ankle brought Ṣìkẹ́mi screaming back to consciousness. She panted, taking quick breaths as she'd seen her mother do during labour, hoping it would make the pain bearable. The pungent, sickly smell of burning flesh permeated the air. She scanned the room with her left eye, since her right one was swollen shut. The room and sleeping platform she lay on looked unfamiliar, but Màmá Lékan's and Màmá Bíọ́dún's faces came into focus. Ṣìkẹ́mi surmised that the person cradling her foot was the local herbalist.

Màmá Lékan rubbed a soothing hand over Ṣìkẹ́mi's head while she spoke to the herbalist. 'Have you cut out all the flesh around the wound?'

'Yes. I've done the best I can. The rest is down to the gods.' The herbalist pulled a poultice of fresh herbs out of a sack and packed it over the wound before binding it with clean cotton rags.

Ṣìkẹ́mi sank back in relief. She didn't think she could take any more pain.

'Here, drink this.' Màmá Bíọdún offered her a bowl, lifting her head off the sleeping platform.

Ṣìkẹ́mi took the bowl and sipped, her body trembling as she did so. It tasted vile, and she pushed the bowl away.

'All of it.' Màmá Bíọdún steadied the bowl so she could drink more.

Once the last drop was gone, Ṣìkẹ́mi fell back against the mat. Her brain felt addled, and her teeth clattered, so Màmá Lékan drew out a heavy wrapper and tucked it round her shoulders. Ṣìkẹ́mi closed her eyes and oblivion found her once more.

NINE

For three days, Ṣìkẹ́mi drifted in and out of consciousness. Once she heard voices from far away. One sounded like her father's, telling her she needed to fight and be strong. Another told her to sleep and stop worrying. One morning she woke sweat-free and sat up for the first time. Hunger pangs rumbled in her belly, and she couldn't remember her last meal. She looked down at her left foot and winced. A fresh poultice lay over the wound, but it could not disguise the discoloured and bloated flesh. She ran her fingers over her right eye. It was no longer swollen shut, and she could see through it, although in a somewhat blurry fashion.

Màmá Bíọ́dún entered the room and saw Ṣìkẹ́mi, and her eyes lit up.

'Ah! You have returned to the land of the living.'

Then Ṣìkẹ́mi's stomach rumbled loud enough to startle the infant strapped to Màmá Bíọ́dún's back. The child wailed and her mother bounced her up and down while dancing on the spot.

'I'll get you some *èkọ*. Something light for your stomach.'
She smiled and left the room.

Ṣìkẹ́mi wrinkled her nose in distaste. She hated *èkọ*, a solid
form of *àkàmù*, made from cornstarch, that took on the acidic
flavour of the leaves it came wrapped in. Then she remembered
she was a slave and lucky to have any food. Màmá Bíọ́dún returned
with the *èkọ* and some spinach stew, which Ṣìkẹ́mi devoured in no
time. Then Màmá Lékan's head peeked through the door.

'How is Ṣìkẹ́mi today?'

Màmá Bíọ́dún smiled and pointed to the empty leaves on
the floor. 'You know what the elders say. "Bàbá is unwell, but
full leaves of *èkọ* are entering his room and empty ones are
coming out."'

Màmá Lékan moved closer to Ṣìkẹ́mi so she could see for
herself. 'Ah! So she is eating. The gods be praised.'

Later that day, Màmá Bíọ́dún allowed Ṣìkẹ́mi to get up and
test her swollen leg. The leg bore her weight with some discomfort but tolerable pain. When Ṣìkẹ́mi hobbled into Màmá
Lékan's courtyard on a makeshift wooden crutch, everyone
burst into applause.

'*Okú oríre.*' Your *orí* has served you well. Back-slaps
followed the felicities, as they congratulated her on her good
fortune. A few rubbed her head in affection, like she was some
kind of talisman. When Bíọ́dún, the child she'd saved, came
over and held her hand, Ṣìkẹ́mi's eyes welled. She sniffled and
wiped her nose with the edge of her wrapper.

'That's enough for today.' Màmá Bíọ́dún took her hand
and led her back to her room in the adjacent compound.

Over the next fortnight, several townsfolk visited the palace to
see the slave who had survived a double cobra attack and lived.

Ṣìkẹ́mi wondered if Rónkẹ́ would too, but she didn't. Instead, Gbénga showed up. 'Enjoy the fame because it won't last, and remember, you are still a slave,' he said, his voice laced with sarcasm.

The words stung, and Ṣìkẹ́mi held up her hands. 'I didn't court fame and I can't control the circumstances.'

Màmá Bíọ́dún entered the room. 'I see you have a visitor.'

Ṣìkẹ́mi watched as Gbénga's torso lengthened, and his manner took on a deference. 'Ah, Màmá Bíọ́dún. I did not know she was staying with you. Thank you for looking after her. She is one of our own, and we miss her.'

'Well, you will have to keep missing her, because she is staying here.'

A speculative gleam entered Gbénga's eyes. 'Ah. I see.' He turned to Ṣìkẹ́mi. 'I hope your recovery is fast. Do not forget your old friends.' He winked as he made his way out.

The conversation felt a little surreal, until Ṣìkẹ́mi realised Gbénga thought she now had powerful benefactors. Màmá Bíọ́dún was Bàbá Kékeré's junior wife and Bàbá Kékeré, the foreman, ran the palace even when he wasn't around. Troubled, her thoughts returned to the unwanted fame. Now she was more recognisable in town, escaping would be harder. Knowing how powerful Madam was, she couldn't imagine anyone would willingly harbour a slave of hers.

Like Gbénga predicted, Ṣìkẹ́mi's fame passed as fleeting as a flash of lightning. Although it took a few more weeks, her eye and foot healed, the latter leaving a star-shaped scar, where the herbalist had excised the venom, as a memento. Now back to health, Ṣìkẹ́mi expected Màmá Bíọ́dún to send her back to the slaves' compound, but nothing happened.

Uncomfortable with the uncertainty, one evening she approached Màmá Bíọ́dún.

'Màmá, shall I return to the slaves' quarters in the morning?'

Màmá Bíọ́dún's gaze shifted from the child suckling at her chest, and her eyes narrowed.

'What for? Are you not happy here? Have I not cared for you like you are my very own?' Her voice rose on the last question, and Ṣìkẹ́mi felt a frisson of alarm.

She fell to her knees. 'Do not be cross with me, Màmá. I thought you would want me to go back once I recovered. You have cared for me well, and I am grateful.'

Màmá Bíọ́dún's tone softened. 'You risked your life for my son. I thought you'd be happier staying here. I can't imagine that life is easy in that compound. I'm happy with the arrangement if you help with chores and care for the children.'

Ṣìkẹ́mi searched Màmá Bíọ́dún's face. 'Won't Bàbá Kékeré and Ọ̀gá Gbénga mind?'

'You leave them to me.'

Ṣìkẹ́mi let out a sigh. 'I'd like to stay.' Then she hovered with indecision. Who would watch out for Kàmọ́rù? She hadn't seen him since her attack and hoped he was well.

Màmá Bíọ́dún interrupted her thoughts. 'Is there anything else?'

'It's just that I used to watch out for a little boy, Kàmọ́rù. Without me there...' Her voice trailed off.

Màmá Bíọ́dún's face softened. 'If that is all, I will arrange for him to be transferred somewhere safer.'

Ṣìkẹ́mi's face split wide open. 'Thank you, Màmá. Thank you.'

. . .

The following day Ṣìkẹ́mi was bent over a raffia broom, sweeping Màmá Bíọ́dún's room, when Kúdí, a servant she'd seen in Màmá Lékan's courtyard, arrived with two wrappers. Màmá Bíọ́dún had promised her those that morning.

'I see you've found yourself a benefactor.' The girl eyed her from head to toe as if she were vermin.

Ṣìkẹ́mi took a step backward, wondering what she'd done to invite such disdain. The girl held up the wrappers, and, as Ṣìkẹ́mi reached for them, she let them fall to the floor. Ṣìkẹ́mi scrambled for the wrappers, sweeping them off the dirty floor.

'Just remember you are a slave, so don't go thinking above your station. You have no friends here.'

Ṣìkẹ́mi watched her go with clouded eyes. People seemed intent on reminding her of her status, as if she needed it. It was clear she had new enemies. Was the girl just motivated by jealousy or was this Gbénga's doing? Given Gbénga's response to Màmá Bíọ́dún, she didn't think he would deliberately antagonise her. She shrugged. She couldn't control the other girl's behaviour, but when she planned her escape she would need to watch out for her.

Ṣìkẹ́mi walked down the centre of Bàdágrì town, a spring in her step. This was the happiest she'd been since her enslavement. While her family dominated her mind at night, during the day there was plenty to distract her from painful thoughts. It was her first time outside the palace walls since her capture six months earlier. Ọba Akítóyè, Bàdágrì's de facto ruler, favoured the white man and his emissaries, who were building a second house for the priests of the white man's god. The Yorùbá called them the faith people. Their first building looked normal, but there were rumours the new one had two levels stacked on each other. Everyone was talking about it and Ṣìkẹ́mi had begged Màmá Bíọ́dún to take her to town to see the marvel for herself.

Beside her, Bíọ́dún skipped along, his hand firmly ensconced in hers. A few paces ahead, Màmá Bíọ́dún led the way with the baby strapped to her back. '*Ẹ̀káàsàn!*' The felicity wishing people a pleasant afternoon rang in the air. Màmá Bíọ́dún stopped to greet everyone she recognised, while Ṣìkẹ́mi curtsied behind her. The noise, smells and sensations all felt different. But then again, compared to the last time she'd been here, so did she.

In the first month following her recovery, her chores were limited to running errands for Màmá Bíọ́dún and Bàbá Kékeré and taking care of their children. Caring for the children had given her a new purpose. She loved showing Bíọ́dún the wonder of nature that surrounded them in the bushes within the palace grounds. And like her brother Lékan, he soaked it up. It wasn't long before the adults recognised Ṣìkẹ́mi's affinity with young children and, during the day, all the toddlers in the compound became her responsibility. She'd been able to wander all over the palace grounds with the children, bringing her one step closer to her goal, although she didn't have a useful plan yet. Somehow, the idea of escape had lost its urgency. Despite the opportunities available, she had done little to plan an escape route and she was unwilling to explore why.

Màmá Bíọ́dún and Ṣìkẹ́mi came to a stop in front of the faith people's building and Ṣìkẹ́mi's mouth opened like a catfish gasping for air. The house stood apart from the others, its brick walls at complete odds with the surrounding bamboo structures. Instead of the traditional thatched roof, a solid flat roof covered the building's first floor, and the incomplete second floor protruded out of it.

Màmá Bíọ́dún pointed out a man in a long, black robe, issuing instructions to the workmen.

'That's one of their priests.'

Ṣìkẹ́mi's eyes bulged. 'But he is like us.'

'Yes. He is one of the returnee slaves freed by the white man. That one is called Àjàyí Káráúdà.'

Ṣìkẹ́mi studied the priest, wondering what kind of name he bore. Àjàyí, she recognised, but Káráúdà sounded foreign. A pristine white collar encircled the neckline of the priest's robe, which, although long like an *agbádá,* had a slim body and sleeves. The priest stopped talking and bent his head over a flat white sheet in his hand. A slim cylindrical object in his fingers moved along the sheet from left to right. Intrigued, Ṣìkẹ́mi squinted, trying to make sense of the man's hand movements.

'What's he doing?'

'He's recording in a book. White people like to record what they said to whom.'

'How will someone else understand what he recorded?'

'They teach each other. Bàbá Kékeré said it's called *ridin* and *raitin.* Just like our *Bàbálawos* teach their apprentices to understand what the Ifá board says, they teach and learn.'

Màmá Bíọ́dún lifted her gaze to the sky. 'We need to go before that rolls in.'

Ṣìkẹ́mi followed Màmá Biodun's fingers. The bands of dark cloud looked far away, but the muggy air signalled an imminent downpour. As they headed towards the palace, Ṣìkẹ́mi's heart filled with hope. She'd seen a freed slave walking in the white man's ways with her own eyes. One day, she too would be free. She just knew it.

TEN

'Ṣìkẹ́mi, stop. Wait for me!'

At Màmá Bíọ́dún's request, Ṣìkẹ́mi did a slow turn. She and Bíọ́dún were several yards ahead of his mother, who, just like she did strolling into town, greeted every familiar face.

'Ṣìkẹ́mi? That's an uncommon name,' said the woman Màmá Bíọ́dún was talking to. 'I met a woman a few months ago at Ìlarǒ who was called Màmá Ṣìkẹ́mi.'

At the woman's pronouncement, Ṣìkẹ́mi's mouth flew open. When she recovered, she closed the distance between them. 'Màmá, did she say anything to you?' Her hand trembled as she grabbed the woman's arm.

The woman swept a speculative gaze over Ṣìkẹ́mi. 'She said she lost a daughter who was ten plus four at the time. Where are you from?'

'I am from Ìsàlẹ̀-Odò, in Ẹ̀gbádò land,' Ṣìkẹ́mi said.

Màmá Bíọ́dún's gaze swivelled between the woman and Ṣìkẹ́mi. 'Madam Tinúbú bought her from the slave market six months ago.'

The woman jerked backward. 'The one who saved your

son? Ah. I was not in town when it happened, so I never met her.'

The woman focused on Ṣìkẹ́mi once more. 'The woman had a child. A boy around ten years old. His name started with K...'

'Kúnlé.' Ṣìkẹ́mi finished the sentence, her eyes dancing. She turned and grasped Màmá Bíọ́dún, her feet bouncing on the spot. 'They are alive! They are alive!'

'Wait,' Màmá Bíọ́dún said. 'It might not be your family.'

But Ṣìkẹ́mi was already hugging her. The similarities were too much of a coincidence. She grabbed the other woman next. 'Màmá, thank you. Thank you!' Then she turned and headed for the palace, dragging Bíọ́dún behind her.

At the palace, Ṣìkẹ́mi wanted to scream her news, but there was no one to listen. Instead she fed the children and got them ready for bed, while her insides threatened to burst. She wished she'd asked if the stranger knew anything about her father. Ìlarǒ was miles away from Ìsàlẹ̀-Odò. Had her màmá gone there to trade, or had the whole family moved to Ìlarǒ? So many questions she wished she'd asked when she had the chance. Still, nothing could dim her joy, because knowing Màmá and Kúnlé were alive was enough. Now she had something to escape for.

Ṣìkẹ́mi spent the next few days considering alternative ways to escape, but she couldn't get within the main gates without Màmá Bíọ́dún or the children. She wouldn't endanger the children by abandoning them while they were in her care. While they were safe from adults within the palace, her incident with the snake showed other dangers lurked. Her best idea was to convince Màmá Bíọ́dún to visit town again and disappear while she was busy chatting with people. All she had to do was encourage Bíọ́dún to stick by his mother while she eased herself in the bushes, and she'd be gone. If she changed into men's clothing, she might avoid recognition in town. She considered stealing a *dànṣíkí* and *ṣòkòtò* from Bàbá Kékeré, but the man was so large she'd drown in them. She'd have to steal some from others in the compound. With her plan all set, Ṣìkẹ́mi turned her attention to getting to town.

One evening, Màmá Bíọ́dún sat on a mat on the veranda, her back against the wall. Around them, conversation flowed as members of the compound joked and shared gossip. Once she had put the children to bed, Ṣìkẹ́mi sat down beside her and, when a lull appeared in the conversation, she seized the moment. 'Màmá, can we visit the town soon?'

Màmá Bíọ́dún turned and looked at her. 'Why? It wasn't that long ago that we went.'

Ṣìkẹ́mi fidgeted with her fingers. 'I know, I just like it there. It's busy and interesting.'

'That's true, but I don't plan to visit town any time soon. We've got all we need.'

Màmá Bíọ́dún rejoined the conversation, leaving a floundering Ṣìkẹ́mi wondering what to do next. She tried twice more, on different occasions, and met the same response. The fourth time, Màmá Bíọ́dún put down the wooden spoon she'd been stirring the beans in the cooking pot with and planted her hands on her hips. 'Adéṣìkẹ́mi, why do you keep insisting on going to town when I've said no three times? What are you not telling me?'

Màmá Bíọ́dún's use of her full given name spelt trouble. Ṣìkẹ́mi stepped back. 'It's nothing. I just wanted to go, is all.' Instead of being subtle, she'd been too obvious, and Màmá Bíọ́dún's glare said she didn't want to hear another word of it. Patience. That was what she needed, and she prayed fervently that the gods would grant her some, because the waiting was killing her.

. . .

Just as she settled the children down, Bàbá Kékeré arrived from his own room to eat with his wife and a deep unease settled in the pit of Ṣìkẹ́mi's stomach. She knelt and greeted him, averting her eyes to avoid the leery grin on his face. Then she began dishing up his and his wife's meal. Once more, she avoided his eyes as she put the food in front of the adults, then she retreated to the courtyard, to ponder on Bàbá Kékeré's behaviour.

Things were different when she first started living with Màmá Bíọ́dún, with Bàbá Kékeré ignoring her most of the time except to send her on minute errands. However, in the last month, Ṣìkẹ́mi's body had changed. The tiny mounds on her chest had each grown to the size of a small mango, and she'd caught Bàbá Kékeré gazing at them with a strange look on his face. The following week, when he visited his wife, he reserved a special greeting for Ṣìkẹ́mi.

'How are you, my good girl?'

Ṣìkẹ́mi looked over her shoulder, thinking he was talking to someone else until she realised he meant her.

More compliments followed, but only when Màmá Bíọ́dún was out of earshot. The first time he sent her to buy kola nuts from Màmá Lékan, who kept a small convenience store in her spare time, he told her to keep the change. She refused it until Màmá Bíọ́dún told her off for being ungracious.

'When an elder offers you a gift, you take it and say thank you.'

Chastened, Ṣìkẹ́mi took the money and thanked Bàbá Kékeré, but her instincts told her something wasn't quite right. He called her his flower that day, which brought back memories of when Fọlárìn's family used to praise her beauty. Surely he couldn't be thinking of making her his third wife? He'd reached out a hand to palm her cheek, but she'd dodged out of the way.

So far, she'd been careful to avoid ever being alone with him. When Màmá Bíọ́dún sent her on errands to him, she always stood at his door to deliver the message, ignoring his invitations to enter.

After Ṣìkẹ́mi cleared their used plates, she disappeared into the courtyard until she heard Màmá Bíọ́dún calling her name. 'Here,' she said, offering Ṣìkẹ́mi a beautiful patterned *àdìre* wrapper. 'Bàbá Kékeré bought it for you, for the palace celebrations for the new yam festival. And this is for me.' She held up another wrapper made of rich *òfì*, the most expensive traditional Yorùbá fabric one could buy. The wide smile on her face showed her delight at Bàbá Kékeré's thoughtfulness.

Ṣìkẹ́mi thought it prudent to act likewise. She gritted her teeth and knelt before him, her body tense. 'I am thankful, Bàbá.'

Bàbá Kékeré smiled, and her skin crawled. For a moment, he looked just like the snake that bit her. She scrambled off her knees back to the courtyard, wishing there was someone she could talk to. The girls her age and older shunned her because of her privilege, and she worried that telling Màmá Lékan might cause her to fall out with Màmá Bíọ́dún. It seemed Bàbá Kékeré was toying with her, but for what purpose she wasn't sure.

That night, the dream came and Ṣìkẹ́mi woke to the feel of something hot and heavy pressing against her back. Then she heard the whisper and her body stilled.

'I'll make it good for you, my flower.'

A wet and sticky tongue licked the back of her ear. Ṣìkẹ́mi's head buzzed and her heart raced. What on earth was Bàbá Kékeré doing with her in his wife's bedroom? Before Ṣìkẹ́mi fell asleep, Màmá Bíọ́dún had gone to sleep in his room. So where was she? She slowed her breathing, feigning slumber, wondering how to extricate herself from the busy hands wandering all over her back and behind.

Sensing she was awake, Bàbá Kékeré clamped a hand over her mouth and Ṣìkẹ́mi felt him pressing hard against her back. She was no match for his strength, but she knew she needed to escape, preferably without waking the children. She relaxed her body and reached a hand behind to stroke Bàbá Kékeré's thigh.

'Argh!' He arched against her. 'My flower... so good.'

The hand on her mouth slipped. She needed to buy time, so she forced the words out.

'I promise not to scream.'

Her assailant relaxed and removed the hand covering her mouth. Ṣìkẹ́mi breathed easier while she considered her options. She knew little of the ways of men and women, but whatever it was she wanted none of it with Bàbá Kékeré. The hands wandering over her grew frantic, pulling at her wrapper, then they cupped her breasts and Bàbá Kékeré moaned. Without warning, he flipped her over, so she was under him, and his thigh pushed between her legs. Ṣìkẹ́mi saw her opportunity and took it. As his face closed in on hers, she rose to meet him and clamped her teeth on his nose.

Bàbá Kékeré yelped, rolled over and collapsed beside her, his hand over his nose. Seizing the moment, Ṣìkẹ́mi scrambled off the mat and fled through the door, her feet flying in no particular direction. I need help, she thought. But who could she go to? Her first thought was Rónkẹ́. She immediately dismissed the idea. She considered Màmá Lékan. The woman was kindness personified, but too close to the problem. She paused and looked up, her heart pulsating from the overdose of adrenalin, and realised her feet had brought her to Màmá Lékan's courtyard anyway. She looked down at her wrapper and cringed at the bloody sight. Before anyone found her, she had to clean herself. She left the courtyard for the bathing area and drew water from the nearby well.

Şìkẹ́mi seethed as she dabbed at her wrapper with vigour, but that simply spread the bloodstains around. Under the cover of darkness, she allowed herself the unusual luxury of venting at this new development. She sank on top of an upturned bucket and, with balled fists, pummelled her own thighs until she was spent. Tears of frustration welled, and she brushed an impatient hand across them as the potential ramifications of biting Bàbá Kékeré's nose hit her. Would he hang about? Would Madam sell her or worse? She needed a friend, but who? The echo of approaching footsteps alerted her to someone else's presence. Still on an adrenalin high, she bolted and ran smack into Rónkẹ́.

ELEVEN

Ṣìkẹ́mi froze and her mouth fell open as Rónkẹ́ came to an abrupt halt. Rónkẹ́'s eyes tracked Ṣìkẹ́mi's tear-streaked cheeks, the wet wrapper with spatters of red, and they grew wider. Still, in a calm voice that belied the gravity of the moment she spoke. 'Is that your blood?'

'No.'

Rónkẹ́ lifted a quizzical eyebrow.

'It's Bàbá Kékeré's. I bit his nose.'

Rónkẹ́ spluttered, and her hand flew to her mouth. Her eyes roamed over Ṣìkẹ́mi from head to toe, then she scanned the bathing area. It was empty except for the two of them. She grabbed Ṣìkẹ́mi's arm and dragged her into a secluded section behind a clump of shrubbery. After checking again that no one was around, she turned to Ṣìkẹ́mi.

'What happened?'

Ṣìkẹ́mi opened her mouth, then closed it, unsure of what to say.

'Did he force you to sleep with him?'

'He tried to. That's why I bit him. To get away.'

Rónkẹ́'s nostrils flared. 'Where was Màmá Bíọ́dún when this happened?'

'She slept in Bàbá Kékeré's room last night.'

Ṣìkẹ́mi watched Rónkẹ́'s lips flatten into a thin line, her eyes blazing with a fury she'd never seen before. Rónkẹ́ shook her head. 'Come with me.' She grasped Ṣìkẹ́mi's arm again and pulled her along.

'Please don't make me return there,' Ṣìkẹ́mi said, when she realised where they were going. Why on earth did these things keep happening to her? Her stomach churned and any time now she was going to retch.

'We have to deal with this. You can't hide from it.'

Then Ṣìkẹ́mi remembered she had left the children in the room with their father. She wondered if he'd stayed to look after them. Unlikely, she thought.

They arrived in Màmá Bíọ́dún's room to find a sleep-tousled Màmá Bíọ́dún staring at her children and the blood-stained mat. She clasped her hands to her chest when she saw Ṣìkẹ́mi, a relieved expression on her face, but that quickly changed to a frown when she noticed Rónkẹ́.

'Ẹ káàrọ̀, Màmá Bíọ́dún.'

Màmá Bíọ́dún returned Rónkẹ́'s terse greeting and immediately turned her attention back to Ṣìkẹ́mi. 'What happened? Did you injure yourself? Why didn't you wake me in Bàbá Kékeré's room? You didn't need to bother Rónkẹ́. You know I am always—'

Rónkẹ́ cut her off. 'It's your husband's blood, not hers.'

Màmá Bíọ́dún's demeanour changed, consternation replacing her initial concern. 'What happened to him?'

Silence greeted her question. Rónkẹ́ fixed her with a hard stare before breaking the silence. 'I think you can guess. Your husband attacked the girl, right here in your room while you were sleeping in his.'

The words spewed out of Rónké's mouth with so much venom, Sìkẹ́mi did a double-take. Rónké stalked forward like a tiger homing in on its prey and Màmá Bíọdún shrank back. 'We both know this is not the first time he's molested young girls.'

'But I didn't think he'd do that to the girl who saved his son's life.'

Rónké's lips curled. 'Well, we both know better now. Where is he?'

'I don't know. He wasn't in his room when I woke and he's obviously not here.'

'Hiding and nursing his injuries, I suppose.' Rónké hissed, then spun on her heels, pulling Sìkẹ́mi along.

Màmá Bíọdún's brows squished together. 'Where are you taking her?'

'To Màmá Lékan.'

'But everyone will find out!'

'Do you have a better solution?'

Màmá Bíọdún looked at the floor, crestfallen. Then she let out a deep sigh.

'I thought not.'

Rónké turned and left, dragging a befuddled Sìkẹ́mi with her. As she followed Rónké, Sìkẹ́mi wondered what had happened to the other girls Bàbá Kékeré had molested, because surely that was her fate too.

Sìkẹ́mi struggled to keep pace with Rónké as she strode across the road to Màmá Lékan's compound. A barely leashed fury convulsed Rónké's entire being, and her grip on Sìkẹ́mi's hand was so tight, Sìkẹ́mi knew it would leave a bruise. At Màmá Lékan's door, Rónké instructed Sìkẹ́mi to wait outside. As she paced the veranda, she heard muffled voices, but couldn't make out what they were saying.

The household was stirring, and soon the courtyard would flood with people. What would the other servants make of her blood-splattered and dishevelled state? Her mind revisited Rónkẹ́'s revelation, and she shivered. The thought of Bàbá Kékeré's intentions filled her with revulsion. Would she always be vulnerable to the whim of others?

Moments later Rónkẹ́ came out, her face still filled with anger, the cords on her neck straining to escape. She invited Ṣìkẹ́mi into the room. 'You will stay with Màmá Lékan from now on.' Rónkẹ́ bit out the clipped instruction.

The image of Kúdí's stark warning floated through her mind. Màmá Lékan's compound would provide no refuge. Her palms felt sweaty, and she lifted her eyes in a plea. 'Please don't make me. People will talk and ask questions.'

'They can ask, but you don't have to answer any of their questions. Màmá Lékan will look out for you.' Before Ṣìkẹ́mi could say anything else, Rónkẹ́ jerked her head in Màmá Lékan's direction, turned and left.

Ṣìkẹ́mi stared at Rónkẹ́'s back, her lips trembling. She turned to Màmá Lékan. 'What did I do to offend her?'

'Argh! Child. It is not you. She has her own demons. Here's a clean wrapper. Go and clean yourself up. It will all blow over soon.'

Ṣìkẹ́mi dragged her quivering legs to the bathing area, her head brimming with thoughts. How was she going to handle the speculation surrounding her change in circumstances? Would Bàbá Kékeré seek retribution? Could she still look after the children? As she collected her bathing water, she realised she'd been here before – enfolded in a blanket of security until it was yanked away, leaving an emptiness in its wake. She couldn't keep doing this. Perhaps it was time she took the lesson her *orí* had been trying to teach her to heart.

She scooped some water out of her bucket and, as the cold

water hit her skin, she renewed her vow. From now on, her key priorities were staying safe and making an escape, and she would do whatever was necessary to make it so.

Màmá Lékan must have warned everyone to leave Ṣìkẹ́mi alone, as no one batted an eyelid when she started sleeping in the woman's room. To her relief, Màmá Bíọ́dún still expected her to look after the children and brought them over to Màmá Lékan's compound. Màmá Bíọ́dún maintained a cordial but somewhat nervous demeanour towards her. She also told whoever asked that Bàbá Kékeré had departed for a farm on urgent business. On the surface nothing had changed, and, as the next few days passed quietly, Ṣìkẹ́mi hoped the furore would die down. But she hadn't counted on Kúdí.

The courtyard in Màmá Lékan's compound teemed with an extra influx of servants pulled from other compounds to prepare food for the impending new yam festival. The towns-folk were expected to gather in the main courtyard, for the Ọba's appearance and blessing. Many of the extra women helping to prepare the food had brought their toddlers along. As such, Ṣìkẹ́mi's small group had swelled so much that Kúdí, Èbùn and Rísí, girls her age, were instructed to help her care for them. An easy conversation flowed between the girls as they rounded up the children and tried to get them to nap.

'I never knew children could wear you out so quickly,' Èbùn said, as she laid a child gently on a mat.

Ṣìkẹ́mi, who was patting a child back to sleep, chuckled. 'I know. They are so energetic. Sometimes it's hard to keep up with such little bodies.'

'Who asked for your opinion, husband-snatcher?'

Ṣìkẹ́mi winced at Kúdí's remark. She'd been waiting for the girl's move for days.

Rísí came to Ṣìkẹ́mi's defence. 'Kúdí! Don't say that. You do not know what happened.'

'Well, you know what the elders say. "The witch cried yesterday, and the newborn died today. Who doesn't know the witch killed the baby?" She's here in Màmá Lékan's room, and Bàbá Kékeré has disappeared. Personally, I feel sorry for Màmá Bíọ́dún.'

Kúdí huffed the final platitude following her metaphor on a sigh. A thick silence followed, and the girls looked at Ṣìkẹ́mi, an expectant expression on their faces. Ṣìkẹ́mi considered saying more, then remembered what Rónkẹ́ had said and clamped her lips together. They could think what they liked. Kúdí backed off when Ṣìkẹ́mi refused to take the bait. But Ṣìkẹ́mi knew it wasn't over.

A week later, having put her young charges down for a nap, Ṣìkẹ́mi strolled to the cooking area, but as soon as she reached Kúdí and her troupe the girls stopped talking. An embarrassing silence stretched for seconds, then Kúdí rolled her eyes, hissed and walked away. With feigned nonchalance, Ṣìkẹ́mi lifted the lid off a water-butt and helped herself to a cooling drink. *She doesn't matter. They don't matter*; she repeated the mantra in her head as she too walked away.

As time passed by, Ṣìkẹ́mi found herself increasingly on the fringe of conversation. She suspected Kúdí of coercing the other servants and forcing them to exclude her. Still, Ṣìkẹ́mi reasoned, it was probably better that way, since it made it easier for her to keep to herself.

Bàbá Kékeré stayed away for six weeks; long enough for his face to heal. Kúdí trilled her welcome when he sauntered across the open yard. '*Ẹkú àbọ̀*, Bàbá!' Then she stopped and gaped. 'What happened to your nose, Bàbá?'

Ṣìkẹ́mi, who'd been playing with the young ones on a mat, stopped what she was doing. She stared for long moments at her attacker, taking in the crescent-shaped scar on his nose, wondering what his reply would be.

'Oh, this little thing. I was rather careless and ran into a tree branch,' Bàbá Kékeré said.

Màmá Lékan snorted from across the yard. 'Tree branches! Those things can mark you almost as well as humans. You must take extra care, Bàbá Kékeré. You know you are not getting any younger.'

Ṣìkẹ́mi bent over, her body heaving silently with suppressed mirth. By the time she looked up, Bàbá Kékeré was gone, but her amused smile connected with the twinkle in Màmá Lékan's eyes. And, for the first time, she felt the heady rush of power; power that came with knowing that she had the upper hand. She'd marked Bàbá Kékeré for life, and it made her feel strong and less of a victim. On that feeling, she fed for days.

TWELVE

Over the following weeks, Ṣìkẹ́mi learned to keep her own company when she wasn't caring for the children. Kúdí waged a war of words, turning anything Ṣìkẹ́mi said into a battle. Hoping the girl would leave her alone eventually, she held her peace. She was right. In time, Kúdí gave up trying to bait her and, along with her friends, blanked her instead.

Now that most of the servants ignored her, it gave Ṣìkẹ́mi an excellent opportunity to observe them unnoticed. Kúdí, she realised, held the others in a grip of fear. Most of them were eager to do her bidding rather than fall foul of her biting tongue or worse. The servants traded in one currency only – knowledge of what was going on with whom and where – and they spent most of their day exchanging it for favours.

So, Ṣìkẹ́mi watched and learned, and there was much to learn. Ifákẹ́mi sneaked out of the compound twice a week to meet up with a street trader for a love tryst. Súnkànmi pilfered minor items from Màmá Lékan's stall when she thought no one was looking. She sold these to the other girls, telling them she got them from town, and they were cheaper than Màmá

Lékan's price, which, of course, they were, since she was getting them for free. As for Kúdí... so far, Ṣìkẹ́mi hadn't caught her doing anything untoward, but she could wait. The girl was bound to have something underhand going on. While her discoveries about the girls were scintillating, she hoped someday to learn something more useful that might help her escape. She already knew Madam and the Ọba were mired in political intrigue that put the royals in danger. Ọba Akítóyè was in Bàdágrì because his nephew Kòsọkọ́, whose father had once deposed Madam's first husband, had deposed him from the Lagos throne. It seemed Bàdágrì was where deposed Lagos kings went to die.

Aided by Màmá Lékan, Ṣìkẹ́mi stayed out of Bàbá Kékeré's way. Nonetheless, his aura hung over the compound like a bad omen and his presence stirred in her a gamut of emotions. Ṣìkẹ́mi often pondered what it meant to be male. To have all that power and strength, and do whatever one wanted, usually with impunity. Images of the female soldiers who captured her always followed these thoughts. If she learned to fight like them, she'd be able to protect herself from most men. But how did a slave transform into a warrior?

Ṣìkẹ́mi wouldn't admit it to anyone, but sometimes she loathed the world of silence that surrounded her. She'd seen almost nothing of Rónkẹ́, who confined all her activity to the main palace courtyard. Màmá Bíọ́dún avoided eye contact with her, never mind conversation, and Màmá Lékan was just too busy. It saddened her to think that, if she died, no one would miss her, except perhaps for the children she looked after.

As she sat in the open courtyard watching over the napping children, the air buzzed with activity and conversation. She closed her eyes and tried to remember her family compound. Bàbá's tall frame, full of strength. Màmá's skin, flawless, the colour of roasted kaṣú. Màmá Aláṣọ's voice, smooth as coconut butter. She remembered the aunties and how she used to cut her eyes at them, much to their annoyance. Apart from Kúdí, she hadn't done that to anyone in months. She tried to imagine how Kúnlé might have grown. Then her thoughts turned bitter as she remembered the days following his birth, the isolation and sorrow. It was how she felt now.

Kúnlé's birth had changed everything. With Bàbá at the farm, almost a day's journey away, she'd stood guard alone in the courtyard, listening to her màmá's groans. Before that, each year, Màmá had drawn a vertical line on her room's wall. Each one of the five lines represented a year since her birth and how long it had taken Màmá to conceive again. Each year, Màmá had said in a voice tinged with sorrow, 'Maybe next year, you'll have a baby brother or sister.' Now, it seemed the child was trying to kill her màmá.

When Bàbá arrived later that evening, she flew at him with arms open wide. He paused long enough to give her the briefest of hugs before rushing to Màmá's room. Moments later, she entered the room just in time to see Bàbá lift the swaddled child out of Màmá's arms. She watched as Bàbá gazed at him with an expression she saw only when he looked at her or Màmá. He never gave her that look again. After that, Bàbá spent minimal time with her, while her aunts took over her re-education. Her cousins, whom she had shunned once too often in favour of her outings with Bàbá, ostracised her and she'd learned to live surrounded by silence until Kúnlé started talking and smiling. But she'd coped then, she reminded herself, and would again.

The next morning, as Ṣìkẹ́mi rolled up the sleeping mats, Màmá Lékan announced she was to take Madam's evening meal to the main palace courtyard. Ṣìkẹ́mi frowned at the news. The new assignment meant encountering Rónkẹ́, since all Madam's meals went through her. Her feelings towards Rónke remained ambivalent. The woman had bought her, then left her in someone else's care for months without contact. The way she'd handed her over to Màmá Lékan still rankled. It reminded her too much of Bàbá's rejection, prompting a desire to stay as far away from Rónke as possible.

'Why me?' she asked Màmá Lékan, wondering if the woman was trying to throw them together.

Màmá Lékan raised an eyebrow. 'Why not?'

The barked question and the expression on Màmá Lékan's face warned Sìkémi not to push. Not wanting to argue with her only ally, she accepted defeat. When Màmá Lékan notified the girls of the change in duties during the morning meal, Sìkémi groaned, fully expecting a comeback from Kúdí, and she wasn't disappointed.

'Why does she always get preferential treatment? I've been begging you to let me take the meals to the palace, and you refused. This isn't fair.' She pointed at Sìkémi. 'She doesn't even want to do it!'

Sìkémi listened to Kúdí's whine through gritted teeth, annoyed that she hadn't hidden her dismay quick enough. Màmá Lékan ignored Kúdí for a while, but the grumbling continued until Màmá Lékan gave in. 'All right! Kúdí, you can take the food tonight and Sìkémi will do it tomorrow, and I don't want to hear another word.'

Kúdí's face lit up with glee. Sìkémi shrugged but felt something was off. If Kúdí volunteered for a job, it was because she stood to gain something. The girl did nothing out of the goodness of her heart. Several times over the past few weeks, Sìkémi had noticed her disappearing from their courtyard when she thought no one was watching. Once, Sìkémi sneaked behind her and followed her as far as the main road that separated Màmá Lékan's compound from Màmá Bíódún's. In the distance, the edge of a white *dànṣíkí* floated in the wind. Then the wearer and Kúdí disappeared.

Ṣìkẹ́mi often wondered whether the man was Kúdí's lover. Kúdí's lewd comments and taunts over the months had erased her innocence and made her wise to the ways of men and women. When she thought back to those last few weeks in Màmá Bíọ́dún's quarters, she couldn't believe how naive she'd been. Focusing once more on Kúdí's request, she wondered whether Kúdí planned to carry more gossip about her to the servants in the main courtyard, or perhaps to Rónkẹ́. She decided to watch her for the rest of the day.

The day was a scorcher, even for the tropics, and Màmá Lékan's compound stood silent and devoid of the usual hum of activity. Most people were sheltering from the energy-sapping heat inside the coolness of their rooms, and the wise seized the opportunity for a quick afternoon nap.

Ṣìkẹ́mi sat under the shaded veranda with Títílayọ̀ draped across her knees, while she braided the child's hair. By the time she finished, the child was fast asleep. So, she laid her down next to her brother, Bíọ́dún. Then she searched for a broom and began sweeping up the strands of hair floating on the ground.

Her aunt, Màmá Aláṣọ, used to say, 'Hair is like a witch. It flies everywhere and gets to places you'd rather it didn't, like your food.' She didn't know why, but of all the things her aunt used to say this one resonated the most. So, while the compound slept, she swept. She bent down to collect the hair into a metal dustpan and noticed a flash of movement. She lifted her head just as Kúdí sneaked out of the courtyard. This was the girl's third time that week.

On the spur of the moment, Ṣìkẹ́mi untied the *ọ̀já* at her waist, draped it over her head and followed. The strip of cloth she'd used to support Títílayọ̀'s bottom when she'd carried her on her back earlier now doubled up as both a disguise and sun shield. Part of her wondered what she was doing, poking her nose into Kúdí's business. If caught, it would make their enmity worse; but information was power and, if Kúdí was up to no good, she stood to gain much by her actions.

Kúdí crossed the road. Then, as if sensing someone was following her, she paused and peeked over her shoulder. Ṣìkẹ́mi dodged behind the bush next to the courtyard's entrance, melding her back against the cool earthen wall. She sneaked a peek. Kúdí was on the move again, picking up pace, her short legs carrying her towards Màmá Bíọ́dún's compound.

Ṣìkẹ́mi kept her distance, waiting for Kúdí to enter the courtyard before sprinting across the space separating them. She arrived at the entrance to Màmá Bíọ́dún's courtyard just in time to see Kúdí walk down the veranda leading to Bàbá Kékeré's room. She should have known! Kúdí's previous sneak-outs had all been when Bàbá Kékeré was in residence. She wondered if Kúdí was satisfying Bàbá Kékeré's carnal pleasures. Given how much the girl knew about the topic, she wouldn't be surprised.

Kúdí rapped her knuckles on Bàbá Kékeré's door. The door opened and Bàbá Kékeré's frame filled the doorway. Kúdí curtsied, and they talked briefly. Then Bàbá Kékeré dipped his hand in his pocket, brought out a tiny vial and handed it to Kúdí before disappearing behind his door. Kúdí turned round and Ṣìkẹ́mi scarpered, realising she wouldn't make it back to her courtyard without being seen. She did the next best thing, diving into the nearest dense shrubbery until Kúdí had walked by and entered Màmá Lékan's compound. Her heart pulsed at the extra shot of adrenalin and her arms stung where the shrubbery had scratched her skin. Brushing the twigs and leaves off her body, she followed at a sedate pace, intrigued by what had just occurred. It could be nothing, but her gut screamed otherwise.

For the rest of the evening, Ṣìkẹ́mi watched Kúdí like a vulture waiting its turn at a meal. When Kúdí left the cooking area with Madam's meal laden on a tray on her head, Ṣìkẹ́mi picked up a bowl of bananas and followed. If challenged, she would lie and say Màmá Lékan had sent her with the bananas. Ṣìkẹ́mi paused at the main courtyard's entrance and watched Kúdí saunter up to a door. Extra guards paced up and down the veranda outside. It would seem the rumours about the danger surrounding Madam were true. Kúdí removed the tray from her head and placed it on a stool outside the door, and Ṣìkẹ́mi waited to see what would happen next.

Kúdí knocked and Rónkẹ́ came out. After exchanging pleasantries, Rónkẹ́ picked a random parcel of *fùfú* wrapped in leaves out of the tray. She opened it, cut a small ball with her fingers, dipped it into the edge of the *ewédú* stew, before lobbing it into her mouth. She nodded, invited Kúdí to follow her and turned. In that split second, Ṣìkẹ́mi caught the treachery. Kúdí slipped a vial out of the top fold of her wrapper and emptied the contents into the stew. She tucked the vial back in her wrapper and, without missing a step, picked up the tray and followed Rónkẹ́ inside.

Ṣìkẹ́mi stood rooted to the spot, as if caught in a trance, wondering if she'd just imagined the scene. Then she snapped back to attention and scurried after Kúdí with her fruit bowl. Without knocking, she entered the room just as Madam asked if Rónkẹ́ had tasted the food.

'Yes,' Rónkẹ́ said, 'but I can again if you like.' Without waiting for a reply, she dipped her finger into the stew.

For a moment, Ṣìkẹ́mi hesitated. The last thing she needed

was to draw more attention to herself, but she couldn't risk Rónké being harmed either. 'Do not touch the food!' Ṣìkẹ́mi screamed as she leapt forward and slapped Rónké's hand away from her mouth. Alarmed and startled, everyone focused on Ṣìkẹ́mi, and Madam's bodyguards rushed in. Kúdí froze, and the tray slipped from her fingers.

'Tell her to taste it,' Ṣìkẹ́mi said, pointing to Kúdí. 'I saw her put something in the food. Tell her to taste it.'

Kúdí shrivelled; her eyes, wide with terror, swept the room, seeking a means to escape, but sword-wielding soldiers blocked the only egress. She fell to her knees, palms open in a plea. 'Please Yèyé, don't make me.'

'What did you put in it?' Rónké asked.

'I don't know, Ẹ̀gbọ́n. Bàbá Kékeré gave me this to add.' She pulled the almost empty vial out of her wrapper and held it up. 'He did not say what was inside.'

One of Madam's bodyguards drew his sword. 'Drink the rest or die.'

'Eh, it wasn't me o.' She wrung her hands in supplication. 'Please forgive me, Yèyé. I did not know.'

'Drink it,' the bodyguard repeated.

Still pleading her innocence, Kúdí lifted the vial to her lips and downed the remaining contents. For an interminable moment, time stood still as everyone watched her. Then, just as Rónké sighed in relief, Kúdí grabbed her stomach and doubled over. In seconds she was writhing on the floor, her face contorted in pain.

'Bàbá Kékeré, you have killed me o!' she moaned.

Rónké took a step backward, her bulging eyes locked on Kúdí's prone form, while Madam's face twisted in anger and disgust. Minutes later, Madam's bodyguards half dragged Bàbá Kékeré through the courtyard into Madam's presence.

'I didn't do anything!'

Even before he appeared, Ṣìkẹ́mi heard Bàbá Kékeré's pleas, which continued until he saw Kúdí, half comatose on the floor, foaming at the mouth. Her cries had faded to pitiful groans.

Bàbá Kékeré held up his hands. 'Ah *Yèyé*, whatever she did, I was not involved.'

'The girl is dying, and she knows it. Why would she lie now?' Madam said. Madam exhaled with a heavy sigh, then she nodded at a bodyguard. While Ṣìkẹ́mi was still trying to decipher that silent communication, Madam rose and returned to her inner chamber, Rónkẹ́ trailing behind her. Ṣìkẹ́mi watched them leave with trepidation. What would happen now?

THIRTEEN

Two guards dragged Bàbá Kékeré, still grovelling and protesting his innocence, out into the courtyard until his pleas became a faint echo in the distance. Two more entered and removed Kúdí's completely still body. A guard pointed to Ṣìkẹ́mi. 'You. Clear the mess.'

Ṣìkẹ́mi dropped to her knees and began scraping the stew into the empty bowl. Her trembling fingers made the task harder, and she had no rags to hand to help. Then she felt a tap on her shoulder.

Rónkẹ́ spoke in a gentle voice. 'Come with me.'

With her heart pounding, Ṣìkẹ́mi stood up, wiped her soiled hands on her wrapper and followed. Inside the adjoining room, Rónkẹ́ stepped aside, leaving Ṣìkẹ́mi facing Madam, who perched on a stool. Ṣìkẹ́mi barely registered the fact that she was inside Madam's bedroom. Her knees trembled, and, partly scared they wouldn't keep her upright for much longer and partly to pay homage, she sank to the floor.

Madam studied her for what seemed like forever, although only a few seconds passed. When she spoke, it was to ask a question. 'You are Ṣìkẹ́mi, the girl who saved Bàbá Kékeré's son from the snake?'

'Yes, *Yèyé*.' Ṣìkẹ́mi kept her head low.

'How did you know she poisoned the food? I am sure you were spying on the girl to make sure it happened. Tell me the truth or you will die.'

Ṣìkẹ́mi jerked her head up, rocking it side to side. She hadn't anticipated the fight for her own life. She took a shaky breath to ease the tightness in her chest. 'No, *Yèyé*, I wasn't. Kúdí sneaked out this afternoon, and I followed her. I saw Bàbá Kékeré give her the vial, but neither of them saw me. I spoke out because I didn't want her to harm anyone.'

'Why did you assume it was poison?' Madam still looked unconvinced.

'This morning, Kúdí insisted she wanted to deliver the food, even though Màmá Lékan asked me first. Màmá Lékan can confirm this. Besides, behind his smiles, Bàbá Kékeré is an evil man.'

Madam exchanged a glance with Rónkẹ́, then her eyes pierced Ṣìkẹ́mi's with a knowing gaze.

'He touched you.'

Ṣìkẹ́mi squirmed under the scrutiny but held Madam's gaze.

'The gods must have a use for you. Your *orí* is strong.' Madam turned and instructed Rónkẹ́. 'Keep her with you at all times.'

'Yes, *Yèyé*.'

Rónkẹ́ grabbed Ṣìkẹ́mi by the arm and led her out to another room in the courtyard. Inside what seemed to be Rónkẹ́'s bedroom, Rónkẹ́ sank onto the edge of the sleeping platform and rested her head in her hands, a dazed expression on her face. Ṣìkẹ́mi observed her in wary silence. When Rónkẹ́ eventually lifted her head, her eyes brimmed with unshed tears.

'Thank you for saving my life,' she said in a shaky voice.

Ṣìkẹ́mi shrugged, as if it meant nothing. 'What will happen to Bàbá Kékeré?'

Rónkẹ́ swiped her tears with the back of her hand. 'They will interrogate him first, but it's the end for him. Madam does not tolerate treachery from anyone.'

Ṣìkẹ́mi thought about his family – Màmá Bíọ́dún and the two children. Without Bàbá Kékeré, their life would be difficult. She wished the woman no harm, and, although the alternative was equally unpalatable, a tinge of regret at the role she played in the tragedy assailed her.

Rónkẹ́ stood up and drew herself tall. 'I need to make sure Madam is comfortable, and that she gets a safe meal tonight. Stay here. Do not leave the room. I will post guards outside the door. Is that clear?' Suddenly brusque, and without waiting for Ṣìkẹ́mi's reply, she slipped out.

Ṣìkẹ́mi plopped herself on the edge of the sleeping platform, as limp as a newly washed wrapper. Her brain processed the latest twist in the saga her life had become. She'd done nothing wrong, yet the burden of Kúdí and Bàbá Kékeré's fall weighed heavily on her mind. Perhaps she shouldn't have got involved, but it was too late for that.

Although ensconced in Rónkẹ́'s room, Ṣìkẹ́mi still heard the palace uproar filtering through. She suspected the news of what had transpired in Madam's quarters was spreading like wildfire. She wondered if everyone would blame her for what happened to Kúdí and Bàbá Kékeré, and how many more enemies she would gain.

Once more, she reviewed the day, wondering what she could have done differently, but came up empty-handed. *Be kind to yourself*, whispered her inner voice. *You followed your instincts and saved at least one life*. The thought cheered her up a bit. Despite her mixed feelings about Rónkẹ́, she would have hated it if the woman came to harm. She wasn't sure whether Madam's last instruction to Rónkẹ́ was a good or bad sign. She'd sought escape, yet here she was, deeply entangled in palace politics. Her thoughts led to her family. What would they think of her escapades? She imagined some of her aunts tutting, telling her she ought to have minded her own business. But on Màmá and Bàbá, she pictured faces full of pride in the woman she was becoming. She forced the thoughts away and studied the room instead.

Rónkẹ́'s room, twice as large as her màmá's, had two distinct spaces: the sleeping area where she was and a living space near the door. Instead of a raffia mat, the sleeping platform, a raised rectangular earthen mound like her parents', was covered in a decadent wadding of cotton batik. A small head pad lay at one end. Several metal trunks decorated in a vivid green and blue pattern leaned against a wall. In the living space, two wooden benches, covered in a beautiful blue cotton batik print and slightly angled towards each other, sat on either side of a cowhide rug. The room spoke of a luxury Ṣìkẹ́mi had never encountered. She scanned the rest of it, and her eyes collided with an almost full-length image of herself on the wall. She gasped. Although she'd seen her own distorted image in pools of water before, never as stark as this. Intrigued, she walked towards the apparition and stretched out her hands until her fingers touched something solid. How was this possible?

For the first time she saw herself fully, noting the large oval eyes and bushy eyebrows ending in a tiny tail. Her màmá was light-skinned, so she had inherited the dark skin and the full lips shaped into a stubborn pout from her father, or so Màmá said. The three tribal marks on each cheek were faint enough to be almost unnoticeable. She liked what she saw, despite the jagged scar running above and extending far beyond her right eyebrow, a result of a palm-tree-climbing escapade. Màmá had threatened to hide her skin when she'd arrived home dripping blood, and as usual Bàbá had mollified her. She ran a finger across the scar; it represented something almost tangible, a link to her past and her family.

She walked back to the sleeping platform and sat down. Somehow, her body stretched out, and she let out a yawn. How comfortable the platform was. If only...

'Wake up, Ṣìkẹ́mi!'

The sound of Rónkẹ́'s voice and the arm shaking her awake drew Ṣìkẹ́mi out of the slumber she'd fallen into.

'How come your sleeping platform is so soft?' she asked, her voice full of sleep.

Rónkẹ́ giggled at the random question. 'It's late, and you need to eat before you sleep.'

At the mention of food, Ṣìkẹ́mi's stomach grumbled, but the thought of visiting the kitchen and facing everyone made her physically ill.

'Don't worry. I've sent for some food for both of us, and Màmá Lékan will make and bring it herself.'

Ṣìkẹ́mi relaxed, confident that Màmá Lékan wouldn't harm a fly. Her mind jumped ahead to what the evening's fracas meant for everyone else in the compound, especially for Kúdí's friends.

Rónkẹ́ saw the wheels turning in her head and cautioned, 'No questions, Ṣìkẹ́mi. Tomorrow will take care of itself. Tonight, we'll eat and sleep.'

Màmá Lékan knocked on the door and entered with a tray of food. 'What a day!' she said. 'Are you both all right?' She scanned them up and down.

Ṣìkẹ́mi nodded, noting the tears in Màmá Lékan's eyes.

Rónkẹ́ took the food tray. 'Yes, we are. Thank you, Màmá Lékan.'

'I didn't know they were planning something.' Màmá Lékan's eyes begged Rónkẹ́ to believe her.

'Màmá Lékan, I am sure you knew nothing of this.'

'If only I'd been more vigilant. Maybe, if I had caught the girl earlier, I might have saved her from her folly.' Màmá Lékan wiped a tear with the corner of her wrapper.

Rónkẹ́ reached out and placed a comforting hand on her shoulder. 'This was not your fault, you hear me? Go to bed. Like I told Ṣìkẹ́mi, tomorrow will right itself.'

After Màmá Lékan left, they both settled down and ate in silence, each engrossed in their own thoughts. Once they had finished, Rónkẹ́ put the empty dishes outside the door for the servants to remove. Ṣìkẹ́mi yawned and wondered where she was supposed to sleep that night. Rónkẹ́ caught her eyeing the sleeping platform and laughed.

'It's okay. It's big enough for two, so you can share it tonight. Tomorrow we'll make plans for yours.'

Ṣìkẹ́mi climbed atop the platform once more and lay down beside Rónkẹ́. Just before her eyes closed, she remembered her *orí* and thanked the god of her ancestors, who, despite the odds, seemed to keep constant watch over her.

FOURTEEN

'Come on. Ṣìkẹ́mi, wake up. It's going to be a busy day, and change is afoot. We need to get moving.'

Rónkẹ́'s words stirred Ṣìkẹ́mi out of the best sleep she'd ever had. She covered her mouth to stifle a yawn.

'We need to bathe, then see to *Yèyé*'s needs.'

Ṣìkẹ́mi nodded, rose and followed Rónkẹ́ to the bathing area. Minutes later, they were back in the room getting dressed.

'What do you think will happen today?' Ṣìkẹ́mi asked.

'A myriad of things. *Yèyé* needs a new foreman, and I need to send for Ọbádínà. Come. We will talk later.'

Ṣìkẹ́mi wondered who Ọbádínà was but shoved her remaining questions to the recesses of her mind. Outside, dozens of armed guards patrolled the veranda, clearly taking the threat on Madam seriously. Rónkẹ́ knocked on Madam's door and Ṣìkẹ́mi was stunned when Kàmọ́rù let them in. After instructing Ṣìkẹ́mi to stay in the outer room, Rónkẹ́ knocked on Madam's bedroom door and entered. Left alone with Kàmọ́rù, Ṣìkẹ́mi turned her attention to the boy.

'How are you? Were you here last night?'

Kàmọ̀rù nodded, his eyes full of understanding. 'I am fine, and I was.'

She must have missed him in the chaos. 'How long have you been here?'

He smiled at her. 'Shortly after your snakebite. You made it happen, didn't you?' Without waiting for a reply, he rushed into her arms and hugged her. Ṣìkẹ́mi gathered him close, enjoying the embrace for a while before letting him go. She scanned the room, taking in its opulence for the first time. They were in a large outer room on par with Rónkẹ́'s living space; only larger and decorated with a rich tapestry of fabrics that covered an assortment of furniture. A huge chair dominated the room, its seat back framed by two intricately carved stiles rising into pointed spindles. It sat on thick legs decorated with carvings depicting Ọya, the river goddess. Several wooden chairs and accompanying footrests completed the furniture. Like Rónkẹ́'s room, an assortment of animal hides, some tan, some the colour of coconut cream, hugged the floor. Ṣìkẹ́mi lingered on the spotted cream and black fur underneath the enormous chair. When Bàbá had told her stories of the bravest leopard-killing hunters, she'd never imagined coming face to face with the creatures' skin.

Several minutes later the interconnecting door opened, and Rónkẹ́ emerged with Madam behind her. As Ṣìkẹ́mi knelt to greet her, Madam took her throne-like seat and gestured to Rónkẹ́.

'Where did Ṣìkẹ́mi sleep last night?'

'With me in my room,' Rónkẹ́ said.

'You'll need a bigger room. Take the other one next to yours. You can use one for living space, and the other for sleeping. Keep Ṣìkẹ́mi as close as possible from now on. Our enemies are now hers.'

'Thank you, *Yèyé*. I will.'

A knock on the door startled them. Kàmọ̀rù opened the door and Màmá Lékan entered, accompanied by a servant bearing the morning meal.

Màmá Lékan curtsied and laid a food tray on a stool. 'I made this myself, and no one has touched it. This tray is for Yèyé.' She pointed to the tray held by the servant. 'That one is for Rónkẹ́ and Ṣìkẹ́mi. Shall I taste the food now in your presence?'

Madam shook her head, so Rónkẹ́ thanked Màmá Lékan and she left. Madam picked up a piece of yam and dipped it into the fried pepper stew in front of her. Just before she put it in her mouth, she paused and fixed Rónkẹ́ with a hard stare.

'From now on you will no longer be my food taster. You are too valuable for that. Appoint a slave for the job.'

'Thank you, Yèyé. May you live long and into old age,' Rónkẹ́ said. She waited until Madam finished her meal and Kàmọ̀rù cleared the used utensils. Then she picked up her tray and beckoned Ṣìkẹ́mi to follow her.

Back in Rónkẹ́'s room, Ṣìkẹ́mi tackled the immediate problem on her mind. 'Who will be the new food taster?'

'Why do you ask? It won't be you, if that's your worry.'

She bit her lips, then blurted it out. 'Please, don't make it Kàmọ̀rù!'

Rónkẹ́ gave her a measured look. 'It is not your place to determine how slaves are employed. What is he to you, anyway?'

Ṣìkẹ́mi paused as she struggled to explain. Eventually, she said, 'I helped him, just like you helped me.' She hoped Rónkẹ́ would understand the analogy.

Rónkẹ́ remained pensive. 'We shall see. I can't promise anything.'

While they ate, Ṣìkẹ́mi sought some answers to the myriad

of questions plaguing her. 'Have you always been Madam's food taster?'

'Yes,' Rónkẹ́ said. 'Since I was a child.'

The question's significance wasn't lost on either of them. Every time Rónkẹ́ tasted Madam's food, she put her life on the line. Ṣìkẹ́mi used to think Rónkẹ́'s job as Madam's personal assistant was easy. Now the significance of the danger dawned on her.

'Did you come here as Madam's slave then?' she asked.

Rónkẹ́ took her time before answering. 'In a way, yes. Madam's father, Olúmọsà, captured my father in the war between the Òwú, Ìjẹ̀bú and Ifẹ̀ people. Madam's first husband died in that war. My father met my mother while still in captivity and had me and my sister. Madam brought me here as her maid when she married Ọba Àdèlé, the current Ọba's older brother.'

'How old were you?'

'Ten. Younger than you were when you arrived.'

A look of understanding passed between them, then Ṣìkẹ́mi's eyes turned contemplative.

'What is it?' Rónkẹ́ asked.

'I never thanked you for buying me; for saving me from being sold to the white man. Thank you.'

'Technically, Madam bought you. I just did the bidding.'

'I don't care. I can't imagine what might have happened otherwise.'

'No snakebite and no Bàbá Kékeré, for starters.'

Rónkẹ́'s eyes glinted with mischief. Ṣìkẹ́mi covered her mouth to stifle the laughter, but it burst out of her throat, and she let it. It felt good to laugh.

'Why did they call him Bàbá Kékeré, anyway? He was hardly the smallest man in town.'

That sent them both into a fit of giggles.

'Well,' Rónkẹ́ said, '*Ọba* Àdèlé first came here from Lagos after his brother Ọ̀ṣinlóku deposed him. Everyone called him Bàbá because he was truly the fatherly sort. When the *Ọba* got his throne back and moved to Lagos, Madam appointed a new overseer, and everyone called him Bàbá Kékeré to distinguish between the two bàbás.'

Now it made sense to Ṣìkẹ́mi. She had always wondered why someone as large as Bàbá Kékeré had such an unsuitable moniker, but she conceded the name suited his unsavoury character. Her thoughts returned to Madam, and she sobered.

'It is good you are no longer the food taster. I wouldn't want anything bad to happen to you.' Ṣìkẹ́mi left unsaid that she had similar feelings about Kàmọ́rù.

Rónkẹ́ smiled. 'Me neither. Any more questions?'

Ṣìkẹ́mi had many. 'Why does Madam look so sad?' She'd seen it that day in the slave market. She knew the woman was widowed, but the melancholy clung to her like a heavy covering.

'Ah! Ṣìkẹ́mi.' Rónkẹ́'s groan made Ṣìkẹ́mi wish she hadn't asked. 'Madam has known much sorrow. She has buried two husbands and both of her sons.'

Ṣìkẹ́mi didn't know what to say. That amount of tragedy would break anyone. That the woman still held herself together was admirable. But she had one more question before she was done. After a respectable silence, she spoke. 'What will happen to Màmá Bíọ́dún? I know you don't like her, but she treated me well. If needed, I'd be happy to speak on her behalf.' She was still worried about the impact of her actions on the woman and her children.

'I don't dislike her, but she has always refused to see her husband for who he is. I warned her not to marry him, but she wouldn't listen.' Rónkẹ́ lapsed into silence and her face took on a faraway look.

Ṣìkẹ́mi wondered if they used to be friends. It would explain the tension.

'Anyway,' Rónkẹ́ said, resuming the conversation, 'that decision is beyond both of us, and you mustn't blame yourself for what happened. That was all Bàbá Kékeré's doing.'

Ṣìkẹ́mi nodded, but, until their fate was settled, she would worry about both Kàmọ̀rù and Màmá Bíọ́dún. However, she'd done her best and now it was up to the gods.

Once Rónkẹ́ and Ṣìkẹ́mi finished their morning meal, they returned to Madam's room, where Ṣìkẹ́mi found her deep in conversation with a handsome stranger. Lithe and fair-skinned, he stood as tall as Bàbá Kékeré. Ṣìkẹ́mi remembered her manners and knelt to greet him.

Rónkẹ́ introduced him. 'This is Bàbá Ọbádínà, *Yèyé*'s husband.'

The surprises kept coming. She hadn't known Madam had a new husband.

Ọbádínà's kind eyes assessed her. 'The girl?'

Rónkẹ́ nodded.

'Who do you think will make a suitable foreman to replace Bàbá Kékeré?' Madam asked, her gaze sweeping over the newcomers. Ṣìkẹ́mi kept silent as Ọbádínà and Rónkẹ́ threw out the names of various servants and Madam turned them down until the names ran out. Ọbádínà paused, a look of deep speculation on his face. 'What if I did it?' he asked.

Ṣìkẹ́mi and Rónkẹ́ both turned to Madam, whose jaw hung slackly.

'Don't look so surprised. We are all stuck here in exile for the foreseeable future, and it's not like I currently have a large army to oversee. I could do it while you take your time to find a suitable replacement. It would be subject to the Ọba's approval, of course.'

Madam mulled on the offer and she and Ọbádínà debated the pros and cons. Finally, Madam agreed, and they both left to converse with the Ọba.

That evening, guards brought Madam news that, under the threat of torture, Bàbá Kékeré confessed to being bribed by Kòsokó's supporters to dispatch Madam in return for full control over her assets. The Ọba subsequently ordered his execution but gave Màmá Bíọ́dún and her children the option to stay on at the palace or return to her family. She chose the latter. Rónkẹ́ also shared the news that the new food taster would not be Kàmọ́rù, and Ṣìkẹ́mi felt the weight lifting off her shoulders.

Late that night, after Rónkẹ́ and Ṣìkẹ́mi helped Madam prepare for bed, they turned and were about to leave when Madam stopped them.

'Ṣìkẹ́mi,' she said, 'for your loyalty and for saving Rónkẹ́'s life, you may ask for a gift. Any gift...'

Ṣìkẹ́mi's heart somersaulted, and a deafening roar filled her inner ears. Then she heard Madam finish her sentence '...except your freedom, so ask wisely.'

Ṣìkẹ́mi's euphoria burst and her breath whooshed out, leaving her as deflated as a cow's empty udder. She stared at Madam, whose earnest expression invited a reply. Flummoxed, she stuttered. 'Erm, erm...' Her voice tailed off, and, as the silence grew heavy, Ṣìkẹ́mi felt herself dangling on a precipice. Chances like this were rare, and she could not afford to squander it. Sweat beaded on her forehead and she swatted it away with a shaky hand. 'May I have until morning to consider my reply?' Her voice came out strong, although her insides were a quivering mess. What if Madam considered the request too bold, too forward?

Madam shifted forward in her chair. No one else moved. Ṣìkẹ́mi held still and, although she fixed her eyes on the floor, she could feel the heat of Madam's gaze searing her from head to toe. Then Madam sighed and leaned back in her chair. 'Fine, you can tell me tomorrow.'

Ṣìkẹ́mi's shoulders flopped, and she let out a sigh. That night, she tossed and turned on Rónkẹ́'s sleeping platform. Madam had already denied her the one thing she wanted. So, what was the next best thing? An image of a female warrior floated before her. The lure of being strong enough, skilled enough to defend herself and those she loved called to her. The idea of avoiding subjugation by another human was one she could not ignore. She debated the options. The temptation to run and find her family immediately was strong. Being in favour with Madam might even give her access to resources that could aid her escape. But escaping would not guarantee she wouldn't be recaptured. Whereas, as a trained warrior, the odds would favour her and her family, when she found them, for life. She would have to delay her plans, but ultimately she would gain skills to keep herself and her family safe from future harm. It seemed the better plan, if Madam could facilitate it. Would she agree to such a thing? She had said *anything*. Ṣìkẹ́mi sank into the mattress, her mind made up.

FIFTEEN

The following morning, Ṣìkẹ́mi and Rónkẹ́ attended to Madam
while servants rearranged Rónkẹ́'s rooms according to
Madam's wishes. Ṣìkẹ́mi kept silent all morning, wondering
when Madam would bring up the question. Ọbádínà came to
visit, and he and Madam completed the reassignment of the
servants to various duties. Then, out of nowhere, Madam said,
'Ṣìkẹ́mi, have you decided what you want?'

At the slight lift of Ọbádínà's eyebrow, she explained the
previous night's conversation. Ọbádínà turned his gaze on
Ṣìkẹ́mi, a soft glimmer of curiosity in his eyes. Although she'd
been expecting it, the question still caught her by surprise. Even
Rónkẹ́ looked curious, as they hadn't discussed it any further.
A tremble coursed through her bones as she knelt before
Madam. She spoke with conviction. '*Yèyé*, I would like to train
as a warrior.'

Dead silence greeted the room. Madam's eyebrows rose so
high, Ṣìkẹ́mi thought they would tip her headpiece off her
head. Then she burst into a roaring belly laugh, to everyone's
startled surprise. 'The girl is a comic.' She laughed some more

and wiped a tear off the corner of her eye. However, her laughter tailed off when Ṣìkẹ́mi's expression stayed the same. 'You really mean you want to be a warrior? But why? That's a man's job.'

Ṣìkẹ́mi shook her head. '*Yèyé*, the warriors who captured me from my village were female.'

'I've never heard of such a thing, and there were no female warriors selling slaves in Bàdágrì the day we bought you. I might have been despondent, but I wasn't blind.'

Ọbádínà put a calming hand on Madam's knee. 'I have heard of such. They are from neighbouring Abomey, and they have been raiding Ẹ̀gbá and Ẹ̀gbádò villages for years.'

'Still, that wish is not within my power to grant. Who would train her? I can't send her off to join the army.'

'I can train her,' Ọbádínà said.

Madam's eyebrows rose again.

Ọbádínà held out his palms. 'Why not? Akítóyè is in exile, and as your new acting foreman I'll be here for a while. Besides, it might solve the other issue.'

Madam's brow furrowed in concentration as she considered Ọbádínà's words.

'*Yèyé*, we're going to check on our room,' Rónkẹ́ said. She tugged Ṣìkẹ́mi's hand and pulled her out of the room.

Outside, Ṣìkẹ́mi turned on Rónkẹ́. '*Ẹ̀gbọ́n*, why did you do that? *Yèyé* will say no. You should have let me plead my case.'

Rónkẹ́ shook her head. 'No. Trust me. Let Bàbá Ọbádínà talk to her alone.'

Back in the room, Ṣìkẹ́mi bounced on her heels, her mind so focused on the two people deliberating her future next door that she didn't notice the extra sleeping platform. She kept glancing at the door. Part of her wanted Madam to say yes to

Ọbádínà's proposal, but it also filled her with trepidation after her experience with Bàbá Kékeré.

She held nothing against the man personally. He seemed personable and kind, but she didn't want to be subject to a man's authority, or be in regular proximity to one. But if her future training depended on a man, that now seemed impossible. She realised she hadn't really thought through the implications of her request. A shudder rippled through her body as she imagined being surrounded by a thousand sweaty male soldiers. She sighed. Working with one man was preferable to an army of them. If only the Yorùbá army had a female regiment.

'Ṣìkẹ́mi, look at your legs.' Rónkẹ́'s voice jolted her out of her introspection.

Ṣìkẹ́mi looked down and her eyes grew round. Ugh! It was her thing of the month. As Rónkẹ́ offered a rag to clean herself with, a new thought crossed her mind, and she wondered out loud, 'Would my monthly cycle interfere with my training?'

'I guess it depends on how badly you want to be a warrior. Why are you interested in being a warrior, anyway?' Rónkẹ́'s eyes sought understanding.

Ṣìkẹ́mi sighed. 'This world is unfair to females. Men rule, they control, they abuse. You should have seen the women who first captured me. When they were attacked, they fought like men, and, although they didn't win, most of them escaped. If I learn to fight like that, I stand a better chance of defending myself against men like Bàbá Kékeré in the future.' Ṣìkẹ́mi thought it prudent to keep her hopes of using her skills to track down and protect her family to herself.

Compassion filled Rónkẹ́'s face. 'Well, I hope you get your wish, and, just maybe, I'll get mine.'

Ṣìkẹ́mi was just about to ask what her wish was, but Rónkẹ́ spoke first. 'Go, clean yourself up.'

An hour later, a knock on the door brought Kàmọ́rù, who

announced Madam needed their presence. They left the room holding hands. In Madam's presence, ramrod-still, Ṣìkẹ́mi waited for her verdict. Ọbádínà's face held a vaguely amused smile that stirred some hope in her, but she couldn't read Madam's deadpan expression, and that worried her.

'You never explained your desire to become a warrior,' Madam said.

Ṣìkẹ́mi opened her mouth, about to repeat what she had told Rónkẹ́ earlier, but she caught Rónkẹ́ shaking her head, her eyes shooting a warning glare. In a flash of inspiration, she paused, reorganised her thoughts and changed her words.

'If you let me become a warrior, like those who captured me, I would serve you better, *Yẹyẹ́*, and protect you with all my strength.'

Ṣìkẹ́mi caught Madam exchanging a glance with Ọbádínà, then her gaze pivoted first to Rónkẹ́, then back to Ṣìkẹ́mi.

'You are a smart girl. It is not the answer to my question, but I will allow it.'

Ṣìkẹ́mi wanted to throw her arms around someone, but instinctively guessed such an effusive display of emotion would be unwelcome in Madam's presence. Instead, she contained her joy, waiting until she and Rónkẹ́ were back together in their room. Then they flung their arms around each other and danced a jig together.

As Ṣìkẹ́mi bedded down that night, something niggled her. Madam, she thought, had given in almost too easily. Ọbádínà had said she was the solution to a problem and Rónkẹ́ had suggested her wish depended on Ṣìkẹ́mi's. But what did it all mean? She tried putting it together, but before her tired brain could probe any deeper, her eyelids fell closed.

. . .

Ten days after Bàbá Kékeré's treachery, and eight months since her capture Ṣìkẹ́mi turned up at the palace guards' training compound. Ọbádínà was already waiting in the courtyard. News had circulated through the palace complex that Madam had granted her wish to become a warrior. Some said she was deluded and Madam insane to allow it. Others noted that her life was already extraordinary, so what difference would one more strange occurrence make?

Ṣìkẹ́mi's skin tingled. She remembered the sword-toting warriors she'd tried to escape; how easily they'd caught her. She couldn't wait to be like them; to have the skills and knowledge to wander the forest without fear, something necessary if she was to find her way back home.

'Good morning, Bàbá.' She knelt to greet him.

Ọbádínà took her in from top to bottom and shook his head. 'That won't do. Come,' he said. He turned and walked towards a room.

Behind him, Ṣìkẹ́mi took hesitant steps, remembering her last time alone in a room with a man. Determined it wasn't happening again, she stood at the door, refusing to budge. A look of confusion crossed Ọbádínà's face. He shrugged, went in, and returned with a pair of shorts and a *dànṣíkí*.

'Go into the room and change. You can't train in a wrapper.'

A prickle of embarrassment flooded Ṣìkẹ́mi's skin. Thanking him, she took the clothing and disappeared into the hut, sliding the internal lock across the door. She felt sheepish now she knew why Ọbádínà had asked her to enter. When she exited the room with her wrapper folded under her arm, Ọbádínà pointed to a stool in the courtyard where she could put it. Ṣìkẹ́mi discarded the wrapper, then turned to Ọbádínà.

'Right. Let's see you run.'

So, it began. Ọbádínà made her run until she begged him to stop, and that was all he asked of her.

Later that evening, Madam requested a blow-by-blow account of Ṣìkẹ́mi's day.

Ṣìkẹ́mi's shoulders lifted in a careless shrug. 'I ran.'

'You ran? That's all you did?' Madam's face wore a bemused expression.

Ṣìkẹ́mi was equally perplexed, but felt it was too early to complain. For the next two days, Ọbádínà made her do nothing else. On the fourth day, he switched things up and made her lift heavy slabs of stone in between each run.

'Run, carry, run, carry, run, run, run.' Ṣìkẹ́mi muttered the mantra under her breath as she repeated each circuit. By evening her muscles raged like an inferno, and the following morning she refused to get out of bed.

'Aren't you training today?' Rónkẹ́'s question dripped with feigned innocence.

Ṣìkẹ́mi pulled her sleep wrapper over her head, burrowed down and mumbled something about not feeling well. Rónkẹ́ relayed the message to Ọbádínà when he came looking for her. She also brought back a reply. 'Ọbádínà said if you don't show up tomorrow, it's all over.'

Ṣìkẹ́mi sighed. What had she let herself in for?

SIXTEEN

The next day, when Ṣìkẹ́mi resumed her training, Ọbádínà had her climbing a wall in the training compound. Later in the evening, Madam asked how her training was progressing.

Ṣìkẹ́mi snorted. 'I am not doing any training. Running, lifting, climbing, but no training.' Her voice took on a belligerent note. 'I don't see the point of it. I don't need anyone to watch me do that. I need someone to teach me how to fight, so that—'

Rónkẹ́ interjected. 'Ṣìkẹ́mi, it's time to clear *Yèyé*'s dishes. It's getting late.'

Ṣìkẹ́mi stopped mid-sentence. Only then did she notice the scowl on Madam's face and the flint in her eyes. She shut her mouth and, following Rónkẹ́'s lead, cleared the dishes and helped tidy up.

Later that evening, back in their room, Rónkẹ́ rounded on Ṣìkẹ́mi. 'Is something wrong with your *orí*?' She dug a forefinger into Ṣìkẹ́mi's forehead. 'Are you that stupid? You asked for this, yet less than a week into it you are complaining.'

Ṣìkẹ́mi's jaw dropped. She'd only seen Rónkẹ́ this angry once before.

'Have you forgotten you are still a slave? Don't let *Yèyé*'s smiles fool you. If she wants rid of you, you'll be gone tomorrow.' Rónkẹ́ snapped her fingers to show just how quickly Madam would get rid of her. 'Of everyone here, you should know better. You saw what happened to Bàbá Kékeré.'

Thoroughly chastened and subdued, Ṣìkẹ́mi thought about how to undo her mistake. But she also wondered at the vehemence in Rónkẹ́'s voice as she chastised her. Was Rónkẹ́ simply looking out for her, or was there more to her training that she didn't know about? She remembered Ọbádínà's words about her training being a solution, and resolved to ask him about it in the morning.

The next morning Ṣìkẹ́mi entered the training courtyard and found Ọbádínà waiting as usual except, instead of his usual placid demeanour, he looked like raging thunder. Before she could utter a greeting, he launched at her.

'So, you think I am wasting your time, do you?'

Ṣìkẹ́mi suspected Madam must have said something.

'Here.' He threw a sheathed sword at Ṣìkẹ́mi before she could blink. On instinct, she reached out and caught the missile hurtling towards her, almost missing it. She took a deep breath and pulled the sword from its leather sheath.

'Lift it high and defend yourself,' he barked, waving a sword of his own above his shoulder.

Ṣìkẹ́mi lifted the sword with both hands and waved it awkwardly, knowing full well she didn't know how to use it. Already her shoulder ached from holding it high. Ọbádínà lunged forward and his blade came crashing down on hers, sending a shock wave through her wrists and forcing her hands to the ground.

Ṣìkẹ́mi dropped her sword and rubbed her aching joints. 'I

can't,' she said. 'Forgive me for what I said to *Yèyé*. I wasn't thinking.' The words flew out of her mouth as if chasing each other.

The rushed apology had the desired effect, and Ọbádínà's face softened somewhat, although his shoulders remained stiff. Ṣìkẹ́mi eyed him, hoping he would relent.

'Why can't you hold up the sword, Ṣìkẹ́mi?' His tone was still sharp.

'Because I'm not strong enough.'

'You are right, and I have designed your training to build your strength. You can't run before you can walk. Do you understand? Look, you have experienced a remarkable year, and you show great promise. If you listen and learn, I can teach you what you need to know. Otherwise, let's stop this now.'

Ṣìkẹ́mi grabbed the lifeline. 'I apologise, Bàbá. I want to learn.'

She still didn't trust him as a man, but he was her best shot at becoming a warrior, and she couldn't risk losing that.

'Right,' Ọbádínà said. 'Let's start with the wall today.'

A month into her training, Ṣìkẹ́mi's arms rippled with taut muscles, the result of all that wall-climbing and slab-lifting. She'd shot up and stood almost shoulder to shoulder to Rónké, who was taller than average. Her training was progressing well and, although Ọbádínà said she still had much to learn, she could already wield the sword with dexterity. The question she wanted to ask him still hovered on her tongue but, not wanting to upset him any further, she held it back.

When she strolled into the training compound that morning, she found Ọbádínà dressed in more formal wear. Instead of his training shorts, he wore full-length trousers and a matching *dànṣíkí*. 'We are going into town today,' he said. Ṣìkẹ́mi looked at her own clothing, wondering if she should change out of her *dànṣíkí* and short trousers, but Ọbádínà waved away her concern.

'No need to change. You look like a boy. It's perfect.'

Ṣìkẹ́mi smiled, taking his words as a compliment. She was delighted and thankful the mounds on her chest had grown no bigger, making it easy to pass herself off as a boy.

'Where are we going?' she asked as they left the compound.

'I am taking you to meet Àjàyí, the white man's priest. He is starting a place of learning to teach the white man's language to our people. You will join them to learn this language, so you are of better use to your mistress.'

Ṣìkẹ́mi gasped. A mixture of surprise, delight and excitement ran through her. Then it hit her, and she stopped midstride. 'It won't work. I don't want to stop my training.'

A wry smile illuminated Ọbádínà's face as he took in the stubborn pout of her lip. He shook his head and chuckled. 'Who said anything about stopping your training? You will attend the place of learning in the mornings and train in the evenings.'

Unconvinced, she stared at him. 'Why can't I start the learning after I finish my training?' Her sole goal was to become a warrior. Anything else was a distraction.

'You can do both at the same time. The matter is already settled, Ṣìkẹ́mi, so move your feet.'

At first, Ṣìkẹ́mi dragged her feet. She had no choice in the matter, but she didn't have to like it. Walking down the streets, she soon realised she looked silly, sulking behind the man, so she picked up speed until she was beside him. As the pair walked up to the Christian mission house, they met Àjàyí, the Black priest, in the yard.

'*Ẹkú àbọ̀*,' Àjàyí welcomed them in Yorùbá.

Ṣìkẹ́mi's eyes narrowed at the man's strange accent. Then

she remembered the priest was a returnee slave who had spent much of his life outside Yorùbáland. She scrutinised the completed two-storey building, now taller than the palace, with several wooden windows adorning fresh white walls. Sunrays glinted off the metal roof sheets capping the edifice, as if paying homage to the stars. Nothing around looked quite like it.

After the usual greetings they followed the priest, who led them into a large sitting room, where he introduced them to a white priest named Henry Townsend. Townsend extended his right hand towards the pair. Ọbádínà grasped it and shook it up and down. Ṣìkẹ́mi stared in confusion. What strange ways the white man possessed; yet soon, those ways might well become hers.

While the adults talked, Ṣìkẹ́mi wandered around the room. It contained only basic furniture; a table, several chairs and a series of wooden shelves on which rested what she thought were rectangular wooden blocks. She had expected an opulence on par with the palace, not this simplicity. Ṣìkẹ́mi wandered off to a shelf and picked up a block. To her surprise, it felt soft, and it fell open, revealing several lightweight white sheets with black markings. She remembered she'd seen the priest holding something similar during her first visit with Màmá Bíọ́dún.

'That's a book,' Àjàyí said behind her.

Ṣìkẹ́mi brushed her hand over the pages, her fingers rustling the whisper-light, crispy sheets. She traced the incomprehensible black etchings, her eyes tracking the two columns down the page. She shut it, returned it to the shelf, then faced the priest. Only one person in the palace could interpret the white man's language, and becoming one of only two would enhance her status.

She lifted her chin. 'Bàbá, can you teach me to understand what it says?'

The priest's eyes creased into a smile. 'That is why you are here. Follow me.'

Ọbádínà interrupted their exit and told Ṣìkẹ́mi a guard would be back to escort her to the palace later. Her face fell as Ọbádínà left. Why did she require a guard escort to the palace? Was it because Madam thought she was in danger, or that she'd run away before completing her training?

Parking the vexing question, Ṣìkẹ́mi followed the priest to another room filled with an assortment of males, some as young as six and some fully grown adults. The room itself comprised a row of wooden benches and tables, and Ṣìkẹ́mi wedged herself on the end of a bench. The priest strolled to the front and stood in front of a black rectangle painted on the wall. 'Today,' he said, 'we are going to learn the white man's numbers.' He turned and drew a line on the black rectangle. 'Repeat after me, *one...*'

Several hours later, Ṣìkẹ́mi returned to the palace, her head buzzing.

'So, what did you learn today?' Madam asked after her evening meal.

Ṣìkẹ́mi's eyes lit up, and she beamed from ear to ear.

'They have numbers just like we do.' She reeled them out, ticking them off her fingers. '*Wọnù, tù, tirì, fọọ̀, faifù, sisì, sẹfùn, etì, nainì, tẹnì!*'

Madam and Rónkẹ́ clapped in delight, but Ṣìkẹ́mi caught them exchanging a sly smile. They were hiding something; but, so long as things worked out for her in the end, she did not care.

SEVENTEEN

Perched high above the forest canopy, Ṣìkẹ́mi wriggled her bottom, shuffling back and forth, to wake her dead leg. The unforgiving tree provided little room for movement and her efforts came to nothing. She grabbed a higher branch and stretched her torso, hoping that would relieve the cramp a little. Nine months into her training, she was the current lookout for Ọbádínà's men, spread out on the forest floor below, processing the men and women from their attack on a nearby village. She was adept at hand-to-hand combat, could wield a spear and sword with dexterity, and was probably the best archer among Ọbádínà's troops. And, aged sixteen, it was her first day in the field.

She looked down at the captives and her stomach lurched at the sight of vulnerable children clinging desperately to their mothers. She looked away, unable to bear the sight. When she'd signed up for the training, it had never crossed her mind that she'd have to raid villages for slaves. The day Ọbádínà informed her she was to join his troops had been one of her darkest. She'd flat out refused.

'What do you mean by no?' Ọbádínà gaped at her, as if she'd grown horns.

'I won't do that,' she said. 'It's wrong. I can't do that.'

'In case you've forgotten, Ṣìkẹ́mi, all you are is a privileged slave. You wanted to be Madam's warrior. This is what Madam's warriors do. How else do you think she got this rich? I can tell you it wasn't from her cocoa plantations. You've got the training, now use it.'

Ṣìkẹ́mi almost broke down. 'Bàbá, please. Assign me to anything else but this.'

'No Ṣìkẹ́mi. I am not wasting all that training, and neither should you. If you can't do this, it's over for you. You won't be much use to Tinúbú either and she'll probably sell you on for a profit. So, think hard before you throw it all away.'

The curt words gave Ṣìkẹ́mi an insight into the soldier he was; someone who had become an army commander worthy of Madam's hand. Rumour had it the *Ọba* himself had chosen him for Madam. Ṣìkẹ́mi watched him leave with clouded eyes. The last nine months had cost her dearly, in broken bones and the wounds that criss-crossed her body, souvenirs collected from various training exercises. She couldn't throw it away, as he said, yet to commit this abomination... In the end, she'd chosen the only option available and here she was.

She looked down again, and the sight of the wailing children overwhelmed her. The contents of her morning meal made their way up her throat. Too late to stop it, she plunged her face into the tree's leafy branches, her body heaving as she retched.

Ṣìkẹ́mi wiped her mouth with the edge of her *dànṣíkí*, looking up just in time to see the silhouette of five men crouching as they closed in on Ọbádínà's camp. They could be villagers trying to rescue their families, or raiders like her. From her height, she couldn't tell, but they did not wear the indigo armbands that set Ọbádínà's troops apart. They had approached while she was retching and were now closer to the camp than her. Her brain ticked, trying to process the ramifications and her next actions. If she did nothing, Ọbádínà and his men would be compromised, and she would have failed in her duty to warn them of danger. After a moment's indecision, she pulled out her bow and arrows. She let three shots fly in quick succession. One by one, men dropped to the ground, leaving just two standing. Then she let out a shrill whistle that alerted the troops, who came running. Ọbádínà's men disarmed the two intruders, tying them up with the other captives.

The threat neutralised, Ṣìkẹ́mi sighed in relief, refusing to think about the men she had dropped. It took her some time to climb down the tree, as she cajoled her deadened left leg into cooperating. Her pulse quickened and her mouth felt dry as she approached Ọbádínà and the men. She lifted her water bottle to her mouth, then, remembering she'd drunk the last dregs ages ago in the tree, she moistened her cracked lips with non-existent saliva. Would the men blame her for almost getting them killed? Still, she'd done her duty, but at what cost?

At the camp's perimeter, her steps faltered as the men turned their attention to her. Then a few rushed forward. Ṣìkẹ́mi resisted the urge to flee. She would die with dignity. The men reached her and, before she could blink, hoisted her on their shoulders. Then they danced her around the camp, chanting, *Befé, bẹẹfẹ o, Ṣìkẹ́mi ti ke ke lulẹ* – Like it or not, Ṣìkẹ́mi has overcome. Bewildered, Ṣìkẹ́mi looked down at the jubilating men while their captives cowered nearby. Then they set her down in front of Ọbádínà.

'Well done, Ṣìkẹ́mi, on your first kill,' he said. 'Today, you have become a warrior, a man indeed.'

Ṣìkẹ́mi looked everywhere but at him and the captives. Why did the accolade feel so hollow? She feared retching again and humiliating herself in front of the men. Ọbádínà, sensing her discomfort, leaned in. 'Breathe, Ṣìkẹ́mi, breathe.'

Ṣìkẹ́mi did as she was told, taking deep breaths.

'What have I always taught you?' Ọbádínà asked.

'It's them or us.'

'It's who?'

'Them or us.'

With a satisfied nod, he returned to issuing instruction to the rest of his crew, letting her be.

Ṣìkẹ́mi and Ọbádínà returned to a palace in uproar. 'Ọbàtálá be praised, you two are back.' Madam stopped pacing and sat in her favourite chair. Rónkẹ́ stood beside her, a worried frown on her face.

Ọbádínà took the seat next to Madam's. 'What's happened?'

'It's Kòsọkọ́. He is raising an army to attack us and has allied himself to the king of Dahomey. Akítóyè is not safe here.' She wrung her hands as she spoke, and Ṣìkẹ́mi saw genuine fear in her eyes as she continued. 'We have asked the British to protect him and their consul, John Beecroft, has agreed to take him to Fernando Po.'

Ọbádínà took her hands in his. 'What about you? Are going with him?'

'No. I'll be fine staying here. Kòsọkọ́ feels threatened by Akítóyè, not me, but we need to be extra vigilant. There are spies everywhere, even here, which is why I am confiding in only you three.'

Ṣìkẹ́mi processed the new development in the light of what she already knew. Over the past year, Kòsọkọ́'s attacks on the family and the town had increased and blossomed into a full-scale war. It had taken Ṣìkẹ́mi a while to understand Bàdágrì's political structure. Her first day in the town, she wondered why a king of Lagos owned a palace in Bàdágrì. Later she learned that Bàdágrì was settled in different waves, by refugees from neighbouring warring countries. Each group settled into distinct parts of the town until the town comprised eight distinct wards, each under chiefs who all collaborated with each other.

'How did *Ọba* Àdèlé establish himself as an overlord over the existing chiefs?' Ṣìkẹ́mi had asked Ọbádínà during a training session. Ọbádínà's face transformed into a smile as he remembered the dead king.

'Àdèlé was very charismatic. The town's history of welcoming refugees made it easy for him to establish himself. It helped that his mother, who was from Bàdágrì, came with him.'

'That doesn't explain how he became more powerful than the other chiefs,' Ṣìkẹ́mi pointed out.

'Until that point, Bàdágrì was a tributary of Lagos. By adopting Àdèlé as their leader, the town broke free from its control and, under his leadership, it became rich enough to rival Lagos.'

That made sense to Ṣìkẹ́mi. In Bàdágrì, money and trade meant everything. Unfortunately, the collaborations had splintered, with some chiefs maintaining their loyalty to Akítóyè and others to Kòsọkọ́. Bàdágrì was now a cesspit of competing interests: returnees setting up new legitimate businesses; slave traders wanting to maintain their current hold and missionaries furthering their spiritual ambitions. No faction trusted the other, which eroded the town's peaceful co-existence.

Later that day, Ọbádínà gave Ṣìkẹ́mi a bag of cowrie shells, her share of the raid's proceeds. In the extra room she kept at the army barracks, Ṣìkẹ́mi cringed as the blood money, her first ever earnings, ran through her fingers. The money signified her road to freedom, an opportunity to amass enough to either buy it or pave the way to a successful escape. But the way she had earned it remained a stain on her conscience, despite her having little choice in the matter. She would earn just enough to fund a successful escape, she decided. In the meantime, she would start studying the forest terrain and hide caches of cowries and weapons to facilitate her eventual getaway.

Two days later, Ṣìkẹ́mi helped Ọbádínà lead Akítóyè, one of his wives and a handful of servants to a British ship in the harbour, and she hoped peace would return.

EIGHTEEN

In a manner reminiscent of her former trips with Màmá Bíódún, Șìkémi strolled through Bàdágrì town centre greeting all the townsfolk she knew. *Pèlę o, obìrin bí akọ*, they replied. It pleased her that they counted her *worthy as any male*. Madam's cronies had started using the moniker to acknowledge her uniqueness when she began training, and it had stuck.

A year after Akítóyè left, Bàdágrì remained on edge. The missionaries tried and failed to mediate between the warring factions. In the ensuing war, Akítóyè's supporters chased their opponents out of town, but those left in Bàdágrì lived under constant threat of retaliation. The hostile environment made slave trading more hazardous than ever.

At seventeen, Șìkémi was leading raids now, the youngest warrior to do so, according to Ọbádínà. The early hunting skills her father taught her had been invaluable, giving her a head start over the other recruits and smoothing her transition into becoming a warrior. Now she remembered those fond moments with Bàbá without the bitterness of the past. She'd accepted her new occupation as a necessary evil and created her own method of atoning for her sins.

To ensure her men's safety, before each raid she worked hard at intelligence gathering using the spying skills Ọbádínà had taught her. Her trips to the town centre served a dual purpose. As she roamed, she searched for traders plying the Bàdágrì-Ìlarǒ route, hoping to hear news about her family. But she also used it to gather information on the British, who were determined to stop the slave trade, and, for this, nothing served her purpose better than her old school.

'Good afternoon, Reverend,' Ṣìkẹ́mi said as she knocked on the classroom door, 'I hope you are well, sir?' She spoke excellent English thanks to her helping Rev. Àjàyí Crowther –whose name she'd first thought was Kárúúdà – translate the English Bible into Yorùbá. As a former prized student, she was always welcome, and it gave Rev. Gollmer, who now ran the school, a chance to show off the school's success.

Rev. Gollmer welcomed her with an open smile. 'My dear man, Ṣìkẹ́mi. It is good to see you. Have you come to see those following in your footsteps?'

While the class stared in open-mouthed awe at the ease with which she and the white priest conversed in English, Ṣìkẹ́mi hid her smile. Even years later, Rev. Gollmer still thought she was male.

She always volunteered to take a class during her visits, and a delighted Rev. Gollmer took a break, leaving her in charge. Ṣìkẹ́mi walked to the front and wrote the words *Current Affairs* on the board with a piece of chalk. Then she turned to the class. 'Tell me, what's going on in our world in Bàdágrì today?'

It was the class's cue. Ṣìkẹ́mi plied the students with questions about the missionaries' and navy's activities and, for a wrap of peanut paste, they told her about the warships in the vicinity.

. . .

A few hours later, back in Madam's quarters, although both Rónkẹ́ and Madam returned her greeting Ṣìkẹ́mi detected a terseness that put her on edge. Not one to prevaricate, she took the plunge. '*Yèyé, Ẹ̀gbọ́n*, have I done something wrong?'

Rónkẹ́ squirmed and wouldn't look at her. Madam coughed and cleared her throat. 'Nothing is wrong, but there is change afoot.'

She shrugged off Madam's words, because the dream always forewarned her of impending doom, and she'd slept like a newborn the previous night. She waited for Madam to continue.

'It is time for you to take your place beside me.'

Ṣìkẹ́mi's stomach quaked. 'What do you mean, *Yèyé*?'

'You will replace Rónkẹ́, because I am releasing her to marry Pedro.'

In a flash, Ṣìkẹ́mi saw all her carefully laid plans dissolving before her eyes. Rónkẹ́ had been dating Pedro, a trader and returnee from Brazil, for a while. Since Madam had not forbidden the romance, she had always assumed she would let Rónkẹ́ leave at some point. But she'd never seen herself as the replacement.

She stood up and paced in front of her owner and mentor. Then she turned beseeching eyes on Madam. '*Yèyé*, we can train someone else to take over. You know I am much more valuable to you conducting raids. No one else brings in as much money as I do. You know this, *Yèyé*.'

She could have absconded right after her training, but she'd wanted to make money first. She'd figured buying her freedom would ensure she didn't spend the rest of her life as a fugitive. While she had a few bags of cowries squirrelled away, it wasn't enough and, without the opportunity to earn more, her goal was untenable. That meant she'd wasted the last year.

'Ṣìkẹ́mi, this was always the plan. You are the solution.'

Madam's voice was quiet but firm.

Ṣìkẹ́mi's head swivelled between the two women, and then it hit her. The problem Madam and Ọbádínà had spoken of the day Madam agreed to her training. But why waste all that effort training her for this?

Madam's voice took on a velvety tone. 'I trust no one else, Ṣìkẹ́mi. You are like my own flesh and blood. These are days of turbulence and treachery, and your military training means I will be safer with you beside me.'

Ṣìkẹ́mi's jaw tightened. That tone worked on Ọbádínà and Rónkẹ́, but it wouldn't work on her. It wasn't just the money. She imagined never feeling the exhilaration the forest gave her again. She couldn't do it. 'Forgive me, *Yèyé*,' she said, then she bolted.

Ṣìkẹ́mi paced the barracks for hours trying to figure out a solution that would make everyone happy, but found none. Later that night, she returned to the room she shared with Rónkẹ́. 'You've always known,' she said to Rónkẹ́, her voice accusing. 'How could you not tell me? You know I love being surrounded by the forest. I can't replace you. That's not me! Living permanently in town would destroy me.' Besides, she and Madam differed in their views on most things, leaving Rónkẹ́ as the mediator between them. She couldn't even begin to imagine the challenge of handling Madam on her own.

Rónkẹ́ glared back. 'Life isn't all about you, Ṣìkẹ́mi. How long have you been here?' Without waiting for a response, she continued. 'I've served Madam almost my whole life, and I was in constant danger every day except for the last two years. So, stop whining about what you want. I deserve a life too, and if I leave it any longer I won't be able to have children of my own.'

She knew Rónkẹ́ was right. 'What do I do?' She plunked

herself down into a chair and cradled her head in her hands. Rónkẹ́ didn't respond straight away, and Ṣìkẹ́mi wondered if she ever would. After a while, she spoke.

'Compromise, Ṣìkẹ́mi. Perhaps you could lead your precious raids once or twice a month? If I train someone else before I leave, they could look after Madam the few times you're gone, although you'll need to increase her security each time you leave.'

Ṣìkẹ́mi didn't like it one bit. It felt like she was dangling under a noose tightening slowly round her neck. Long after Rónkẹ́ began snoring, Ṣìkẹ́mi lay awake considering her options. She envisaged a time when, well past her prime, she would be of no use as Madam's protector, but she couldn't wait that long to find her family. Fleeing was her only option, but Madam would hunt her down, if only to make an example of her. For that plan to work, Madam would have to believe her dead. Her head turned over the intricacies of trying to fake one's own death. Where would she even begin? She loathed agreeing with Rónkẹ́, but for everyone's sanity, she needed to convince Madam to accept a compromise.

Ṣìkẹ́mi visited the next day, hoping to find a relaxed Madam to ensure any possibility of a smooth conversation. Instead, she found Madam in her living room, nose scrunched, her head cocked to the right, as a hairdresser wove rows of flat-weave plaits into her silver-black stresses. The air reeked of camphor and sulphur from the balm the hairdresser used to moisturise each row of plaits. Rónkẹ́ was out meeting Pedro, which meant there was no buffer between her and Madam. She'd have to manage on her own. She squared her shoulders. It would be good practice for later.

Ṣìkẹ́mi knelt and used her most reverent tone. '*Yèyé...*'

'Umm?' Madam raised an arched brow, her eyes squinting from the pain inflicted by the pull of the hairdresser's fingers.

'Forgive my behaviour yesterday. It was the shock speaking.' She paused, gauging Madam's reaction to her words. Madam didn't move a muscle, so she carried on. 'As you said, I will take Ẹ̀gbọ́n Rónkẹ́'s place at your side, but I have a proposal that may benefit us both, if you permit me to explain it.'

Madam adjusted her wrapper. 'Go on.'

Ṣìkẹ́mi took a deep breath and dived in. 'If you allow me to conduct raids twice a month, it will keep me strong and in shape, so that I can do my duty well and protect you with my life.' Since Madam said nothing. Ṣìkẹ́mi continued. 'I will also train one of my men to watch over you in my absence, and I will deliver double the normal profit.'

Madam's eyes blinked rapidly, and Ṣìkẹ́mi hoped the bait had worked.

'Twice a month?' Madam said.

'Yes, Yèyé.' Ṣìkẹ́mi held her breath.

'Fine. I agree.'

Ṣìkẹ́mi breathed again. But she had one more issue to address. Madam's wealth was heavily dependent on the slave trade. They would all benefit if she diversified and strengthened other income streams.

'Yèyé, there is one more thing. I hear some local farmers are using techniques introduced by the white man. They are more profitable, and I think we should look into it.'

Madam's arched brows puckered into a puzzled frown. 'What for? My farms are doing fine. Besides, since when did farming become more profitable than enslaving?'

Ṣìkẹ́mi sighed inwardly. 'Yèyé, it might be if we changed our farming methods. Forgive me for quoting a proverb in your presence. The elders say twenty children cannot play together for twenty years. Change is coming. Don't you think we should prepare for it?' She'd kept her tone light, hoping not to antagonise Madam, who rarely responded well to uninvited suggestions from others.

With a hint of impatience, Madam brushed the hairdresser's hands out of her head and focused her full glare on Ṣìkẹ́mi. 'So, you are now my foreman, eh? You think you know more about my business than I do, eh? Watch yourself o, Ṣìkẹ́mi. Know your place.'

Ṣìkẹ́mi fell silent at the veiled warning, and watched as the hairdresser placed tentative hands back on Madam's head, waiting several seconds before resuming. Ṣìkẹ́mi dropped the matter, hoping to try again another day. She had a win. There was no need to jeopardise it.

NINETEEN

OCTOBER 1851, BÀDÁGRÌ

Ṣìkẹ́mi hummed the words of a Yorùbá ballad as she heaved a large bag of cowrie shells onto a table in her room. Three and a half years later, she was still a slave, albeit a rich one. She'd inherited Rónkẹ́'s rooms next to Madam, but she still kept her room at the barracks, since it suited her raids better. As she counted her profit in the dim lighting, she reflected on the strange duality of her current life. In the year and a half since Rónkẹ́'s departure, when she wasn't in the forest conducting raids she spent her time as Madam's confidante and companion. She also ran an extensive spy network, from which she mined information – something almost as valuable to Madam as gold.

Her relationship with Madam was difficult, and she hadn't realised how big a buffer Rónkẹ́ was between them until she was gone. She lacked Rónkẹ́'s tact and geniality, and her penchant for saying exactly what she thought didn't always go down well with Madam or her guests. Nowadays, Ṣìkẹ́mi watched everything she said and every twitch in Madam's brow. The situation was only tolerable because her fortnightly jaunts to the forest gave them both respite and ensured her money pot continued to grow, and now she could make her move.

Ṣìkẹ́mi separated the profit into two parts, one for Madam and one for herself. She scooped the two piles of cowrie shells into sacks and moved them across her room to the hideaway under her bed. Then she opened the door carved into the wooden floor and shoved the sacks into the cavern within. She would deliver Madam's in the morning.

It surprised Ṣìkẹ́mi, how quickly her money grew. She'd developed a highly efficient raiding strategy by only selling strong and healthy people. It gave them a better chance of survival and the strongest slaves held the highest value, meaning a tidy profit. Her transactions were quick, because she had cut out the haggling by prearranging the price for each slave. It saved time and reduced the likelihood of being caught. Her team was large, and, like her mentor before her, she shared the profit with her men, but she struck often, and her success rate made it cost effective. Madam always paid her a tenth of whatever she delivered. She suspected Madam knew she was creaming her profits, but Madam was shrewd and no other warrior in her retinue brought her as much profit as Ṣìkẹ́mi did.

Ṣìkẹ́mi picked up her sponge and headed for the bathing area, needing to wash away the day's grime. Later, as her head hit her pillow, her thoughts turned to Rónkẹ́. She ought to pay her a visit and check how she and the little one were doing, but first she would ask Madam to name the price of her redemption.

In the early hours, Ṣìkẹ́mi, a light sleeper, tuned in to the background noise invading her sleep. She knew something was amiss the second her eyes opened. She gathered her clothing, dressed and set out for Madam's quarters. As she strode through the courtyard the sounds, no longer muted, flew at her from all angles. Kòsọkọ́, Akítóyè, the white man; the words reached Ṣìkẹ́mi's ears, carried on the wind's sail. She quickened her steps. *What has Kòsọkọ́ done now?*

She entered Madam's living room and found her and Ọbádínà head-to-head, so deep in conversation that, despite her knocking, they missed her entry. She coughed.

Madam looked up. 'You're back. You are your father's daughter. We were just talking about you.'

Ṣìkẹ́mi's heart lurched at the mention of her father, but she tamped down the feeling. She knelt to greet them both, marvelling at the Yorùbás' absurd view that entering a room just as people finished talking about you affirmed your paternity. 'The palace is buzzing. What's happened?'

The glint in Madam's eyes gave away her delight. 'Akítóyè is back, and the British have agreed to help him regain his throne.'

Ṣìkẹ́mi blinked. 'How will they do that?'

'First, they will send a delegation to negotiate with Kòsọkọ́.'

Ṣìkẹ́mi couldn't fathom Kòsọkọ́ giving up the throne willingly. 'Won't that defeat the objective?'

Madam's face split into an evil grin. 'It's Kòsọkọ́ we are talking about. He will refuse their offer and give them the excuse they need to attack.'

They clearly had it all worked out, but it all sounded ominous, especially since the British had been resolute in not involving themselves in the fracas. 'What will the British gain in return?' she felt compelled to ask.

'Akítóyè promised to stop the slave trade.'

Ṣìkẹ́mi hiked a single eyebrow. 'The *Ọba* agreed with that?'

'Yes, he did.'

Ṣìkẹ́mi searched Madam's face for any sign of disapproval of such an agreement and found none, although an inflection in her voice suggested she wasn't sharing everything. Still, if the end of the slave trade was part of the deal, perhaps it included the release of existing slaves. She might as well find out before handing all her money to Madam. On a whim, she decided to delay posing her question to Madam.

'So, what now?' she asked instead.

'We prepare for war and wait,' Ọbádínà said.

Ṣìkẹ́mi contemplated the idea of going to war. The last one had changed nothing, but perhaps the involvement of the British would make a difference, and, if it brought the emancipation of slaves, it would be worth it.

'I told you so,' Madam said a few days later, adjusting her wrapper as they strolled from the Ọba's quarters. 'Kòsọkọ́ refused to grant Beecroft and his men an audience.' She clapped her hands with relish, her eyes glinting in anticipation of sharing the rest of her news with Ṣìkẹ́mi. 'The British will attack Lagos tomorrow, with a contingent led by Commander Forbes.'

'What do we do in the meantime?' Ṣìkẹ́mi asked.

Madam lifted a shoulder. 'We'll wait here for news from the British.'

The following evening, in the middle of a training session with her men, Ṣìkẹ́mi paused as the pounding of feet outside the courtyard alerted her to trouble. The town crier burst into the courtyard, then stopped to catch his breath.

'Bàbá Gbohùn-gbohùn, why are you running about in this sweltering heat?' Ṣìkẹ́mi asked.

The wizened old man drew a few steadying breaths before plunking himself on a stool. 'Eh, we are in trouble o!' He clasped his head with both hands.

'What do you mean, Bàbá?'

'Ah! The British o! They failed o! Kòsọkọ́ beat them back, and they have retreated to the sea with their injured and dead comrades.'

A gasp lit round the courtyard, and soon it teemed with people who'd heard the town crier's voice. Dread descended on the palace as people pondered the ramifications. If the British couldn't remove Kòsọkọ́, who could? Ṣìkẹ́mi found herself at the centre of a frenetic burst of activity as she and Ọbádínà increased palace security. A reprisal from Kòsọkọ́ and his allies seemed inevitable, so Madam's personal troops joined the *Ọba*'s army and Ṣìkẹ́mi stationed soldiers all along the palace perimeter wall as they waited.

A day later messengers arrived from Beecroft, and the *Ọba*, Madam and his commanders joined them in secret meetings behind closed doors. Beecroft intended to launch another attack, this time with a larger fleet and the palace army.

With the war imminent, Ṣìkẹ́mi wanted to know Madam's intentions concerning her own slaves. One evening, she broached the question. '*Yèyé*,' she said, careful with her words. 'If *Kabiyèsí* signs the treaty, how does it affect the business?'

'My business? It doesn't.'

Madam's inscrutable face almost made Ṣìkẹ́mi think she'd asked a stupid question. She tried again. 'Doesn't the treaty depend on not trading in slaves?'

'Mmm. You think so? Let me tell you how it is done.' Madam gestured with her fingers. 'They will do their own thing over there, and I will do mine here. After all, they are signing a treaty with Akítóyè, not me.'

'*Kabiyèsí* won't be happy.'

Madam broke into a dry chuckle. 'Since when has that been a problem? Who placed him on the throne? Is it not me? Is it not my money that has kept him fed and happy in Bàdágrì for years? Hmph!'

Madam hissed the last words through her teeth and rolled her eyes. It signalled the end of the discussion. Ṣìkẹ́mi shook her head. Was Madam that naive, or just blinded by her own sense of self-importance? The information gathered through her extensive spy network confirmed the British wanted the trade stopped at all costs and the treaty would include a proviso covering existing slaves. But her instincts told her no one would give up such a lucrative trade for nothing. Although the missionaries and British emissaries talked about stopping the trade on humanitarian grounds, she was convinced they had more insidious motives.

What was also becoming clear was that Madam had no intentions of honouring the treaty, which led Ṣìkẹ́mi back to two options – running away or buying her freedom, of which she preferred the latter. But would Madam agree? Madam's volatile nature made her prone to rash decisions and Ṣìkẹ́mi didn't want to push her into selling her to someone else. She needed to proceed with caution when approaching Madam, and her success would depend on choosing the right time and words. She only wished she could shake off the nagging feeling she was asking for the impossible.

Under the cover of darkness, Ṣìkẹ́mi sneaked into the mission house graveyard. An eerie, oppressive silence hung in the air, punctuated only by the occasional hoot of an owl. The elders believed visiting the graveyard at night, when the spirit world was most active, invaded their realm and invited evil into one's life. And that made the graveyard the perfect hiding place for her extra loot. No one else would dare and she could always pay the local Ifá priest later to atone for her transgressions.

Ṣìkẹ́mi's visits to the mission house had always served a dual purpose; after each class finished, she would visit with Rev. Gollmer. Later, she would join the evening service and say a prayer to the white man's god. She'd long ago decided one could never have too many gods. Then, on her way out, in the dark, she'd visit the graveyard.

She paused at Mrs Gollmer's grave and made the sign of the cross with her fingers. The priests did it often, like it was some kind of talisman, so she followed suit. The poor woman had died of malaria fever within months of arriving. It made Ṣìkẹ́mi wonder what motivated white folk, who seemed both traitor and saviour to the Africans. Many braved the harsh conditions of the African soil and almost certain death to bring the salvation of their foreign god. Yet, their kin still bought slaves under their very noses. The previous day, the priests had celebrated Christmas, a festival meant to bring goodwill to all men, yet any time now Beecroft's guns would rain on Lagos. It was a puzzle that vexed her often.

She moved to the next grave and, after confirming she was alone, she stooped and, with the hoe she'd brought, dug into the ground until she struck something solid. Never knowing where she'd be had forced Ṣìkẹ́mi into planning several contingencies and her money was scattered around different locations, from the town graveyard to the depths of the forest. The once brilliant idea was becoming a hindrance, as retrieving her buried treasure was increasingly difficult. Still, she reasoned, it was better to have access to some money than none. She opened the metal box, retrieved several strings of cowrie shells and tied them round her waist.

The elders had a saying: 'If you sprinkle cold water on the ground ahead of you, you will walk a dust-free path.' The money would smooth her way, provided she survived the battle. She stood, ready to leave. Suddenly, an ear-splitting boom resembling the sound of a hundred thunderbolts reverberated in the air, and the ground shook. The battle for Lagos was on.

As she jogged back to the palace Ṣìkẹ́mi hoped Rónkẹ́ and her family would be safe. Rónkẹ́'s move to Àgùdà on Lagos

Island nearly broke her. 'Why can't you stay in Bàdágrì?' Ṣìkẹ́-mi's eyes had begged. But Pedro insisted his business would flourish better in Lagos and Ṣìkẹ́mi couldn't fault the argument. The constant skirmishes between Akítóyè and Kòsọkọ́ had caused a trade embargo that cut Bàdágrì off from much of the produce from the hinterlands. From a trader's perspective, Lagos was a far more lucrative place of abode.

Nonetheless, Rónkẹ́ was the closest thing she had to a sister, and she missed her with a frightening intensity, emotions that always led to thoughts of her birth family. Those feelings came with a curtain of melancholy that reminded her of Madam when she first met her, so she suppressed them. She reckoned the busier she kept, the less time she spent thinking about feelings, and, if she didn't think, she couldn't hurt.

TWENTY

Early the next morning, Ṣìkẹ́mi, Madam and the rest of Akítóyè's retinue loaded themselves into several canoes and sailed towards the Lagos coastline. Ṣìkẹ́mi gasped as the flotilla came into sight. The sea bobbed with a mass of boats covered and led by four British warships – HMS *Bloodhound*, HMS *Teaser*, the *Victoria* and the *Harlequin*. The warships towered over the boats like giant monsters. Ṣìkẹ́mi's men rowed Madam to a smaller British ship for safety. Then they formed the flotilla's rear guard against any surprise attacks by Lagos' Dahomean allies.

All day Ṣìkẹ́mi concentrated on staying alive, as both sides took casualties with neither gaining the upper hand. The British cannons made an unholy, almost deafening racket, and from the shore Kòsokó's war guns returned the volley, filling the air with the putrid stink of rotten eggs. Ṣìkẹ́mi thought it rather ironic that Kòsokó bought his arsenal from the Europeans he was now at war with.

The battle raged all night and, the next day, a cannon from Lagos narrowly missed Ṣìkẹ́mi's boat. Ṣìkẹ́mi and the men rowed a sharp turn to avoid the turbulence caused by the passing missile, and in doing so upset the boat's balance. For a minute, as they scrambled to right the boat, Ṣìkẹ́mi thought she might die. Shortly afterwards, luck favoured the British. They blew up Kòsokó's royal arsenal and the town's defence collapsed.

A collective gasp rent the air on Ṣìkẹ́mi's boat as they closed in on the Lagos coastline. On Ṣìkẹ́mi's prior visit to Lagos as Rónkẹ́'s guest, it had heaved with traders dripping in the wealth gained from slavery. Foreigners, the British, Brazilians, Portuguese, Spanish and even Italians hustled beside traders from all over Yorùbáland. The European presence led to a rush of buildings springing up along the waterfront. Now the entire coastline blazed, and plumes of thick black smoke rose in majestic columns high above the skyline. Against the sky's dark curtain, burnt-out carcasses of former dwellings lined the coast, their naked roofs sticking out at awkward heights and angles.

Much to Ṣìkẹ́mi's relief, on the morning of 29 December 1851 they made landfall. They found the town covered in a cloak of soot and empty, except for the elderly and young, the inhabitants having fled inland or further down the coastline. The British led Akítóyè ashore, and the few remaining chiefs swore allegiance to him. Three days later, Akítóyè signed a treaty with the British and the task of rebuilding the town began.

A soft sea breeze blew in the wind as Ṣìkẹ́mi made her way down to the Àgùdà area of Lagos with an urgency in her step. Leaving the salty, fishy smell behind, she turned a corner and the thudding in her chest reduced. A smile broke over her face and her pace slowed down to a leisurely stroll. Apart from the occasional scorched wall and the strong smell of charred wood,

the area bore little sign of the trauma of the recent battle with
the British.

The once swampy area had sprung a few more dwellings
since her last visit. Ọba Ìdéwù, who preceded Madam's
husband's second reign, granted the land to the Brazilian
returnees. The Yorùbá nicknamed the returnees '*Àgùdà*', hence
the locality's name. Since then, dozens of them had settled in
the area. Skilled craft workers, the Àgùdà wasted no time devel-
oping the area into a bustling neighbourhood. Their dwellings
announced their new-world origins, boldly setting them apart
from the indigenous mud houses.

Although she'd only visited it once, it didn't take her too
long to find Rónkẹ́'s house. The modest building stood one
storey high, like most of its neighbours. The dwelling was
created for a single family, unlike the sprawling traditional
compounds on the rest of the island that hosted multiple
extended families. Built of brick and domed with an iron-
sheeted roof, its external façade bore the intricate designs so
common among the returnees.

For a moment, Ṣìkẹ́mi paused and admired the frontage,
painted in a cream colour, with an enormous doorway framed
by stone pillars. Curved windows, longer and larger than those
in the mission house in Bàdágrì, lined the building's front. Each
one was framed by an intricate arched relief etched into the
wall. The beautiful brown wooden shutters set into the
window frames stood in sharp relief, while still creating a
welcoming buzz. Underneath each window, patterned etchings
mimicking the cream and brown colours on the wall and
windows formed a frieze that stretched along the building's
front.

Ṣìkẹ́mi used the large iron knocker on the front door and
waited. The door opened and Rónkẹ́'s startled face spread into
a wide grin. She opened her arms to envelop Ṣìkẹ́mi, who

stepped into the warm embrace. Rónké looked well, and the roundedness prodding Ṣìkẹ́mi's stomach as they hugged told her she was carrying again. She loosened her embrace a little to give Rónké room to breathe.

As they stepped over the threshold, Ṣìkẹ́mi noticed Rónké's attire. Under her wrapper, which was tied at the waist, she wore a *bùbá*. The modern invention was fashioned out of three rectangular pieces; a central piece with a neck-hole and two pieces for the sleeves. The missionaries frowned on the Yorùbá females' utilitarian wrapper, which left them with bare shoulders. Nowadays, the younger females wore the top as an additional cover-up.

Ṣìkẹ́mi smiled. It seemed Rónké was fast becoming a fashionable woman, a signal the old ways were changing. Yet, a part of her worried that not all change was good for her people. She couldn't shake the feeling the British were up to no good and her instincts had never failed her yet.

Ṣìkẹ́mi followed Rónké into her hallway and took off her flat sandals. Then Rónké led her into the living room and offered her a seat. Ṣìkẹ́mi mewed a sigh of appreciation as her bottom sank into a plush brown armchair. The Àgùdà sure knew how to make comfortable furniture, and it was wonderful to relax without the constant threat of censure, if only briefly.

Rónké took a seat opposite an ornate coffee table. 'I bet the last few days have been busy.'

Ṣìkẹ́mi nodded. Rónké didn't know the half of it. 'Yes, they have been. This is the first opportunity I've had to check on you.'

Rónké smiled. 'We were fine. The British informed the Àgùdà of their plans and we sought shelter further inland that week.'

Ṣìkẹ́mi's eyes roamed over her mentor, taking in the gentle swell of her belly. She practically glowed, and Ṣìkẹ́mi wondered what carrying another human inside her body would feel like. It wasn't something she thought of often, because embracing motherhood required a lot of precursors she didn't want. She'd have to allow an intimacy she'd permitted no man so far. Then, there was the matter of her freedom. Having a child without it would consign the child to misery. Perhaps one day...

Ṣìkẹ́mi changed her line of thought and asked after Rónkẹ́'s husband. 'How is *Ẹ̀gbọ́n* Pedro?'

'He is well; out conducting business. How is *Yèyé*? I trust all is well in her world now Akítóyè has his throne back?' Rónkẹ́'s breathy laugh showed how well she knew Madam and Ṣìkẹ́mi sniggered.

Rónkẹ́ fixed Ṣìkẹ́mi with a stare. 'Really, how is *Yèyé*?'

'She is well; busy planning palace renovations and forging alliances with the remaining chiefs.'

'Does that mean you'll be in Lagos for the foreseeable future?'

'Yes, on and off, in between raids.'

Rónkẹ́'s face darkened. 'Why are you still conducting raids? We heard the British demanded an end to the trade in return for helping Akítóyè.'

'That's true, but you know *Yèyé*. She can't wait to rebuild, and palace reconstructions require money. She never intended to relinquish the trade.'

Rónkẹ́ was silent for a minute. Then she turned her full gaze on Ṣìkẹ́mi, her brows furrowed, a sad expression marring the beautiful face. 'Don't you tire of it all? Does it not bother you that you are doing to others what was done to you?'

Rónkẹ́'s words touched a nerve and Ṣìkẹ́mi's throat clogged. She looked down, trying to get her feelings under control. When she raised her head, unshed tears shimmered in her eyes. 'What do you want me to say? I am a slave who does her owner's bidding to survive.'

'But the misery the ongoing slave trade causes...' Rónké huffed out the unfinished sentence.

Ṣìkẹ́mi sighed. Rónké had learned of the experiences of those sold to the Americas through Pedro, who strongly opposed the trade. 'I know,' she said. 'But I didn't start this evil, and I can't stop it.'

An uncomfortable silence permeated the air as they each pondered the vile trade and their role in it. To come to terms with what she did, Ṣìkẹ́mi had created rules for herself. She never raided villages directly, always stealing captives off others on their last leg to the coast, a trick learned from her own capture. She freed the young, the women and the elderly she came across. Hopefully, the young would grow into adults who would continue the next generation of Yorùbás, and the elderly would grow old in peace or until they were next raided. In return, she also hoped the gods would reward her by reuniting her with her family someday.

Rónké interrupted the silence. 'Would you stop if you could?'

Ṣìkẹ́mi considered the question. Would she? Nothing else gave her the same heady exhilaration – the power and excitement she felt when she was on a hunt. It was also wrong, and, once the thrill abated, guilt and sorrow took its place, leaving her tossing well into the night. Given a chance, she would choose a different life.

'Ẹ̀gbọ́n, I would. I hope Yèyé will let me buy my freedom so I can stop. Do you think she would?'

Rónké searched Ṣìkẹ́mi's face for the truth, and Ṣìkẹ́mi bore the scrutiny. Then Rónké broke the stare and shrugged. 'Who knows, with Yèyé?'

Rónké dropped the subject as her daughter, Àdùnní,

padded into the room, rubbing sleepy eyes. Rónké pulled her forward and introduced her to Ṣìkẹ́mi. 'See, this is your Auntie Ṣìkẹ́mi.'

Àdùnní hung back, hiding her face behind her mother's wrapper. Ṣìkẹ́mi chuckled at the moniker, reminiscent of the way the British addressed their elders.

'Come Àdùnní,' Ṣìkẹ́mi said. 'See my broad shoulders? Would you like to sit on them?'

The child's head bobbed up and down behind her mother's wrapper. Ṣìkẹ́mi held out her hand and, after a few tentative peeps, Àdùnní reached for her. Ṣìkẹ́mi swung her up in one clean swoop and the child squealed in utter delight.

Ṣìkẹ́mi spent the rest of the afternoon playing with Àdùnní and catching up on Rónké's news. It was a while since she had interacted with young children, and it reminded her of the days before her training when she had looked after the palace's children. Flashes of when she played with her brother resurfaced from deeply buried memories, and her face clouded over. It seemed she could never escape the dark thoughts. If alive, he would be much taller now, perhaps even betrothed.

Rónké exhaled with a sigh that broke through Ṣìkẹ́mi's thoughts.

'That sounds heavy,' Ṣìkẹ́mi said. 'What's on your mind?'

'What if you ran away from Madam? We could shelter you and petition the British to intercede on your behalf.'

Rónké looked hopeful, but Ṣìkẹ́mi shook her head. It was an option she had considered briefly before discarding it. As a favoured slave, she had power, but as a runaway slave, she'd be everybody's target. In addition, no slave owner allowed their slaves to escape without consequences, as it encouraged others to do likewise.

'I don't want to spend the rest of my life as a fugitive. *Yèyé* would never forgive me, and her reach is long and far beyond Lagos. I intend to find my family and I wouldn't want them in harm's way. Besides, your neighbours might not like you harbouring me. Keeping me here might give their own slaves ideas and no one really wants their slaves freed. I don't want to cause trouble between you and your neighbours or between you and *Yèyé*.'

Ṣìkẹ́mi watched Rónkẹ́ process that thought. It surprised her somewhat that the Àgùdà returnees, who were previously enslaved themselves, owned domestic slaves. It was one of the reasons she was convinced nothing could end the trade and it helped assuage some of the guilt she felt at her own clandestine activities. If emancipated slaves felt comfortable owning slaves, who was she to question the status quo?

Rónkẹ́'s lips firmed, an expression Ṣìkẹ́mi knew too well. 'I still want to. I'll talk to Pedro and see what we come up with.'

Ṣìkẹ́mi felt like arguing, but it would be pointless. Like Madam, once Rónkẹ́ got hold of an idea she was loath to drop it. Ṣìkẹ́mi knew she was only trying to help, but her plan wouldn't work. If she did invoke the treaty, she would do so under her own steam. However, she was convinced the only thing that might induce Madam to part with her would be several large sacks of cowrie shells. Ṣìkẹ́mi almost had enough, and the idea of buying her freedom from Madam with Madam's own money somehow seemed both ironic and befitting.

TWENTY-ONE

Ṣìkẹ́mi mulled over Rónkẹ́'s words as she plodded back to the palace. The evening din of travellers heading home after a hard day's trading permeated the air and people jostled for space on the crowded street. Lost in thought as she was, her shoulder collided with something solid. Ṣìkẹ́mi blinked rapidly as she focused on the man in front of her. She and the stranger both muttered apologies and went their separate ways, but something about him bothered Ṣìkẹ́mi. She turned round and watched the stranger's back as he strode away. 'Fọlárìn,' she whispered. Then she shouted. 'Fọlárìn!'

The stranger stopped and turned round. Ṣìkẹ́mi's heart pumped so hard it roared in her ears. It was Fọlárìn! The handsome boy had grown into a breathtaking man; still with the angular jaw, symmetrical eyebrows and those eyelashes. Beneath the triangular flare of his nose, a neat moustache framed his bow-shaped top lip, growing downwards into a compact beard. Despite her height, he towered over her, his short trousers and *dànṣíkí* revealing muscled arms and legs. She couldn't stop staring at him, and as she gawked a slow rush of butterflies stirred low in her belly. The gods must have worked extra hard carving out his features, she thought.

Fọlárìn walked back to her, a puzzled frown on his face. 'Do we know each other?'

The old habit resurfaced. Ṣìkẹ́mi couldn't help playing with him. 'You mean you don't recognise the face of your wife-to-be?'

Fọlárìn's face remained blank as the seconds ticked by, then his eyes rounded like an owl's. 'Ṣìkẹ́mi? Is that you?' He grabbed her and twirled her around.

'Stop that. Put me down at once!' She batted the strong arms that held her, her eyes sparkling in delight.

Fọlárìn put her down, then stood back to examine her closely, taking in her cropped hair, the *dànṣíkí* and trousers. He shook his head repeatedly. 'What has become of you?' The question held no censure, just wonder.

Even after he put her down, Ṣìkẹ́mi's skin still tingled where he had touched her. She ignored the sensation. 'Come,' she said, leading him to a *dongoyárò* tree by the roadside. 'There is much to share. Let's talk in the shade, unless you are in a hurry.'

For the next few minutes, they caught up with each other's lives. Fọlárìn told her he was sold to Madam Ẹfúnṣetán Aníwúrà, a powerful contemporary of Madam's who lived in the city of Ìbàdàn and became her adopted son's companion. He was in Lagos with his master on business, and they would return to Ìbàdàn in the morning.

'So, you became a warrior, ẹhn? You were always different.' His eyes flashed. 'I am glad things worked out for you.'

'Thank you. Màmá and Kúnlé were seen in Ìlarǒ a few years ago. Once I buy my freedom, I will search for them. Do you know what happened to your family?' she asked.

Ṣìkẹ́mi registered the moment Fọlárìn's body stilled. His eyes clouded, and he shook his head.

'What is it?' she asked.

'I met someone from the village last year. He said most of the villagers were captured and sold to the Americans. He was sold to a Lagos chief, but he swore he saw both our parents and Kúnlé marched off to a ship.'

Ṣìkẹ́mi sagged, her head shaking. 'No, that's not possible. The woman I spoke to said the Màmá Ṣìkẹ́mi she met had a child about Kúnlé's age whose name also started with a "K". It has to be them.'

Fọlárìn stared at her, his eyes full of compassion. He reached out a hand and touched her hand. 'Ṣìkẹ́mi, it was Bàbá Làmídì. Surely, he can't have been mistaken, given how well he knew your family.'

As the words sank in, Ṣìkẹ́mi heard the roar of a rushing wind, and her knees gave way. Fọlárìn caught her just in time, lowering her to the ground, before kneeling beside her. With eyes snapped shut and her head doubled over, she drew her knees to her chest, grasped her head in her hands and rocked her body on the spot. Waves of desolation washed over her, the barbs hitting her skin like tiny arrow heads.

Fọlárìn put a warm hand on her shoulder. 'Pẹ̀lẹ,' he said. 'I know it is tough news.'

Ṣìkẹ́mi shuddered. If true, everything she lived for was gone. The chances of Bàbá Làmídì, her father's close friend, misidentifying her family were low to none.

'What are you going to do now?' Fọlárìn's voice sounded faraway.

Ṣìkẹ́mi pulled herself together and lifted her head. 'I don't know.' Freedom seemed pointless with no one to share it with. She stood up.

Fọlárìn rose too. 'Will you be all right?'

She nodded and hugged him. Then they parted ways.

Ṣìkẹ́mi dragged her feet back to the palace in a haze. What were the odds of encountering Fọlárìn in Lagos, only to discover her family gone? She was glad he hadn't been shipped to the Americas, but her heart bled for her family. A sudden rush of emotions flooded her once more. She gasped and doubled over as they threatened to overwhelm her. She gulped several deep breaths until she felt in control once more. Despite the blow, she was alive, and she still had Rónkẹ́. A nugget of hope resurfaced. The seer had said she would return home. Surely he would not have said that if there was no one to return to. She would petition Madam for her freedom and invoke the British treaty if need be.

Madam lifted her chin, swung it left, then right, as a myriad of expressions flashed across her face. In front of her, Ṣìkẹ́mi held a long-handled mirror framed in red mahogany wood. Madam's fingers made repeated jabs at a section of the headpiece sticking out at an awkward angle. 'Why won't it stay in place?' she muttered aloud.

The servant who had toiled over the intricate design hovered, her face clouded with worry. Every poke from Madam's fingers increased the risk of the headpiece unravelling. Ṣìkẹ́mi hid an amused smile behind compressed lips. She understood the girl's anxiety since they'd already spent half an hour on it. After a few tucks here and there, Madam's face settled into a semi-satisfied grin. She stood up. 'Right! I am ready for the day.'

The servant exhaled an audible sigh. Ṣìkẹ́mi gathered her courage. It was time. She knelt before Madam. '*Yèyé—*'

A loud knock made everyone turn.

Kàmọ̀rù's head appeared. 'There is a messenger here, Yèyé. Kabiyèsí wants to see you now.'

'Tell him I am on my way.' Madam turned to Ṣìkẹ́mi. 'You heard the boy. Whatever you wanted will have to wait.'

Ṣìkẹ́mi snapped her jaw shut and pursed her lips. It had taken hours of psyching herself up and practising the right words, and the Ọba had just derailed her plan. She stood up and followed Madam.

As they strolled past curious palace dwellers, Ṣìkẹ́mi cast a practised eye over her mistress. Madam adored being right at the heart of power. Judging by the number of visitors she hosted daily, Ṣìkẹ́mi knew Madam was busy brokering as much favour as her money could buy. She had thrown herself into the business of rebuilding the palace and donated a sizeable portion of her wealth to it, much to Akítóyè's delight.

The main palace building housing the throne room came into view, towering above the rest of the complex. Ṣìkẹ́mi took her time admiring the edifice that had replaced the old palace ruins. 'It looks good,' she said. The recent upgrade had transformed parts of the old structure into a two-storey building. Now, with a long Brazilian-styled portico topped with an undulating domed roof, it rivalled the mansions of the wealthiest returnees.

Madam nodded. 'You know what the elders say. When the king's house burns, it only makes it more beautiful. Do you know Portuguese traders helped build the original building over a hundred years ago?'

Ṣìkẹ́mi winged an eyebrow. 'I didn't know our people dealt with white folk that far back.'

A ghost of a smile flitted over Madam's face. 'Then they respected us as equal trading partners. Now...' She left the sentence trailing.

Ṣìkẹ́mi wondered if Madam's impending meeting with the king was linked to the fact that he had met with Beecroft just the day before. As Madam said he would, Akítóyè ignored her trading activities, despite his treaty with the British. Not only was she trading slaves for guns, her private army was now larger than the king's. Palace gossip suggested neither the king nor Beecroft were happy about it. For both their sakes, she hoped Beecroft's visit was unrelated to Madam's summons, because she was done prevaricating, and she needed Madam in a good mood to ask for her freedom.

'*Kabiyèsí o!*' Ṣìkẹ́mi and Madam chorused, as they knelt and paid homage to the monarch, who sat on a high-backed beaded throne. Decked in a brocade *agbádá*, matching *ṣòkòtò* and an embroidered white cap, he cut an imposing figure. Beside him sat the *Eletú Òdìbò*, his prime minister. Apart from an odd assortment of furniture, the throne room looked rather sparse and uninspiring, a sign the redecorating was ongoing.

'Welcome, *Yèyé*.' With a flick of his wrist, the king waved his *ìrùkẹ̀rẹ̀* at his sister-in-law, welcoming her with the horsetail insignia. Then he invited them to rise and offered Madam a stool. Ṣìkẹ́mi stood behind Madam and waited.

'You sent for me, *Kabiyèsí*? I hope I am not too late.'

'Ah! *Yèyé*, no time is too late or early for you. Let the servants bring you something to drink.'

The king turned to the servant next to him. 'Bring some water for *Yèyé*.' As the servant scurried to do the king's bidding, he turned his attention back to Madam. 'Will you ask your warrior to wait outside?'

'Outside? Is something wrong, *Kabiyèsí*?'

'This word is for your ears only. Ask her to wait outside.'

Madam pressed her lips into a tight grimace, but she could

not outright defy the king in the presence of a slave, so she nodded at Ṣìkẹ́mi. Ṣìkẹ́mi curtsied and took her leave, waiting outside the throne room entrance. She cocked her ears, but the conversation in the room was too muted for her to catch their words. However, she didn't have to wait long.

A few minutes later Madam burst out of the throne room, her earlier sunny disposition gone. 'Come, we are leaving!' Madam's entire body shook with concealed fury, as she took long strides towards her own quarters.

Ṣìkẹ́mi eyed her with concern. 'What happened?'

Madam launched into a diatribe. 'Ẹhn, me, a whole me! Has he forgotten who I am? He wants me to return to Bàdágrì, after everything I have done for him. Did I not put him on the throne?' She beat her chest with her right hand as she spat the words. 'Okay. We'll see who outlasts the other. Me or him.' She clicked her fingers. 'Ṣìkẹ́mi, are you still gawking behind my back, or are you paying attention?'

Ṣìkẹ́mi hurried after Madam, her mouth half-open. She'd expected the king to voice his displeasure, but not outright banish his sister-in-law. 'I'm here, *Yèyé*. Yes, I am paying attention.'

'We are going back to Bàdágrì. You hear me? He and Beecroft can have Lagos. We'll see what good it does them.'

At a loss, Ṣìkẹ́mi nodded. 'Yes, *Yèyé*.'

Ṣìkẹ́mi's stomach roiled as the ramifications of Madam's banishment sank in. The *Ọba* had truly scuppered her plans. Akítóyè's treaty did not cover Bàdágrì, which meant if Madam refused her request she could not appeal to the *Ọba* or the British. Worse still, an incandescent Madam was not a kind one. Broaching her freedom now would likely tip the woman over the edge, risking Ṣìkẹ́mi being resold or even death.

Ṣìkẹ́mi spent the rest of the afternoon listening to Madam bemoan the ungratefulness of the king she helped to the throne. As they packed for departure the following morning, she contemplated her future; one without the family she hoped for; one without Rónkẹ́. She'd barely been able to tolerate Madam when Akítóyè lived in Bàdágrì. The future, with a slighted Madam, looked very bleak indeed.

TWENTY-TWO

Ṣìkẹ́mi leapt through the air and landed feet first and combat ready in front of a new opponent. All around her, in the earthy throes of battle, feet thundered, dust swirled, and an unearthly roar filled the air. She sized up the man, taking in the double-edged sword swaying in his right hand. No match for her, she surmised, as she took an offensive stance and thrust forward. For minutes their feet danced to the primitive sound of clashing blades, as Ṣìkẹ́mi and her opponent mirrored each other's movements, searching for a weakness.

Then Ṣìkẹ́mi noticed another opponent creeping towards her. With lightning speed, she freed her second sword from its sheath, twisted sideways, thrusting both swords, each into the stomachs of her opponents. Her jaw clenched at the satisfying crunch of metal meeting bone. Without pause, she moved on to the next opponent, continuing the slaughter, her troops following her lead, making quick work of the enemy, until they all lay dead or scattered.

Ṣìkẹ́mi did not waste valuable time pursuing her fleeing foes. Instead, her men gathered the bound captives into a row.

While her troops stood guard, she inspected the captives. Moving down the line, she separated them into two groups: the young, weak, old, suckling babies and their mothers in one group, and everyone else in the other.

Next, Ṣìkẹ́mi did a quick visual count of her troops, nodding with satisfaction that all twenty stood before her. 'You know what to do,' she said to her second-in-command, Odùtọ́lá. He took ten of Ṣìkẹ́mi's warriors, who gathered the strongest captives into a huddle and started setting up a temporary camp. Ṣìkẹ́mi and the rest of her troop herded the remaining captives back through the forest.

A few minutes into the trek, Ṣìkẹ́mi paused and addressed the sniffling women and children.

'Today, the gods have smiled at you, but if you want to live, you must be silent. I will guide you to the nearest village. You can find your way home from there.'

The captives grew quiet as they absorbed the news, their eyes asking what their lips would not utter.

'The others won't be returning with you. Their fate is up to the gods now.'

A few more whimpers greeted Ṣìkẹ́mi's announcement, making her scowl.

'If you make any more noise, I will leave you here and you can take your chances with the next lot of raiders or wild beasts. The choice is yours.' Her announcement achieved the desired effect. Mothers hushed their children, some covering the errant mouths with their hands. Ṣìkẹ́mi nodded, and her men led the way.

Ṣìkẹ́mi wasn't sure why she continued to free the weaker captives. It wasn't as if the gods might reward her for it. When she first returned from Lagos, she'd paid traders from Ìlarǒ and its neighbouring villages to search for her family and report back to her, but it had all been in vain. After months of fruitless searching, what hope she had left petered out, and she came to believe Fọlárìn's information. With nothing to leave Madam for, her focus shifted. Now, eighteen months later, she raided to avoid Madam's company and to gain wealth, and she didn't care about much else.

As Ṣìkẹ́mi and the captives trekked through the forest, morning turned to afternoon. Shards of afternoon sunlight filtered through the giant trees like triangular prisms, filling the forest floor with an ethereal haze and lending it a mystical air. The chatter of baboons and chimpanzees mingled with the sweet chirps of the paradise flycatcher, camouflaging her captives' heavy breathing. Many were still children and Ṣìkẹ́mi knew they found the trek arduous and the forest terrifying. But thanks to Ọbádínà's training, to her it was home and sanctuary; the place where she felt most at ease.

The thinning forest trees and a huddle of raffia rooftops in the distance signalled they were fast approaching the edge of a village. Ṣìkẹ́mi stopped the trek and addressed her unwanted captives. 'Keep walking in that direction until you reach the village. May your gods guide your path.'

'Thank you!' The heartfelt expression of gratitude rumbled through the captives as Ṣìkẹ́mi turned and led her men away.

The sun hung low in the evening sky by the time Ṣìkẹ́mi returned to base camp. They spent the next two hours resting and preparing for the night trek, and, once darkness enveloped them, Ṣìkẹ́mi gathered her troops and the captives. Guided by hand-held fire lamps, they headed towards the coast. A day later, in the dead of night, she marched her human loot into a tiny creek that emptied into the ocean.

Although British naval vessels still patrolled the Atlantic coastline, detaining any slavers they caught and freeing the captives, Ṣìkẹ́mi had quickly figured out how to evade their clutches. The mangrove provided excellent cover for her illicit activity, its giant roots the perfect hiding place for the dug-out boats she used to transport her captives.

Ṣìkẹ́mi reduced any potential losses by using several boats. Her dug-outs were nimble enough to hide in the myriad of tiny creeks and rivers, where the larger ships could not follow. If accosted, her men would abandon the boats and swim to safety. She might lose one or two cargo loads, but the others would compensate for it. But she rarely did.

At the creek, surrounded by the chirps of the night forest, Ṣìkẹ́mi supervised her men. Once they finished loading all the canoes, the flotilla set off, with two warriors rowing and one guarding the slaves. Their destination? One of the several mud banks lining the Bàdágrì coast for her appointment with Domingo, the Brazilian slave trader. This was her life now, and for the most part she was content.

It was mid-morning the following day before Ṣìkẹ́mi appeared before Madam with two sacks full of cowrie shells. She hefted both sacks onto Madam's coffee table just as a commotion in the background caught her attention. She leaned out of Madam's window and spied the town crier in the distance. Alert and on edge, she opened the door and paced. The frown on her face mirrored Madam's, because a running town crier meant only one thing.

Minutes later, huffing, the town crier prostrated before Madam. '*Yèyé*, may you live long. May evil never darken your door again.'

The room stilled at the ominous words.

'What happened?' Ṣìkẹ́mi asked.

'Ẹ̀hn, it is Akítóyè, o!'

Madam stiffened at the mention of the Lagos king. 'What do you mean? Akítóyè?'

'Ẹhn, he is dead o!'

Madam slumped into a chair, her mouth wide open. 'Ẹhn, you lie. Say it again.'

The town crier remonstrated with his hands. 'Ah, *Yèyé*, you heard me the first time.'

Ṣìkẹ́mi didn't blame the town crier for not wanting to repeat himself as the bearer of bad news. She studied Madam's slackened jaw and bulging eyes. Although she hadn't forgiven her brother-in-law for banishing her, the two had been allies far too long for the death not to affect her. Eventually Madam found her voice. 'So, what killed Akítóyè?'

'Ah, *Yèyé*, it is death o!'

Madam leaned forward and clapped her hands in the town crier's face. 'Bàbá Gbohùn-gbohùn, what is wrong with you? I mean, what kind of death?'

'Ẹhn, don't mind me. They just said he died. Nobody knows what of.'

Madam looked bewildered. 'Hà. How can he just die? What kind of misfortune is this?'

'I don't know, *Yèyé*. May the gods preserve us.'

'Um.'

A moment of silence prevailed, then Madam stood. 'Ṣìkẹ́mi, we are going to Lagos.'

Ṣìkẹ́mi frowned at the pronouncement. Were they even allowed in Lagos? '*Yèyé*,' she said, 'did the banishment order end with the king?'

Madam shrugged. 'I don't care. They are not burying him without my presence.'

. . .

Back in her room, Ṣìkẹ́mi cursed as she pulled out bags of cowries from her underground safe. Living with Madam was a never-ending trial. She'd tried remonstrating with her, reminding her of what happened the last time in Lagos. Her business in Bàdágrì was blooming, and the British ignored her. What more did she want? But, bent on meddling with the succession process, Madam would not reconsider.

Ṣìkẹ́mi cringed, remembering Madam's frenzy the last time they were in Lagos. Madam would expect her to continue business as usual, which meant scouting new, safe raiding routes and an end to her well-ordered existence. She wished the woman wasn't so addicted to power and politics. She sighed and tried to console herself. Perhaps it was time to reconsider that treaty. Assuming they weren't expelled the moment they arrived, it might be her last shot at freedom on her own terms.

TWENTY-THREE

Another bead of sweat rolled down Ṣìkẹ́mi's brow. She grimaced as she swiped it with the back of her hand, then wiped her hand on her *dànṣíkí*. She wished she'd brought a hand-fan along. Like the other dignitaries, a slave stood behind Madam, fanning her with a large peacock-feather fan. Ṣìkẹ́mi's skin caught a whiff of the humid breeze following each downward stroke of the fan, but it did little to ease her discomfort. She checked the sky and frowned. The impending rain shower would temper the heat, but it would turn the palace front into a mud bath, and, given the high-ranking officials about, that would be disastrous.

They'd been back in Lagos for five months and were now seated among a long row of dignitaries and kingmakers. Further to her right, the newly crowned *Ọba* Dòsùnmú sat next to the new British consul, Benjamin Campbell, and other representatives of the British monarch. Behind them sat members of the royal family. Nearby a group of drummers, clad only in white wrappers, beat their *gbèdu* drums with so much vigour, Ṣìkẹ́mi feared the drums' skins would burst. In front of the dignitaries, as far as the eye could see, the palace courtyard teemed with *Ẹ̀yọ̀* masqueraders, covered head to toe in white shrouds, capped with wide-brimmed hats.

The masqueraders, of every shape and size possible, some undoubtedly hiding children beneath their shrouds, made a spectacle of epic proportions. Clustered in groups denoted by different-coloured hats rimmed with white tassels, they bobbed up and down as they moved their feet to the drumbeat. Each masquerader held a thin, long stick with ends shaped into a flat tongue, and the sticks swayed in the air in tandem with their owner's movements. In the centre of the throng, two masqueraders tested each other's mettle, smacking their sticks together. Around them, some masqueraders leapt several feet into the air, while others twisted their shrouded forms up and down in a swirl of synchronised movement. The crowds behind them roared at their antics, their noise mingling with the sounds from the drums and stamping feet, creating a deafening cacophony.

The festival, the first of its kind to honour the dead *Ọba* Akítóyè, was nearing its pinnacle. The leaders of the masquerade procession neared the new king and paid homage, while a praise singer extolled their beauty and ancestry. Then they danced away from the king, back towards the town centre.

Ṣìkẹ́mi scanned the heavens again. The clouds were rolling in fast. Campbell and his countrymen wouldn't appreciate being caked in the mud that would accompany the thunderstorm. She studied the dignitaries from Madam to the new *Ọba* on his throne. They all smiled and joked, pointing out the antics of the masqueraders. Yet, despite the outward appearance of civility, the *Ọba* led a troubled court. Beecroft and Akítóyè's deaths within two months of each other had ushered in a new regime and politics that had Madam reeling.

An hour later, with the last echoes of the drums fading in

the distance, the first droplets hit the raffia canopy sheltering the dignitaries. Everyone rose at once, hastening their farewells to the new king in a bid to outrun the downpour.

Back in her room, Madam tutted about the king and his new-found friends. 'The young these days; they have no respect for their elders.' She huffed as she took off her regalia.

Madam was referring to Dòsùnmú's reluctance to take advice from his aunt. Despite Madam's best attempts to plant herself at the centre of court life, Dòsùnmú had blocked her every move. The thirty-year-old king was much closer to Ṣìkẹ́mi's age and preferred younger advisers and the counsel of the British, who had backed his ascension.

'He surrounds himself with slaves and the sons of slaves,' Madam said, her voice laced with disdain. Ṣìkẹ́mi raised a sardonic eyebrow at Madam's reference to the British-educated returnees who made up the bulk of Dòsùnmú's advisers.

'And as for Campbell...' She hissed, showing her disgust for the latter. Her lack of access to the king riled her to no end, and she detested the new consul. Brash but astute, Campbell was an expert at wheedling and more than Madam's match. In the impending battle between the two, Ṣìkẹ́mi wondered who would win.

Ṣìkẹ́mi had no sympathy for Madam. Although it wasn't her place to say, 'I told you so', her constant silence left Madam in no doubt of her views, which only made Madam crankier. But Ṣìkẹ́mi no longer cared. She ignored the woman's tantrums. Besides, as Ṣìkẹ́mi suspected she would be, the woman was too busy brokering power to notice Ṣìkẹ́mi's increased absence. Madam had less need for security, since the British had contained Kòsọkọ́ at Èpé, miles down the coast. So, even when she wasn't raiding, she spent more time in the forest than at the palace. Madam was captaining a sinking ship, and Ṣìkẹ́mi was ready to bail when it sank.

Soon after Ṣìkẹ́mi settled Madam into her quarters, Ọbádínà came to pay his wife a visit. Ọbádínà was judicious in his visits to his wife whenever she was unhappy. He barely visited Madam in Bàdágrì. A man of simple tastes, he'd told Ṣìkẹ́mi he preferred a quiet life when he wasn't fighting somebody's war, so Ṣìkẹ́mi was surprised to see him.

As they both sat down for a meal, Madam resumed her complaints about Dòsùnmú. 'Dòsùnmú is allowing his Àgùdà and Sàró friends to control access to trade at the ports. When I requested an audience, he had the nerve to send a message that he was too busy. Ẹhn!' Madam slapped her hands against her thighs. 'Too busy for me, Ọ̀ṣuntinúbú, the wife of a king. Three kings have come and gone. Me, I am still here. And he says he's too busy? Hmm. You know what the elders say: when large sorrows overwhelm you, little troubles take advantage.'

When no one responded to her rant, Madam focused her laser eyes on Ọbádínà. 'Can you get me an audience with him?'

'Me?' Ọbádínà raised both hands, his body jerking backward. 'You know I have no influence over that one. He has appointed a new commander over his army, and I am lucky I still have a job.'

Madam hissed and rolled her eyes. 'The proverbs say children who know how to wash their hands will eat with their elders. These days, it seems they have no desire for their elders' presence.'

The room lapsed into silence while Madam and her husband finished their meal. Once the meal was over, Madam broke the silence. 'Ṣìkẹ́mi, could you see that the *Eletŭ Òdìbò* gets the gift I prepared for him earlier?'

'I plan to have a servant deliver it this evening,' Ṣìkẹ́mi said.

'No. I want you to take it to him now.'

Ṣìkẹ́mi straightened, surprise etched on her face. It was a minor errand usually assigned to the household servants. But, at Madam's insistent stare, she swallowed her irritation and rose.

'Yes, Yèyé. I will see to it now.' As Ṣìkẹ́mi stood, Ọbádínà pulled his chair closer to his wife's and, before she even left the room, they started whispering. Ṣìkẹ́mi thought the whole thing rather strange – the errand seemed fabricated to get rid of her – but she welcomed the respite.

Madam had been at her most miserable in Bàdágrì, making life difficult for everyone in her household. Ṣìkẹ́mi had barely held on to her sanity and her forest excursions had become an increasingly necessary outlet for her frustrations. Once, she'd summoned enough courage and asked Madam to name her price for her freedom. Madam became so incensed she'd threatened to sell Ṣìkẹ́mi to the first white man she found. After that, Ṣìkẹ́mi had kept her peace. Now, she could petition the new king and invoke the treaty agreement.

Ṣìkẹ́mi delivered Madam's parcel to the chief. The man's eyes held a faint twinge of interest that Madam had sent Ṣìkẹ́mi instead of the usual servants, but he held his tongue. Ṣìkẹ́mi reassessed her opinion of him. He was greedy like the other chiefs Madam courted, but he was also astute, and, by the looks of it, discreet. That might work to her advantage, Ṣìkẹ́mi decided.

Ṣìkẹ́mi strolled back to the palace, taking delight in the lively Lagos streets. It had taken aeons for those who fled during the British siege to return. Lucrative deals between locals and Europeans had created a trade boom, infusing life into the city once more. Traders lined both sides of the street, peddling their wares and jostling for attention. 'Move out of the way!' A porter burrowed through the crowded street with a wooden cart full of fresh yams. As Ṣìkẹ́mi stepped aside, a soft hand touched her arm. 'Oranges round and fresh. Please buy my oranges,' a young girl implored, and lifted an orange towards Ṣìkẹ́mi's nose. She smiled and shook her head. The palace already heaved with oranges. A tap on her shoulder made her swivel round, alert and ready for combat.

Fọlárìn lifted a placating hand. 'It's just me. I called your name, but you seemed lost in thought.'

Ṣìkẹ́mi's shoulders relaxed, but she took a step backward. 'Fọlárìn. How are you?'

At the lukewarm welcome, Fọlárìn's smile faltered. 'I am well. You?'

Ṣìkẹ́mi shrugged. She'd never considered what to say if they ever met again. Although he had done no wrong, somehow her brain tied him to the moment she lost all hope, and for now she wanted nothing to do with him. He was a reminder of everything she had lost. '*Liar*,' a voice in her head echoed. He was still devastatingly handsome, and her breath hitched as she took him in. With brutal intent, she tamped down the invading thoughts, nodded and made to sidestep him.

'Wait! Why are you being so rude?' He grabbed her arm, and Ṣìkẹ́mi's eyes narrowed. 'I hoped I'd find you in Lagos. I have something important to tell you.'

Ṣìkẹ́mi hitched her eyebrows. The last time they met, he'd given her the worst news of her life. What more could he possibly say? The bump in the middle of his throat bobbed, piquing her interest.

He started. 'You see...'

'Look, I am in a hurry. Please say whatever it is, so I can be on my way.'

Fọlárìn moistened his lips, then started over. 'I owe you an apology. Don't be cross, but I was wrong, and you were right all along. Your family is alive and well in Òké-Ọ̀dán. It's halfway between Abẹ́òkúta and Ìlarǒ.'

Ṣìkẹ́mi's jaw dropped, and a stunned silence followed. Then a blind fury consumed her. 'You mean for the last two years I have grieved for nothing? Why should I even believe you?' Several passers-by stopped and gawked as the wind carried the aggression in her voice.

An angry vendor waved them away from her stall front. 'I beg you. Please move away from my stall if you want to fight. Don't bring your bad aura here.'

Fọlárìn took several steps and turned to her. 'I apologise for how you've felt. I only shared what Bàbá Làmídì said. There was no reason to disbelieve him. You said so yourself.'

Ṣìkẹ́mi planted her hands on her hips and thrust her chest forward. 'You don't know how I've survived the last two years; what I have done.'

'But I have apologised.'

'Well, it's not enough.' She folded her arms over her torso and tapped her foot.

Fọlárìn's lips thinned. He drew himself tall and threw his hands up. 'I can only apologise. And this new you...' He paused, searching for the words, while his fingers pointed in accusation. 'You've changed, and it's not for the better.' He turned and walked away, leaving Ṣìkẹ́mi gawking at his back.

Ṣìkẹ́mi pulled herself together and stumbled through the streets. How she got back in one piece, she'd never know. In the privacy of her room, she let go and wept. She cried for all the years she hadn't and for the joy of renewed hope.

Later that evening, a calmer Ṣìkẹ́mi reviewed the day's events. She hadn't even asked him how he'd found her family. Was his information reliable this time round? Her instincts told her he wouldn't have sought her out unless he was sure. She remembered his parting words, and a tinge of regret filled her. She scrunched her nose with a rueful grin. They both disliked the new her. But that would all change now. The wonder of the discovery left her feeling as buoyant as a cloud. She could dream again, and, for the first time in years, she burst into laughter; a deep, guttural belly roar.

TWENTY-FOUR

A month later, Ṣìkẹ́mi stood at the edge of the clearing while her men prepared their campsite for the night. The sun sat low in the sky, its departing halo leaving behind a palette of bright blue-orange streaks. She was back on the job at Madam's insistence, despite the higher risk of capture since the British had redoubled their efforts to stamp out the trade. Two more raids and she was done. She was willing to offer Madam most of her wealth for her release, with other options available if unsuccessful.

Deep in thought, she turned and walked towards a cluster of dense trees nearby. Behind her ear, mosquitoes buzzed, following her, unwilling to let such a prized meal out of their sight. She swatted them away and enjoyed a moment of relief before they encircled her again. She shook her head, a rueful smile hovering on her lips. There was nothing peskier than a hungry mosquito.

She lowered herself on to a damp fallen tree trunk beneath a giant Ìrókò tree, stretching her knotted muscles as she did so. Behind her, the muted chatter of her men filtered through. She was near enough to hear them, but far enough to gain some thinking space. It had been a hot, dank and tiring day shadowing a raiding party, and now she needed to decide the best strategy for engaging the enemy in the morning. She felt the rustle of tree leaves behind her, then her second-in-command, Odùtọ́lá, emerged. She inclined her head, and he sauntered over to where she sat, perching on the edge of the same log. Together, they enjoyed the quiet for a while.

'We will engage tomorrow?' Odùtọ́lá broke the silence.

Ṣìkẹ́mi nodded. Odùtọ́lá had worked with her for years and could often read her mind. Her eyes wandered over him, taking in the broad shoulders and finely sinewed biceps. The oval eyes set into his mahogany face sported permanent crinkles at the corners and his full lips often curved into an endearing smile. Tall, athletic and attractive, he reminded her often of Fọlárìn, but without the cockiness she found so unappealing in the latter. He served her well and was the only other human she trusted to any degree besides Rónkẹ́.

'Is something else bothering you?'

Ṣìkẹ́mi sighed, wondering whether she was making something out of nothing. 'Àkàndé.' She bit out the name.

Odùtọ́lá nodded. 'Has he done or said something stupid?'

'You mean apart from the usual?' She grinned, flashing her teeth. 'Not yet. But I sense it's only a matter of time.'

'The boy is an irritant. At his worst, he's a downright fool. Shall I get rid of him before he gets someone killed?'

Ṣìkẹ́mi pondered the question. The boy was bright and ambitious, but his arrogance eclipsed his potential. 'Not yet. Let's wait and see. We might reform him yet.'

'All right. As you say.' Odùtọ́lá's smile bathed her in warmth as he stood and headed back to the group.

Ṣìkẹ́mi sensed Odùtọ́lá had deeper feelings for her, although he hid them well. Every so often, she caught a look of longing on his face, although he never gave her cause for concern. However, while she liked him, whenever she was with Odùtọ́lá she did not feel an iota of the excitement she felt standing next to the adult Fọlárìn. Her determination to do life alone served her well and, although she would never admit it, she was afraid of the potential consequences of letting her guard down. Besides, she was just biding her time, knowing her future lay in the search for her family. So, it seemed counterintuitive to embark on a romantic dalliance. But, once in a while, she imagined what the warmth of another human would feel like if she let go of the constraints she'd built around her life.

Ṣìkẹ́mi quietened her personal thoughts and, once more, embraced the silence as her mind plotted the morrow's attack. A second rustle of feet made her turn, thinking Odùtọ́lá had forgotten something, but the person walking towards her was the errant Àkàndé. Ṣìkẹ́mi tensed, her body alert. The young man, only recently assigned to her battalion, spelt trouble. Rudeness, subverting orders, acting without permission were just a few of the infractions laid at his feet in barely three weeks. If she was being honest, she saw something of her own youthful arrogance when Ọbádínà first started training her. Ọbádínà had given her a second chance, and she would do the same, if the fool would learn.

Ṣìkẹ́mi watched him approach and, without asking permission, he perched himself on the spot just vacated by Odùtọ́lá. Ṣìkẹ́mi sighed and her mouth tightened. She straightened her spine and hardened her voice. 'I did not invite you to sit. What are you doing here when everyone is working hard at setting up camp?'

'Everyone is, except you.'

Ṣìkẹ́mi's already tight jaw tensed even further. She bit her lips to stop herself from screaming. Instead, she stood up, turned and faced him full on, thankful for her height, which helped her stand shoulder to shoulder with most of her team. 'You and I are not mates. I am your superior. You do not tell me what to do and you do not talk to me that way.'

'Come, now. Don't be like that. You know I like you and I am better for you than Odùtọ́lá. If he can sit here, why can't I?'

Ṣìkẹ́mi did a double-take. She had not expected his romantic notions. 'Àkàndé, if you value your position in life, you will stop this behaviour and listen to—'

Before Ṣìkẹ́mi could finish her sentence, Àkàndé stood up, clamped a hand round her arm and pulled her body close to his. Ṣìkẹ́mi's startled surprise lasted but a second. Acting on pure instinct, and in one swift motion, she grabbed him by the waistband of his ṣòkòtò and hefted him over her shoulder. As he sailed over her head, she turned round in time to see him land at her feet, face down. Then she grabbed his arm, twisting it in a corkscrew motion behind his back. Àkàndé screamed as his shoulder popped out of its socket, and that brought the men running. They found Ṣìkẹ́mi standing over Àkàndé, her foot planted in the middle of his back.

'If you ever lay your hands on me again, you will not live to see the sun rise. Do – you –hear – me?' Ṣìkẹ́mi punctuated each word.

'Yes,' he said, breathing through the pain.

Ṣìkẹ́mi yanked on the arm she was still holding. 'I did not hear that.'

He screamed the reply. 'Yes! I hear you, Ọ̀gá.'

Ṣìkẹ́mi hissed, dropped the arm and walked away while her men helped up the miscreant. She heard another scream as they popped his shoulder back into its socket. That ought to teach him, she thought.

Ṣìkẹ́mi stomped through the forest for ten minutes as she

fought to bring her temper under control. She'd never had to discipline a team member that way. Most of them were in her team because of her reputation and because they respected her. Perhaps she should get rid of him after all, but he was a referral from Ọbádínà's friend, and she didn't want to disappoint her old mentor. Grimacing, she walked back to the camp.

As she brushed through the forest foliage, Şìkẹ́mi thought of how she felt when Àkàndé mauled her. He'd reminded her of the weasel, Bàbá Kékeré. Apart from Fọlárìn's impromptu hug, she'd never let a male touch her since that night. Her revulsion for some men, and desire for others, particularly Fọlárìn, puzzled her. Fọlárìn was unattainable, but Odùtọ́lá was within arm's reach. Dare she explore a romantic connection with him? The temptation to be intimate with another human hovered like a whisper. What would it feel like to lie flesh to flesh with a male? The thought sent a delicious quiver coursing through her veins.

But Àkàndé's behaviour highlighted the potential difficulties if she lost her men's respect. Starting a romance with Odùtọ́lá could cause resentment among her troops and lead to more insubordination. Would Odùtọ́lá feel entitled if they became mates? Should she consider finding Fọlárìn again, or take what was within her grasp?

The thoughts circled her head, with no straightforward answers. She needed feminine advice, she decided, and there was no one better than Rónkẹ́. It was time to visit her childhood mentor again – after dealing with the most pressing matter.

TWENTY-FIVE

Ṣikẹ́mi swung her feet off her bed. The thoughts swirling in her head had made sleep difficult. She'd eventually dozed off fitfully, only to be woken by the early-morning calls to prayer from the nearby mosque. She had rehearsed several scenarios, choosing words, then discarding them. Should she do it in front of Ọbádínà, who now visited his wife frequently, or when Madam was alone? She hadn't a clue and decided she'd follow the wind and be guided by Madam's mood. In her room, ten sacks of cowries lay waiting. She prayed the gods would grant her wish.

Much later that day, Madam sat in her living room, regaling Ọbádínà with the exploits of her day, the meetings she'd had with various chiefs and, of course, the different ways she planned to thwart Campbell's plans for Lagos. When a lull appeared in the conversation, Ṣikẹ́mi seized the moment and knelt. '*Yèyé*.'

When Ọbádínà and Madam focused on her, Ṣikẹ́mi continued. 'May your days be long. May the gods continue to prosper you. All your endeavours will turn to good. And may only good health be your portion.'

Madam and Ọbádínà chorused, '*Àṣẹ́!*' to each prayer. Then they waited for Ṣìkẹ́mi to continue.

'*Yèyé*, concerning the matter of my freedom...' She paused, searching for the right words. 'I appreciate all you have done for me, and all the opportunities you have given me. I am fortunate to have such a kind mistress. However, some time ago, I received news that my mother and brother were alive. I therefore seek your benevolence once more and ask that you free me in return for a hundred thousand cowries.' A pulse ticked in her neck as she waited for Madam's response, but she willed herself to stay calm.

Madam fixed Ṣìkẹ́mi with a haughty stare, and for several seconds said absolutely nothing. When she opened her mouth, Ṣìkẹ́mi tensed.

'Mmm... Ṣìkẹ́mi, where has all this money come from? Because I know the ten per cent I have given you over the years could not have amounted to this much.'

The question Madam delivered with such deadly intent caught Ṣìkẹ́mi by surprise and she scrambled for an appropriate answer.

'*Yèyé*, it is the dregs of your wealth. You taught me well. I took those lessons to heart and invested the money you gave me; a little here and there. Even as the gods made you prosperous, they showered the remnants of your blessings on me. That is where it came from.'

'Hmm. Well said.' Ọbádínà's head bobbed up and down. The mischievous glint in his eye showed his pleasure at the by-play, and Ṣìkẹ́mi couldn't tell whose side he was on.

'Well, the stony part of this issue is that I need you, Ṣìkẹ́mi. As you say, I have looked after you well. Should I not now reap the rewards of my investment? Now is not a good time for you to leave. Perhaps in five years we can talk.'

Ṣìkẹ́mi found herself clenching and unclenching her fists.

Unsure what to do, she schooled her face, thanked Madam for her consideration and rose. Madam and Ọbádínà fixed her with a stare, but Ṣìkẹ́mi smiled and sat back in the chair she had occupied earlier. After a brief pause, Madam and Ọbádínà resumed their conversation as if nothing untoward had happened.

Ṣìkẹ́mi tuned them out. Inside, she fumed, outraged at the idea of serving another five years. If Madam wanted war, she would get it, and Ṣìkẹ́mi was determined to emerge the victor.

Ṣìkẹ́mi dragged her feet as she entered the *Eletǔ Òdìbò*'s compound. She'd come at night to avoid any news of her activities making their way back to Madam. As she entered his presence, she knew there was no turning back from her chosen course. 'Good evening, Bàbá.' She prostrated before the kingmaker, who was second only to the king. He was also the second person to occupy the post since Ṣìkẹ́mi had lived with Madam. When he had dethroned Akítóyè, Kòsọkọ́ had executed the previous post-holder. That *Eletǔ Òdìbò* was a friend of Madam's. This one, not so much, and Ṣìkẹ́mi hoped to use it to her advantage. Madam remained indebted to the man and several other traders in town, despite the king's order to settle her affairs.

'Welcome, Ṣìkẹ́mi. *Obìrin bí akọ.*' The *Eletǔ Òdìbò* fussed as he picked up scattered gourds and offered her a seat.

Ṣìkẹ́mi smiled at the moniker she hadn't heard in a while. She glanced around the shabby, dark living room, with its three hard wooden benches, two stools, and not a single rug in sight. The stale stench of empty palm-wine gourds filled her nostrils, and she tried not to wrinkle her nose. She wondered how the man spent his money, since there was little evidence of it around. Then she remembered he had seven wives and an uncountable number of children. That, plus the alcohol, probably accounted for most of it. Short and wiry as he was, with a huge gap where his front four teeth should be, Ṣìkẹ́mi couldn't understand how he attracted one woman, let alone seven. One of life's mysteries, she was certain, or perhaps it was the power.

The chief took an empty bench. 'How can I help you?' he asked.

'Ẹhn, Bàbá, it is more a matter of what I can do for you.'

The man leaned forward, his beady eyes lighting up. 'I am listening.'

'I know that Madam owes you and several traders large sums of money. Despite *Kabiyèsí*'s instruction, she has no intention of paying it back. You see, it is a deliberate ploy to reduce your cash flow because she feels excluded from the trade deals the British are offering the Àgùdà and Sàró. If you are interested, I can continue to keep you abreast of her plans.'

The chief sat silently for a while, sizing up Ṣìkẹ́mi, knowing this offer had a price. 'I see,' he said finally. 'And what do you want in return?'

'Well, Bàbá, I wished to buy my freedom and Madam has refused. I would like to petition the king under the British treaty. If you support it and put in a good word on my behalf, I would be forever grateful.'

The chief nodded emphatically. 'Ah Ṣìkẹ́mi. That is a small thing. Do not worry at all. It is done.'

Ṣìkẹ́mi rose, and the chief saw her out. At the door, he winked at her. 'Do look after yourself and your mistress.'

Ṣìkẹ́mi froze, and for a minute she wondered if the man was trying to add her to his conquests. Then she recovered and bade him goodnight. As she took a brisk walk back to the palace, doubts assailed her. Had she done the right thing, involving the *Eletǔ Òdìbò* in her plans? If anyone had the king's ear, it was him, but his overeagerness in accepting her offer made her worry about his reliability. She shrugged. The deed was done.

Days later, Ṣìkẹ́mi strolled through the Àgùdà area, noting the multi-storey dwellings with their fancy windows and grandiose doors that had sprung up since Akítóyè's second reign. She walked up to Rónkẹ́'s door and knocked. Hers was the only place outside the forest she could relax. Moments later, the door opened to Rónkẹ́, dressed in a floor-length European frock, a startling vision of modernity. Her youngest child, a boy, was balanced on her hip, while Àdùnní, who'd grown a lot taller since Ṣìkẹ́mi last saw her, clung to her mother's skirt.

The delight on Rónkẹ́'s face caused warm butterflies to swarm inside Ṣìkẹ́mi's belly. Rónkẹ́ reached out and wrapped her free arm round Ṣìkẹ́mi, drawing her into a hug. Ṣìkẹ́mi responded by wrapping both her arms round Rónkẹ́. The two clung together for minutes before Àdùnní's plaintive 'Màmá!' made them spring apart. Ṣìkẹ́mi reached down and hefted Àdùnní into her arms. The child squealed.

'Do you remember me, Àdùnní?' she asked as she walked into the lobby.

The child nodded emphatically. 'Auntie Kẹ́mi!'

Ṣìkẹ́mi's face split into a grin at the child's abbreviation of her name. No one had ever called her Auntie, but she liked it. 'That's right!' She burrowed her head into Àdùnní's chest, tickling her as she did so. That brought a fresh round of giggles from the child.

'Come and sit down,' Rónkẹ́ invited as she moved into her living room. 'How have you been? So much has happened since I last saw you.'

Ṣìkẹ́mi nodded as she sat with Àdùnní balanced on her knee. She reached out a hand to stroke the toddler's head. The boy squirmed and hid his face in his mother's bosom. Ṣìkẹ́mi gave him an indulgent smile before turning to answer his mother's question.

'It has. Our world is changing so fast, I can hardly keep up with it. So much change, whether or not one wants it. How are you?' She shifted the focus back to Rónkẹ́. They would get to her problems soon enough. Rónkẹ́ didn't seem to mind the deflection and proceeded to give Ṣìkẹ́mi an update on her life.

Eventually, a lull in the conversation allowed Ṣìkẹ́mi to broach the real reason for her visit. 'How did you decide Pedro was right for you?' she asked.

Rónkẹ́'s eyes lit up with a mischievous spark. 'Well, apart from his handsome face...' She giggled and fanned her face with her hand. 'Seriously, I think it was his kindness that won me over. Why do you ask? Do you have a suitor?'

Ṣìkẹ́mi squirmed, refusing to meet Rónkẹ́'s eyes.

'Ṣìkẹ́mi?'

'Not really, I just wondered... considered the possibility.'

'Who is he? I never saw you show interest in a man while I lived with Madam. He must be special.'

Ṣìkẹ́mi fidgeted with her fingers for a while, then decided to be honest. Otherwise, what was the point of her visit?

'Actually, there are two. Odùtọ́lá, my second, and Fọlárìn.'

Rónkẹ́'s brow creased. 'Fọlárìn?'

Ṣìkẹ́mi told her about Fọlárìn and their accidental meetings.

'Well, you may never see Fọlárìn again. Has Odùtọ́lá said anything?'

'No. But I see it in his eyes.'

'How do you feel about him?'

'I like him. But I don't want to risk the other men thinking he gets special privileges. I don't want their insubordination.'

Rónkẹ́ lowered her head in silence for a minute. When she

raised it, Ṣìkẹ́mi saw sympathy in her eyes, but she clearly had no answers that Ṣìkẹ́mi hadn't thought of herself.

For the next few hours, Rónkẹ́ played the perfect host and Ṣìkẹ́mi forgot her troubles. She laughed more in an afternoon than she'd done the entire month. She ought to visit Rónkẹ́ more often, while she still could.

'Tell me,' Rónkẹ́ said suddenly. 'Are you and *Yèyé* getting on any better?'

The complete change of topic caught Ṣìkẹ́mi by surprise. Her smile dimmed a little, and her lips curled in a sardonic twist. 'The British and Dòsùnmú shun her, so *Yèyé* is incandescent with rage and almost obsessive in her quest for power. Her current priority is building an army to eclipse the king's.'

'So, the rivalry between them is ongoing?'

'*Yèyé* counteracts his orders and defies him openly, like she has a death wish. She's worse than ever.'

'Have you asked her to free you?'

Ṣìkẹ́mi nodded. 'I offered her a hundred thousand cowries. She told me to return in five years.'

Rónkẹ́'s eyes grew round. 'You have that much money?'

Ṣìkẹ́mi shrugged. They both lapsed into an uncomfortable silence, each lost in their own thoughts.

Rónkẹ́ spoke eventually. 'I know you don't want it, but our offer is still open.'

Ṣìkẹ́mi waved her away. 'No. I don't want you involved. I have already approached the *Eletǔ Òdìbò* for his support.'

Rónkẹ́ huffed. 'That old fool? He can't see beyond the end of a battered palm-wine gourd.'

Perhaps it was Rónkẹ́'s tone, or the ring of truth in her words, but Ṣìkẹ́mi's teeth clenched. 'I know he's a drunk, but I'm supplying him with information about Madam, in return. It's a business transaction, and drunk or not he likes money.'

'I don't understand why you trust him over me. He may be

the prime minister, but Pedro has superior connections with the British.'

'He is discreet, unlike the others. I felt I could trust him.'

Rónké snorted. 'Have you seen him drunk? How discreet do you think he is then?'

Ṣìkẹ́mi didn't know how or when their voices rose several notches. She looked down to find Àdùnní tugging her *dànṣíkí*, eyes wide with fear, and the toddler burrowed into his mother's shoulder. Ṣìkẹ́mi's shoulders flopped as she picked up the little girl and hugged her, while Rónké soothed the toddler.

'Forgive me. I'm doing the best I can.' She whispered the words over the child's head.

Rónké nodded, accepting the apology.

Ṣìkẹ́mi put Àdùnní down, distracting her with a cowrie shell. 'It's time I left.'

She felt miserable, the afternoon glow having disappeared. At the door, Rónké hugged her. 'Whatever happens, I will be here for you.'

Ṣìkẹ́mi hugged her back and left.

TWENTY-SIX

The sea looked rougher than usual today, but Ṣìkẹ́mi's swimming skills were better, so she swam for shore at a leisurely pace. She no longer experienced the paralysing fear that had gripped her when she first found herself surrounded by water, and the shoreline within sight boosted her confidence. As she swam, her powerful strokes cut through the waves, eating up the distance. Almost there, she paused and trod water, enjoying a brief rest.

Suddenly, the water at her waist darkened. Beneath the waves, several short, pointy spears encircled her. Agitated, she dived underwater, trying to assess the threat. The spears descended with her, blocking her exit. Flapping her arms, she resurfaced, as an irritating echo from the past rang out. 'Ṣìkẹ́mi, move! You are in danger!'

Ṣìkẹ́mi cussed. As if she didn't know that! And why was Màmá Péjú poking her nose into Ṣìkẹ́mi's business, anyway? She was grown now and didn't have to obey her aunt any more. Ṣìkẹ́mi turned round and noted the spears had parted, creating a clear path through the circle, albeit in the wrong direction. She started forward, planning to swim through the gap and around them, but, just before she could dive, the water formed a high-speed bubble, racing straight at her. She gaped in surprise as a large needlefish flew out of the depths and slammed into her, impaling her shoulder on its beak. Ṣìkẹ́mi screamed and everything turned black.

Ṣìkẹ́mi's body bolted upright, her heart galloping as if it had just run a mile. Disoriented, she scanned her immediate surroundings, taking in her men, who lay scattered, napping under the shade of the trees in the camp they'd set up. She gulped deep breaths and expelled them slowly in an effort to still her racing heart, and as she did so the nightmare receded, leaving her listless.

Ṣìkẹ́mi rarely thought of Màmá Péjú, preferring to concentrate on her parents and brother when she allowed herself the luxury of thinking about family. Màmá Péjú's voice embodied the less pleasant aspects of her childhood. The fact that the woman had invaded her dream put her on edge, but she didn't want to brood on it during a high-stakes raid.

Wanting to be alone with her thoughts, she stood up and walked to the edge of the clearing, as she often did when seeking solitude. She didn't like raiding along the Lagos route. It was less familiar and far too dangerous, but Madam was spending money like it was water and demanded more raids to replenish her coffers. Ṣìkẹ́mi obliged, to stay out of her way, while waiting for Madam to self-combust. She found an upturned log and perched her bottom on it. The last time she dreamed of drowning, she had consulted an Ifá priest, who had told her it was her *orí*'s way of warning her of impending danger or change. The priest's words did not surprise her, since all her previous episodes had preceded a major incident in her life. If this was another premonition, she wondered what the future held.

Her men were stirring from the brief rest, and Ṣìkẹ́mi planned to lead them further into the forest before nightfall. Out of the corner of her eye, she noticed Odùtọ́lá in a heated conversation with another soldier. Then he rose and made his way across the clearing towards her. Ṣìkẹ́mi read his body language; the deep scowl marring his features, and the heaviness in each step. When he reached her side, he sank to the floor.

'What is it?' Ṣìkẹ́mi asked.

He stayed silent for a moment before replying. 'You won't like it.'

'Tell me.' Her voice was sharper than intended, heightened by her recent dream.

'It's Madam. She and Ọbádínà are planning to attack Àgùdà tomorrow.'

'What!' Ṣìkẹ́mi screeched, before reining in her voice so as not to alarm her men. 'Are you sure?'

'Yes. Bello's sister works in the kitchen and picked up the chatter. He says she's reliable.'

Ṣìkẹ́mi's thoughts raced a hundred to the second. Now it all made sense. Madam and Ọbádínà's frequent clandestine meetings; and on each occasion Madam had contrived to send her on a meaningless errand. She'd also been happier, but Ṣìkẹ́mi had assumed it was because Campbell was back in England on leave. Her thoughts went to Rónkẹ́ and her husband. Would Madam have warned them? She hoped so. Then she remembered the dream. Her instincts kicked in and her heartbeat ratcheted upwards once more. Was the dream warning her of this? She needed to reach Rónkẹ́ before Madam put her plan into action.

'I'm aborting the raid,' she said to Odùtọ́lá.

Tipping his head to one side, he eyed her in surprise. 'You've never done that before.'

'I have to warn Ẹ̀gbọ́n Rónkẹ́.'

'Surely Madam would have alerted her.'

'She didn't tell me. What does that tell you?'

Odùtọ́lá stayed silent for a while, then offered a suggestion. 'Why don't you let me lead the raid while you turn back?' His eyes lit up, and Ṣìkẹ́mi realised he relished the opportunity for more responsibility. She shook her head and watched the light dim in his eyes.

'Not this raid. It's not that I don't trust you to do the job well. The terrain is unfamiliar and the risks too high.' Plus, she'd never forgive herself if anything happened to her men in her absence. 'I'd only be distracted worrying about you all, which means I won't be much use to Rónkẹ́ either. Gather the men and lead them back. I'll take two men to the rendezvous spot with Domingo's men, then head to Àgùdà.'

Odùtọ́lá nodded and gifted her one of his gentle smiles before lumbering back to the group.

Ṣìkẹ́mi chose two companions, Òjó and Dàda, for her journey to Domingo's base. They were both in their prime, eager to please, but level-headed. She could rely on their obedience and resourcefulness. She moved swiftly, eager to get there before dusk so she could travel through the night to Lagos and arrive in time to pre-empt Madam's strike. It was fortunate that she was less than a day's trek from the meeting point.

Her thoughts turned to her future. She needed to prepare for the changes ahead if the premonition came true. Perhaps it was time to consider running away, although her mind rejected the thought with every fibre of her being. She wondered if Odùtọ́lá would consider leaving with her, then shook her head.

Unlike her, he was no slave and had family members in Lagos. He shouldn't have to give that up.

It wasn't long before Domingo's base camp came into view and, as she had expected, the sky welcomed them with a crescent-shaped white glow. They'd made good time, moving at a faster pace than her entire troops could have. As they neared the outer perimeter, Ṣìkẹ́mi grew tense, her earlier dream warning her to be cautious. She slowed her steps and lifted a fist to warn Òjó and Dàda to do the same. They were good lads; they slowed their movements to mirror hers immediately. Still obscured by trees shooting far into the sky, the camp appeared busier than usual, and Ṣìkẹ́mi spied the silhouette of several men in the distance.

The trio crept forward with great care, crouching low until they reached the edge of the camp. Ṣìkẹ́mi peered through the trees, assessing the scene, then she drew a sharp breath and froze. Dressed in long-sleeved coats belted at the waist and with their trousers tucked into calf-high boots, these were not Domingo's men. Domingo used locals as his intermediaries, and they dressed accordingly. Ṣìkẹ́mi knew without a shred of doubt that in broad daylight those coats would be red, the hallmark of the British troops.

She pulled her men back and made a hasty retreat, but in his hurry Òjó tripped over a log. The unexpected thud as he landed startled a flock of birds nesting on a tree nearby, and they took flight, squawking as they flew. That set off a chain reaction, causing a group of monkeys on low-hanging branches to chatter madly, alerting the British soldiers to their presence.

Ṣìkẹ́mi hauled Òjó to his feet. Then she heard the unmistakable sound of someone moving a musket from half-cock to full-cock. 'Move!' she hissed. 'Go!' They broke into a run, headlong into dense foliage, hoping it would give them better cover. As they ran, the first shot rang out and a bullet travelling at speed whizzed past Ṣìkẹ́mi's head. She dodged, zigzagging as she burrowed through the vegetation. A second later, she stumbled as something slammed into her, but she kept moving. Soon the sounds died away, and, once Ṣìkẹ́mi thought there was a safe enough distance between them, she slowed down and signalled her men to stop. Shaken, Òjó and Dàda nodded, their torsos bent over, as they pulled deep breaths into their lungs.

Ṣìkẹ́mi sank to the forest floor, shaking her head from side to side, struggling to process what had just happened. A single word percolated in her mind. Betrayal! But by whom? Someone must have told the British about the handover location and it had to be one of her men. Ṣìkẹ́mi changed it often for extra security, and within her battalion less than a handful of people knew the precise meeting point of any single raid.

Her mind circled to Odùtọ́lá. His news of Madam's treachery had set her change of plan in motion, but he'd offered to lead the raid instead of her. So, it couldn't be him, unless he was planning on handing himself over to the British. She felt pressure building behind her eyes and her heartbeat spiked. Who would do such a thing? She pinched the bridge of her nose, trying to contain her frustration. Somebody was going to pay for this. She just didn't know who yet.

Ṣìkẹ́mi took a swig from the leather water pouch dangling on a string round her neck. But despite the drink her throat clogged, and an unfamiliar vice gripped her chest, making it hard to breathe. The faster she pulled in the air, the harder it was. *Slow down!* A voice from the past jogged her memory. It was Màmá Aláṣọ, trying to calm her down after she'd fallen out of a tree and started hyperventilating.

Ṣìkẹ́mi stilled her body, took a deep breath and counted. *One, two, three...* She exhaled on the tenth count and did it again and again. It didn't take long before the adrenalin that had fuelled her hasty retreat started receding and she was back in control of her body. Then, an unfamiliar sensation coming from her shoulder imprinted itself on her consciousness. She turned her neck to inspect it and gasped as a fiery furnace burned along her left collarbone. She paused the motion, reached over with her right hand, and her fingers made contact with a sticky wetness where her clothing clung to her shoulder blade.

'I've been shot,' she muttered aloud, which made Òjó and Dàda swivel round, looks of horror plastered on their faces. 'There's no need to worry,' she lied, 'but I need your help to stop the bleeding.'

The two men stepped closer, eager to help any way they could. There was no exit wound, so Ṣìkẹ́mi surmised the bullet was still lodged in her body. Together, Òjó and Dàda made a makeshift bandage from the clean rags they carried in their satchels for emergencies and tied it round the wound.

'We've got to get back to Lagos. Help me up,' Ṣìkẹ́mi said.

Òjó and Dàda flanked her and helped her to her feet. Her teeth clattered, the shock setting in. She tensed her jaw and dug deep. 'Let's go.' Slowly, they moved forward.

In her wildest dreams, not once had Ṣìkẹ́mi imagined she'd be trudging through the forest, bleeding and dependent on her men. It was her worst nightmare come true. Refusing to show weakness, she pushed herself through each step by sheer force of will, focusing on the next mile ahead. But her wound continued to seep, and as her lifeblood drained, and her steps grew slow and weary, Ṣìkẹ́mi realised she was in real danger of not making it to Lagos alive.

Pushing the pain to the recesses of her mind, she visualised each of her men, cataloguing her recent interactions with them. She wondered if she'd missed signs of their duplicity, but nothing came to mind. Then, out of nowhere, it hit her. Àkàndé! He'd interrupted her meeting with Odùtọ́lá and one of Domingo's men when they were determining the drop-off point. She'd paused the meeting and waited until she heard his receding footsteps. What if he'd circled back? He was one of two men absent for health reasons, and the only one with a grudge against her. He had never openly defied her again after she dealt with his insubordination, but she always felt his animosity towards her whenever in his vicinity. It had to be him, and she couldn't wait to confirm her suspicion. That was sufficient motivation to keep going.

TWENTY-SEVEN

At first, Ṣìkẹ́mi kept a reasonable pace with her men, determined to reach Lagos before sunup, when Madam would put her plan into action.

'Ọ̀gá, please rest.'

Ṣìkẹ́mi gave Dàda and Òjó a baleful glare. They'd been urging her to take breaks every few miles, but she had ignored them. However, for the first time since her capture as a child, she was finding the trek through the forest arduous.

'Let us carry you,' Òjó said, his eyes pleading.

The idea of being carried sent a shudder through her. 'No, I will walk with my own two feet.' Sandwiched between them, shoulder to shoulder, as she was, they were practically carrying her anyway, she reasoned, and pride would not let her give them the permission they sought.

But Òjó wasn't done. 'Ọ̀gá, if we take turns carrying you, we will be faster.'

Ṣìkẹ́mi ignored their entreaties and pushed forward. As the night wore on, she dragged one exhausted foot after the other. Soon, the trees blurred into one long flurry of green. At some point, they stopped to rest and, in a moment of clarity, she realised her error. She didn't know why she hadn't thought of it sooner.

She turned to Òjó on her left. 'Òjó, I want you to go ahead, and go straight to Ẹ̀gbọ́n Rónkẹ́. Tell her to leave Àgùdà, because Yèyé is planning to attack the area.'

Òjó, shook his head. 'Ọgá, I can't do that. If I leave you with Dàda, you will bleed to death before you get to Lagos. We have to stay together.'

Ṣìkẹ́mi mustered all the strength she could in her weakened state. 'Òjó, that's a direct order.' Even if it sounded more like a plea, she was still his boss.

Òjó planted his feet on the ground. 'Ọgá, you can discipline me later, but I will not leave you.'

Ṣìkẹ́mi cursed. She was both pleased and annoyed at his loyalty. 'Fine. We should get moving then.' At the curt command, the men stood to attention and helped her up.

Daylight hovered on the skyline before they emerged from the forest into the Lagos metropolitan area. Soon Madam's compound came into view, and Ṣìkẹ́mi heaved a sigh of relief. After falling out with the new royal, Madam had built a new complex, including a small barracks, outside the palace, for herself and her personal retinue. She housed the rest of her growing army in new barracks on one of her kola-nut farms on the mainland. The small barracks had its own entrance and courtyard, and Ṣìkẹ́mi hoped her men could sneak her into her room before anyone saw her. She also needed to get a message to Rónkẹ́.

The last few steps were the worst. Ṣìkẹ́mi's breathing grew shallow, and her men all but dragged her along. They turned a corner, entered the barracks' courtyard and ran smack into Odùtọ́lá. His jaw slackened as he took in the spectacle they made.

'Good grief, what happened?' It was a good question, Ṣìkẹ́mi thought. Then darkness descended, and oblivion claimed her.

Ṣìkẹ́mi's eyes flew open, and she rammed a fist into her mouth to stifle the scream attempting to escape. Someone was poking her shoulder with a hot iron rod. At least that was how it felt.

'Shh! It's all right. I am just feeling for the bullet.'

Ṣìkẹ́mi relaxed at Odùtọ́lá's soothing reassurance and lifted herself into a seated position. Then she remembered passing out in the courtyard. Her skin flushed at the thought of her men carrying her unconscious form into her room.

'We need to get the bullet out. Drink some of this.' Odùtọ́lá handed her a flask of *ogogóró*, the local gin. She took several swigs and passed the flask back.

'Here, bite on this.' He gave her a piece of wood and Ṣìkẹ́mi bit down on it, bracing herself. The next minute, shards of pain erupted like a shower of burning stars, radiating out from her shoulder to every part of her being. As Odùtọ́lá's finger dug deep into the wound, she was tempted to shove him aside, and probably would have had she the strength. But common sense told her he needed to retrieve the bullet if she were to stand any chance of recovery. She held tight, chomping on the piece of wood in her mouth as if her life depended on it, which it did.

'I've got it.'

Ṣìkẹ́mi's body sagged at the unmistakable satisfaction in Odùtọ́lá's voice. She spat out the wood and panted, taking several shallow gulps of air, followed by deep ones. The pain receded somewhat, becoming just about tolerable.

'I need more *ogogóró*.' She sagged against her bed, her eyes pleading.

Odùtọ́lá passed her the flask, and she took another swig.

'We'll need to wash it out and pack it with some herbs to help it heal. I'll let Màmá Lékan take over.'

Only then did Ṣìkẹ́mi realise her childhood carer was in the room. Ṣìkẹ́mi nodded and sank backward on her bed as Màmá Lékan took over.

For the next few days, Ṣìkẹ́mi hovered in the land between the living and the dead. Shadows came and went. She thought she heard the ghosts of her parents whispering to her in the dark, and even Madam's voice. Then the dreams came, and the waters threatened to drown her for good. Somehow, she battled them all, fought through it and emerged one morning to sunshine streaming into her room.

Her eyes roamed the room and found Màmá Lékan, sat in a corner. A slave pottered, tidying the room. 'What day is it?' Ṣìkẹ́mi asked.

'I see you've returned to us.' Màmá Lékan shook her head, a rueful smile on her face. 'You had one foot in heaven and the other here on earth. Even Madam was worried.'

Ṣìkẹ́mi flinched at the mention of her owner.

Màmá Lékan rose from her chair, poured some water in the jug next to her into a cup, and handed it to her. 'You must be parched. Have some water.'

Ṣìkẹ́mi sat up, took the cup and thanked her, swallowing the contents in a single gulp. 'What day is it?' she repeated.

'*Ọjọ́ ẹtì.*'

Friday. She was injured on Monday. Ṣìkẹ́mi did the arithmetic. She trained her eyes on Màmá Lékan. 'Have you heard from *Ẹ̀gbọ́n* Rónkẹ́? Is she okay?' Her voice wobbled, and she hated the vulnerability it portrayed.

Màmá Lékan turned her eyes away and said nothing.

'Màmá Lékan?'

'She is fine.'

The brusqueness in her voice belied what came out of her lips. 'Màmá Lékan, please tell me the truth.'

Màmá Lékan sighed. 'She and the children are safe.'

Ṣìkẹ́mi heard a 'but' in there somewhere. 'She and the children?' Then her addled brain made the connection, and her eyes flew wide open. 'Pedro!'

The sadness in Màmá Lékan's eyes confirmed her fears. Ṣìkẹ́mi stood up and staggered as the room swam before her. Màmá Lékan put a restraining hand on her good shoulder.

'Slow down. You are not fit to go anywhere.'

'But I must go to her!'

'In your current state? You'll collapse there, and she'll have to care for you as well as her children. There'll be plenty of time later. Now rest.'

Màmá Lékan's voice brooked no argument, and, even though Ṣìkẹ́mi was long past taking orders from anyone but Madam, she found her torso pushed back into her bed. Tears of frustration welled in her eyes. She detested feeling weak and helpless, but she couldn't do anything about it. She closed her eyes as the tears seeped through, then mercifully, sleep claimed her once more.

TWENTY-EIGHT

Ṣìkẹ́mi dragged her feet, the impending visit filling her with dread, as she noted the burnt-out shells now dotting each Àgùdà street. Some houses were luckier than others and stood untouched beside their grotesquely misshapen neighbours. A deathly stillness hovered in the air. No sounds of children playing in the streets or mothers chattering on balconies.

Ṣìkẹ́mi had thought of little else since learning of Pedro's death. She hadn't seen Madam since she'd regained consciousness and had no desire to, although she knew she couldn't avoid her forever. She'd processed the disaster every which way and still wondered if she could have prevented it, perhaps by paying more attention to Madam and Ọbádínà. From various sources she learned that, with Ọbádínà's backing, some of Madam's men stirred up rioters who went through Àgùdà attacking people and burning houses. Ṣìkẹ́mi still could not fathom why Ọbádínà, one of the fairest people she knew, had supported the venture and why neither he nor Madam had warned Rónkẹ́. It seemed such was their hatred for the returnees.

Her thoughts shifted to Rónkẹ́. Òjó had delivered Ṣìkẹ́mi's

message to Rónkẹ́, but when he got there Pedro was not at home. Rónkẹ́ warned her neighbours and with her children fled to safety, but Pedro, on hearing rumours, went back home and found it on fire. He thought his family was inside and died trying to save them. Ṣìkẹ́mi couldn't even begin to imagine Rónkẹ́'s pain, and it was all because of her. If she'd been more careful leaving the rendezvous site; if she'd swallowed her pride and allowed her men to carry her, she might have arrived in time to make a difference. This was all her fault, and it couldn't be undone. She wondered how Rónkẹ́ was faring with the friendly neighbours offering her temporary shelter.

Ṣìkẹ́mi broke out of her maudlin thoughts when something hard hit her back. She turned round and found a group of children pelting her with tiny stones. 'Go back to where you came from,' they screamed, their little faces contorted in fear and anger. It seemed news had travelled that one of Madam's soldiers was walking their streets. She ignored the children and quickened her pace.

She found the house Màmá Lékan had described and knocked. The door opened and Ṣìkẹ́mi confronted a stranger, whose mouth firmed into an angry grimace.

'What do you want? We don't need the likes of you here. Haven't you done enough?'

'Please.' Ṣìkẹ́mi kept her voice low. 'I need to see Ẹ̀gbọ́n Rónkẹ́. I wasn't involved in what happened.'

Angry eyes looked her up and down. The woman hissed, turned and walked away. Ṣìkẹ́mi entered, closed the door, followed the sound of voices into a large room, and came to an abrupt stop. The room was filled with women all dressed in black and in their midst sat Rónkẹ́, a forlorn expression etched on her face. Ṣìkẹ́mi barely recognised the face marred by sunken eyes and hollow cheeks. The chatter died down as everyone stared at the newcomer.

Ṣìkẹ́mi shrank into her *dànṣíkí*. She had never experienced so much hostility directed solely at her, all at once. Rónkẹ́ lifted her head, noticed her and drew a quick intake of breath.

'I'm so sorry.' Ṣìkẹ́mi fell at her feet and grabbed her ankle in supplication. 'I never knew. They kept it from me.'

Rónkẹ́ swatted her hand away. 'How is that even possible? How could you not know? Next to her husband, you are the closest person to her. And you let this happen. I will never forgive you.'

Ṣìkẹ́mi's heart sank, as each word lodged in her heart like a tiny barb, tearing her apart, piece by piece. '*Ẹ̀gbọ́n*, I promise you, I did not know, or I would have warned you even if I couldn't stop it. I tried to warn you but was wounded on my way from a raid.'

Tears ran down Rónkẹ́'s face. 'I know. Your life is all about the raids. I guess you were too busy running them and making money to notice what was happening right before you. Go. Enjoy your wealth. I hope it makes you happy.' She lifted the hem of her gown and used it to wipe the tears from her face. 'Go!' she repeated.

'Please *Ẹ̀gbọ́n*. Forgive me. Let me stay.'

As Rónkẹ́ dissolved into tears, the woman who let Ṣìkẹ́mi in tapped her shoulder. 'You have said your piece. Please leave now. This is more distressing for her.'

Ṣìkẹ́mi rose to her haunches, undecided. She sought Rónkẹ́'s eyes once more, pleading through the silent communication. Rónkẹ́ stared back, her eyes soulless. Ṣìkẹ́mi felt a burning sensation sear her throat. She stood and left.

The stone-throwers had disappeared, fortunately. She didn't know how she might have responded otherwise. She returned to the barracks with haste. Bitter bile filled her throat as she strode, head low, shoulders hunched over. She considered the unfairness of it all – Rónkẹ́, widowed, with two young mouths to feed.

Back at the barracks, Ṣìkẹ́mi hid in her room for hours. There was no undoing what had happened. Nothing would bring Pedro back. Would Rónkẹ́ see through her pain to forgive her someday? She doubted it. Her mind circled to the empti-ness in that shared final stare; Rónkẹ́'s friendship, the one thing she valued the most, turned to dust. She felt the headache build, tiny prickles behind her eyes amplifying the pain. Then the searing loss pierced her heart, just as if someone had plunged a dagger in and pulled it out. She clutched her midrib, fighting for breath. Then the dam burst, finding expression in an almighty howl that, once she started, she couldn't stop. The sounds, deep and guttural, forced their way out and her body shook from the sheer exertion of it, until, spent and tired, she fell limp onto her bed. If anyone in the compound heard her, they stayed clear, although she was past caring.

Hours later, hollowed out and empty, Ṣìkẹ́mi gathered her travelling essentials together. There was no point in moping around the compound and she wanted to avoid Madam, lest she was tempted to murder her. She sent for Odùtọ́lá. He arrived, took one look at her, and nodded. 'I shall get the men together.'

'Thank you,' she whispered to his retreating back.

Ṣìkẹ́mi strode up and down, eyeing the ill-gotten reward of a hard night's labour. Before her, a large group of captives cowered, heads hanging down, while her soldiers milled around the perimeter of the large clearing. Odùtọ́lá stood nearby, waiting for her instructions, watching her every move, but Ṣìkẹ́mi ignored him, concentrating on her loot. Then she moved forward and started separating the captives into two groups.

A quiet gasp echoed round the clearing as Ṣìkẹ́mi continued her task, a job she'd recently delegated to her men. At a loss for what to do, they sought Odùtọ́lá's guidance, a questioning gaze on their faces. Sensing the fury simmering beneath Ṣìkẹ́mi's polite veneer, Odùtọ́lá shook his head, a sign that they should stand down. The men nodded and followed his lead.

Ṣìkẹ́mi eyed her new captives, mostly a mix of strapping young men in their early prime, adolescents and pre-adolescents. She suspected their original kidnappers had split them from their womenfolk before starting the southbound trek. 'You.' She jabbed a finger in the chest of a young man, separating him from the others. Her men moved forward and led him to a corner, forming a second group. Ṣìkẹ́mi moved on to the next victim, her fingers clenching and unclenching as she paced. She had hoped the raid would dull her seething anger and slake her thirst for vengeance. But a black mist still raged within her. She longed to make someone pay; her obvious target was Àkàndé. However, she had it on good authority he was hiding out at Madam's large barracks under Ọbádínà's protection. She couldn't prove he'd sold her out yet, but she'd learned he led the Àgùdà rioters, which was a good enough reason to run her sword through him.

From the back of the huddle, Ṣìkẹ́mi spied a captive taking tentative steps backward. He looked young, teetering on the brink of adulthood. The boy cast a nervous glance about. He was going to make a run for it. Lightning fast, she snatched a whip out of the hands of one of her men. It sailed through the air before connecting with the boy's flesh. He screamed in agony.

'Where do you think you are going?' Ṣìkẹ́mi's hardened voice rang out, and, before the boy could answer, she retracted the whip, then lashed out again and again. The whip crackled as it met its target, then recoiled before flashing out again. While the remaining captives huddled, Ṣìkẹ́mi's men stared, mouths half-open, the uncharacteristic behaviour rendering them mute. The lashings and the boy's screams continued until Odùtọ́lá stepped forward and touched Ṣìkẹ́mi's raised arm.

'Ọ̀gá, I think he has learned his lesson.'

Ṣìkẹ́mi's arm paused mid-motion as Odùtọ́lá's quiet words penetrated her fog. She dropped the whip. 'What are you staring at?' she yelled, before stalking off into the surrounding forest. Her men averted their gazes and began processing the rest of the captives.

For about half a mile, Ṣìkẹ́mi tramped through the forest, angry at Madam, the world, but mostly at herself, for taking her frustration out on the teenage captive. She heard Odùtọ́lá's footsteps shadowing her, although he stayed a safe distance away. Slowly, her anger dissipated, and her jerky strides slowed until she came to a stop. Odùtọ́lá did likewise, keeping more than an arm's length between them. A thick silence reigned, but Odùtọ́lá watched and waited until Ṣìkẹ́mi's stiff shoulders started to heave. Then she grabbed her middle and curled over.

Odùtọ́lá took the few remaining paces and closed the gap between them. He wrapped his arms around Ṣìkẹ́mi, drawing her into an embrace, and rocked them both on the spot. Ṣìkẹ́mi stiffened for a moment, then relaxed and melted against him. Her body trembled as violent shudders ran through her, and as she wept her silent tears soaked through his *dànṣíkí*. Odùtọ́lá held on, his hand running circles over her back, his lip murmuring words in her ear, although none of them registered.

Ṣìkẹ́mi lost track of how long they stood in silence, locked in the embrace. She'd stopped crying but clung to him like a limp seaweed. Somehow, his hand had moved lower, and now rested on the gentle flare of her hips, where mother nature declared her femininity despite her best efforts to camouflage it. She stayed pliant in his arms, and his hand moved again, tentative fingers skimming her rear, searching. She felt his desire awaken as his manhood stirred. In an instant, something shifted and Ṣìkẹ́mi's body went rigid. Odùtọ́lá stilled his wandering hands and waited. After a few seconds, Ṣìkẹ́mi released her hold on him and stepped backward.

Her tear-stained face met his. 'I'm sorry,' she said. 'I can't.'

Odùtọ́lá lifted his arms in surrender. 'I understand. We shall speak no more of it.'

Ṣìkẹ́mi smiled into the darkness. 'I like you, you know. It's just... me.' She finished the word with a sigh.

Odùtọ́lá nodded as if he understood, although his face told a different story. 'Shall we head back?' He turned, and she followed.

TWENTY-NINE

Following the *Ọba*'s hastily delivered summons, Madam dressed with care. The mulish expression on her face showed she was in fighting form and ready for the impending show-down. For several weeks after the riot, Ṣìkẹ́mi had used her recovery as an excuse to avoid Madam. Months later, they had settled into the habit of circling each other, never speaking of the dreadful tragedy that stood large between them. Ṣìkẹ́mi tried to spend the barest minimum of time in Madam's presence. They hardly ever conversed, their communication limited to terse commands and polite responses. If Madam felt any remorse at Pedro's death, she didn't show it, and Ṣìkẹ́mi had long stopped caring about Madam's welfare. Still, for now their fates were inextricably linked.

A few days earlier, Ṣìkẹ́mi had visited the *Eletǔ Òdìbò*. This time, the chief welcomed her with a cool reserve, and Ṣìkẹ́mi understood his position. After the Àgùdà riot, the missionaries, businesses and the British put tremendous pressure on the *Ọba* and his chiefs to catch and punish the offenders. Rumours of Madam's involvement were rife, but no one could confirm

them, and without proof *Ọba* Dòsùnmú couldn't move against
the perpetrators. That was why Ṣìkẹ́mi visited the chief.
Odùtọ́lá had led a covert investigation and confirmed that
Àkàndé, who was now Ọbádínà's second-in-command at the
main barracks, boasted that he led the riot. He'd also suggested
he would soon be Madam's chief of staff.

The chief led Ṣìkẹ́mi to a secluded room in his compound.
'These are troubled days,' he said.

Ṣìkẹ́mi accepted his explanation. 'Indeed, Bàbá. That is why
I am here.' She told the chief about Àkàndé's betrayal and all
she knew of Ọbádínà and Madam's involvement. The chief
wore a sympathetic smile as his eyes bored into hers. 'Are you
willing to stand publicly and repeat what you have told me?'

Ṣìkẹ́mi took a deep breath. 'I am,' she said. 'What will you
do now?'

'I shall relay the information to the king. Any decisions are
up to him.'

'What about my freedom, Bàbá?' She hoped their agreement still stood.

'Don't worry. The king will release you, whatever else
happens.'

With that reassurance, Ṣìkẹ́mi left, and, although she felt a
bit like the faith people's Judas, her choices were limited. That
Ọbádínà had promoted a member of her regiment without
telling her told Ṣìkẹ́mi her own position was at risk. So, she'd
acted before Madam did. All she could do now was watch her
back and await the gods' verdict.

She forced herself to make conversation. '*Yèyé*, why do you
think *Kabiyèsí* sent for you?'

'Hopefully to tell me where my husband is.'

Madam's voice betrayed her anxiety and irritation. No one
had seen Ọbádínà for days. Rumour had it the *Ọba* had
arrested him. Ṣìkẹ́mi had walked behind Madam when she

marched to the palace and publicly decried the king. The king hadn't responded to Madam's outburst until the summons delivered that morning. Whispered rumours in town suggested the British consul, Campbell, had returned from leave in England, which might explain the summons.

Ṣìkẹ́mi marvelled that Madam seemed oblivious to her own self-destruction. Madam risked being banished like before, but Ṣìkẹ́mi doubted the thought had crossed her mind.

She couldn't resist posing the next question. 'What if the *Ọba* banishes you again?'

Madam took her time answering. 'He can try, but he needs the approval of most of the chiefs, and I have them in my pocket. Also, if that were the case, one of them would have warned me.'

Madam's voice brimmed with confidence, a confidence Ṣìkẹ́mi did not share. She could not imagine Campbell ignoring the Àgùdà riot, given how important the returnees were to British trade. The British had proved their mettle by deposing Kòsọkọ́ and keeping him away from Lagos. Would they mete out the same punishment to Madam? She reckoned they would find out soon enough.

The trek to the palace took mere minutes. A small contingent of white soldiers dressed in their red coats milled around the palace's outer courtyard, a sure sign Campbell was about. A heightened tension filled the air as two guardsmen met them in the king's inner courtyard, ready to lead them to the throne room. The inner courtyard brimmed with people and, as they passed, Ṣìkẹ́mi recognised several of the paramount chiefs' guards. She knew this was no ordinary meeting.

Ọba Dòsùnmú I sat resplendent in full regalia in the overcrowded throne room. Decked out in a floor-length, flowing, purple *agbádá* and a gold beaded cap, topped with a red tassel on his royal head, he appeared more mature than his age. Campbell and all the paramount chiefs formed a semicircle around the *Ọba*, who sat in the middle. Madam's eyes widened, and she released a sharp gasp as her brain registered the significance a little too late. A bead of perspiration broke out on her forehead, and Ṣìkẹ́mi knew it was from trepidation rather than the heat. This would be a public spectacle and, by the looks of it, none of the chiefs Madam bribed had pre-warned her.

Madam and Ṣìkẹ́mi paid homage, and the *Ọba* invited Madam to take a seat in the middle of the semicircle formed by the chiefs. Madam's hands shook as she adjusted the chair before sitting on it. Ṣìkẹ́mi knelt behind her, head bowed, but a ripple of delight coursed through her veins even as she kept her face blank. It was time Madam experienced the terror she often inflicted on others.

'*Yèyé*,' *Ọba* Dòsùnmú said, affording her the respect due her age, 'Ẹ̀hn, thank you for coming.' He adjusted his *agbádá*. 'As you can see, our friends from the queen's land are here. They are not happy about the incident in Àgùdà. What do you say to this?'

Madam bowed again. '*Kabiyèsí*! May you live long. I had no part in that incident. I was not there. I was visiting family here that day.'

'Ẹ̀hn, *Yèyé*, those who survived the massacre identified your soldiers as the culprits.'

'Ah! *Kabiyèsí*, if they know the culprits, why aren't those men before you? Why are they pointing fingers at me?'

Madam stared at the *Ọba*, her eyes defiant. He stared back, their minds locked in a contest of wills. Then the king broke the impasse and glanced at Campbell. Ṣìkẹ́mi clocked the imperceptible nod.

'Ẹ̀hn, *Yèyé*,' the *Ọba* said, 'we have settled the matter with our friends. You are to move to Abéòkúta with all your men and household. You must never return to Lagos. If you do, I cannot protect you. Do you understand?'

Şìkémi hid her gasp. Abéòkúta! Even though it was Madam's ancestral home, she hadn't been there since she married Ọba Àdèlé over two decades earlier. She'd suspected the king might banish Madam to Bàdágrì, like before, but this was much worse.

Madam fell to her knees before the king. 'Kabiyèsí, do not do this. You know how loyal I have been to your house, to your father, and before him to your uncles. I would never do anything to jeopardise your house. Please do not let the white man do this to me.'

'My hands are tied, Yèyé. It is done and you must leave. May the gods watch over you in Abéòkúta as they have done here.'

As if primed, all the chiefs chorused, 'Àṣẹ́!'

Şìkémi focused on the king, expecting him to address her and pronounce her release, but he did nothing. She swallowed and sought the Eletǔ Òdìbò. Their eyes met briefly before he looked away.

Madam rose, knowing it was indeed done, and, with all the dignity she could muster, walked tall out of the assembly. Şìkémi stood, her mind blank. Had the Eletǔ Òdìbò reneged on their agreement? She felt like screaming but didn't think it was a good idea. Her stomach churned and her legs felt weighted down as she followed her mistress. Staying with Madam was no longer a tenable option, much less a banished Madam.

That evening, Ọbádínà showed up at Madam's compound, having been released by the king and also being under orders to move with her to Abéòkúta. The king had given them five days to leave. Once the household retired, Şìkémi sneaked out to the chief's house and met an unsmiling guard at the door. She handed him a bag of cowries. 'Please tell the *Eletǔ Òdìbò* Ṣìkẹ́mi is here to see him.'

The guard gave her a cursory glance and pocketed the bag. 'I know who you are, but the chief is not receiving visitors today. I will let him know you called.'

Ṣìkẹ́mi's mouth opened and closed. She tried speaking, but the words deserted her. Her hands itched. Retrieving her money wouldn't require much effort, but assaulting the man at his post would cause unnecessary trouble. She turned and stomped away. For the next two nights, she tried again, and met with the same response. The chief was not receiving visitors. Her throat thickened as she turned away the third time, a heaviness filling her from the inside out. Each hour saw her freedom slipping away like grains of sand sifting through her fingers. She didn't know whether it was the *Ọba*'s desire to see her gone or the *Eletǔ Òdìbò*'s. Either way, Lagos was as dangerous to her as it was to Madam. With one day left, Ṣìkẹ́mi realised a new future loomed. She made up her mind. She would follow Madam to Abẹ́òkúta, and, with some luck, escape from there.

Ẹkáàrọ̀ o. Ṣé dada lẹ jí. The words echoed through the neighbourhood, as Ṣìkẹ́mi strolled down the short distance from the campsite hosting Madam's army to Madam's new house. Their journey to Abẹ́òkúta over several days, through dangerous territory, had forced her and Madam into close proximity. Unable to relinquish her disdain for Madam, Ṣìkẹ́mi had maintained a polite distance. She still did, focusing on daily tasks while she made her final plans. Anger filled every waking moment and, whenever she found herself near Madam or Ọbádínà, she thought she would burst a blood vessel. She knew what she must do, but the unfairness of it made her fume.

She approached the house and exhaled a soft sigh at the absence of the throngs she'd tolerated for six weeks. Two weeks after arriving in Abẹ́òkúta, she'd gone to Madam's house and found people amassed up front. The crowd parted to let her through. Then they all cheered and clapped.

'What was that about?' Ṣìkẹ́mi had asked Màmá Lékan when she entered the house.

Màmá Lékan grinned. 'They were waiting for you.'

'Me, why?'

'Ah. You haven't heard the story.'

Màmá Lékan explained how, a few years earlier, the neighbouring Dahomeans had nearly captured the city before the
Ẹ̀gbá forced their retreat. After the battle, the Ẹ̀gbá gathered the
bodies of their defeated foes and realised their enemies were
female. The market women composed a song mocking the
men, which annoyed them enough for the king to ban it.

'What has that got to do with me?' she said.

'They heard Madam had a female warrior. They came to see
for themselves.'

Ṣìkẹ́mi tolerated the scrutiny because the number of
gawkers diminished daily. But the damage was done. The
unwanted notoriety had thwarted her plans to keep a low
profile until she escaped, and people now recognised her almost
everywhere.

Ṣìkẹ́mi walked down a side alley to the back of the house.
Her eyes followed the men hoisting the last bit of corrugated-
iron sheeting over the rafters covering the servants' quarters.
Satisfied they were on track, she strolled back to the front. The
main building was built in record time by Madam's army. The
modest, two-storey brick house embraced the budding African-
Brazilian architecture, with intricate ochre motifs and friezes
carved into the plasterwork. Large, shuttered casement
windows provided much-needed ventilation, and the carved
wooden door was as impressive as any seen in Àgùdà. Ṣìkẹ́mi
was surprised Madam didn't build something more opulent,
but her prudence was wise, given trading opportunities were
less lucrative in Abẹ́òkúta compared to Lagos or Bàdágrì.

Thanks to the generous land donated by Madam's father,
Olúmosà, the building boasted expansive courtyards to the
front and back that allowed for large communal gatherings.
The front courtyard was the designated venue for Madam's

house-opening party in three days. Ṣìkẹ́mi wandered across the courtyard, making a mental note of where to seat the expected dignitaries, who included the chiefs who welcomed Madam to the town. She doubted the missionaries, who had a powerful presence in the town, would attend. They were steadfast in their contempt for Madam, deeming her a threat to their missionary efforts and the peace of mind of the freed slaves. Still, the party was the talk of the town, and that morning Madam sent a large bag of cowries to the rain-catcher to ensure nothing threatened her festivities.

As Ṣìkẹ́mi stood in the front yard, half-heartedly supervising the men arranging furniture, her mind zeroed on the chatter of the two women in the courtyard's periphery. She studied the younger of the women, the personal maid of Madam Ẹfúnṣetán Aníwúrà, Madam's guest, and Fọlárìn's owner, who had arrived from Ìbàdàn early that morning for the house opening. They were introduced then, although Ṣìkẹ́mi paid little attention to the maid because she was fixated on Madam Ẹfúnṣetán, whose fame preceded her.

Ẹfúnṣetán was striking – as tall as Madam, with a medium build. Her ebony skin bore no wrinkles and Ṣìkẹ́mi surmised she was a few years younger than Madam. A firm jaw framed her square face, the classic African nose offset by a full lower lip. Like Madam, three vertical tribal marks on each cheek marked her as Ẹ̀gbá. The women were similar, exuding power and wielding authority with ease, but where Madam's demeanour bordered on the morose Ẹfúnṣetán oozed warmth. She broke into an amiable smile for all who greeted her. Still, if the rumours were true, that killer smile hid a ruthless heart.

Ẹfúnṣetán's diminutive maid seemed too young and inexperienced for her role, but Ṣìkẹ́mi knew looks could be deceiving. She wondered how they would manage the demands of both women, even for a few days. But none of it mattered, because she'd soon be gone.

Two days later, the increasing sound of gentle ripples flowing over the pebbled riverbed filled the air, bringing a soothing calm to Ṣìkẹ́mi's troubled heart. As she drew nearer the embankment the camp's chatter disappeared, leaving a quiet calm behind. The Ògùn River, a mere stone's throw away, glistened in the darkness, the moonlight turning its waters black. It was the lifeblood of the Yorùbá nation, flowing from the hinterland all the way down to the coast, and a main source of transporting goods and cargo.

She sniffed the air and tweaked her nose, noting the rank smell of decaying blood from the abattoir a little upstream. Despite the stench, she came here as often as she could; the river's soothing sounds made up for the assault on her nostrils. She stilled, recognising the soft footsteps behind her. Odùtọ́lá. When he reached her side, she acknowledged his presence with a slight nod. Together, they strolled closer to the river's edge. When they reached the banks, Ṣìkẹ́mi stopped and stared.

'Are you all right?' he asked.

Ṣìkẹ́mi turned and faced him. He'd always been able to read her different moods. She tried to hold back the pools of tears hovering, but a tiny escapee trickled down the corner of her eye.

Odùtọ́lá lifted a finger to flick it away. 'You are leaving.'

She sniffled but said nothing.

For the second time in his life, he grabbed her hands and drew her close to his chest. They stayed silent like that for aeons until a hoot from an owl startled them both. With a shaky laugh, Ṣìkẹ́mi straightened and took a step backward, but Odùtọ́lá held on to her hands.

'Let me come with you,' he said.

For several minutes, she remained silent. Then she sighed. 'I can't let you. You are a free man. I cannot be responsible for turning you into a fugitive.'

'Why not wait a few more months and ask her again? Perhaps we can get the town elders to intervene on your behalf.'

Ṣìkẹ́mi shook her head. 'I have given her everything I have, and I have nothing more to give. Every month I spend with her is time not spent searching for my family. I am not getting any younger and if I am to find my family alive I must search for them now.'

Odùtọ́lá digested her words in silence. 'When? How?' he asked, eventually.

'No. I don't want you involved and, for your sake, the less you know the better.' The hairs on the back of her neck prickled. She glanced over her shoulder, but they appeared to be alone.

'This is goodbye then?'

'Yes, it is.'

'Then let's sit for a while.' Odùtọ́lá sank down onto the grassy bank, pulling her hand along. Ṣìkẹ́mi followed him down and he scooted closer, draping an arm around her shoulder. She tensed for a minute, then relaxed and leaned into the embrace. Together they lay back and watched the stars, each deep in thought, until Ṣìkẹ́mi broke the silence, rolling on her side to face Odùtọ́lá. Sensing the shift, he did the same so they lay facing each other.

Ṣìkẹ́mi reached out a hand and trailed a finger down his jaw. She swallowed. 'Thank you,' she said.

He caught her hand. 'What for?'

'Everything. I'll never forget your kindness and loyalty.'

In response, Odùtọ́lá leaned forward and touched his lips to her forehead. 'It was my privilege.'

Ṣìkẹ́mi entwined her fingers in his, then pulled him up. It

was time. Silence enveloped them once more as they made their
way back to the camp.

'More wine!' Madam Ẹfúnṣetán held out her cup in front of
Ṣìkẹ́mi, her obsidian-coloured eyes flashing daggers, daring a
refusal. Ṣìkẹ́mi clicked her fingers at a servant, who hurried to
do the woman's bidding. Beside her, cackling like someone
deranged, Madam showed similar signs of being inebriated.

She lifted her half-empty cup. 'Me too!'

Ṣìkẹ́mi's gaze flitted between the women. Madam always
maintained a certain level of sobriety in the past, so it was quite
riveting seeing her a little less in control for the first time. When
most of the dignitaries left the house-opening ceremony a few
hours earlier, Madam and her house guest had retired to her
room with a keg of palm-wine. It was now past midnight, with
the results unfolding before her and neither woman wanting to
sleep.

Ṣìkẹ́mi observed the time trickling away with increasing
unease. Under different circumstances, she might have found
the mutual admiration blossoming between the two women
somewhat endearing. Earlier, they'd swapped childhood stories.
Both women were born in Abẹ́òkúta to warrior fathers and
mothers who were seasoned traders. Soon after, they moved on
to discussing their sorrow over losing children – Madam's two
sons and Ẹfúnṣetán's only daughter. An uncomfortable silence
followed, leading to both women imbibing excessive amounts
of alcohol.

As far as she knew, Madam didn't have close friends.
Women who feared her, yes. Women who hated or envied her,
absolutely. But a genuine friend to share her sorrows with? Her
closest relationships had been with Rónkẹ́ and Ṣìkẹ́mi, and
those no longer existed.

While focused on her own thoughts, Ṣìkẹ́mi had missed the start of the women's current conversation. Now they were busy regaling each other with their most outrageous exploits.

'I told him to... take her head off.' Ẹfúnṣetán made a slicing motion with her fingers.

Madam jerked upright, spluttering into her palm-wine. 'What! Why?'

Ẹfúnṣetán lifted her shoulders and dropped them. 'She disobeyed me.'

Even half drunk, Madam's business acuity asserted itself. 'Why didn't you just let her deliver her baby, then sell them both? Seems like a waste of two humans to me.'

Ẹfúnṣetán dissolved into a fit of giggles. 'Where's the fun in that?' Then she paused and her face looked serious. 'You'd think the others would learn, but no.' She shook her head and hiccupped. More laughter followed.

So, the rumour that the woman often beheaded her slaves was true!

'Well, I have done nothing that crazy, and they sent me here. Look at us both!'

Madam stood up and staggered onto the sturdy, low table in the room's centre. Ṣìkẹ́mi hovered behind her, unsure of what to expect. With jerky movements Madam lifted one foot, then the other, until she was balanced on the table. Then she bent her knees, jutting out her bottom, and jiggled her hips. 'Pàreke!' she crooned, dancing to her own imaginary music. Not to be outdone, Ẹfúnṣetán pulled off her sandals and joined Madam on the table.

Ṣìkẹ́mi eyed the table, hoping it would hold their combined weight, but she didn't want to tempt the gods. She really needed to get the situation under control. She had wanted them drunk and sleepy, not rowdy, and time was ticking.

'Yèyé, the table might break.' She kept her tone soft, fearful of arousing Madam's anger, which was the last thing she needed.

'Are you saying I'm heavy?'

Ṣìkẹ́mi pretended she hadn't heard the slurred words. Instead of responding, she signalled the servants with a discreet nod towards the alcohol. Immediately, they started to pack the palm-wine away. After studying both women, she decided to tackle Madam's guest first.

'Màmá, please let me escort you to your room,' she said, addressing Ẹfúnṣetán.

'No, she's sleeping in my room tonight.'

Ṣìkẹ́mi raised a surprised brow at Madam's slurred words, but Ẹfúnṣetán saved her from having to reply.

'No, I'll go to my room. I will be more comfortable there.'

Ṣìkẹ́mi let out a grateful sigh. Ẹfúnṣetán staggered off the table, prompting Ṣìkẹ́mi to offer her arm. She handed the woman to her maid. Then she helped Madam down and into a chair. 'I'll be right back, Yèyé,' she said, as she followed Ẹfúnṣetán out.

After seeing them safely to their room, Ṣìkẹ́mi left Ẹfúnṣetán to her maid's ministrations and hurried back to Madam, whom she found slumped on a chair, snoring away. Thankful for the quiet, and with the help of another servant, she bustled Madam into her bed. Then she took the oil lamp, bid the servant goodnight, and left Madam's room for the last time.

THIRTY-ONE

Ṣìkẹ́mi stretched her aching muscles as she strode through the building, down the stairs and into the back courtyard. In the empty courtyard, she found a cooking stool and perched her bottom on it. Then she put out the lamp in her hands and drew a deep cleansing breath as darkness enveloped her and the quietness soothed her jangled nerves. She just needed a moment to gather herself before putting the rest of her plan in motion.

Lost in thought, she didn't notice anything unusual until someone slipped a thin rope over her head and yanked it backward. Her heart hammered against her ribcage as she choked. She grasped the rope, trying to fight whoever was strangling her, but her adversary was strong. In the ensuing struggle, Ṣìkẹ́mi kicked her legs out in front of her, striking a lidded empty water can, which clattered onto the floor. The noise must have startled Ṣìkẹ́mi's attacker as he dropped the rope and fled, leaving Ṣìkẹ́mi gasping for breath.

When her heartbeat slowed sufficiently, Ṣìkẹ́mi stood. She had suspected someone might try to kill her and was surprised it hadn't happened sooner. Alert and cautious, she felt her way through the darkness back to her room. She undressed with haste, pulling off her party garb and donning a simple *dànṣíkí* and short trousers.

Once dressed, she fell to her knees and felt for the hole she'd cut into the wooden floor underneath the bed. Then she lifted out the cowrie shells, some in satchels, others strung like beads. She tied all the strung cowries round her waist underneath her *dànṣíkí*, then heaved the satchels over her shoulders, so they criss-crossed over her front and back. She winced as the combined weight aggravated the bruise forming on her collarbone.

The heavy bags would slow her down, she realised. The problem with cowries was the need to carry thousands of them, and she needed the money to ease her path. Who knew what dangers lay ahead? But she knew her limits. Huffing, she removed two bags and left them for whoever was lucky enough to find them, thankful for her other contingencies. On her way to Abẹ́òkúta, each time she attended to her toileting needs she buried a few bags in selected spots in the forest. She hoped they would still be there when she returned to reclaim them.

She looked around the room. Apart from her money and weaponry, she was taking nothing. She had arranged for some money to be delivered to Màmá Lékan and Rónkẹ́, after she was gone. Rónkẹ́ and her two kids had returned to Abẹ́òkúta with them and now lived with Rónkẹ́'s family. Rónkẹ́ still refused to see her, and Ṣìkẹ́mi had given up on a reconciliation.

She gave the room a final glance, then left. A mile away in the woods, a horse was waiting for her. She moved fast, and it wasn't long before she found the horse still tethered where she'd left it in the early hours. It nickered at her approach. She ran her hand gently down its mane, soothing it into submission. She saddled the beast and heaved herself onto its back. Then she attached two of her cowrie bags to the saddle, keeping the rest on her person.

Horses were not her preferred mode of transport. Madam kept a few, but Ṣìkẹ́mi found their gait nausea-inducing. Still, she needed a great distance between her and Madam as quickly as possible. She gulped, dug her heels into the horse's sides, and held on to the reins.

Ṣìkẹ́mi stopped and peered into the darkness, concentrating on the various sounds filling the air. The birds called and a variety of insects buzzed, but nothing sounded unusual. Yet she couldn't shake the sense that for the past few minutes someone had been following her. A queasiness settled into the pit of her stomach. She'd ridden the horse along a well-worn track for several miles, but as the forest grew denser she set it loose and continued on foot. Her unease increased. A crackle here, an echoed footstep there. Unnerving, but never quite enough to pinpoint. The person was good; possibly as good as Ṣìkẹ́mi herself, which was worrisome, if not downright frightening.

The money bags weighed her down, as she had suspected they would, and the earlier slight ache from the bruising round her neck was now a full-blown throb. As she debated discarding a couple more bags, she heard the unmistakable sound of twigs crackling beneath a foot. In an instant, her weariness disappeared. Tense and alert, she scanned the surrounding forest. In the darkness, her eyes saw nothing, but her instincts told her she wasn't alone.

'Who are you? Show yourself!'

Silence greeted her pronouncement. Ṣìkẹ́mi huffed. The person following her seemed content remaining in the shadows, but why? She checked her weapons, just in case; her bow and arrows, a dagger and her faithful sword. Then she pressed on, hoping the looming daylight would bring better protection, or, better still, a friendly village.

She had headed south when she left, following the same trail they'd journeyed from Lagos to Abẹ́òkúta. She reckoned the day would break in about three hours, and she knew she was close to where she'd stashed her last set of cowrie shells. Something urged her to discard the heavy weight slowing her down, but she'd spent years working hard for the money and was loath to throw it away. She quickened her pace, having decided to make a quick stop and add some of it to her already buried loot.

Less than an hour later, she arrived at the crossroads marked by a giant Ìrókò tree. The elders revered the Ìrókò tree, believing in its malevolent powers, so it made the perfect hiding place. She stopped and listened again. Then she stooped, offloaded the heavy bags, pulled out her hand shovel and started digging. If she dug fast, she could leave in minutes.

'Are you looking for these?' She heard the chinks as a bag of cowries landed near her feet. Without turning, she knew the voice. Àkàndé. She should have known.

'You are losing your touch, Ṣìkẹ́mi. Surely Ọbádínà taught you better than that.'

Ṣìkẹ́mi rose and turned round. She took in her enemy, the cruel, twisted smile and the evil glint in his eyes. Ṣìkẹ́mi recognised the look – that of a hunter playing with its prey. She could take him, but her instincts urged caution. She felt for her sword.

'Don't even try it. You are surrounded.' As he uttered the words, several soldiers emerged from the forest. They'd been waiting, which meant she'd been careless en route to Abẹ́òkúta, and it was about to cost her. She counted eight men and weighed her chances. She could dispatch three, maybe even four, before they overwhelmed her. For once, she wished she'd accepted Odùtọlá's offer. It might have evened the odds and given her a fighting chance. Her brain processed several scenarios. She didn't win in any of them.

'Look, I'd rather take you in alive. There's more glory for me, as the man who bested you. But we will kill you if we have to. The choice is yours.'

Ṣìkẹ́mi processed the truth in Àkàndé's words. Why hadn't the gods warned her of this predicament? Then she remembered she hadn't slept and therefore couldn't dream. Her mind slipped back to her first capture when she was fourteen and her companion, Fọlárìn's, easy capitulation. She'd thought him weak then. Now she saw the wisdom in his actions. She remembered her childhood trip with her mother to the seer. He'd predicted she would make it home. Maybe this wasn't the end. She could die fighting now or take her chances with the gods. Slowly, she raised her hands in surrender.

'You didn't anticipate this, ẹhn? You think you are a man's equal. Better even. But you are wrong. You are just a woman, albeit an unusual one.'

Ṣìkẹ́mi held her tongue, recognising Àkàndé was baiting her, revelling in his one-upmanship. A good soldier knew when to quit. Instead, she studied him. Ọbádínà had obviously seen Àkàndé's potential and trained him as her replacement. Ṣìkẹ́mi wasn't too proud to acknowledge that his success in tracking her through the forest meant he was at least as good as her. Yes, she'd been careless, but so was everybody sometimes.

Àkàndé ordered one of his men to gather up her stuff and tie her hands. A young soldier stepped forward, almost reverent and apologetic. Ṣìkẹ́mi smiled, giving him the permission he sought. It seemed even Àkàndé's men admired her. The rope felt strange as it wrapped around her wrists. How many times had she led captives to their fate in the same manner? The gods had a sense of humour, and right now she was their joke.

Relieved of all its burdens, the throbbing in her neck lessened and a thought crossed her mind. She turned to Àkàndé and caught him eyeing her chest, his face a mix of contempt and pure lust.

He moved closer and whispered in her ear. 'We could settle this with an arrangement.'

Ṣìkẹ́mi kept her face placid and let her silence do the talking.

'Fine. Have it your way. It's your downfall.'

'Tell me,' she said, as he moved away, 'did you send someone to strangle me last night?' The question had puzzled her all night.

Àkàndé let out a short snort. 'That was hardly a strangling. You are still here, aren't you? It was just an incentive to make sure you didn't postpone your escape.'

'So why didn't you just kill me?'

'And let you die a murdered hero? No, it's much better if you are branded a coward and runaway.'

Ṣìkẹ́mi had to concede the point, and, in a moment of clarity, realised her obsession with money had contributed to her easy capture. She should have let the money go and changed her direction of travel.

'Tie her feet too,' Àkàndé said to the man who tied her hands.

Ṣìkẹ́mi waited while Àkàndé's men gathered their belongings, then the group set out. The rope tying her feet together was just wide enough for a slow shuffle. It would be a long, slow trek back to town, and the fault was all hers.

THIRTY-TWO

News of Ṣìkẹ́mi's failed escape spread like wildfire and people came out of their houses to watch the spectacle as Àkàndé led her through the town. He'd retrieved her horse on their way back and now sat atop it like royalty, while Ṣìkẹ́mi shuffled behind him. Being a market day, the streets were busier than usual, and the heavy traffic slowed their progress. It reminded her of her entry to Bàdágrì so many years ago. *Perhaps someone will save me like the last time*. But she knew she was kidding herself. Unless the gods performed a miracle, she would probably be dead by sundown.

People on their way to the market stopped and gawked as she passed by. The whispers flew past her ears. *Ṣìkẹ́mi, Tinúbú's she-warrior. Did she run away? What was she thinking?* Some reached out to touch her, as if to check that she was human. Ṣìkẹ́mi kept her head down and focused on putting one foot in front of the other as they drew near to Madam's house. Humiliation was not a new meal to her, but it was years since she'd last tasted it.

Àkàndé had sent one of his men ahead and, when they

entered Madam's front courtyard, they found all the servants already gathered. Ṣìkẹ́mi spied Màmá Lékan in a corner, wiping tears from the corner of her eye with the edge of her wrapper. She looked away, unable to bear the woman's sorrow. Àkàndé led her to the furthest corner of the back courtyard, next to the pit latrines. Then he ordered his men to tie her to a tree and watch her. As the sun blazed down on her, her predicament reminded her of the night things unravelled for Bàbá Kékeré. She would probably meet the same fate. A bitter taste rose up the back of her throat. Then she reminded herself that, compared to most slaves, she'd enjoyed a good life.

While Ṣìkẹ́mi waited, the servants' children gathered, forming a circle around her, their faces scrunched. Ṣìkẹ́mi understood their confusion; the soldier who regularly gave orders was now shackled to a tree. Then Màmá Lékan appeared with a stick in her hand.

'Shoo!' she said, brandishing the stick at the children. 'If I catch you, you'll be sorry.'

The children scattered in all directions, squeaking as they went. Màmá Lékan approached her. 'Do you need anything? Water?'

Ṣìkẹ́mi's eyes smarted. She swallowed the lump in her throat. 'No, Màmá Lékan. But thank you. For everything.'

Màmá Lékan nodded and left her in peace.

On her walk of shame, she'd had plenty of time to think about her mistakes. She'd been short-sighted in her single-minded desire for self-sufficiency and hadn't appreciated all those who had helped her on the way. Màmá Lékan, in particular, came to mind. Ṣìkẹ́mi had never truly acknowledged her unwavering devotion, nursing her through two major injuries. Kàmọ̀rù too. Although she kept tabs on him, she never really did much for him. Now the end was near, she added them to her failures with Rónkẹ́ and Odùtọ́lá and wished she'd done better. Except for Rónké, she'd kept people at bay, to prevent them from hurting her; but she'd hurt them in turn, and was hurting now anyway.

The shadows moved across the courtyard, and afternoon turned to evening. Then the servants began placing chairs and mats in the courtyard, which soon filled with chattering people. Madam's extended family, friends, servants and neighbours formed a circle, kneeling, sitting or standing, while the elders took the chairs, leaving three central ones unoccupied.

A hush descended, killing the chatter as Madam came out, led by Ọbádínà and followed by her guest Ẹfúnṣetán. They walked to the centre of the circle and took the three empty seats. Ṣikẹ́mi stiffened her spine and lifted her chin, preparing herself for the trial ahead. She hoped it would be quick, and that whoever was tasked with killing her did it humanely.

A voice, unmistakably Àkàndé's, rang out. 'Bring the slave woman here.'

Ṣikẹ́mi kept her chin up as the man guarding her untied her bindings and led her to the centre of the gathering. A low murmur rumbled through the crowd. 'What a pity,' she heard several people mutter. Àkàndé came forward, grabbed her shoulders and forced her to kneel in front of Madam.

'Yèyé, I found her deep in the forest on the way to Lagos. She was digging up bags of money she hid there earlier. Ask my men. They can bear witness.'

Madam shifted forward, an elbow resting on a knee, her right hand fisted under her chin. She stayed like that, studying Ṣikẹ́mi while everybody held their breath. Finally, she spoke.

'Untie her.'

Men shuffled forward to remove Ṣikẹ́mi's shackles.

'Ṣikẹ́mi,' Madam said, 'give me a good reason for this absurdity. Did you really run away? After everything I have done for you, given you? This is how you repay me?'

Ṣìkẹ́mi lifted her eyes and met Madam's. She would not lie.

'*Yèyé*, you knew I wanted to find my family.'

'What family? You have no proof they are alive. Have I not treated you as a daughter? Have I not given you everything a mother should? You have dined at the feet of kings. What other slave can say that? What other family do you need?' Madam lifted her hand in question.

'I am sure she had help,' Àkàndé said. He signalled, and a section of the crowd parted. Ṣìkẹ́mi's hand flew to her throat as she watched Àkàndé's men lead Odùtọ́lá forward, bound in ropes, in clothes half-torn. A bead of dried blood clung to his brow from a gash in his temple and his lips appeared bruised and puffy. She closed her eyes and shook her head from side to side. This was not supposed to happen. The men pushed Odùtọ́lá forward and made him kneel beside Ṣìkẹ́mi.

'Odùtọ́lá, tell me this isn't true,' Madam said to the newcomer. But Odùtọ́lá stayed silent, staring at the floor.

Ṣìkẹ́mi hissed and dug her elbow into his ribs. 'Tell them it's not true,' she whispered furiously, but Odùtọ́lá didn't budge. Ṣìkẹ́mi's pulse raced. Was he staying silent out of some wrongly placed sense of loyalty towards her, or had they cut out his tongue?

Ṣìkẹ́mi turned her full gaze on Madam. '*Yèyé*, in the entire time I have been with you, have I ever lied to your face?' Her voice trembled even as she spoke.

A gasp echoed through the crowd. Madam shook her head.

'Then believe me now when I tell you Odùtọ́lá had no part in this. Do whatever you want with me, but please do not punish an innocent man.'

Madam held Ṣìkẹ́mi's gaze for a long minute. Then she nodded. 'Okay. Let him go. Take care of his wounds,' she ordered.

Ṣìkẹ́mi let out a huge sigh, and a peace settled over her. At least she wouldn't have Odùtọlá's death on her conscience. She rearranged her face, ready for the trial to continue.

Àkàndé's men helped Odùtọlá to his feet, and Ṣìkẹ́mi tracked his progress as they led him away. Darkness had descended during the proceedings and the servants lit some oil lamps. It created a surreal atmosphere, almost like a vigil for the dead. Appropriate, Ṣìkẹ́mi thought, given her impending death.

'Well, you know the penalty for runaway slaves. Death, or I can sell you to the Europeans. The choice is yours.'

Ṣìkẹ́mi turned, opened her mouth, ready to state her preference, and in that split second caught a glint in the crowd. She'd almost missed the silver arrow-shaped tip of a spear. She turned back to the crowd, searching. That section held no soldiers, so why would someone be holding a spear? Alert, she checked the perimeter again. Someone was in danger. But who? She took a step towards Madam.

'*Yèyé*, there's danger here. I can feel it.' Her tone held a note of urgency.

Madam looked at Ọbádínà. Ṣìkẹ́mi did the same. 'Trust me on this,' she said. He knew her instincts were rarely wrong.

Ọbádínà nodded and Madam, her guest and Ọbádínà all stood at once.

'Lead them indoors and I'll cover the rear,' Ṣìkẹ́mi said, as she sprang into action.

A murmur ran through the crowd at the trio's abrupt departure. Then, out of nowhere, a spear came hurtling towards them. Ṣìkẹ́mi lunged forward with an outstretched hand, ready to grab its shaft. She staggered as her body bore the full force of the flying object, pushing her to her knees. Winded, she rose just as servants and soldiers wrestled the would-be assailant to the ground.

People scattered in all directions as they realised something was amiss. Ṣìkẹ́mi glanced at the house. Although Ọbádínà and the women had reached the door, there could be more danger lurking inside. She ran, covering the women as Ọbádínà led them upstairs to the safety of Madam's room.

Inside, Madam collapsed on a chair while Ọbádínà did a quick sweep of the interconnecting rooms.

'Well, that was interesting,' Ẹfúnṣetán said, staring at her host. 'Is your household always this exciting?' Then she noticed the spear in Ṣìkẹ́mi's hand. 'Wait, let me see that.'

Ṣìkẹ́mi looked at the spear, a bewildered expression on her face. Then she handed it over.

'I've seen this before,' Ẹfúnṣetán said, as she traced the long iron-forged handle with a finger. 'In Ìbàdàn. I am sure of it.'

A short silence followed, then Ọbádínà's eyes widened. 'The assailant was after you?'

'Possibly.' Ẹfúnṣetán turned to Ṣìkẹ́mi. 'Did they catch him?'

'They caught someone.'

'I want to see him.' Ẹfúnṣetán rose and made for the door.

Ọbádínà rushed after her and blocked her egress. 'Wait, it could be dangerous out there. Stay here with Ṣìkẹ́mi. I'll find out what's happening and report back.'

Ẹfúnṣetán settled back down on one of Madam's chairs, a full pout on her lips as Ọbádínà slipped out. In his absence, the women stared into space and a thick silence descended. Ṣìkẹ́mi settled her gaze on the old spotted rug Madam had brought with her from Lagos. She remembered the first day she saw it in Madam's room. This might be the last. She passed a weary hand over her face, the thought of another trial making her shudder. She really wished the day was over.

A knock on the door announced Ọbádínà's return. 'I have good and bad news,' he said as he settled into a chair in front of the

women. 'The good news is they caught him.' He turned to
Ẹfúnṣetán. 'But you were right. He is a slave from Ìbàdàn. His
master promised him his freedom if he killed you, but he won't
name his master. He'd rather die.'

'Oh, he will, but he might enjoy a nicer death if he cooper-
ates,' Ẹfúnṣetán said.

'Well, I'm glad I wasn't the one putting you in danger. Still,
we have the matter of one runaway slave to settle.' Madam
nodded in Ṣìkẹ́mi's direction.

Ẹfúnṣetán followed Madam's gaze until her eyes rested on
Ṣìkẹ́mi. She studied her for several seconds, like someone
inspecting an object for sale. 'She did save our lives,' she said.

'Your life, you mean. In any case, if I don't punish her it will
give all my slaves permission to run away. I can't do that.'

'Fine, give her to me.'

'What!' Three voices echoed in the room.

'I said give her to me. You don't want her. Without her, I
might be dead.' A mischievous smile curved her lips. 'You don't
like wasting slaves. You said so yourself, remember? Besides, she
may well prove useful.'

Then, as if nothing untoward had happened all evening,
Ẹfúnṣetán fluffed down her wrapper. 'I'm tired,' she said. 'I
can't take any more excitement, and I am going to bed. You!'
She pointed at Ṣìkẹ́mi. 'Say your goodbyes and be ready to leave
for Ìbàdàn in the morning.' With that, she flounced out of
Madam's room.

Later, Ṣìkẹ́mi settled Madam down one last time, and as she
turned to leave Madam whispered in the dark, 'I would have
released you. I just wasn't ready to be alone yet. You should
have waited a little longer.'

Ṣìkẹ́mi pondered the words as she stumbled past the
soldiers Ọbádínà had posted on guard for the night. Why
hadn't she said so instead of the blunt refusals? If she'd

known, she would have waited. *Would you?* her inner voice mocked.

Ṣìkẹ́mi found herself at the bottom of the stairs, although she couldn't remember how she got there. So much had occurred. She wasn't sure where to sleep. Her room on the top floor near Madam's didn't feel appropriate any more. She wondered whether the money she had left behind was still there. It might prove useful after all, and Àkàndé had taken everything she had except the strings round her waist.

She turned and crept up the stairs. To her surprise, the money bags were still there, barely concealed next to the bed. Slowly, she picked them up, and sank on to the bed. What had she done? Now she was heading to Ìbàdàn, a city much further away from her intended destination. Would she ever get home with the scrapes she kept stumbling into?

Ṣìkẹ́mi stood up, went downstairs and knocked on Màmá Lékan's door. The door opened, Màmá Lékan drew her into a hug, and Ṣìkẹ́mi burst into tears.

THIRTY-THREE

TWO MONTHS LATER, SEPTEMBER 1856, ÌBÀDÀN

Ṣìkẹ́mi thought she would die of boredom, if it were possible. As she passed the men guarding Ẹfúnṣetán's sprawling compound, they nodded, but none attempted to engage her in conversation. For once, Ṣìkẹ́mi wasn't afraid to admit her loneliness. The only upside to being Ẹfúnṣetán's slave was the chance to reconnect with Fọlárìn. But the one person she'd hoped to see in Ìbàdàn had failed to materialise, and she dared not ask about him for fear of drawing unwanted attention.

Ṣìkẹ́mi took her tenth lap around the compound, which was built atop one of the seven hills surrounding the city. From the hilltop, Ìbàdàn lay, spread out, compound after compound packed next to each other, the rectangular shapes creating an interconnecting labyrinth of dwellings. The hum of the city filled the air, a mix of human conversation, baying livestock and the bustle of movement. She needed to burn some energy, so she picked up the pace, breaking into a light jog around the rectangular space.

Since arriving, she'd learned the city grew from a war camp and was ruled by military men under a single general. Like

Tinúbú, Ẹfúnṣetán enjoyed showing off her she-warrior. Ṣìkẹ́mi had already escorted her to the homes of several business associates and political allies, including the general. But there was little else to occupy her time when she wasn't accompanying Ẹfúnṣetán or running errands for her. So, she walked several laps around the compound's perimeter each day for exercise. She missed training with her men, the forest; things she'd been so eager to leave behind when she ran from Tinúbú. It made her wonder what she would do with herself if she ever gained her freedom.

Ìbidún, Ẹfúnṣetán's personal maid, came out of the main building in the compound, a two-storey structure, which housed Ẹfúnṣetán and her closest attendants. The house held two large sitting rooms and three small bedrooms on the ground floor, and four large bedrooms on the upper floor, one of which Ṣìkẹ́mi shared with Ìbidún. A corridor and a central stairwell divided the rooms on both floors. The rest of the compound was arranged in the traditional manner, with single-floor rectangular buildings around a central courtyard. Two buildings contained several rooms for staff and slaves. One stood as an open, but roofed, outdoor kitchen, and the last block housed the latrines and bathrooms. Ìbidún dipped a little curtsy to Ṣìkẹ́mi. 'Màmá wants to see you now,' she said.

Ṣìkẹ́mi nodded, hoping Ẹfúnṣetán would put her to good use. She followed Ìbidún indoors, noting how the compound guards followed the sway of the girl's hips as she moved. Ìbidún was about sixteen, with a pretty heart-shaped face and bright, curious eyes that drew you in. Her fair skin alone was enough to garner unwanted attention, so much so that the household called her *Òyìnbó*, the Yorùbá nickname for white folk. The girl hero-worshipped her, and Ṣìkẹ́mi was at a loss as to why. She didn't want the responsibility of looking out for anyone but herself, so she'd tried discouraging her. She barely spoke to the girl, answered the barest minimum of questions, and rebuffed all Ìbidún's efforts at making friends. Yet the girl continued to fetch her bathing water and wash her clothes, even though Ṣìkẹ́mi asked her not to.

She knew she was being mean, and her lips twisted at the self-imposed irony – she was lonely but didn't want to make friends. She decided to break the silence. 'How is *Yèyé* doing today?' She didn't know why she called Ẹfúnṣetán *Yèyé*, since the woman was much younger than Madam Tinúbú. Force of habit, she guessed, and because Ẹfúnṣetán exuded the same presence, and wielded as much political power and authority as her peer.

The girl smiled. 'She is much better. You will soon see.'

The last two months had been eye-opening; the similarities between Tinúbú and Ẹfúnṣetán were much stronger than she imagined. A month after their arrival, Ẹfúnṣetán became listless and moody, alternating between fits of anger and bouts of weeping. She barely ate, wouldn't bathe, and saw no one except Ìbidún, who had spent the last few weeks coaxing her to leave her bedroom. It reminded her of Madam Tinúbú's mood swings, and she wondered which Ẹfúnṣetán she would find that morning; the vivacious socialite or the vicious enslaver.

Ìbidún led Ṣìkẹ́mi across Ẹfúnṣetán's living space right into the connecting room, which served as her bedroom. It was her first time in Ẹfúnṣetán's inner sanctuary. Her new mistress sat in front of a large oval standing mirror as a servant fussed over her. Ṣìkẹ́mi's eyes roamed the room, noting its simplicity. Light from a single window bathed the room, making it appear more spacious than it was. Instead of animal skins, raffia mats decorated the room's floor. Unusually for a woman of Ẹfúnṣetán's wealth, the furniture was sparse: a small bed, some wooden stools, several large metal trunks and a mirror, something in high demand among the wealthy Yorùbá.

Ṣìkẹ́mi's wandering eyes returned to their starting point and collided with Ẹfúnṣetán's in the mirror. She braced herself as their gazes held, each taking the measure of the other. Ẹfúnṣetán's face wore an inscrutable mask that Ṣìkẹ́mi found impossible to read, and a shiver fluttered down her spine. She lowered her eyes. In Ẹfúnṣetán she sensed a dark viciousness that far eclipsed that of her previous mistress.

Groomed and dressed in a colourful cotton wrapper and matching *gèlè*, Ẹfúnṣetán looked ready to live again. According to Ìbidún, Ẹfúnṣetán believed enemies in her compound were trying to kill her. Ṣìkẹ́mi saw no evidence of such but couldn't dismiss the possibility, given she knew the slaves in the compound feared her and none showed her any affection. That, combined with Ẹfúnṣetán's legendary reputation for wickedness and the assassination attempt at Abẹ́òkúta, meant she couldn't entirely dismiss Ẹfúnṣetán's concerns. The question was whether the danger stalking Ẹfúnṣetán resided within or outside her compound.

Ẹfúnṣetán broke the silence. 'You've been here for months now. Tell me. Which of the chiefs you've met do I need to worry about?'

Ṣìkẹ́mi gulped at the unexpected question. Her mind circled through the chiefs and zeroed in on Látoosà, the general. His smile never seemed to match the coldness in his eyes whenever he met Ẹfúnṣetán. Proud and formidable, he'd given himself the title *Ààrẹ̀ ọ̀nà kàkanfò*, deeming the previous ruler's title of *Báalẹ̀* beneath him.

'The general,' she said. 'He dislikes... no, detests the fact that he needs you.'

Ẹfúnṣetán lifted an eyebrow that suggested she knew that already. 'Go on. Who else?'

Ṣìkẹ́mi thought of Bàbá Fábùnmi, and an amused smile hovered on her lips. Ẹfúnṣetán was well endowed, front and back. The desire in Bàbá Fábùnmi's eyes when he focused on Ẹfúnṣetán's chest or the roll of her bum cheeks as she walked was comical. She caught Ẹfúnṣetán's glower in the mirror and wiped the smile off her face.

'Do share, Ṣìkẹ́mi. Who do you find so amusing?'

The bite in Ẹfúnṣetán's tone cautioned her, but something of the old impetuous Ṣìkẹ́mi surfaced. 'Erm... it's Bàbá Fábùnmi.' She paused, wondering whether to finish her sentence, then shrugged. 'He would like to bed you.'

Ìbidún released a shocked gasp. Ṣìkẹ́mi kept her face deadpan, and in the silence that ensued she wondered if she had a death wish. But Ẹfúnṣetán had asked, and she had answered. She glanced at Ẹfúnṣetán. Doubled over, the woman's body juddered. Then she made a gurgling sound, and a frisson of alarm shot through Ṣìkẹ́mi. Before she could react, Ẹfúnṣetán erupted into a belly roar of laughter. Ṣìkẹ́mi and Ìbidún shared a surprised look, then both joined in.

Ẹfúnṣetán came up for air. 'That old goat. He's as old as my grandfather. I wonder if he can still get his little thing up.' She crooked her forefinger as if mirroring the man's appendage, then she cracked up once more. When her laughter petered out, her head lifted and she resembled a lion about to pounce. Ṣìkẹ́mi stood to attention.

'You will serve me well,' Ẹfúnṣetán said, a note of satisfaction in her voice, and Ṣìkẹ́mi realised she'd just passed a test. 'I don't need a slave raider or warrior. I have more than enough of those. But I need a spy. And for that, you will do. You may go where you want in my household, but keep your eyes and ears open. If a bird sneezes, or a dog talks, I want to be the first to hear about it. Understood?'

'Yes, *Yèyé*,' Ṣìkẹ́mi said, glad that her new role was clearer.

'Now, I want you to take a message to Chief Ògèdèngbé, and you don't need a guard watching you any more.'

Sìkẹ́mi listened to the message, relieved she was no longer under the watch of the guards who had tailed her every move since she arrived. She bowed and left her mistress's chambers.

'Sìkẹ́mi, wait for me.'

Sìkẹ́mi swivelled round at the sound of Fọlárìn's velvety tone. She'd waited months for this moment. The longer she waited, the more she fantasised about it. And now he was finally standing in front of her. Beside him walked another young man, one she recognised as one of Ẹfúnṣetán's guards. Her breath hitched as an uncharacteristic shyness invaded her. She couldn't help being drawn to him. A part of her marvelled at the attraction, given how much she had loathed him as a child.

'I heard Madam Ẹfúnṣetán brought you to me. That must be a story in itself.'

'You think I came looking for you? You flatter yourself.' Sìkẹ́mi's face split into a grin as the old banter between them resurfaced. She was glad he didn't bear a grudge at their angry parting, something she'd regretted.

'Me? I know better. How are you?' He moved into step beside her, while the other man kept a respectful distance behind them.

'I am well. I'm on an errand for Madam.'

'I know. I saw you leave the compound.'

'So, you are back with Kúmúyilò?' No one had mentioned either man since she'd been in residence. At one point, she'd thought she'd misheard Fọlárìn when they met in Lagos.

'Uh-uh.'

'How long before your next travels?'

'Who knows? Kúmúyilò goes where the wind blows, and where he goes I follow.'

Ṣìkẹ́mi mulled over that and wondered about his life in Ẹfúnṣetán's household. 'Well, it is great seeing you again.'

'I feel the same way.'

Ṣìkẹ́mi smiled before she pointed. 'I have reached my destination.' It hadn't taken long.

Fọlárìn nodded. 'Go and deliver the message. I will wait here for you.'

As she entered Chief Ògèdèngbé's house, Ṣìkẹ́mi felt a new lightness in her spirit, and she wondered if Fọlárìn felt the same.

Ṣìkẹ́mi completed her errand, and as Fọlárìn walked her back to Ẹfúnṣetán's compound she seized the opportunity to apologise. 'Forgive me for my behaviour in Lagos. It was a difficult time.'

Fọlárìn beamed at her. 'Forget about it. It's in the past.'

They settled into the walk, taking it slow, along the dusty, noisy streets, neither eager to reach their destination.

'We mustn't be seen together. It will cause trouble,' he said as they neared the compound. 'But I would like to see you again.'

Ṣìkẹ́mi's heart leapt, but she was puzzled. 'Aren't you staying in Madam's compound?'

'No. Kúmúyilò has his own house.'

Ṣìkẹ́mi mulled over his words. With a single glance, Fọlárìn had ignited novel sensations within her. Stuff she had never felt before. She'd been able to walk away from Odùtọ́lá, but for some reason this allure was far stronger. They'd have to be cautious, though, because Ẹfúnṣetán forbade her slaves of opposite genders from fraternising, with severe punishments for those who disobeyed.

'I would like that, but how do we avoid getting caught?'

She glanced at Fọlárìn, who wore a knowing expression. It reminded her of the cocky boy of her childhood, although now he exuded a quiet maturity that had been missing before; perhaps one born of suffering. His eyes did funny things to her, and she hoped she had the same effect on him.

Fọlárìn gestured at the guard accompanying them. 'Múfútáò here is my friend. He will keep our secret. You can sneak out of the compound on the nights he is on duty. Someone will be waiting to lead you to a friend's house where we can meet.'

It sounded workable except... 'I won't always know in advance which nights I can sneak out. How would you know when to wait?'

'When you think you can get away, signal to Múfútáò at sundown and he'll send me a message. I'll wait, whether or not you come.'

Ṣìkẹ́mi thought it over. She was almost certain the spark she felt was mutual, and she couldn't wait to explore it. She'd made no plans to escape, because Ẹfúnṣetán's men monitored her every move, but, with Ẹfúnṣetán relaxing the rules, she could consider the possibilities once more. In the meantime, she'd savour life's pleasures and explore what she'd been missing.

THIRTY-FOUR

'How do you do that?'

Ṣìkẹ́mi groaned. 'Do what?'

No longer used to sharing her personal space, she often found Ìbidún's incessant chatter tiresome. It was bedtime, and, given her earlier meeting with Fọlárìn, she needed some quiet time to think about her future.

'Know what people are thinking. The things you told Màmá this morning.'

It was something Ṣìkẹ́mi did by pure instinct, but how did one explain that? She sat up. 'When you spend as much time as I do watching people, you learn to notice what their bodies are trying to hide. My màmá used to say, "Elédùmàrè gave us only one mouth, but two eyes and ears, for a good reason." You learn so much more when you watch and listen.'

Ṣìkẹ́mi lay down on her bed and faced the wall, signalling the end of the conversation. Ìbidún was quiet for less than a minute before she spoke again. It kind of reminded Ṣìkẹ́mi of her younger self with Rónkẹ́.

'Why did you become a warrior?'

The question, delivered in a quiet voice that lacked Ìbidún's usual chirpiness, piqued Ṣìkẹ́mi's interest. She turned round and eyed Ìbidún, who perched on the edge of her bed with her hands clasped together. Somehow, Ṣìkẹ́mi sensed the girl wanted, no, needed, a thoughtful response. She relented. 'There's no straightforward answer. I was always different as a child. I loved the forest, hunting, climbing trees; all things girls shouldn't do, I was told. I was captured by the Dahomey female warriors. That's where I initially got the idea.'

Ìbidún nodded. 'I heard of those. They are the ones who nearly captured Abẹ́òkúta. I suppose it was a good way to learn to protect yourself.'

The girl was smarter than Ṣìkẹ́mi had first assumed. Ṣìkẹ́mi scrutinised her again, picking up on subtle cues; the trembling hands and the agitated way her foot tapped the floor. 'Who do you need protecting from?'

Ìbidún squirmed and looked down. 'I can't tell you that, Ẹ̀gbọ́n.'

At least she didn't deny it. Ṣìkẹ́mi had noticed the girl's nervous twitches earlier, a behaviour absent until Fọlárìn and his master appeared. A worrying thought crossed her mind. Was one of Kúmúyilò's men harassing her? Fọlárìn? Although, she didn't think he was the sort. Perhaps it was even Kúmúyilò himself. An image of Bàbá Kékeré's grubby hands roaming her body popped into her head, and she recoiled in revulsion. She wouldn't let that happen to Ìbidún on her watch. She probed further.

'I hear Madam's son, Kúmúyilò, has returned.'

Ìbidún flinched as if she'd been slapped, confirming Ṣìkẹ́mi's fears. Not wanting to distress the girl further, she changed the subject. 'I can teach you to protect yourself, if you like.'

She regretted the words as soon as they left her mouth, but Ìbidún straightened her shoulders and her face lit up. 'Thank you. Thank you! Màmá can't find out. She won't like it and it does no one any good to upset her. But it would make me so happy.'

Ṣìkẹ́mi bit her lips, knowing she couldn't retract the offer. 'Doesn't she trust you?' She was curious as to their relationship. She didn't know how the girl came into Ẹfúnṣetán's service.

'She does. We are family. She is my mother's cousin. Still, I prefer to stay clear of trouble. Her anger isn't something you want to see.'

Ṣìkẹ́mi didn't want to skulk around, hiding from Ẹfúnṣetán while teaching Ìbidún. 'We have to tell her. I don't want trouble either, and I don't think *Yèyé* will appreciate us hiding it.'

Ìbidún's shoulders slumped, and the light left her eyes. 'We can't. She'll demand to know why, and I can't tell her. Forget about it.'

Ṣìkẹ́mi watched Ìbidún's face shut down. She put out the lamp and went to sleep, leaving a conflicted Ṣìkẹ́mi staring into the darkness.

Ṣìkẹ́mi understood the girl's beauty made her vulnerable, something she couldn't ignore. A slow smile broke over her face. Training the girl would occupy her time, and outwitting Ẹfúnṣetán and her informants among the servants and guards would add some much-needed excitement to her daily existence. She lay back down and started plotting.

Five days later, Ṣìkẹ́mi melded into the shadows as she sneaked along the veranda edging the dark courtyard on her way to see Fọlárìn. At the entrance to the courtyard, Múfútáò gave her a quick nod, and she slipped out. In the alleyway, a boy in his teens waited for her. 'Come this way,' he whispered as he led her away. Remembering her aborted escape from Tinúbú, Ṣìkẹ́mi hoped she wasn't walking into a trap, but she'd come armed just in case. If it came to it, she'd die standing. The boy led her through three alleyways before slipping into a small courtyard. Ṣìkẹ́mi followed him and collided with Fọlárìn. 'Shush!' He put a finger to her lips before she yelped.

Fọlárìn led her to a small room lit with a hurricane lamp. A small bed covered with a clean cotton sheet and a single stool were its only furniture. Ṣìkẹ́mi sat on the edge of the bed and Fọlárìn took the stool.

Her gaze flicked round the room. 'Where is your friend?' She still felt uncomfortable in a confined space with a man, even if it was Fọlárìn, and she was prepared to defend herself if necessary.

As if sensing her unease, Fọlárìn moved his stool backward, creating some space between them. 'My friend is in his brother's room nearby. I promise you are safe here and we won't do anything you don't like. Let's just talk.'

And talk they did. Ṣìkẹ́mi discovered Fọlárìn's first master, a cruel man, had whipped him often for the tiniest infractions. On an errand, Fọlárìn came across a gang of boys pummelling Kúmúyilò into the ground. He'd felt compelled to help Kúmúyilò escape. Subsequently, Kúmúyilò took him home to Ẹfúnṣetán, who bought him off his master.

A lull in the conversation allowed Ṣìkẹ́mi to ask a burning question. 'Did you and Kúmúyilò receive combat training?'

'Madam Ẹfúnṣetán arranged training for the household a few years ago. She even took part in it.'

Ṣìkẹ́mi's eyes nearly popped out. No wonder the woman wasn't impressed with her when they met. 'Ìbidún, her personal maid, isn't trained,' she said.

'Perhaps she joined the household afterwards.'

Ṣìkẹ́mi eyed him for a moment, her eyes dancing. 'So how good are you and Kúmúyilò?' Although her question was deliberate, she kept her tone light.

'Ṣìkẹ́mi, you do not need to fear me. It is probably the other way round. Our training was basic and, from the rumours I heard, you are an accomplished soldier.' His pride in her was unmistakable.

Ṣìkẹ́mi relaxed, feeling that if it came down to a battle between her and Kúmúyilò she stood a good chance. Changing the subject, she asked the next pertinent question.

'Have you heard any more news from Òké-Ọ̀dán?'

'Yes, I have.'

Ṣìkẹ́mi jerked off the edge of the bed.

Fọlárìn stood, and his arms reached out and held hers. 'Calm down. I didn't run into your family, if that's what you are thinking.'

Ṣìkẹ́mi's hopes plummeted.

'But I met someone from Òké-Ọ̀dán who confirmed they are there, and I sent them a message that you were alive and well.'

It was the best news Ṣìkẹ́mi could have hoped for. She grabbed him and locked him in a hug, clinging on as if her life depended on it. His arms wrapped around her, and they clung to each other until Ṣìkẹ́mi registered the thudding of Fọlárìn's heart. Or was that hers? It was difficult to tell. She drew back, giving them some space, and swatted his hand. 'Why didn't you tell me this when we met a few days ago?'

His face split into a saucy grin. 'Because we couldn't do this then.' He pulled her close again. 'See how my heart beats for you? Even at fifteen, I felt this way, but couldn't express it.'

Ṣìkẹ́mi giggled. 'So, you picked a fight every time we met?'

'Well, at least we were talking. It was better than nothing or that disdain-filled glare you used to send my way.'

Ṣìkẹ́mi was silent for a while as she stood nestled in Fọlárìn's arms. The unfamiliar mix of calm and excitement left her bewildered but pleasantly surprised that she liked it. Eventually, she broke the silence. Her fingers gestured between them. 'What do we do about this?'

Fọlárìn raised a shoulder. 'Enjoy it?'

She needed more than that. 'Then what?'

Fọlárìn's eyes narrowed. 'I don't know.'

She detached herself and stepped back. 'We can't conduct clandestine meetings forever, and you know the consequences if we are caught. We need to think about the future.'

Fọlárìn folded his arms over his chest. 'We shouldn't worry about that now. Can't we just explore these feelings first? You're always too many steps ahead.' The needling tone reminded her of the teenage Fọlárìn.

Ṣìkẹ́mi stepped towards the door. 'I need to get back before I'm missed.'

As she turned the latch, Fọlárìn's hand closed over hers. 'Please don't go like this.' His voice softened. 'I apologise. I shouldn't have said that. Don't end this before it's begun. Give us a chance.'

Ṣìkẹ́mi sagged against him and nodded. An hour later, she was glad the pitch-black darkness gave them excellent cover, ensuring no one recognised them. At the courtyard entrance, they said goodbye and, as she scurried to her room, she reflected on the conundrum: she and Fọlárìn mixed like oil and water, yet both ingredients made a great pot of stew.

Several days later, Ṣìkẹ́mi entered Ẹfúnṣetán's living room and found her deep in conversation with a stranger. Neither noticed her entry, and Ṣìkẹ́mi used the moment to observe them without censure. The man was in his prime, tall and muscular. His *dànṣíkí* hung flat from his shoulders, with no hint of the paunch that graced the bellies of the rich. Ṣìkẹ́mi coughed, and they both looked up. 'Good morning, *Yèyé*.' She knelt to greet her mistress, then stood up.

'So, this is the abomination?'

The unveiled insult shook Ṣìkẹ́mi to the core, and she felt her skin burn in humiliation. No one had called her that before. She assumed this was Kúmúyilò, judging by both the open hostility and his confidence in Ẹfúnṣetán's presence.

Ẹfúnṣetán's eyes lit up as if she was anticipating Ṣìkẹ́mi's response.

But Ṣìkẹ́mi wouldn't be drawn. 'Good morning,' she said to the stranger. She dipped her knee in a slight curtsy, then she kept quiet, waiting for his next move.

Kúmúyilò leaned back in his chair and his eyes travelled over Ṣìkẹ́mi, from head to toe, as if assessing her and finding her wanting. She understood now why the man terrified Ìbidún. Ṣìkẹ́mi returned the favour with a steely, unrelenting glare. This man would not intimidate her. Seconds ticked by. Then, as if sensing her resolve, Kúmúyilò broke the eye contact and resumed the conversation with his mother, as if she wasn't there.

Ṣìkẹ́mi exhaled and used the opportunity to study her new opponent. Attractive enough to turn heads, he carried himself with the arrogance born of wealth and power. His shaved face bore no tribal marks, leaving him with clean, smooth skin, which was unusual. The cruel twist of his lips before he dismissed her hinted at a malevolent nature. She didn't know why he considered her a threat, but there was no mistaking that he didn't want her in Ẹfúnṣetán's household. He reminded her of a snake waiting to strike. She needed eyes at the back of her head around him, she decided.

It was a good thing that she had already started tutoring Ìbidún, who'd bribed another servant to keep watch on Ẹfúnṣetán whenever they practised. They'd found a clearing near the pit latrines. It wasn't the ideal training space, but no one lingered there, which gave them the privacy they needed. Ṣìkẹ́mi had taught her basic moves she could surprise an opponent with. Not enough to cause long-term harm, but enough to enable a quick escape. She hoped for Ìbidún's sake that Fọlárìn was right about Kúmúyilò's fighting skills, because with his size Ìbidún's training so far would make little difference. Perhaps it was time to show her some more sophisticated moves.

THIRTY-FIVE

Ṣìkẹ́mi sneaked into the building and climbed the stairs quietly, hoping Ìbidún was fast asleep. She'd told her she was training alone to maintain her own fitness, but Ìbidún's knowing look said she believed otherwise.

Her weekly meetings with Fọlárìn were usually the high-light of her week, but this meeting hadn't gone to plan. The rumour mill intimated that Kúmúyilò was plotting to kill his mother. Ṣìkẹ́mi wanted to use Kúmúyilò's attack as a smoke-screen to slip away unnoticed, but she hadn't been able to convince Fọlárìn of Kúmúyilò's intentions, let alone plan a joint escape. She was tempted to go it alone, but her previous attempt highlighted the risk, and she didn't want to leave Fọlárìn behind.

She turned the door handle slowly, stepped inside, and came to an abrupt stop. Ìbidún sat on her bed, with knees drawn to her chest, red eyes and a tear-stained face. Ṣìkẹ́mi scrambled onto the bed and wrapped her arms around her. Although initially she had found Ìbidún bothersome, she'd grown fond of her and now treated her like a younger sister, much as Rónkẹ́ had her. Her heart thumped madly. 'What happened?' The silence stretched, and, in the pit of her stomach, she knew. 'Was it Kúmúyilò?'

The girl's head bobbed.

Ṣìkẹ́mi went rigid. 'I'm going to cut his thing off.'

Ìbidún's hiccup morphed into a half-giggle. 'No need for that. I got away by using a move you taught me.'

A smile broke on Ṣìkẹ́mi's face as she rubbed Ìbidún's back in a circular motion. 'Well done! So why are you still crying?'

Ìbidún drew back and wiped her eyes with the edge of her wrapper. 'What if he tells Màmá and she punishes me?'

'Surely Yèyé won't take his word over yours? You are family, after all.'

'He's done it to other girls before. She always sided with him, despite witnesses. And when those girls fell pregnant, she blamed them.'

Ṣìkẹ́mi's optimism dimmed a little, but she donned a brave face. 'Don't worry, he won't tell her. Can you imagine him admitting to anyone that a mere girl outwitted him?'

'He won't tell her that. He'll lie, with the same result.'

'No, he won't, trust me. Now go to sleep. We will sort it out in the morning.'

Ìbidún lay back and folded her arms over her chest. 'Who is he? The man you sneak off to.'

Ṣìkẹ́mi tensed at the sudden change of topic. 'I don't know what you mean.'

Ìbidún's smile was sly. 'Is it Ẹ̀gbọ́n Fọlárìn?'

Ṣìkẹ́mi drew back, stood and paced the room. If Ìbidún knew, who else did?

Ìbidún watched Ṣìkẹ́mi, her face furrowed in concern. 'Don't be cross. I shouldn't have asked.'

Ṣìkẹ́mi eyeballed Ìbidún. Although Ìbidún was chatty with

her, elsewhere she was a model of discretion. She could trust her, she decided.

'Yes. We are from the same village. We were betrothed as children. How did you find out?'

Ìbidún shrugged. 'You told me to watch and listen. Whenever he visits with Kúmúyilò, you seem to glow.'

Ṣìkẹ́mi cringed. Was she that obvious? Knowing the girl would hound her for more, she took charge.

'Go to sleep, Ìbidún. We can talk tomorrow.'

The girl tittered as she rolled on her side. 'It's already tomorrow.' There was silence, followed by a murmur. 'I'm glad I have you on my side.'

Ṣìkẹ́mi frowned as she settled on her lumpy mattress, her mind processing Ìbidún's whispered words. She liked the girl, but her attachment would only complicate matters when she left. Leaving Ìbidún behind at the mercy of Kúmúyilò's whim wasn't ideal, but a few more choice lessons would ensure she could defend herself from anyone. She shifted focus to the other two problems. How did she warn Kúmúyilò off without making a bigger enemy of him, and who else knew about Fọlárìn and her? She'd been so blinded by her emotions that she hadn't taken sufficient precautions, and that could be costly. To reduce suspicion, she would need to avoid visiting Fọlárìn for a while.

'Good afternoon Bàbá.' Ṣìkẹ́mi sounded breathy as she bowed before Chief Ìbikúnlé. She'd sprinted the last few steps to get out of the pelting rain and her wet *dànṣíkí* clung to her curves, making a mockery of her masculine bow.

'Good afternoon, Ṣìkẹ́mi. I see you brought showers of blessings. Are you well? How is your mistress?'

'She is well, Bàbá, as am I.'

The chief offered her a seat and some water. Ṣìkẹ́mi took both and thanked her host. Since hearing whispers of Kúmúyilò's plan, she'd taken her spying role more seriously and visited Ẹfúnṣetán's allies weekly for information that would benefit them both. Ẹfúnṣetán sent the chiefs bags of cowrie shells, from which Ṣìkẹ́mi pilfered small amounts, much as she had from Tinúbú. She might not be a liar, but she had no problems thieving if it served her purpose, and the money would be useful when she escaped.

Ṣìkẹ́mi noticed the chief's unease as he shifted about in his seat, throwing nervous glances at his two sons, playing a game of *ayò* in the corner. Nostalgia flooded her. She had watched her father and uncles play the game so often under the shade of the *dongoyárò* tree in her family courtyard.

The chief coughed. 'Mm, how can I help you today, Ṣìkẹ́mi?'

She took her cue from him. 'Ah, Bàbá. Nothing much. *Yèyé* wanted me to check on your well-being. It's been some days since you last spoke.'

'Ah. Thank her for me, o. As you can see, I am well, and the gods favour me.'

An uncomfortable silence ensued, and Ṣìkẹ́mi took sips of water to fill it. Once she had finished her cup, she stood. 'Bàbá, it's good to know you are well. I shall be on my way, and I will deliver your message to my mistress.'

The chief stood alongside her. 'You know, I haven't been out today. I think I shall take a walk and see my friend up the road.' He addressed his sons. 'Tell your mother I won't be long. I'm going to visit Ifáyẹmí.'

'We will,' they said without looking up.

The chief walked Ṣìkẹ́mi several yards up the road before he stopped and focused his attention on her. 'Ṣìkẹ́mi, a well-trained child only needs half a sentence to make sense of the rest. Are you listening to me?'

'Yes, Bàbá.'

'Good. Tell your mistress the elders say, if the death in your household doesn't kill you, the one outside can't. They also say the backyard is where the enemy dwells, and the betrayer lives inside the house. I have not spoken in half sentences. Do you understand me?'

'Yes Bàbá, I do.'

The chief nodded. Ṣìkẹ́mi thanked him for his wise words and walked back to Ẹfúnṣetán's compound, impervious to life around her. She jumped at a shrill whistle, and stepped back as a battalion of soldiers marched by, teasing the young female traders by the roadside. Ṣìkẹ́mi rolled her eyes at their ribaldry. If she hadn't been in men's clothing, they would have targeted her too. The city heaved with young soldiers, Ìbàdàn having multiplied several times over as people displaced by the wars made it their home. The new warlords, with their grand ideas of building an empire to replace old Ọ̀yọ́, were constantly warring with other Yorùbá cities.

As the soldiers' noises died away, Ṣìkẹ́mi returned to her musings. The chief's words confirmed her suspicions and the rumours. But how did she relay the message to Ẹfúnṣetán, given her own interest lay in the woman's demise? Yet if she didn't, she risked Ẹfúnṣetán finding out she was hiding information, which could complicate matters.

Ṣìkẹ́mi entered the courtyard and ran smack into Kúmúyilò. The hairs on her arms stood to attention as they eyed each other. Ṣìkẹ́mi made the first move. 'You are just the person I hoped to see.'

A slight tightening of Kúmúyilò's mouth showed he doubted that. He crossed his arms. 'Does my mother know you trained her maid to defend herself?'

Ṣìkẹ́mi hadn't expected the directness. 'That maid is your cousin. Does your mother know you attacked her?'

Kúmúyilò shrugged his shoulders. 'You can tell her, but she won't believe you.'

'I would not tempt the gods if I were you. Trust me when I tell you she will believe me. I don't care what you do with anyone else, but leave that child alone.'

She went to walk past him, and he grabbed her arm. Ṣìkẹ́mi braced and drew herself tall. She looked him in the eye. 'Unless you want to put your combat training to the test, I suggest you take your hands off me.'

The quick lift of Kúmúyilò's brow showed his surprise that she knew about his training, but he held her for a moment longer, his eyes challenging. His fingers drummed a light beat on her upper arm. 'Words are like eggs. Once they break, you can't put them back together. You should watch what you say to me, as I'll soon be in charge here.' He thrust her away.

'Thank you,' Ṣìkẹ́mi said, and a look of confusion crossed his face, not knowing he had unwittingly given her the confirmation she needed.

Later that night, Ṣìkẹ́mi relayed the exchange to Ìbidún, whose eyes grew rounder by the second. Even though she didn't tell her about Kúmúyilò's last threat, the girl's next words confirmed what she knew.

'You shouldn't have said anything. Now he will come after you.'

'Don't worry about me. I can take care of myself. Besides, I am a slave. I do not matter to anyone.'

'You matter to me, and I don't want anything to happen to you.'

'It won't. I promise.'

Ìbidún twiddled her thumbs idly for a while. Then she cast Ṣìkẹ́mi a side glance. 'You know he's not even a blood relative.'

'Kúmúyilò?'

'Uh-uh. No one knows who his family is. A hunter in Màmá's family found him at the base of an Ìrókò tree and brought him to Màmá, who had just lost her daughter. He is cursed, that one, and he will be the end of her.'

Ṣìkẹ́mi suspected Ìbidún had heard the rumours, too. 'All we can do is keep our eyes and ears open and stay one step ahead of him.'

She hadn't figured out how yet, and she needed to speak to Fọlárìn soon.

Ṣìkẹ́mi picked up a bucket and pretended she was heading for the bathroom. At the compound's perimeter, she gave Múfútàò a quick nod, dropped the bucket and slipped out. A few minutes later, she knocked on the door of their rendezvous venue; Fọlárìn opened it and pulled her in. Once their initial pleasantries were over, Ṣìkẹ́mi turned serious, because she really needed to convince him this time.

'Fọlárìn, I'm afraid I have bad news to share.' She explained the chief's warning, Kúmúyilò's attack on Ìbidún and what he'd said when she challenged him, and, as she spoke, Fọlárìn shook his head repeatedly. When she finished speaking Fọlárìn remained silent.

'You must have seen signs of his cruelty over the years. You can't tell me you didn't know he molested the slave girls.'

'I think you misunderstand him. And the girls are slaves.'

Ṣìkẹ́mi rounded on him. 'What? You mean like you and me?'

'Of course not. You are different.'

'Tell me how. Because I can defend myself? So defenceless women are fair targets? I thought better of you than this.'

Fọlárìn looked shamefaced. 'I'm sorry. I wasn't thinking. But I really don't think he's as bad as you paint him to be.'

'Why are you so blinded by loyalty that you can't see the truth? He will attack his mother and I won't wait to see what happens afterwards, so you'll need to pick a side.'

Ṣìkẹ́mi made to leave, but Fọlárìn drew her into his arms, his hands kneading the skin up and down her back, soothing her anger away. For a while she remained rigid, then time seemed to stop as Fọlárìn leaned forward and his lips met hers questioningly. As she leaned into the caress, Ṣìkẹ́mi felt herself come alive. Her body pulsated with need, and she thought her heart would burst. Her fingers explored his face, his head, everywhere. He pulled her forward, and they tumbled onto the bed. Before she could think, they were engaged in intimate acts she'd never imagined possible. She paused for a moment and voiced her concern at the potential ramifications of what they were doing.

'Don't worry, I will take care of it,' he whispered in her ear, and the world righted itself.

Minutes later, in the afterglow, she lay replete, surprised at the wonder of what she'd experienced. Just thinking about it still made her tingle. She rolled onto her side to look at Fọlárìn and her mouth dropped open. He was fast asleep, head lolled to one side, gently snoring.

Carefully, she left the bed, and as she dressed a coldness invaded her limbs, despite the room's stuffy heat. Part of her understood Fọlárìn's reluctance to admit what he must know to be true, because that meant acknowledging the coming change. But she was done trying to convince him. It was time for him to choose his own path. She tiptoed to the door, turned, drank in the sight before leaving.

THIRTY-SIX

'Ẹkáasàn. Ṣé dada ni?'

Ṣìkẹ́mi heard Ẹfúnṣetán long before she came into view. Her mistress sat resplendent in a brown velour wrapper and *gèlè* on the house's front veranda, calling out felicitations to acquaintances who passed by. A slave stood by, fanning her with a raffia fan. On a stool beside her, Ìbidún's fingers worked, deftly shelling melon seeds, which would be grounded and made into *ẹ̀gúsí* soup, a favourite of Ẹfúnṣetán's, later.

Ṣìkẹ́mi approached and knelt. '*Ẹkú ílé, Yèyé.*' She was returning from Chief Fábùnmi, who wouldn't look at her as he took Ẹfúnṣetán's generous bribe. Something was definitely up.

Shrewd eyes appraised her. 'Kú àbọ̀ o. I hope you have useful information today?'

Ṣìkẹ́mi nodded. For weeks, she'd fobbed Ẹfúnṣetán off, unsure of how much to share of what she'd learned, and it was clear her patience was running thin. If she didn't stop prevaricating, the woman would march off and confront her allies herself. She came clean. 'Yes, *Yèyé.* I have a message from Chief Ìbikúnlé.' She'd decided to share the man's proverbs.

Ẹfúnṣetán rose. 'Come, let's go inside and talk.'

Ṣikẹmi followed Ẹfúnṣetán to her living room, which was better decorated than her bedroom. Ṣikẹmi suspected that was because she hosted the chiefs in it often.

Ẹfúnṣetán sat down in a comfortable armchair. 'I'm listening.'

Ṣikẹmi knelt and delivered the message exactly as she had heard it six weeks earlier. Ẹfúnṣetán sat back in her chair for several seconds, then a speculative gleam entered her eyes. 'Who do you think he's referring to?'

Ṣikẹmi wasn't falling for that. '*Yèyé*, it could be anyone. They say all lizards lie with their tummy to the ground, so we don't know which ones have a bellyache. It could be any family member.'

'Or servant or slave like you,' came the sharp rejoinder.

Ṣikẹmi rocked back on her heels. She held up her hands. '*Yèyé*, my hands are clean. Perhaps you should consult the Ifá priest to shed some more light on the matter.'

But Ẹfúnṣetán wasn't done. 'I heard you've been teaching Ìbidún to fight behind my back. What is that for, if you don't wish me harm?'

A bowl clattered to the floor in the corridor. Ìbidún rushed in and knelt before Ẹfúnṣetán. 'Màmá, forgive me. That was my doing. I asked *Ẹ̀gbọ́n* to teach me so I could protect myself from unwanted attention. I didn't mean to upset you.'

'Who's been bothering you?' Ẹfúnṣetán barked.

Ìbidún flinched but held her nerve. 'No one in particular. The city is swarming with soldiers, and I'm out on errands often.'

Ẹfúnṣetán lifted a sardonic eyebrow at Ṣikẹmi. 'Is this true?'

'Yes, *Yèyé*, it is,' Ṣikẹmi said.

Ẹfúnṣetán tried to outstare her. Ṣikẹmi held the gaze. The Yorùbás had a saying. *In the eyes, you find the true discernment of words.* Ẹfúnṣetán seemed satisfied. 'All right, but we have to be vigilant.'

Ṣìkẹ́mi pressed her lips together. She couldn't agree more. Ẹfúnṣetán's attack on her had caught her by surprise, and, in future, she wouldn't be sharing bad news, she decided.

The last two months in Ẹfúnṣetán's household had been uneventful, yet an air of imminent disaster hovered over the compound like the smell of rotten eggs. Ṣìkẹ́mi lost count of how many times she passed whispering servants, who stopped and pretended to be busy. Her proximity to Ẹfúnṣetán alienated her from most of them, and Ṣìkẹ́mi couldn't blame them, since she'd done little to foster any deep relationships bar those with Múfútàò and Ìbidún.

An afternoon of exercise left her hot and sweaty, so she strolled to her room for a quick change of clothing and found Ìbidún staring into space. Ẹfúnṣetán, in bed, recuperating from a recent fever, had reduced her demands on Ṣìkẹ́mi, but doubled Ìbidún's work. The girl looked like she carried the universe's weight on her flimsy shoulders. 'How are you?' she asked.

Ìbidún shrugged. 'I'm all right. You know how she is. She's asleep now.'

'Shall we stroll to the market together?'

'What, now?'

Ṣìkẹ́mi shrugged. 'Why not? You've not left her room for days. It will be good to stretch your legs and get some air.'

Half an hour later, they entered Òjé market, the oldest in the city, named after a Yorùbá sub-tribe who had emigrated south after the empire collapsed. A canopy of corrugated-iron sheets topped the stalls far into the horizon, providing much-needed shade for the swarms of traders and customers. As they strode down a wide lane of vegetable stalls, the fragrant smell of fresh mint hit Ṣìkẹ́mi's nostrils, transporting her back to her mother's courtyard. For a minute she revelled in the memory of her màmá making vegetable stew, until Ìbidún's words cut through the market din. '*Ẹ̀gbọ́n*, are you all right?'

Ṣìkẹ́mi blinked, realising she'd stopped, but a few strides caught her up. 'Don't mind me. I was somewhere else. Tell me, what are the servants saying about Kúmúyilò and *Yèyé* these days? I can tell something is going on.'

Ìbidún gave her a cautious glance before answering. 'They think he is going to attack her soon.'

Ṣìkẹ́mi took a deep breath. 'May I ask why you've not told her?'

'What's the point? She won't believe evil of him, and you saw what happened when you delivered Ìbikúnlẹ́'s message. I'm not letting her accuse me.'

'If she dies, life will be difficult under Kúmúyilò. Have you thought of that?'

'I'm not staying here. I'm going with you.'

The girl knew she was leaving. Ṣìkẹ́mi shook her head. 'You can't do that.'

Ìbidún opened her mouth.

'Wait, let me finish. I'll be a fugitive, possibly for the rest of my life. I may never settle down among my kin. You don't want to live like that, moving frequently, afraid of capture. Why don't you go back to your family in Abeokuta?'

'I've got no one there who cares about me. Both my parents are dead.'

Ṣìkẹ́mi did a double-take. 'You never said so.'

Ìbidún shrugged. 'I don't like to talk about it.' She was silent for a while, then she spoke. 'Where will you go when you leave?'

'Òkẹ́-Ọ̀dán, where my family is, at least to start with.'

Ìbidún's brows dipped inwards. 'That's funny. Someone visited Madam with Kúmúyilò a few days ago. I'm sure they mentioned Òké-Ọ̀dán.'

Ṣìkẹ́mi's heart skipped a beat. 'Really? What happened after?'

'Nothing, they left together.'

Ṣìkẹ́mi mulled over Ìbidún's revelation, wondering what business Kúmúyilò had with Òké-Ọ̀dán. For a second, she visualised a grown-up Kúnlé, then dismissed the thought. He couldn't possibly be friends with Kúmúyilò. She could find out by asking Fọlárìn, but she hadn't seen him since the night they were intimate, and she wasn't keen on doing so any time soon.

'I am still coming with you when you leave,' Ìbidún said.

Ṣìkẹ́mi winced. 'Shall we discuss it again later? Look! We've walked the entire length of the market. Let's buy some food on our way back.' She led Ìbidún to a citrus fruits stall and picked up a sweet orange, bouncing it in her hands. Introduced by the Europeans, they grew larger and juicier than the African cherry oranges nestling beside them.

'How much are the white man's oranges?'

'Four cowrie shells a basket,' the stall owner said.

Ṣìkẹ́mi shook her head. 'One.'

'Ha! *Ẹ̀gbọ́n*. That's too little. Two, please.'

Ṣìkẹ́mi turned and walked away.

The vendor sighed. '*Óyá*, come and buy!'

Ṣìkẹ́mi returned and exchanged a cowrie for a basket. It wasn't often that she bought things – she often relied on her owners' groceries – but it was good to know she could still haggle with the best of them.

Ṣìkẹ́mi's heart raced as she surveyed the terrifying band of masqueraders encircling her. She'd escaped the sea only to face this

*additional threat. The bare-chested masqueraders wore grotesque
masks smeared with streaks of blood and billowy raffia skirts that
jiggled up and down as they stamped their feet. The masks'
slanted eyeholes and grilled mouths added a touch of menace to
the ensemble. Belled anklets round each bare foot produced a
dissonant chime that mingled with the racket from the trampling
feet, forcing Ṣìkẹ́mi to cover her ears with her hands.*

*Every time Ṣìkẹ́mi tried to break out of the circle, the glis-
tening chests closed in around her, pushing her back. An
unbidden terror gripped her throat, and she froze as their leader
advanced and inched his face into hers. Suddenly, he tore off his
mask. Ṣìkẹ́mi opened her mouth and screamed.*

Ṣìkẹ́mi jackknifed upright. Her hand clawed at her throat as she
tried suppressing the overwhelming queasiness in her stomach.
She scrambled off her bed, but, before she could reach the
bedpan Ìbidún kept under her bed for night emergencies, her
stomach heaved. She clamped a hand over her mouth and
snagged the pan just as its contents came spilling out.

'Are you all right?' Ìbidún, who was asleep minutes earlier,
hovered beside her, her eyes seeking assurance.

Ṣìkẹ́mi swiped a hand over her mouth, pushed the pan
under her own bed and lay back down. She couldn't remember
the last time she felt this grotty. She checked her forehead with
the back of her hand, but it didn't feel unduly warm, so it
couldn't be fever. What had she eaten the night before? Had
someone tried to poison her? Ìbidún, whose eyes were latched
on the wall etchings beside Ṣìkẹ́mi's bed, showed no signs of
being ill.

'Ẹ̀gbọ́n,' Ìbidún said, 'when did you last see your thing of
the month?'

Transfixed, Ṣìkẹ́mi did the calculation and, in the deafening

silence that followed, the answer hanging on both their lips led
to a new stark realisation.

Ṣìkẹ́mi rolled off the bed clutching her stomach, past the
metal pan holding the vomit that had prompted the question in
the first place. She needed air. Air to breathe and think. She
staggered to the wooden window, opened it and peered
unseeing into the dark, dusty courtyard outside. Like a
drowning person, she dragged in breath after breath, in, out, in
again. A darkness threatened, but she couldn't let it pull her
under.

Fọlárìn did this.

No. You did this. You both did.

Could she avoid Ẹfúnṣetán's death sentence? The woman
always beheaded her pregnant slaves.

You've cheated death before. You can do it again.

Ìbidún joined her at the window, putting a comforting
hand on her shoulder as Ṣìkẹ́mi gulped at the air. A lightness
overcame her, and her last thought as she succumbed to the
darkness was, 'Can one breathe too much air?'

Ṣìkẹ́mi came to on the floor with an anxious Ìbidún
alternatively sprinkling water on her face, then fanning it away.
'What happened?' she asked.

'You fainted.'

A baffled frown snaked across her face, then it all came
crashing back. She slapped her head with both hands. *'Orí mi o!*
What have you done?'

'I don't think you can blame your *orí* for this predicament,
Ẹ̀gbọ́n.'

Ignoring Ìbidún's smirk, she clambered across the room to
the etchings. She'd used the method to monitor her cycle long
before she learned to read and write, and the habit had stuck.

She scanned the chalk markings, each row of six vertical marks crossed with a single diagonal mark, as the nausea threatened again. In her entire life, she'd never been late. Six weeks overdue, she surmised, which gave her a maximum of two months to solve the problem before she began to show. She plunked herself on the edge of her bed.

Ìbidún offered her a clay bowl of water, which she sipped, gargled and spat into the pan. Then she poured some in her palm and rinsed her face. Somehow, that made her feel better.

'What are you going to do?' Ìbidún pressed. 'I know a herbalist who can help.'

Ṣìkẹ́mi wondered how the girl knew so much despite her young age. Then she realised Ìbidún must have known some of the women in the household who had faced this situation before. They both knew her options were limited. Escape, abort the child, or die. She couldn't escape until Kúmúyilò killed his mother. She rejected the other option, since this could be her only chance to have a child. Someone to love and who would love her back unconditionally. 'I need time to think. To process this,' she said.

Their eyes met, Ìbidún's pensive. Time was the one luxury she didn't have. If the other slaves discovered her secret, death would come swifter than an eagle's dive. She clasped her head in her hands once more, hoping for clarity. Starting a romance with Fọlárìn had been a mistake; the flirting, the come-hither looks. She should have ignored the spark, the way his nose flared when he looked at her hips and how his glances made her blood sing. They both knew the penalty for getting pregnant. But he had promised to take care of it. He was supposed to have spilled his seed on the ground.

The voice in her head taunted. *That's what you get when you rely on men's promises.* After years of rigid self-discipline, why did she lower her guard? Because he was a part of her elusive past and she'd longed for the company of someone who valued her as a woman, not a warrior slave. And look at where that had led her.

Unable to bear the circling thoughts, she lay down and curled up under her cover, but her thoughts returned to the dream, which had taken on a new form. What truly terrified her was that the face she'd seen staring back at her after the masquerader unmasked himself was her brother's. Ṣìkẹ́mi prayed with all her might that he was safe, because she couldn't imagine escaping only to find her family incomplete.

Exhausted, she popped her head up and addressed Ìbidún. 'Please tell *Yèyé* I am unwell.' She lay down once more and closed her eyes. Tomorrow would take care of itself, she decided.

THIRTY-SEVEN

A gentle shake of the shoulder roused Ṣìkẹ́mi from sleep. She yawned, stretched and sat up. 'What time of day is it?' she asked as Ìbidún handed her a cup.

'We've just had our afternoon meal. I told Màmá you are unwell, so you don't have to worry about getting up today.'

Ṣìkẹ́mi eyed the concoction. 'What is this?' It smelt as evil as it looked.

'It's something to keep the retching at bay.'

Ṣìkẹ́mi sipped, and the instinct to gag overwhelmed her. 'This tastes terrible.' Not wanting to prolong the torture, she paused, took a deep breath, and slurped the rest in one go. She hoped the medicine would help her get back on her feet before the servants' tongues started wagging. Her lower limbs felt heavy. She swung them off the bed and made a cautious effort to stand. The room swam, mirroring the tumbling in her stomach. She collapsed back on the bed and puffed. 'Surely this malady can't just be because I'm with child. Women do this effortlessly every day, so what's wrong with me?'

Ìbidún gave her a sympathetic smile. 'Some women have it

worse than others. The medicine will work soon, and you'll feel better. Shall I bring you some *àkàmù*?'

Ṣìkẹ́mi shook her head and lay back down, her brain once more focused on her predicament. 'I could beg *Yèyé*'s forgiveness. Perhaps she would let me live. I saved her life once.' She knew the answer to her voiced thoughts even before Ìbidún spoke.

'A debt she repaid by bringing you here instead of letting Madam Tinúbú sell or kill you. She has killed slaves for less and, if she let you live, she'd be giving others permission to follow suit.'

Ṣìkẹ́mi's eyes searched Ìbidún's. 'I don't know what to do.'

'*Ẹ̀gbọ́n*, one more day of thinking won't do you any harm.'

Ṣìkẹ́mi nodded, settled back into bed and pulled her sleep cover over her head.

Three days later, Ṣìkẹ́mi was still in bed, and Ìbidún hovered over her in between attending to Ẹfúnṣetán's needs. 'You need to eat,' she said, offering Ṣìkẹ́mi a bowl of *àkàmù*. But Ṣìkẹ́mi burrowed deeper underneath her cover, trying to shut out the world for just one more day.

'*Ẹ̀gbọ́n*, this is unlike you. You are a warrior. Get up and fight for your child.'

The words washed over Ṣìkẹ́mi.

'The servants are whispering and Màmá is getting impatient with your absence.'

Ìbidún's warning on the third night penetrated Ṣìkẹ́mi's fog. The idle chatter of the slaves and servants would cause untold harm if she didn't act. Ìbidún had told them she was suffering from fever, but most fevers lasted three days or less.

The next morning, she woke to sunshine streaming into the

bedroom. It was probably mid-morning, and she was alone. She swung her feet over the edge of the bed, then paused, checking if the rolling sickness would hit again. It didn't, thanks to the concoction Ìbidún kept plying her with, and she heaved a sigh. She sent a silent thank-you to the gods for sending Ìbidún her way. After giving herself a pep talk, she considered her options. She was determined to keep the child, whether or not Fọlárìn wanted to be involved. But he had a right to know, and it might influence his decisions. With her thoughts settled, she rose, ready to begin her day.

'Pẹ̀lẹ. Are your bones stronger?' As she wandered through the courtyard, everyone Ṣìkẹ́mi met asked the same question. She thanked them for their well wishes as she strolled by, testing her physical strength and mentally preparing herself for the days ahead. The fresh air felt wonderful on her skin, and she lifted her face to catch the early-afternoon sunrays, glad she'd made the effort. From the corner of her eye, she spied Múfútàò, patrolling a section of the compound. She walked towards him, intent on making contact.

'Tonight,' she said, when she was close enough to ensure no one would overhear her.

He gave a slight head-shake. 'They will both be here tonight.'

Ṣìkẹ́mi kept her voice low. 'Can you arrange for me to speak to him here, while Kúmúyilò is dining with *Yèyé*?'

Múfútàò inclined his head. 'I'll try.'

Ṣìkẹ́mi swallowed, smiled and walked on. Refreshed from the short walk, she presented herself to Ẹfúnṣetán, who was entertaining representatives of the market women's league. She entered the room, and silence descended as several goggle-eyed women tracked her approach. Ṣìkẹ́mi prayed her belly would behave and she wouldn't embarrass herself. She knelt in greeting.

'*Pèlé o*! Are you feeling much better?'

'Yes, *Yèyé*. I am. Thank you for letting me rest.'

Ẹfúnṣetán looked her over as if to reassure herself that Ṣìkẹ́mi was well indeed. 'Since you feel better, could you check on Chief Fákórede and Chief Ifáyẹmí? Ìbidún just left for your room. She was going to do it, but I'd rather you did.'

Ṣìkẹ́mi excused herself. She wondered whether she was up to traipsing around town, but realised she had to unless she wanted to arouse suspicion. On her way to her room, she noticed the queasiness had eased. It was probably nerves at seeing Ẹfúnṣetán for the first time in days. She found Ìbidún on the verge of leaving. '*Yèyé* wants me to deliver the message,' she said, as she picked up the satchel at Ìbidún's feet.

'Are you well enough?' Ìbidún asked without looking at her. 'I'm happy to do it.'

'Yes, I am, thanks to you. I took a short walk before talking to *Yèyé*. I feel stronger.'

'All right,' Ìbidún said, with her gaze fixed on the floor.

Ṣìkẹ́mi glanced at the floor, wondering what Ìbidún found so riveting. Baffled, she eyed the girl, taking in the droopy shoulders and clenched jaw. 'What's the matter? You look like someone died.'

Ìbidún kept her eyes down and twisted her hands.

'Ìbidún. Please tell me what the problem is?'

After several moments of twiddling her thumbs, she sighed. '*Ẹ̀gbọ́n*, let's wait until you are back.'

Ṣìkẹ́mi tapped her feet against the floor. 'Ìbidún, I'll spend the rest of the afternoon worrying about whatever this is. Just tell me now.'

Ìbidún flopped onto her bed. 'Do you remember I told you

about the man who visited with Kúmúyilò and talked about
Òké-Òdán?'

Sìkẹ́mi nodded, encouraging her to continue.

Ìbidún moistened her lips.

'Ìbidún, just say it.'

'He's your brother, and Kúmúyilò has imprisoned him. I
heard him telling Yèyé when he visited her this morning. They
are keeping him as a means of controlling you.'

The satchel dropped and Sìkẹ́mi's mouth fell open. 'Kúnlé?' She took a step towards Ìbidún and stopped. 'Are you sure?'

Ìbidún stared at her with a look akin to pity.

Sìkẹ́mi flopped onto her bed as the new situation sank in. If
Ìbidún's information was accurate, she couldn't leave without
her brother. It also explained the last twist in her dream. But
why would he search for her in Ìbàdàn? Then she remembered
Fọlárìn saying he'd sent a message to her family. Perhaps he'd
come looking for Fọlárìn? Fọlárìn would have told her,
unless... he didn't know! She kneaded the back of her head
where a headache was forming. Her life just kept getting more
bizarre.

She picked the satchel off the floor.

'Where are you going?' Ìbidún sounded worried.

'I need to think. I might as well do it while I run the
errand.' Quietly, Sìkẹ́mi let herself out.

By the time Sìkẹ́mi had completed her errands, she was certain
of one thing – she needed to speak to Fọlárìn. Only he could
provide insight on where Kúmúyilò might have stashed her
brother. She asked Ẹfúnṣetán to excuse her from attending to
dinner on the pretext that she hadn't fully recovered, and the
afternoon's errands had tired her more than she expected.

Ẹfúnṣetán dismissed her and instructed her to be ready for work in the morning.

Later that evening, as Ẹfúnṣetán dined with her son, Ṣìkẹ́mi waited for Múfútáò's message. A young slave soon knocked and informed Ṣìkẹ́mi that Múfútáò wanted her in the courtyard. She rewarded the child with a cowrie shell, accompanied by strict instructions not to tell anyone about it.

Outside, Múfútáò signalled that Ṣìkẹ́mi should leave the courtyard and, just beyond the exit, she found Fọlárìn waiting. 'Come,' he said, leading her to their usual meeting place.

'Won't Kúmúyilò wonder where you are?' she asked.

'I told him I felt unwell.'

Once they had privacy, Ṣìkẹ́mi braced herself. 'I am with child,' she said bluntly, knowing there was no easy way to deliver her news.

Fọlárìn staggered to a chair and sat, his eyes wide. 'You are sure?'

'Yes, and there's more. I'm not sure how they met, but Kúmúyilò has imprisoned my brother. I know it's a lot to consider. So, when you've processed this, if you have any insights on locating Kúnlé, please let me know.' She stood and left without waiting for a response.

As she strode to Ẹfúnṣetán's compound, Ṣìkẹ́mi took in the sights. Night-time rendered most neighbourhoods pitch black. However, here, some of the wealthier households mounted torches on their perimeter walls like a homing beacon, and as the tongues of fire danced in the breeze they warmed Ṣìkẹ́mi's heart. They reminded her of her stints in the forest, where she had relied on fire for warmth and protection. She'd survived so much in her young life, and she wasn't giving up now. If it was her last mission on earth, she would rescue her brother.

Instead of returning to her room, she hid in a courtyard nook until servants brought Ẹfúnṣetán's dirty plates out to be washed. Kúmúyilò always used the back courtyard exit, and he soon appeared in the doorway. Ṣìkẹ́mi watched him shiver and draw his dànṣíkí closer, as if to ward off the cold. Then he moved, taking long strides towards the exit. She moved fast, beating him to it, and melded into the shadows beyond the guards' sight. She had no intentions of harming him yet but, just in case, she followed him until they were far enough that no one would hear his shouts if he cried for help.

'I heard you are holding someone calling himself my brother.'

Kúmúyilò's steps slowed, and he turned round. 'Ṣìkẹ́mi, why are you stalking me like a thief in the night?' His eyes narrowed, and he tucked his hand in his pocket.

Ṣìkẹ́mi watched him just in case he was reaching for a weapon. 'You should let the poor soul go, because my brother died many years ago.'

'Are you sure?' He pulled out his hand and stretched it towards her. 'The man who came looking for you claimed you gave him this. Do you recognise it? He said you would.'

Ṣìkẹ́mi reached for the bracelet, and she couldn't stop the tiny gasp of recognition that flew out of her lips. It was the bracelet her mother had given her; the one she gave Kúnlé the day before raiders ransacked their village.

A triumphant gleam entered Kúmúyilò's eyes, and his voice hardened. 'Stay out of my way and my business, or you'll never see your brother again.' He turned and disappeared into the shadows, leaving a stunned Ṣìkẹ́mi in his wake.

THIRTY-EIGHT

Kúmúyilò moved at such a pace that Ṣìkẹ́mi thought his heels were on fire. He slowed and glanced over his shoulder, forcing Ṣìkẹ́mi to duck behind a stranger to avoid being seen. The woman gave Ṣìkẹ́mi a suspicious glare, but Ṣìkẹ́mi ignored her. She could just about see Kúmúyilò's cap in the distance, so she picked up speed to avoid losing him. She wanted to know his destination.

It had been two weeks since she told Fọlárìn about Kúnlé and the child, and she hadn't heard from him since. She'd tried to monitor Kúmúyilò when she wasn't running errands, but so far had learned nothing about Kúnlé's whereabouts. She'd checked Ẹfúnṣetán's dungeons without success.

Ṣìkẹ́mi had been walking by his house on her return from an errand when she spotted Kúmúyilò leaving. The shifty way he kept looking over his shoulder caught her attention, and on the spur of the moment she followed him, hoping to discover something that might aid her cause.

Kúmúyilò's steps slowed as he reached his destination, and it didn't surprise Ṣìkẹ́mi to see him slip into the general's compound. If the general was sponsoring Kúmúyilò's treachery, Ẹfúnṣetán didn't stand a chance. She hurried after him. At the entrance to the general's compound, she met an unfamiliar guard. So, with a brazen smile, she squared up to him. 'I'm with Madam Ẹfúnṣetán's son.'

The guard didn't return her smile, but after a moment's hesitation he let her in. In the distance, the edge of Kúmúyilò's *dànṣíkí* disappeared into the general's courtyard and Ṣìkẹ́mi suspected he was heading to the general's meeting room. At the courtyard entrance, she met another guard. This one recognised her, and, just in case she needed help later, with a wink she palmed a small bag of cowries into his hand as she passed by. In the slaves' and servants' world, money was key.

At this point, Ṣìkẹ́mi ran out of ideas. She needed to eavesdrop on the meeting room conversations, but following Kúmúyilò was not an option. She reassessed the situation, noticing the window in the meeting room's end wall and the tiny alleyway between that wall and the adjacent block. It made for the perfect hiding spot.

Ṣìkẹ́mi skirted back the way she came, nodding to the guard at the courtyard's entrance. He gave her a puzzled, but nonchalant, glance. Outside, she strode down the length of the wall towards the gap between the buildings, which provided another entrance into the courtyard. She hoped any guard watching that section would be just as amenable, because disarming him would cause a commotion she'd rather avoid. To her relief, the area was empty of guards, and she crouched under the window as the conversation filtered out towards her.

'So when will you act?'

Ṣìkẹ́mi's head snapped back as she recognised Bàbá Fábùnmi's voice.

'In three days. I have put two trusted slaves on it,' Kúmúyilò said.

'What about Ṣìkẹ́mi's brother? Do you still want me to hold him?'

That voice belonged to Chief Ifáyẹmí. The snake. He was manipulating both sides, and no wonder she hadn't been able to find Kúnlé in Ẹfúnṣetán's dungeons. Even so, she was relieved. Ifáyẹmí's only interest was money, so it might be easier to secure Kúnlé's freedom than she had first thought. She tuned back in to the conversation.

'Yes, for now. I haven't decided his fate yet.'

'You are sure the plan will work, and the slaves won't betray you?' the general asked.

'I have promised them their freedom, something they can't get otherwise.'

A silence filled the air, followed by shuffling feet. Ṣìkẹ́mi wondered which slaves Kúmúyilò had bribed, but she had all the information she needed. She crouched through the alleyway and left.

Five minutes into her walk, a shoulder tap made her spin round. Her shoulders relaxed, and she eyed Fọlárìn, who didn't look too well compared to the last time they had met.

'We need to talk,' he said.

She cocked her head. 'You've had two weeks to talk. Why now?'

'I know. I'll explain later. You were right about Kúmúyilò, and I've discovered your brother's location.'

'As have I. So, there's nothing to talk about.'

'Ṣìkẹ́mi, listen to me for once in your life. Meet me tonight.'

Ṣìkẹ́mi went rigid. She closed her eyes and took a deep breath, ready to bellow at him. When she opened her eyes, he was gone. She stood there shaking in disbelief, then fumed all the way back to Ẹfúnṣetán's compound. The nerve of the man; ordering her about after two weeks of inaction.

. . .

Birds chirped; cicada beetles sang. The rainy season was at its peak and the showers had returned, leaving Ṣìkẹ́mi completely at home as she trudged through the forest. Madam was visiting friends in a nearby town, so for the past two nights she'd sneaked out to stash a few weapons on her intended route out of the city. Ṣìkẹ́mi believed the gods were smiling on her because Múfútàò was on night duty that week.

The last few raindrops fizzled away, leaving the forest sounds less muted, and her feet squelched as they moved through the muddy forest floor. She paused, thinking she heard a faint echo of footsteps. The scene was eerily similar to when she had left Tinúbú. She shook her head. Her brain must be playing tricks on her.

The forest floor crackled again and Ṣìkẹ́mi tensed. She ducked behind a tree and pulled out her sword from its scabbard. At the next footstep, she whirled forward and stood facing her shocked would-be attacker – Ìbidún. The girl clasped her throat in utter terror. Ṣìkẹ́mi sheathed her sword. Then she grabbed Ìbidún's arms and shook her hard.

'I could have killed you! What were you thinking?'

The girl's teeth clattered. 'I'm sorry. I thought... you were leaving me behind.'

The air whooshed out of Ṣìkẹ́mi, and she let go of Ìbidún. Her own heart thundered as if she'd just done a sprint. The girl was supposed to have gone with Ẹfúnṣetán, but she'd said she was unwell. 'You can't just follow me like that. It's too dangerous, and I wasn't leaving. I was just preparing and stashing some weapons along the route.'

Ìbidún's eyes widened as she took in the assortment of weapons peeking out of the sack slung over Ṣìkẹ́mi's shoulders. The money Ṣìkẹ́mi had pilfered from Ẹfúnṣetán and the little she'd brought from Abẹ́òkúta had been handy.

'Promise me you'll never do that again. You'll need to

follow my instructions while we are here. Your survival depends on it.'

Ìbídún's shudders had abated now that Ṣìkẹ́mi had released her. 'I promise,' she said.

Ṣìkẹ́mi closed her eyes and breathed deeply, trying to regain some calm.

'Where are we going?' Ìbídún asked.

Ṣìkẹ́mi rolled her eyes. 'We are there, actually.'

'Oh.'

Ṣìkẹ́mi bet she wasn't expecting that.

'So, what do we do now?'

'We dig.' They were at the base of a large ùbé tree and Ṣìkẹ́mi threw her the hand spade she had brought along. While Ìbídún dug, Ṣìkẹ́mi reorganised her plans. When the hole was big enough, she placed an assortment of knives and a spare sword wrapped in cotton in it.

Ìbídún eyed the bundle. 'What about your other sword?'

'We can't traipse around here without protection.' She shook her head in despair and Ìbídún looked sheepish. 'Come on. Let's cover this and return to town.'

When they were close to Ẹfúnṣetán's compound, Ṣìkẹ́mi stopped. 'Go on home. I will be along shortly. I need to do something first.'

Ṣìkẹ́mi watched Ìbídún's mouth firm into a mutinous pout that reminded her of her younger self.

'I'm staying with you.'

Ṣìkẹ́mi suspected she had feigned the illness to keep tabs on her. She shook her head. 'Fọlárìn asked me to meet him. That's where I am going.'

Ìbídún shrugged. 'I'm coming with you.'

Ṣìkẹ́mi sighed. 'Fine, it's getting late. Let's go.'

As they neared the meeting point, Ṣìkẹ́mi thought she heard someone following them. She pulled Ìbídún into an alleyway and hushed her to silence. She waited a few seconds, then stepped into the street, but she saw no one she recognised, and nothing seemed suspicious. She grasped Ìbidún's hand, and they hurried to their destination.

Fọlárìn's brows lifted when he saw Ṣìkẹ́mi and Ìbidún, but he masked his surprise quickly and offered them seats. Ìbidún sat next to Ṣìkẹ́mi, her gaze flitting back and forth between her and Fọlárìn.

Fọlárìn coughed, the sound tinged with embarrassment. Ṣìkẹ́mi helped him out. 'She caught me hiding weapons in the forest and won't let me out of her sight. You'll have to speak in front of her.' She lifted and dropped her shoulders.

Fọlárìn breathed in deeply, as if preparing for battle. 'I apologise for not believing you earlier. I find it hard to believe anyone would actually want to kill their own parent.' Then, realising what he had said out loud, he clamped his hand over his mouth and stared at Ìbidún in horror.

'It's all right. She already knows Kúmúyilò's plans for *Yèyé*.'

'And she isn't horrified?'

'She's not really Kúmúyilò's mother, and she's never been one to me,' Ìbidún said, trying to be helpful.

Ṣìkẹ́mi rolled her eyes, and Fọlárìn chuckled. 'I guess that explains it. Was I alone in my ignorance? She's given him everything, so it's difficult to understand why he would harm her.'

'Greed,' Ṣìkẹ́mi said. 'So, what changed your mind?'

'I overheard him the night you waylaid him in the alley. I came back to the compound and waited, wanting to talk to him, but you beat me to it. I've spent the last fortnight searching for Kúnlé and he is at—'

'Chief Ifáyẹmí's,' Ìbidún said, and they both turned in surprise.

'How...?'

Ìbidún beamed at them. 'I watch and listen, then, like you, Ẹ̀gbọ́n,' she pointed her fingers at Ṣìkẹ́mi, 'I bribe the right people.'

The girl was a wonder, Ṣìkẹ́mi thought, and far more resourceful than she'd given her credit for.

'So, what now?' Fọlárìn asked.

Ṣìkẹ́mi laid out her thoughts. 'For the right price, Ifáyẹmí will release him. Yèyé will return tomorrow and Kúmúyilò will strike the day after. We'll need to get Kúnlé out of Ifáyẹmí's compound and leave town that night, but we'll need to confirm Yèyé is dead, or she'll pursue us.'

'Why do you think Kúmúyilò won't follow us?' Ìbidún asked.

Fọlárìn raised an eyebrow. 'Us?'

'She wants to leave with me, but I've said no. It won't be safe for her.'

'You still haven't answered my question,' Ìbidún said.

Ṣìkẹ́mi spoke. 'He'll be too busy consolidating his power to find the time, and I'll cause more trouble than I'm worth, whereas Yèyé would be the town's joke if she let a slave run away with no repercussions. She has more to lose.'

'Why can't she come with us?' Fọlárìn asked, gesturing towards Ìbidún.

'Apart from the dangers and difficulties of living on the run, even if Kúmúyilò didn't care, her family might think we kidnapped her for leverage and force Kúmúyilò to track her down.'

Ìbidún stood and glared at Ṣìkẹ́mi. 'I've already told you my parents are dead. I have no siblings, and no one's checked on me since I came here. Why would they now?'

Fọlárìn interjected before things got too heated. 'How about a compromise?' Ṣìkẹ́mi tried to speak, but Fọlárìn held up his hands. 'Hear me out.' He took Ìbidún's hand. 'Ṣìkẹ́mi has taught you enough that you can protect yourself physically. Stay here. Once we're settled and safe, I promise we'll send for you.' His eyes sought Ṣìkẹ́mi's agreement. Ṣìkẹ́mi scowled but nodded reluctantly. It was the best compromise under the circumstances.

Ṣìkẹ́mi gestured to Fọlárìn. 'Back to the real problem; we need to rescue Kúnlé and monitor what's happening at the house simultaneously, so we'll need to split up. I'll monitor the house and you can rescue Kúnlé. Then we can rendezvous at an agreed location.'

'And I'll just sit back and watch,' Ìbidún muttered, her face dark. Then she brightened. 'You've both forgotten something important. What will you do about Màmá, if Kúmúyilò's plan fails?'

There was a long silence, then Ṣìkẹ́mi decided she wasn't discussing killing Ẹfúnṣetán in front of her relative. 'Nothing. We'll know how much threat we'll face in the future and prepare for it.'

'I have something to add,' Fọlárìn said. 'I contacted all the slaves and servants who are loyal to me. They want to come too.'

Surprise lit Ṣìkẹ́mi's face. 'Really? How many?'

'Eight. And they all have some combat training. It will even the odds and give us a fighting chance if we meet resistance on our way out of town.'

Ṣìkẹ́mi nodded. 'Let's end this. I'll catch up with you tomorrow to finalise plans.' She pulled Ìbidún's hand. 'Come on.'

Ìbidún stood reluctantly and stared at Fọlárìn. 'You promise you'll send for me?'

He met her gaze. 'I swear it, in Ifá's name.'

THIRTY-NINE

The waters parted for Ṣìkẹ́mi, much like they did for Mósè in the faith people's holy book, and her feet squelched on the wet, sandy seabed, as she trod to the shore. Then a staircase appeared in the sky. Her heart fled to her mouth as, compelled by an invisible force she found impossible to resist, she took each heavy step upwards. In the clouds, she found herself on a window ledge peering down into Ẹfúnṣetán's bedroom. Ẹfúnṣetán lay sprawled and asleep, her semi-naked body half-shielded by the bedcover as a shadowy figure towered over her. Mesmerised, Ṣìkẹ́mi watched a dagger descend slowly. She urged it on. This was what she wanted; needed; but before the dagger struck its mark, the scene dissolved, and the wind transported her back to the shore.

Ṣìkẹ́mi's eyes flew open, and, after calming her thudding heart, she rose. As she washed, she brooded over the dream. It confirmed Kúmúyilò's impending plan, but the frustrating way it concluded left her wondering whether the plan would fail. Freedom was so close, she could almost taste it, but if Ẹfúnṣetán survived it would shatter her hopes of reunion with her family, because she wouldn't put them at risk. She had to make sure Ẹfúnṣetán died, yet something about that expediency niggled her. With drooping shoulders, she went about her day, the burden she carried weighing her down.

Perhaps it was Ṣìkẹ́mi's imagination, but the entire household also seemed on edge, probably spooked by the mysterious disappearance of the household cats the previous night. The servants had found their bowls full of food in the morning. It didn't help that people believed cats had a sixth sense, which drove them away from home just before their owner's demise. Ṣìkẹ́mi thought neither the servants nor the cats were wrong, given it was the day of Kúmúyilò's planned attack.

Ṣìkẹ́mi hoped to spend most of her last day with Ìbidún. However, to her dismay Ìbidún claimed she needed to complete several errands for Ẹfúnṣetán that took her out of the compound. She returned to their room just before the evening meal. 'Use this as you see fit, until we send you word,' Ṣìkẹ́mi said, handing Ìbidún a large bag of cowries. Ìbidún accepted the gift with tears in her eyes. Then she thanked Ṣìkẹ́mi before stuffing the bag into a trunk beside the wall.

At supper, in contrast to Ìbidún's glumness, Ẹfúnṣetán appeared high-spirited and keen to discuss her recent visit with family. 'Màmá Ifọn asked after you. She wondered if you were married yet,' she said, addressing Ìbidún in between mouthfuls. Then she squinted as if trying to solve a difficult problem. 'How old are you now?'

'Twenty, minus three,' Ìbidún said.

'Why don't you have any suitors?' Ẹfúnṣetán asked, still squinting.

Ṣìkẹ́mi caught Ìbidún's quiet snort, followed by, 'As if anyone would dare around you,' and stifled her own giggle.

Ẹfúnṣetán leaned forward. 'What did you say?'

'I am waiting on the gods to favour me, Màmá.'

Ẹfúnṣetán's hand paused on its way to her mouth. 'They should hurry before you grow too old.' Then she lobbed the morsel into her mouth.

Ìbidún pinched her lips together and her face turned morose again.

'What is wrong with you tonight?'

Ìbidún's spine straightened at Ẹfúnṣetán's sharp tone. 'I don't think I'm fully recovered. May I go to bed?'

'Go.' Ẹfúnṣetán waved her away and Ìbidún scampered off. Then Ẹfúnṣetán turned her attention on Ṣìkẹ́mi. 'Tell me some stories to make me laugh.'

Ṣìkẹ́mi sighed. Ẹfúnṣetán's gaiety bordered on the manic and signalled an impending mood crash. Reminding herself she would soon be gone, she gathered her thoughts and began regaling her with stories of Madam Tinúbú's exploits in Bàdágrì and Lagos.

Three hours later Ṣìkẹ́mi crept to her room and found Ìbidún's bed empty. Deflated, she plopped herself down. She wanted to say a final goodbye but suspected Ìbidún didn't and was hiding elsewhere. She resisted the temptation to search her out. Instead, she lit an oil lamp and took up guard at the window on the top landing overlooking the courtyard, opening it just wide enough to peer through.

On the precipice of a new dawn, Ṣìkẹ́mi's past floated through her mind; all the decisions leading to this point, her regrets and her joys. She thought of the shattered lives her slave trading had caused, her broken relationships – some she regretted more than others; the new ones she'd forged that signalled a new day. She only hoped that, as she moved forward, she'd live a life with more integrity than she had up to that moment. So why was she sitting here awaiting Ẹfúnṣetán's execution? Ṣìkẹ́mi wrestled with the conundrum as her conscience laid siege to her mind. She needed Ẹfúnṣetán dead. Yet death at the hands of the orphan she saved didn't seem right.

A shadow flitted across the courtyard, and her heartbeat spiked. Out of nowhere, her throat clogged and emotions she could only describe as a mixture of guilt and compassion assailed her. She peered through the gap again and saw a man's silhouette. Someone was definitely coming. She picked up the lamp, wheeled round and headed for Ẹfúnṣetán's room. She opened the door and entered. '*Yèyé*, you need to leave your room. It's not safe here.' Although she spoke with urgency, Ẹfúnṣetán didn't stir. Ṣìkẹ́mi moved closer and saw that Ẹfúnṣetán lay sprawled at an awkward angle on her bed, in her wrapper and *bùbá*, and with shoes still on her feet. Beside her on a stool sat a half-drunk cup of water. Even if she'd been exhausted, why hadn't she taken off her shoes?

She lifted Ẹfúnṣetán's arm, and it dropped like a rock. She felt beneath Ẹfúnṣetán's nose, and the cool breeze of her exhaled breath grazed Ṣìkẹ́mi's skin. Wondering why she was so unresponsive, Ṣìkẹ́mi shook her again, hard, and Ẹfúnṣetán's eyes snapped wide open. But when she tried to speak, she couldn't work her jaw. In a flash of understanding, Ṣìkẹ́mi realised someone had poisoned her bedside water to paralyse her and make the assassination easier.

As Ṣìkẹ́mi bent to lift her, Ẹfúnṣetán's eyes widened in terror. 'I'm moving you to somewhere safe,' Ṣìkẹ́mi said, but, before she could move, the door opened.

Ṣìkẹ́mi dropped Ẹfúnṣetán's dead weight back onto the bed and spun round to face the attacker. She drew her own weapon as the attacker lunged forward, brandishing a dagger. Strong and burly, the assailant was more than Ṣìkẹ́mi's match. Ṣìkẹ́mi tackled him, but he took her down with him. For minutes, they grappled on the floor, each trying to gain the upper hand. Ṣìkẹ́mi hoped Ìbidún, wherever she was, wouldn't wake and come running straight into danger.

The assailant rolled Ṣìkẹ́mi over, so she was under him. She saw the glint of his dagger as his raised hand descended. She bucked, but too late. The dagger pierced her flesh, and a searing pain scorched her arm. As her assailant pulled away, Ṣìkẹ́mi lifted her knee and delivered a sharp kick to his groin. Stunned, he grunted and gasped, and his hold on her slackened, giving Ṣìkẹ́mi the opportunity she needed. She grasped his arms, rolled him over so she straddled him and, with a single stab, delivered the killing blow. She flopped back and lay panting on the floor beside the man's flaccid body. A quick glance at her injury told her it was minor.

'Wh-at's ha-ppe-ning?' Ẹfúnṣetán's slurred and barely recognisable words penetrated Ṣìkẹ́mi's daze.

Ṣìkẹ́mi stood up and surveyed the bloody scene. It seemed the poison's effect was temporary. 'Can you move, *Yèyé*?'

Ẹfúnṣetán moved her head, but nothing else. Ṣìkẹ́mi hovered with indecision. She hadn't thought through her decision to help the woman. Now she had one more complication to resolve. She picked Ẹfúnṣetán up and carried her to the room she shared with Ìbidún and laid her on Ìbidún's bed.

'*Yèyé*, once more I have saved your life, so you owe me my freedom. I want you to know this was your son's handiwork. Please heed my warning. Kúmúyilò plotted this with others, and he will probably try again.'

Ẹfúnṣetán shook her head from side to side in denial, but Ṣìkẹ́mi ploughed on.

'If I were you, I'd trust no one, not the general or Chief Ifáyẹmí or Bàbá Fábùnmi. They all knew about this. I will get Ìbidún to help you before I leave. I need you to swear in Ifá's name that you won't pursue me.' She paused and made eye contact.

'Thank you. I swear in Ifá's name that I won't.' The weak voice and shimmering tears in Ẹfúnṣetán's eyes made Ṣìkẹ́mi feel sorry for her. She wiped the bloody dagger and placed it between Ẹfúnṣetán's teeth. Ẹfúnṣetán bit down on it to seal the oath. Then Ṣìkẹ́mi retrieved her knife and left without a backward glance.

Ṣìkẹ́mi was back in familiar territory, in her beloved forest. It didn't matter to her which forest it was, so long as she was surrounded by nature. Yet she was anything but happy. Each step felt laden, her heart weighed down. This was becoming a habit, she thought as she examined her emotions once more. She was on her way to fulfil a life's dream. In hours, she would see her brother, and, in days rather than weeks, hopefully, her parents. So why did she feel so miserable?

This heaviness in her spirit, the feeling that someone had ripped out a part of her heart, seemed odd. In her head, the decision to leave Ìbidún behind made sense, but her heart disagreed. She wished she could have said goodbye. After depositing Ẹfúnṣetán in their room, she'd searched the house in vain, eventually leaving Ẹfúnṣetán to the care of the only servant she found. The others had either been instructed to leave or they had possessed sufficient insight to use their own initiative.

As soon as she'd emerged into the back courtyard, she'd seen a shadow fleeing and suspected that was the lookout for Kúmúyilò's dead assailant. She'd left immediately, not wanting to be there when the household discovered the dead slave. She wondered if she should go back for Ìbidún, but her feet kept carrying her forward to the rendezvous point with Fọlárìn and the others. Their plan was to offer Ifáyẹmí a bribe, and, if that failed, to break Kúnlé out by force. If their plan worked, they should be well on their way. Her mind returned to Ìbidún, and she hoped the girl would forgive her.

Engrossed in the personal introspection, Ṣìkẹ́mi almost missed the forest camp a few feet ahead. She stopped and, camouflaged by the trees, assessed the situation. Two swordsmen guarded the camp, while two men warmed their hands over a campfire. Something about them seemed vaguely familiar. She searched but saw no one else. Thankful she had spotted them in time, she continued on a side path. Suddenly, a voice rang out. 'Stay exactly where you are.'

Ṣìkẹ́mi heart sank as she turned and faced none other than Kúmúyilò, with two other men, who both stood trying to tie the drawstrings of their ṣòkòtòs. They had likely been relieving themselves outside the camp she'd inadvertently stumbled across. Ṣìkẹ́mi took a step backward and pulled out her dagger. The two men stepped forward, flanking her, but keeping a safe distance. One of them whistled, drawing the attention of the other four in the camp. Ṣìkẹ́mi suspected they were camping in the forest to provide Kúmúyilò with an alibi for his where-abouts during his mother's assassination.

Ṣìkẹ́mi's brain worked furiously, trying to figure out her next move. Kúmúyilò wouldn't fight unless he had to, prefer-ring others to do the hard work for him. Even if he attempted to, he could not match her skill. The other six men were unknown quantities. She recognised two as soldiers in Ẹfúnṣetán's army. She hoped they were the only trained ones. It would even the odds a bit, especially if she tackled those two first.

Ṣìkẹ́mi stalled for time, as she prepared herself mentally for the biggest battle of her life. After coming this far, she wasn't prepared to lose. 'I thought you were busy dispatching your mother,' she said, taking up a defensive stance as one man moved forward, dagger in hand.

'As you can see, I am nowhere near my mother. Whatever happens to her has nothing to do with me.'

The man closed in on Ṣìkẹ́mi. As they circled each other, she kept her eyes on him, even as she spoke to Kúmúyilò.

'We both know that's a lie. Fábùnmi and Ifáyẹmí, I understand, but what's in it for the general?'

Kúmúyilò's tiny gasp revealed his surprise at how much she knew. Good – she needed to keep him on his toes. 'You should know your mother is still alive.'

'So, you helped her? I wondered if you might. It doesn't matter. I will try again after I'm done with you.'

Her opponent lunged forward and Ṣìkẹ́mi sidestepped him. She swung round and pulled him into a headlock before slicing his throat. He crumpled to the ground. So, this was the plan? Tire her out with idiots, to make the work easy for the actual soldiers? Still, she had a trick or two up her sleeve. He wanted his men to toy with her while he watched, but that worked in her favour, as she could dispatch them one at a time.

She addressed Kúmúyilò. 'You didn't answer my question. Why the general?'

Kúmúyilò laughed. 'He owes my mother too much money, and he's worried she's getting too powerful for her own good.'

'So, you sold out your own mother for what? Money? Power? After she picked you up from the forest floor and nurtured you as her own?'

Kúmúyilò's face clouded with rage. 'You know nothing of my relationship with her, and it's none of your concern. After today, you will resemble the thunderstorm that threatened but failed to shed a drop. No one will even remember your name.'

Another man came forward, swinging a sword with the confidence of someone well trained. Ṣìkẹ́mi pulled hers out, and they ducked and dallied for a few minutes while Kúmúyilò enjoyed the blood sport. The man soon joined his comrade on the floor, but Ṣìkẹ́mi knew she was tiring. The baby she was carrying didn't help. Would the remaining men still fight if they knew she was pregnant? Should she risk telling them? She addressed Kúmúyilò again. 'Why are you risking these young men's lives? Are you afraid to fight me like the man you claim to be?'

Kúmúyilò's sneer disappeared, replaced by a scowl as the other men cackled. Good. She wanted them to relax. It might throw them off their guard and make them careless.

But Kúmúyilò upped the stakes. He gave his men an imperceptible nod, and the remaining men moved as one, encircling her. She danced in the middle of their cordon, her heart sinking. She would kill two, maybe, before one of them ended her life. Still, she'd die fighting. She lunged, and the battle begun.

For aeons, blades clashed, as bodies twisted and turned. They were playing with her, she realised, like a cat played with a mouse. Knowing the end was near, she sent a final prayer to the gods, thanking them for a life well lived and asking that her spirit might rest with the ancestors. Then just as she lost all hope, above the melee of the grunts and stomping feet, she heard the unmistakable sound of horses' hooves. Startled, the soldiers raised their heads at the incoming disturbance, and Ṣìkẹ́mi thanked the gods as Fọlárìn and several sword-brandishing men emerged through the trees.

FORTY

The rest of the battle was short and swift. Fọlárìn's men evened the odds, and Kúmúyilò's men were soon dead or incapacitated. When at last the battle sounds died, and the men dismounted, Ṣìkẹ́mi gave Fọlárìn a quick hug, before searching for her brother among the men. The wide smile and gap between his front teeth gave him away. She ran at him, swept him off the ground, twirling him around like he was a child.

'Is that really you, Ṣìkẹ́mi?' Kúnlé asked, staring at her in disbelief. 'You have the strength of a hunter. I always knew I'd find you.' Then he threw his arms around her. Ṣìkẹ́mi pulled him close and for minutes they clung to each other in silence.

Unbridled joy coursed through Ṣìkẹ́mi's veins as she clasped him to her chest. She'd imagined this scene a thousand times, but nothing could have prepared her for the overflow of emotion now flooding her being, such that she thought she might explode. The thudding of heartbeats registered in her consciousness, a synchronised pulsating force, as their hearts chased each other in tandem. Sharp prickles stabbed her eyes, and she tried to stem the flow of tears. Then she realised these were tears of joy. So, she let them fall, revelling in the release they brought. She felt almost complete.

Moments later, she pulled back and noticed Fọlárìn and the men dealing with the corpses strewn around. She turned her attention back to her brother and whispered the urgent query. 'Màmá and Bàbá?'

A grin split his face. 'They are well.'

The remaining tension left her body, and she pulled him close for a quick hug before she finally let him go. 'Did Kúmúyilò or Ifáyẹmí hurt you?'

'No. They treated me well, mostly. Why does Kúmúyilò hate you so?'

Ṣìkẹ́mi gave him a lopsided smile. Even her brother had noticed the animosity. Before she could reply, Fọlárìn interrupted the reunion with a frown on his face.

'We may have a problem,' he said, pointing at the downed men. 'Kúmúyilò escaped with another man, so Ìbidún could be in danger.'

Ṣìkẹ́mi swivelled on her feet. 'What do you mean?'

'Ìbidún secured Kúnlé's release before we got there by telling Ifáyẹmí Ẹfúnṣetán sent her, which is why we arrived so early.'

Ṣìkẹ́mi realised Ìbidún must have used the money she gave her earlier and had probably saved her life as a result. 'No wonder I couldn't find her. Did she return to Ẹfúnṣetán's afterwards?'

'No, she insisted on coming with us, and that's the problem. When we heard clashing blades about half a mile away, we stopped and hid her. She was supposed to go home if we didn't return for her soon, but if Kúmúyilò finds her before we do he could take his anger out on her. We need to move now!'

By the time Fọlárìn finished speaking, Ṣìkẹ́mi was already in a horse's saddle. She pulled Kúnlé up behind her and rode off as if her life depended on it.

'Let me lead the way,' Fọlárìn said, galloping behind her, forcing her to slow down and let his horse pass. Then she picked up speed again.

Bare minutes later, they came across Ìbidún's prone form on the forest floor, eyes closed, a crimson patch spreading across her chest. Ṣìkẹ́mi scrambled off the horse and rushed to the injured girl.

'Ìbidún? Ìbidún!'

Ìbidún's eyes opened, and a weak smile crossed her face. 'They found you.'

'Yes, they did, when I needed them most, thanks to you. Who did this to you?' Ṣìkẹ́mi asked, just to keep Ìbidún talking.

'Kúmúyilò tried to make me return with him. I refused. His guard lost patience with us arguing about it and stabbed me to force Kúmúyilò to leave with him.'

Ṣìkẹ́mi heard Fọlárìn and his men dismounting next to her. 'Do you have any clean rags?' she asked. Someone thrust a clean cloth into her hands and she pressed it against Ìbidún's wound to stem the flow of blood. After several minutes of applying pressure, she spoke. 'I am just going to check the wound to see how bad it is,' she said as she lifted Ìbidún's *bùbá*. Her jaw clenched when she saw the deep laceration underneath her fifth rib. Her forehead creased at Ìbidún's laboured breath and short rasps. She was losing her. 'Ìbidún, stay with me. You hear me? Stay with me!'

The girl's eyes closed, and her head lolled backward.

Ṣìkẹ́mi lifted helpless eyes to Fọlárìn, who was crouched beside her. One of the men spoke. 'Igbó-Orà is a brief ride from here. We can get help for her there if we hurry.'

Nodding quickly, Ṣìkẹ́mi got back on the horse. Fọlárìn and the men lifted the unconscious girl up, cradling her against

Ṣìkẹ́mi's chest. Fọlárìn mounted the horse and took the reins, and they rode off.

The gentle rise and fall of Ìbidún's chest told Ṣìkẹ́mi the girl was asleep. She felt Ìbidún's forehead and sighed in relief. Her skin felt cooler, a sure sign the fever was breaking. For the last three days, as Ìbidún fought and resisted death's call, she'd prayed to the gods like never before. Ògún, Ifá, Ṣàngó, Ọbàtálá and any other god who cared to listen. She'd even sent a few words to the faith people's Jésù.

Fọlárìn entered the dark room and put a comforting hand on Ṣìkẹ́mi's shoulder. He watched Ìbidún for a few minutes before speaking. 'She sleeps. You should eat and then rest. I'll keep watch over her for you.'

Ṣìkẹ́mi drew a pained breath and gave him a weak smile. She couldn't remember the last time she ate, and she hadn't slept since they arrived at Igbó-Orà. Every time her eyes closed, all she saw was Ìbidún, unconscious in her arms, and she knew it was her fault. A fresh wave of guilt crashed over her, filling her with self-loathing. She still couldn't comprehend the girl's determination to follow her, despite the danger.

She stood and stretched her torso before exiting the room. Outside in the courtyard, she thanked the villagers who had taken them in and the medicine woman who sat mixing a healing poultice for Ìbidún's wound. Nearby, Kúnlé and the band of men who had followed Fọlárìn helped the villagers repair a thatched roof. Kúnlé waved at her, and she waved back. With all her energy focused on Ìbidún, they hadn't talked much. She'd been terrified of losing the girl. When Ìbidún started murmuring incoherent words in her delirium, Ṣìkẹ́mi had turned to Fọlárìn. 'Why didn't she stay with Ẹfúnṣetán or return with Kúmúyilò?'

Fọlárìn had taken her hand. 'Because she cares for you. To her, the danger was worth the risk.'

'But why me? I told her I was just a slave.'

Fọlárìn massaged her cold fingers as he spoke. 'You gave her more than Ẹfúnṣetán ever did. You inspired her, just like you do me and the men who followed me.' He paused, as if searching for the right words. 'On our way, she told me she wanted to be like you. I think the self-defence training did it. Before that, she lived in constant fear of Kúmúyilò. You were the first person to consider her needs and do something about it. You are a leader among men and a kind one, at that. That is why I choose you, if you would have me.'

Their eyes met, and, even in the moment's sorrow, Ṣìkẹ́mi felt the heat spear her body. She'd touched her forehead to his in an unvoiced promise. They would talk later, not while they kept vigil and the girl's life hung in the balance. Meanwhile, Ṣìkẹ́mi promised the gods she'd cherish each day if they spared Ìbidún's life.

'Ṣìkẹ́mi, come, she's awake!' Fọlárìn's voice roused Ṣìkẹ́mi out of her reverie. She ran back into the dark room and knelt beside Ìbidún. She grasped her hand and stroked it. 'Ìbidún, how are you feeling?'

'Ẹ̀gbọ́n, I am thirsty.'

Despite Ìbidún's obvious weakness, a dazzling smile broke over Ṣìkẹ́mi's features as her eyes met Fọlárìn's across the mat. 'We can do something about that. First some water, then some àkàmù if you can hold it down.'

She wanted to gather the girl in a hug, but feared disturbing the wound and hurting her, so she held herself back. Instead, she gave Ìbidún's hand an awkward pat. Then she rose and wandered back into the courtyard. She lifted her face to the heavens and let it bathe in the sunlight. As her skin warmed, the heat radiated inwards, thawing her heart until she felt she would burst with joy. In the sky, an eagle flew by, its wings soaring and swooping in a majestic display of freedom, echoing exactly how she felt.

She let go of the burdens and they melted away, leaving her feeling weightless and free. She revisited all her experiences since leaving her father's house; the tears and sorrows that led her to this place of strength and wholeness. The gods were gracious indeed.

Three days later, Kúnlé led Ṣìkẹ́mi, Ìbidún and the men into Òké-Òdán. The village was stirring, the sound of hooves pounding the dirt drawing people from their compounds. As her body swayed in tandem with the horse's gait, Ṣìkẹ́mi's stomach rolled in anticipation of reuniting with her family after several years apart.

Most of her family and Fọlárìn's mother had survived the village sacking because Fọlárìn's father and two of her uncles defended them and paid with their lives. Màmá Aláṣọ, too, was now with the ancestors. After months of searching, Bàbá had found the rest of the family in Ìlarǒ, after which they moved to Òké-Òdán. Ṣìkẹ́mi wondered if her life might have been different if she hadn't chased after Bàbá's knife.

A sizeable crowd of villagers soon formed a procession behind the riders strutting through the village. Ṣìkẹ́mi's heart hammered a new beat as the main thoroughfare ended, and Kúnlé's horse veered into a side lane. After Fọlárìn's message reached their village, her mother had sent Kúnlé to find her and, if possible, buy her freedom. First, he had travelled to Lagos, then he followed her trail to Abẹ́òkúta and finally to Ìbàdàn, where he fell into Kúmúyilò's clutches.

They dismounted outside the compound's perimeter wall and tethered their horses to trees. Then Kúnlé took her hand and led her into the courtyard. A middle-aged woman with greying temples stood in the middle of the courtyard with a bowl full of corn feed and chickens clucking at her feet. At the sound of footsteps, she turned. Then, as if in slow motion, the bowl dropped, her jaw slackened, and she lifted her hands to her head, before breaking into a run towards Kúnlé.

Ṣìkẹ́mi smothered a grin as her mother clung to Kúnlé, chiding that he'd been gone for months and she'd thought she lost everyone important to her. Kúnlé endured the scolding with a smile. Then he released her and said, 'Màámi, I want you to meet someone.' Only then did Màmá register the other strangers with her son. Kúnlé pulled Ṣìkẹ́mi forward and placed her hand in Màmá's. A look of confusion crossed Màmá's face until Kúnlé said, 'Here's your warrior daughter.'

Ṣìkẹ́mi could have laughed as her mother took in her *dànṣíkí* and wide trousers. She took a step backward, then another forward, then she broke into a dance and song. 'Villagers stand up and dance with me, villagers stand up and rejoice with me, because my gods have exalted me.' Then she clasped Ṣìkẹ́mi in a vice-like grip, clung to her and wept.

The commotion must have roused her father, as he came stumbling out of the building, scratching his head. He took one look at Kúnlé and ran towards them. He engulfed them in the biggest hug possible and his words echoed the wonder on his face. 'Ṣìkẹ́mi, is this really you?'

Ṣìkẹ́mi swallowed and nodded, before including him in the embrace, and, as their tears mingled, she thanked the gods, who had fulfilled their promise. Ṣìkẹ́mi, *Obìrin bí akọ*, the warrior woman and stolen daughter, had finally made it home.

EPILOGUE
APRIL 1922

Underneath the giant leaves of the *dongoyárò* tree, Ṣìkẹ́mi sat with children gathered at her feet, in the compound she and Fọlárìn had built, and in which they had raised five children. Now she couldn't count her grandchildren.

'Màmá Olópă, tell us another story.'

'Which one would you like me to tell, Ayọ̀bámi?' Ṣìkẹ́mi smiled at her grandson. The boy was always hungry for stories.

'The one about the girl who escaped from Ẹfúnṣetán.'

For a minute, Ṣìkẹ́mi smiled and remembered the years gone by. Within a decade of her escape, the British annexed Lagos, and soon the rest of Yorùbáland fell. They lumped her people and hundreds of other conquered nations into a single entity called Nigeria. The British left puppet kings on their thrones to manage local customs and affairs, but with no actual power to control the wealth of their land. Those who resisted found themselves staring down the wrong end of a barrel and forcibly deported from their motherland.

Her focus returned to the squirming bottoms. 'All right. Are you all ready?'

Several heads bobbed up and down.

'Àaló o.' Ṣìkẹ́mi spoke the age-old story starter, passed down the generations, since the forefather, Odùdúwà, founded the Yorùbá nation.

'Àalò!' The children sang the reciprocal response.

'There was once a little girl...'

The children sat enraptured as she told them a sanitised version of how she escaped Ẹfúnṣetán's clutches. Ṣìkẹ́mi spied Adéńrelé's raised finger. He was Ìbidún's and her brother, Kúnlé's, grandson, and he'd interrupted the juiciest part of the story. 'Adéńrelé, what is your question?'

'How did the girl escape when she was surrounded by soldiers?'

'Wait for the rest of the story, Adé. You need to learn patience. Màmá Olópǎ hasn't got to the bit where help arrived.'

Ṣìkẹ́mi cackled. That was Ìfẹ́bòmi, her oldest grandchild. Bright and fiery, she reminded Ṣìkẹ́mi of her younger self.

The family called her Màmá Olópǎ, after the British appointed her as head of the local constabulary and the òpǎ, her baton and the main insignia of her post had become her nickname.

From the doorway, Morádéún, Ṣìkẹ́mi's daughter-in-law, signalled with her eyes. Ṣìkẹ́mi brought the story to a close although the children moaned. As Morádéún rounded them up and led them inside, Ṣìkẹ́mi leaned her eighty-seven-year-old bones back into her wicker chair and glanced at the three head-stones jutting out of a clump of bushes in the courtyard. Màmá, Bàbá and Fọlárìn. She'd outlived them all. Madam Tinúbú and Ẹfúnṣetán too. Madam had wormed her way into the hearts of the Ègbá, who made her their minister for women's affairs. She'd died in her sixties of natural causes. Kúmúyilò had tried again and eventually murdered his mother. The Ègbá had demanded justice for their daughter. To appease them, the general executed the slaves who followed Kúmúyilò's orders and removed him as the head of Ẹfúnṣetán's family.

Ṣìkẹ́mi smiled. Her life had been blessed. She'd taken Ìbidún's lesson to heart and been the richer for it, enjoying a life filled with joy, laughter and companionship. The British had plundered the land's spoils, while their queen, Victoria, got richer by the day. But they managed the impossible by stopping the evil slave trade and the drain of the land's sons and daughters to the Americas. The warring Yorùbá tribes had found a peace of sorts, while, ironically, the Europeans ended up engaging in their own world war.

Her hands felt cold and numb despite the warm night, so she pulled up the velvet wrapper covering her knees and draped it around her shoulders. She closed her eyes and listened to the night's song. The crickets chirped; the birds tweeted. It was as close as she got to the forest nowadays, but it was more than enough.

AFTERWORD

In the UK, the year 2020 saw a seismic shift in public opinion about the legacies of slavery. History warred with itself, as those responsible for the past brutalisation and enslavement of others were called to account. Statues in honour of past slave owners came tumbling down and conversations about restitution became more open.

That year, I discovered a hidden history in my family that would once more shift my concept of self on its axis. I had a recent progenitor who, as a prisoner of war and victim of the Yorùbá civil wars (1789–1893), was held in domestic slavery. I had grown up knowing I was a descendant of royalty, but now I knew I was also a descendant of a slave.

As a child, I queried the scant information on that side of the family and my parents provided an explanation that satisfied my childhood curiosity. I believed that story until, in 2020, a chance conversation with my mother about my memoir, *Coconut,* unveiled the truth. I suspect the truth was suppressed because my culture considered slavery a shameful heritage, and today there are parts of Nigerian society where descendants of slaves are still ostracised and excluded from their communities. Faced with this revelation, I battled with reconciling this aspect of my heritage and identity with the prevailing cultural labels and stigma.

That year, I also came across an article in the Nigerian newspaper the *Premium Times*. It was written by Abdulbasit

Kassim, then a visiting doctoral fellow at the Institute for the Study of Islamic Thought in Africa at Northwestern University. The article called for the spotlight to be shone on African slave traders, who were equally revered and complicit in the transatlantic trade.

Two such giants came to mind: Madam Ẹfúnpòròyè Tinúbú (AKA Madam Tinúbú) and Madam Ẹfúnṣetán Aníwúrà, who both have statues honouring them in major Yorùbá cities. In the mid-1800s, a period of huge political turmoil in the Yorùbá kingdom, both women emerged as dominant figures and rose to positions of great wealth and power. At a period when such attributes were the sole preserve of men, I wondered how they managed it. But, while I learned much at school about the transatlantic slave trade, I was taught nothing about these women's roles in it.

As I pondered the fate of my progenitor, it occurred to me that, while information abounds about slavery in the Americas, the individuals caught in the domestic markets and the locals who exploited them for profit are largely unknown. As I imagined what life could have been like for my progenitor, my protagonist Adéṣìkẹ́mi (Ṣìkẹ́mi) was born.

Although *The Stolen Daughter* is all fiction, I set this product of my imagination within a real historical context, with real political players, at the dawn of British colonisation.

While life for domestic slaves in Africa could be brutal, it was possible for them to rise to prominence within their new families. For example, King Jaja of Opobo, kidnapped and sold into slavery as a child, became the head of his family and a city founder. Our heroine's story reflects this possibility.

Finally, if reading this has made you wonder why I am cagey about naming my progenitor, it is because I wish to protect extended family members who are yet to come to terms with this knowledge. Thank you for choosing to read *The Stolen Daughter* and I hope you enjoyed this rollercoaster ride through an interesting time in African history.

GLOSSARY

Ààrẹ̀ ọ̀nà kàkanfò: Generalissimo

Àdìre: Tie-dye fabric

Agbádá: A long billowing top worn by males

Àgùdà: Term for Afro-Brazilian returnees

Àkàmù: A breakfast porridge made from cornstarch

Àmàlà: A starchy food made from sun-dried yam flour

Àṣẹ́: So, may it be (as in Amen)

Aṣọ: Cloth/clothing/fabric

Ayò: Wooden board game

Báalẹ̀: Title meaning 'Head of the land'

Bàbá: Father or form of address for an older man

Bàbá Gbohùn-gbohùn: Town crier

Bàbálawo: Medicine man/priest

Bùbá: A traditional top worn by females

Cowrie shells: Empty, small to large sea-snail shells traditionally used for currency in Africa and the Middle East

Dànṣíkí: A shorter (hip- to knee-length) top worn by males

Dongoyárò tree: Neem tree

Ẹ̀bà: A starchy staple made from grated, fermented and fried cassava grits

Ẹfun: Chalk

Ẹ gbà mí!: Help me!

Ẹ̀gbọ́n: Elder

Ẹ̀gusí: A traditional stew made out of the seeds of the white-seed melon (Cucumeropsis mannii)

Ẹkáàrọ̀: Felicitation used in the morning similar to 'Good morning' when addressing an elder

Ẹkáàrọ̀ o. Ṣé dada lẹ jí?: Good morning. Did you wake well? (As spoken to an elder)

Ẹkáasàn: Felicitation used in the afternoon similar to 'Good afternoon' when addressing an elder

Ẹkáasàn. Ṣé dada ni?: Good afternoon. Are you well?

Ẹ̀kọ (food): A more solid form of *àkàmù*

Ẹkú àbọ̀: Welcome home

Ẹkú ílé: A greeting for those you meet at home

Elédùmàrè: Supreme being; creator of heaven and earth

Ẹ pẹ̀lẹ́: A commiseration or general greeting used in a wide range of circumstances (this form is used to address an elder or superior. See *pẹ̀lẹ́* below)

Ewédú: Jute leaves; a leafy green vegetable

Ẹyọ̀: Masqueraders/festival celebrating key events in Lagos

Fùfú: A starchy food made from grated, fermented cassava

Gbẹ̀du: Drum used only during the *Ẹyọ̀* festival

Gèlè: Headpiece created out of a rectangular piece of fabric

Ifá: The Yorùbá god of divinity, wisdom and intellectual development

Ìgbàdí: Waist beads used as a female fashion accessory and for holding up sanitary wear

Ìrùkẹ̀rẹ̀: A hand-held accessory often used by royals as an insignia and made from horsetail hair

Kabíyèsí: A felicitation used to honour and address kings similar to, 'Your Majesty'

Kaṣú: Cashew

Kékeré: Small

Kú àbọ̀: Welcome

Màmá: Mother or form of address for an older woman

Ọba: King

Ọbàtálá: Yorùbá deity, tasked by the supreme to create humans

Obìrin bí akọ: Woman like a man

Òfì: Most expensive traditional woven fabric

Ọgá: Boss

Ogogóró: Local gin

Ògún: Deity; god of iron and war

Ọjá: A strip of fabric used like a sling to support a baby's legs and bottom when carried on the back

Okú oríre: A felicitation – Congratulations on the effectiveness of your o*rí*

Olorì: Title of a king's wife

Orí: Personal deity who looks out for your well-being

Oṣùka: A round piece of fabric used as a headrest to cushion heavy loads

Ọya: Deity; river goddess; goddess of divinity, femininity, fertility, beauty and love

Óyá: Imperative; similar to 'right' or 'that's it'; 'let's go'; 'come on'

Pèlẹ o: A commiseration or general greeting used in a wide range of circumstances (this form is used to address a peer or subordinate)

Ṣàngó: Deity; god of lightning and thunder

Sàró: Abbreviated term for Sierra Leonian returnees

Ṣòkòtò: Ankle-length trousers

Yèyé: Form of address used for female elders, particularly royals

A LETTER FROM FLORENCE

Dear reader,

I want to say a huge thank you for choosing to read *The Stolen Daughter*. If you did enjoy it, and want to keep up to date with all my latest releases, just sign up at the following link. Your email address will never be shared and you can unsubscribe at any time.

www.bookouture.com/florence-olajide

I hope you loved *The Stolen Daughter* and if you did I would be very grateful if you could write a review. I'd love to hear what you think, as it makes such a difference helping new readers to discover one of my books for the first time.

If you're reading on a Kindle, the app allows you to post a review when you finish the book, and I'd love it if you could please spare a minute to share your thoughts no matter how brief.

I am always thrilled to hear from my readers and you can get in touch through social media or my website.

Thanks,

Florence

KEEP IN TOUCH WITH FLORENCE

www.florenceolajide.com

facebook.com/florence.olajide
x.com/florenceolajide
instagram.com/flora.jide

ACKNOWLEDGEMENTS

I would like to thank:

My editor, Nina Winters, for her patience and continuous encouragement even when I hadn't a clue what I was doing.

The wonderful team at Bookouture, especially Jacqui Lewis, Anne O'Brien, Hannah Snetsinger, Sarah Hardy, Eileen Carey and Kim Nash for all your support and help in bringing this to life.

Claire Bord, with whom I birthed the original idea. Abi Dare – as usual, your advice was invaluable.

Tola Okogwu, Penny Langston, Louise Ishani and Sade Fadipe for the invaluable feedback that helped shape and reshape my ideas.

Naomi Wright, for sketching my beautiful muse.

My church family, in particular Maria Warren, Bola and Val Mogaji, Mwamba Sawyer, Jennifer and Eric Okoh, Rod and Penny Langston for the meals and wheels.

My 'Fostered' family: Remi, Gloria, Sade, G-man, Antony, Dee, Ronke, Toyin, Kofo and Richard. It's been wonderful getting to know you all.

Deji and Dotun Okubadejo – you keep me grounded. May our travels inspire our imagination even more, and maybe I'll get to write about those next.

My family for their unwavering support and love. You spur me on to greater things.

My husband and love. Thanks for being my hands and legs this past year. I couldn't have done it without you.

And finally, to God, my maker, for giving me the strength and will to plod through the pain and physiotherapy each day, and for surrounding me with love and a mass of helping hands.

PUBLISHING TEAM

Turning a manuscript into a book requires the efforts of many people. The publishing team at Bookouture would like to acknowledge everyone who contributed to this publication.

Commercial
Lauren Morrissette
Hannah Richmond
Imogen Allport

Cover design
Eileen Carey

Data and analysis
Mark Alder
Mohamed Bussuri

Editorial
Nina Winters
Ria Clare

Copyeditor
Jacqui Lewis

Proofreader
Anne O'Brien

Marketing
Alex Crow
Melanie Price
Occy Carr
Cíara Rosney

Operations and distribution
Marina Valles
Stephanie Straub

Production
Hannah Snetsinger
Mandy Kullar
Jen Shannon

Publicity
Kim Nash
Noelle Holten
Jess Readett
Sarah Hardy

Rights and contracts
Peta Nightingale
Richard King
Saidah Graham

Milton Keynes UK
Ingram Content Group UK Ltd.
UKHW031116251024
450128UK00003B/57